THE SHOP

This book was originally published in a slightly different format by Breakaway Media in March 2011.

Thomas & Mercer first edition, February 2012.

Published by Thomas & Mercer
P.O. Box 400818
Las Vegas, NV 89140

ISBN-13: 9781612182698
ISBN-10: 1612182690

THE SHOP

J. CARSON BLACK

THOMAS & MERCER

To John Lescroart, for helping me become a better writer. You are the class of any field.

ACKNOWLEDGEMENTS

It takes a village to raise a book. Many thanks to my agent, Deborah Schneider, and to Courtney Miller and Charlotte Herscher for making this the best book it can be.

For your practical help, support and encouragement: Chris and Marcelino Acevedo of Clues Unlimited; Maynard Allington; Lori G. Armstrong; John Cheek; John Garrett; Alison Gaylin; Liam Hopper; Carol Jose; John Lescroart, Lee Lofland; Carol Davis Luce; Donald Maass; Daniel Piel; George, Cliff, Barb, and Daniel McCreedy; Michael Prescott; Diana Ross; Don and Rose Shepperd; Lynn Spencer, Karin Tabke; Bonnie Toews and Elaine Walsh. To Barbara Schiller, Darrell Harvey, Janice Jarrett, Robin Williams, Solange Jarrett-Williams, Edie Laude, Jennifer Jarrett, Celia and Dale Halstead, and Lafayette and Beth Barr. Thanks also to Southwest Crime Ink: Elizabeth Gunn, J.M. Hayes, and Susan Cummins Miller.

Special thanks to William Simon, a.k.a. The Caped Crusader. Without you, this book could not have been written.

Once again, as always, thanks to my mother, Mary Falk, and my husband (and partner in crime), Glenn McCreedy.

PROLOGUE
MEMORIAL DAY WEEKEND
ASPEN, COLORADO

Landry thought: *The kid's positively giddy.*

Landry had been getting comfortable with the night, watching from the woods as the party wound down at the house on Castle Creek Road, people getting into their expensive cars and driving away, leaving just the core group.

Shortly after, the young man came out and made his unsteady way to the deck railing. He had spiky hair and a scarecrow frame. He looked down at the rushing water, then up at the stars. Landry could see his smile even from where he was. The kid's skinny arms hugged his body, as if he couldn't quite believe his good fortune. Tipsy—more than tipsy, inebriated—but something had delighted him, thrilled him. Something had gone very right for him today.

The young man twirled around, looking at the stars. Mesmerized by them. He could have been the leading man in his own musical—the wonderful story of his life. He could barely contain his joy. He had less than an hour to live.

*   *   *

As they reached the walkway, Landry said, "Gloves and masks from now on."

They split up. Jackson would go in first, through the back door. Landry and Davis would go in the front. Green would remain outside; he was surveillance only.

They waited for Jackson to report in. "Upstairs clear."

"How many?"

"Two. The couple. They were laying in bed."

"Lying," Landry said.

"What?"

"Lying in bed. Not laying."

A pause. Then, "Roger that."

Davis opened the front door in one smooth, quick motion, and they stepped inside.

The lights were on. Landry saw the expensive furnishings and enormous stone fireplace, cataloging these things briefly before dismissing them. His eye was on the four targets. Three of them were sleeping: a male and female entwined on a zebra skin near the fireplace and a young woman crashed out on the couch. The fourth was in the process of walking unsteadily toward the kitchen. He was the kid Landry had seen twirling under the stars. A lot worse for wear. He'd done some steady imbibing, or toking, or snorting, since last Landry saw him on the deck.

The kid looked at them. His eyes had difficulty tracking. He said, "You should've come earlier, there was a lot more food."

Landry fell into step with the kid and put an arm around his shoulder, casually pulling him around so he held him from behind. He slit the kid's throat and dropped him like a sack of grain. Dead in eight seconds.

Davis finished dispatching the couple as Landry turned his attention to the sleeper, who was half-sitting, half-lying, her head resting against the couch back. Some sixth sense must have awakened her because she cocked her head upward, her eyes bewildered.

Startled.

He'd seen her before. It came to him—Brienne Cross. One of those celebrities in the news all the time. His daughter had a poster of her up in her room.

He hesitated just long enough for alarm to dawn in her eyes, which dismayed him. He touched a finger to his lips, letting her know it was all right, and pulled her up toward him with one hand. He drew his knife across her throat with the other.

Her mouth went slack. The light in her eyes died. He let her back down on the couch, gently.

"Four here," he said into the radio. Thinking: *Brienne Cross*.

Jackson joined them. There were six people dead. All in all the operation had taken fewer than five minutes.

Landry looked at Jackson. Jackson shifted his feet, then started back toward the stairway. His reluctance was clear. He might not do a convincing job.

Landry said, "I'll do it."

* * *

The couple lay in bed, naked above the sheets. They looked peaceful despite their slashed throats. Landry crossed himself, trying to think of what he did next as gutting a deer. They were dead; they would feel nothing. But their mutilation bothered him.

Done, he glanced around the room, which now resembled an abattoir. His regret at the desecration of these young people was eclipsed by the satisfaction of a job accomplished with flawless precision. It had taken him three and a half minutes, including painting the two eights on the mirror with the woman's blood.

As he started down the stairs, Landry thought about the girl on the couch, the look in her eyes: frightened, then trusting, and finally, empty.

His daughter wanted to grow up to be Brienne Cross.

They were almost out of there. One last check of the perimeter and—

Then he heard sirens. They were a long way off but coming fast.

Simultaneously, Green's voice crackled in his ear.

"Police heading this way."

"Where?"

"Up from the valley. Two units."

"We're out of here."

Landry turned off the lights and slipped out the back door. The sirens screaming in the night now. His mind ranging far ahead as he tried to make sense of this. He wasn't worried about escaping. What worried him was something else.

Who had betrayed them?

He melted into the woods, found a suitable vantage point, and stretched out, stomach-down, on the ground. Relied on his training to make himself part of the forest.

Cataloging faces, phone calls, names. *Who?*

The lights burst through the trees below, blinking white, red, and blue. Engines straining. In his mind's eye he saw them swerving in at the house, slamming into park—

But that did not happen.

The cars did not slow. They rocketed past, two Pitkin County Sheriff's cars.

It was okay.

No one had betrayed them.

As the sirens receded, he spoke into his radio. "Wait where you are until I give the signal."

1
MEMORIAL DAY WEEKEND
NICK

It came to Nick Holloway, gradually, that he was lying on cold hard concrete. Something above held him fast. His shirt was hooked on the undercarriage of a car.

He managed to get loose, tearing his shirt in the process, and crawled out from under. Enveloped by the stench of motor oil, shaking and sick, Nick finally realized where he was: the two-car garage beneath the Aspen house.

The last thing he remembered was talking to a guy named Mars at the *Soul Mate* wrap party. He'd never seen Mars before. It was an exclusive wrap party—just Brienne Cross, the contestants and their guests, himself, and the crew. But Nick remembered talking to the mysterious Mars, the two of them sitting on the back deck, the movement of Castle Creek rushing underneath the slats making him dizzy.

After that it was lights-out.

Nick pulled himself to his feet. His legs didn't work very well, and the smell of flowers and cut lawn sickened him. He became aware of the bright yellow ribbon stretched across the entrance to the garage. Written on the tape were the words "CRIME SCENE DO NOT CROSS."

A policeman behind the tape stared in at him, mouth open in shock. Then he started yelling.

*　　*　　*

A Pitkin County Sheriff's detective with long legs, big shoes, and a face like a hatchet put him in the front seat of a brown Chevy Caprice, exactly the kind of car Nick had described in his thriller, *Hype.*

"Do you have some ID?" the detective said.

Nick had a question of his own. "Do you know how I ended up in the garage?"

"I thought maybe you could tell me that."

Nick realized that he had to stare at the air conditioner vent in the cracked dash to avoid spinning. "I have no idea."

"ID," the detective reminded him quietly.

Nick shifted to pull his wallet out of his back pocket and nearly passed out. He stared at the vent until the double vision stopped. "Jesus."

Hatchet Face took the wallet and looked at his driver's license. "Nick Holloway. I've heard that name before."

"Maybe it was my book, *Hype.* Number thirteen on the *New York Times* Best Seller list."

"I don't read. The wife does, though. It's not about vampires, is it? She loves that stuff." Hatchet Face had his license out and was tapping it against his leg. "Did you know the people in the house?"

Nick noticed the past tense. He wondered if the cast and crew had blackballed him, but that seemed silly. The aspirin taste seeped into his mouth again—he was going to be sick.

"Mr. Holloway."

But Nick had already passed out.

*　　*　　*

They resumed the interview in the emergency room. They had plenty of privacy. It had been two hours, and a nurse had poked her head through the curtain once, ducking out instantly in case anyone asked her for anything. Nick lay in a surgical gown on the crank-a-bed. Hatchet Face, Detective Derek Sloan, sat on a plastic chair.

"You mean they're all dead? Brienne? Justin? All of them?"

Nick wasn't quite able to grasp it, but he knew it was huge. Logically, he understood that he had just escaped death, but in his current state, he was unable to assimilate it.

Sloan switched his ankle from one knee to the other. "You have any idea how you came to be in the garage?"

"Nope." Nick told the story again: He remembered talking to Mars on the deck. Feeling pretty good. Then looking down at the rushing water between the slats of the deck, feeling sick. "I think I was looking for a bathroom."

"That's the last thing you remember?"

"Until I woke up under an oil pan."

"You were writing an article for *Vanity Fair*?"

"A series, actually. 'The Reality Show Diaries.' Not my choice for a title. I was thinking more along the lines of 'Sucking Up for Fun and Profit.'" Once again it hit home that all of them had been killed. If he hadn't been in the garage, he would have been killed, too.

The detective questioned him about his presence in the garage at length, and also asked if he knew of anyone who would want to kill everyone in the house. He mentioned white supremacists.

The room began to spin again.

Somebody in blue scrubs bustled in and told Sloan to leave.

2
SIX WEEKS LATER
JOLIE
NORTH FLORIDA

The pond behind Jolie Burke's house was about two-thirds the length of a backyard swimming pool. She figured it would take her eight strokes to reach the opposite bank.

During the day, the pond was opaque. The shadows were deep and almost impossible to look into. Little bubbles spiraled up near the bank where decaying vegetation and cypress trees met.

Never once had she contemplated swimming in it.

That had changed this morning, when Jolie looked at the pond from her yard.

One minute it was a normal day, close and sticky, the sun hot on the top of her head. Her mind was still on her parents' first home, which she'd walked through the day before.

Then the feeling came up, fast, and gripped her hard. Her heart pounded. Her hands and feet went numb. She couldn't get her breath.

Jolie knew it was the pond.

She forced herself to move, to turn around and walk back into the house. The feeling of doom followed her into the kitchen. She sat down on a chair at the kitchen table.

She sat in the chair for maybe half an hour. Time seemed to expand. The clock ticked loudly. Her cat, Rex, begged for his food, but she couldn't stand up to give it to him.

Finally, legs shaking, she rose to her feet and fed the cat, then went to the bedroom and put on the clothes she'd laid out the night before. She left the house and got into the car. By the time she drove into the parking lot at the Palm County Sheriff's Office, Detective Jolie Burke felt almost normal.

* * *

After dinner, she walked out onto the screened-in porch and looked in the direction of the pond. The trees were black against the sky. Between the trunks, she could see the faint glimmer where a slice of moon was reflected in the water.

Jolie made the decision then. She went back to the bedroom and pulled on her swimsuit, nosed her feet into her flip-flops, grabbed a towel from the linen closet, and slapped down the path and through the gate to the pond's edge. *We're going to fix this thing once and for all.*

The moment she hit the path, the feeling started to build.

By the time she reached the bank, there was thunder in her ears. Her heart pounded.

Then the chasm started to open up beneath her feet.

Ignore it.

She stepped up to the edge of the pond. The world seemed to slither from view. Her legs shook. She dug her toes into the damp earth. Whether this would result in a dive or keep her chained to the ground, Jolie wasn't sure. Just then, the phone rang inside the house.

It startled her so much, she almost sat down. Instead, she sprinted for the back door, thinking: *I'll be back later, and we'll finish this.*

* * *

The person on the phone was Lonnie Crenshaw, the Palm County Sheriff's Office dispatcher.

"We have a report of shots fired at the Starliner Motel in Gardenia, and at least one gunshot victim. The victim is deceased. Can you take this?"

"Sure."

Jolie held on to the phone with one hand and stripped out of her swimsuit with the other. She walked to the closet and eyed blouses and slacks on a row of hangers. Grateful for the distraction. She would put the other stuff—the terrifying notion that this weird phobia was here to stay—out of her mind. "What's the situation? We're backup for the Gardenia PD?"

"Negative. They're asking for one of ours to work the case." There was a pause. "The deceased is Jim Akers."

"*Chief* Akers?"

"That's right. Are you sure you want to take this?"

It took a moment for the magnitude of the situation to sink in. Adrenaline surged as she realized both the opportunity this presented and the possible pitfalls.

"You want Louis to take it?"

"No," she said. "I'll get there as soon as I can. Who's there?"

"Gardenia PD. We have two units of our own on the way."

"Tell them to stay out of my scene."

3

Gardenia lay twenty-three miles inland from Meridian Beach, on a straight two-lane highway running through flatwood forests, scrubland, and cypress sloughs.

The Starliner Motel was a gray cinder block building with turquoise doors. The office jutted out toward the street. Ten units stretched off to the right. An oleander hedge ran alongside the motel, paralleling the railroad tracks. The oleander's leaves looked yellow. Maybe it was from the glow of the sodium arc light above, or it could be due to the sulfurous pall cast by the Gardenia paper mill.

A little over a month ago, two people died here. Now there was another death.

Room nine was the second-to-last unit on the end. In addition to the sheriff's and Gardenia PD units parked out front, Jolie spotted the chief's navy Crown Vic parked nose-in to the room. A Gardenia PD officer stood just outside the open door to the room. His job was to keep unauthorized people out of the scene. He took it seriously—Horatius at the Bridge.

Jolie put on gloves and booties, took out her camera, and walked past the deputies, giving them a friendly nod. She tried not to be distracted by the smells coming from the room: gunpowder and the stench of meat left out too long.

It didn't help any that the rotting meat was Jim Akers, a man she'd met on at least four occasions. The thought of him inside this sordid little motel at the edge of town depressed her to a depth she had not expected.

"Are you the responding officer?" Jolie asked the Gardenia cop.

"Yes, ma'am."

"Has anyone else been inside?"

"No, ma'am, I preserved the scene."

She stepped through the doorway.

The chief lay faceup across the bed. His feet were on the floor, as if he had been sitting on the edge of the bed and then decided to lie back. He wore jeans, a polo shirt, running shoes.

He'd been shot above the right ear. His head was turned to the side, away from the point of entry. Blood seeped into the bedspread like an inkblot. The contents of his head—blood, a few flecks of bone, and brain matter—had been flung against the wall and the headboard like pudding.

I bet you don't miss a thing.

Something he'd said to Jolie once. She didn't recall the context, but he was right about that.

She tried not to miss a thing.

Jolie thought about everything she knew about him, which wasn't much. He did flirt with her once at a picnic, in an offhand kind of way. It didn't bother her because there didn't seem to be anything behind it. She'd seen him with his wife and daughter— they looked like a happy family to her.

Jim Akers was an uncommonly handsome man. Now all that was gone.

Jolie surveyed the room, which reminded her of the places she and her dad had stayed in on their way back from New Mexico. Hundreds of miles a day, but the rooms were all alike. In small towns whose names she'd since forgotten, or places just off the freeway.

She raised the camera and took photos of the man on the bed.

*　　*　　*

The crime scene technicians came in. Jolie watched them for a while before going outside in the hot, damp air, inhaling the heavy scent of magnolias along with the residual incinerator stink of the paper mill. She could taste the copper of his blood, and every once in a while the spoiled-meat stink seemed to blow out of the room, bloated and huge. She looked at her notes under the porch light.

She wondered what the chief had been thinking, if he knew it was coming. Was there time to think? Did he close his eyes and pray? Or did he just give up and let it happen?

Jolie concentrated on the list of Akers's possessions: wallet, change, comb, ID, pocket litter.

Something was missing.

Two things, actually. His cell phone, and his service weapon. Jolie doubted that a cop, even an administrative cop, would go anywhere without his service weapon.

And it was strange he had no cell phone. A police chief was on call, always. These days, how many people left their cell phones behind?

She stepped off the walkway and motioned the responding officer over. His nameplate said "Collins." "Did you know the chief well?"

He seemed calm, but his eyes were like two blue holes in his head—shock. "Yes, ma'am. Pretty well. It's a small department."

"What kind of service weapon did he use?"

"An S&W model 66 .357 Magnum. The short barrel. Same as everybody in the PD."

It occurred to her that there might be another explanation for the missing weapon and phone. It was a fleeting thought—way out of left field. She dismissed it immediately as outlandish.

But the feeling, small and uncomfortable, grew behind her solar plexus.

"What kind of holster?" she asked.

"A belt holster, ma'am. Standard issue."

She liked his succinctness. "Did he have a backup weapon?"

He stared into the room, watching one of the crime scene techs examining the bloody headboard. The tech was a woman, short and squat, hair done up in an elaborate bun. "He had one in an ankle holster. Don't know the make or model, though."

"Did he wear them regularly?"

"Yes, ma'am." He looked puzzled. "Why wouldn't he?"

Jolie went back into the room. Gently, she lifted the polo shirt up with a gloved finger.

No belt holster. Not even a belt.

No backup gun, either.

4

The motel owner, Royce Brady, hovered outside the tape. He was a wiry man with a complexion like a gingerbread cookie. He wore a Hawaiian shirt and shorts and white socks and sandals and a hearing aid. Jolie took him to the motel office.

"A woman called the office and said she heard gunshots," Brady told her. "Said she was driving by and heard the shots."

"What time was this?"

"About ten? Not sure, though."

"What did you do?"

"I called room nine. The chief of police was right here in my motel, so I called him. When he didn't answer, I went down the row and looked in each room." He added, "That's when I found him."

"Did Chief Akers ever check into one of your rooms before?"

"No. Kind of took me by surprise."

"What was his demeanor?"

Brady shrugged. "Same as he always was. Calm, friendly."

"Did you see him with anyone?"

"No, but I'm inside here mostly. I leave the guests alone. They check in, and after that, what they do is their business."

"You know him well?"

"I know everyone in this town. He was here during the standoff, the hostage situation. Worked the phone right here in the office, tried his best to get that sick asshole to come out." He stared forlornly at the parking lot. "That poor young lady who was killed, she was my daughter's age. A real nice girl. Piled all her used towels in the sink so the maid didn't have to stoop to pick them up. Always left a good tip, too. Can't think a medical rep makes that much, but she was considerate like that. How'd I know, when I gave her the key, I was signing her death warrant? There must be a curse on that room."

"What are you saying?"

"It's the same room."

Jolie couldn't believe what she was hearing. "Luke Perdue and Kathy Westbrook—that happened in room nine?"

"Yes, yes, room nine. I spent a ton of money to clean up the mess, finally got it ready for paying customers, and now *this* happens!"

*　*　*

Jolie went outside into the warm night and stared up the walkway in the direction of room nine. Room nine. *The same room.* She thought about the two missing weapons. The missing phone. Thought about the woman who called the motel about gunshots.

A theory forming. Just a theory. Nothing to get excited about.

A woman called the office to complain about gunshots, and Royce Brady went to check the rooms. He found Chief Akers dead on the bed of room nine.

Room nine, the same room where Luke Perdue had taken Kathy Westbrook hostage a little over a month ago.

Lots of elements here. Coincidences.

Jolie had been a cop for nine years. She saw it as a huge responsibility. People depended on her, every day. They looked to her for help.

The hostage, Kathy Westbrook, had depended on Chief Akers to get her out. She would have taken comfort in the knowledge that the cavalry had come for her. The chief of police had been right here, in this motel, negotiating for her release. She would have thought he wouldn't let her come to harm.

But she was wrong.

5

The meat wagon was backed up as close to room nine as possible, doors open. A flatbed had already taken the chief's Crown Vic to impound.

Jolie found a woman with an elaborate hairdo in the bathroom, removing the clear plastic liner from the wastepaper basket. Jolie noted the two beer bottles inside the liner as well as a crumpled-up Kleenex. The beer fit in with her theory, but it could fit in with any theory. As the woman walked it out of the bathroom, Jolie caught a sharp smell—a cross between rubbing alcohol and perfume. It reminded her of something, but she couldn't remember what.

"Do you know if there was GSR on his hands?" Jolie asked.

The woman pushed up at her glasses on the bridge of her nose with a gloved finger. "Randy did that."

Randy, the other tech, was assisting in the removal of the body. The victim was zipped up in the body bag on the gurney, ready to go.

Jolie said to Randy, "Was there any gunshot residue on his hands?"

"No. Why would there be?"

"You did bag his hands, didn't you?"

"I didn't think it was nec—"

"Please open the bag."

"I don't want to break the seal."

"Open the bag."

He shot her a resentful look and pulled the zipper open. The death stench billowed out.

She leaned forward and looked at the hands. No visible evidence of gunshot residue. In between the waves of death smell, Jolie got a whiff of the same odor she'd smelled in the bathroom—a sharp, alcohol-based scent.

Randy bagged the chief's hands and zipped up the bag. "Anything else?"

She heard the resentment in his voice, and was surprised by it. "Make sure his hands are swabbed and tested for an alcohol-based product. All right?"

He nodded. She saw the tiredness in his eyes under the harsh yellow light. He'd probably worked the day shift and then come out here at night. Jolie knew this happened a lot, understaffed as the crime scene unit was. "I'm hoping you'll do this yourself," she said. "It's very important, and it could make the difference in this case."

"Okay, I'll make sure it gets done."

"Thanks." As she stepped outside, Jolie's gaze strayed to Stearing Automotive across the street.

Stearing Automotive had figured prominently in the standoff last month. Jolie pictured one FBI sniper and his spotter lying flat on their bellies on the roof, and the other FBI sniper and his spotter positioned on a railroad car. The railroad car had been stopped dead on the tracks that bisected Kelso Street.

Jolie thought about the philosophical rift between hostage negotiators and tactical teams. There was even a joke about it.

The hostage negotiator says after a two-week standoff, "We're beginning to make real progress."

Ten minutes after hostage negotiations begin, the SWAT team leader says, "Told you it wouldn't work—time to go in."

True.

Jolie thought about Chief Akers working the phone, trying to bring Kathy Westbrook and her kidnapper out safely. After hours of painstaking negotiations, two people still ended up dead.

She checked her watch. Seven a.m. She wanted to get to the Akers house early so that Akers's widow, Maddy, would hear about her husband's death before it made the news.

But Jolie's guess? Maddy Akers already knew.

6

NICK

ORANGE COUNTY, CALIFORNIA

One minute Nick was ahead of the other car, and the next, the jogger crossed in front of him.

They'd dragged from the light and were coming off the curve by the park when the jogger trotted out onto the road. Three in the morning—and there was a jogger crossing the street! Nick hit the brakes, and the car slewed sideways and jounced against the curb.

Everything stopped.

First thing he realized—the airbag didn't deploy.

Second thing he realized—he was unhurt. Maybe banged up a little. But unhurt. The seatbelt had saved him. His car was in the right lane but turned backwards—he'd done a complete one-eighty.

Nick put a hand up to touch his face and smelled the alcohol on his own breath.

Had to get out of here.

Because the airbag hadn't deployed, he could drive away. There would be no drunk driving charge, if he could just get this thing straightened out and go, soon. But what about the other driver?

What about the jogger? Bemused—it must be the shock—he looked around. The other car was gone. The jogger was gone.

He got out, shakily, dread building. Peered under the car—no jogger.

Almost cried with relief. He looked around. The street was empty.

Just the six-lane road, the park on the right, the sodium arc lights staining everything orange.

Son of a bitch—lucky as usual.

Get the hell out of here. He forced himself to move. Got back in and turned the car around, worried that at any minute a speeding car would come around the curve and ram right into him. But his luck held. He took the back streets home. Driving like a little old lady.

*   *   *

Back inside his condo, he sat on his couch and stared out the window at the darkness. Thinking: *How lucky can you get?*

First, he'd survived the massacre at the Aspen house. And now, he'd driven away from an accident which could have killed him, the other driver, or the jogger. He'd even avoided a drunk driving charge.

I've been spared.

That was the bottom line. He'd been spared. And for what? His new thriller was dead in the water. He had to have a follow-up. Nick had a three-book deal, and this was the third book.

But he couldn't get past chapter four.

A deadline was looming. It was his last thought before he fell asleep.

*   *   *

His cell woke him. A text from one of his more ardent fans.

The message said, "When can we meet?"

Never, he thought.

To be fair, this guy wasn't hurting for money—Frank was some big muckety-muck in the government. He was just a pest— a glommer-on. He had a manuscript in his closet and wanted something for nothing, just because they were related—cousins, several times removed, if the guy was to be believed.

First e-mails, then phone messages, now text messages.

Get a life.

Outside, it was sunny. Another beautiful California day. Nick stared at the sky. Feeling better.

Much better.

Maybe it was the accident—the feeling he'd cheated death once again. But this morning he'd awakened full of purpose. Nick had been trying to come up with the idea for another book, but nothing had interested him—until now. This story was different. This story had been dropped in his lap.

The best ideas always came like this, on waking. Before he even got up to take a leak.

He felt excitement building, the sense of *purpose*, deep in his gut.

Nick had found his inspiration.

7

Chief Akers's house sat on a street dead-ending at a small public park. The yard was dominated by a moss-draped oak and a fish pond. A boat was backed into the carport, which was otherwise empty.

Maddy Akers drove a GMC Yukon.

Jolie pressed the buzzer and waited. No one answered. She rang again. Then knocked. Mrs. Akers either wasn't at home or she was in a deep sleep.

A car turned onto the street from the main drag. From the sound of the engine, it was a four-banger.

The car did a funny thing. It came to a stop three doors down, in the middle of the street. Jolie was a defensive driver and could read car body language—most good drivers can.

This car—an old Toyota Corolla—braked, then crawled forward to the next driveway. The driver executed an awkward turn, rushed and sloppy.

The driver's head swiveled back in Jolie's direction, long hair flipping with the motion. Either it was a female driver or a Lynyrd Skynyrd fan. The Corolla went back up to the road, blinker on, and turned right. Too far away to see the license plate.

Jolie's own take-home vehicle was a Crown Vic with black-walls. It was supposed to look like a civilian's car, but the jack-in-the-box clown on the antenna didn't fool anybody. She'd been spotted.

She jogged to her car, started it up, and followed.

On Kelso, Jolie saw the Corolla up ahead, stopped at the light. She stayed in the other lane and to the left, behind an old truck. The Corolla only went a city block before turning in at Bizzy's Diner. The parking lot was already full. Jolie cruised by, parked at the convenience store next door, and watched in her rearview as the woman got out. The woman was slight and pale. Lackluster red hair fell straight from a middle part. Low-riding jeans. The woman held a ratty shoulder bag close as she jabbered on the cell phone held to her ear. She snapped the phone shut, dumped it in her purse, and walked across the parking lot as if someone might jump out at her at any minute.

Jolie ran the plate: 1989 blue Toyota Corolla, belonging to one Amy Perdue.

Luke Perdue, the hostage-taker at the Starliner Motel, had a sister.

It was in the paper and on the news.

*　*　*

Bizzy's: pebbled gold water glasses, rabbit-warren rooms, mismatched tablecloths, Friday night catfish buffets. Jolie parked herself at a table in one room where she could look through the doorway and see Amy Perdue in the other.

The woman was still on the phone. She looked more than nervous; she looked scared.

Jolie ordered a big breakfast. The waitress, Eileen, had big platinum curls. Eileen's son, a Marine lance corporal, came back from Afghanistan with a severe head injury. On Eileen's days off, she drove three hours to the VA hospital in Biloxi, and three hours back, to visit her son, even though he would never recognize her again.

Eileen never mentioned her son, but she'd been quick to offer Jolie her condolences when her husband died. With Danny, most people pretended it never happened. Even people Jolie worked with and saw every day, people who had worked with him, too. Ignore it and it will go away.

Eileen came by with Jolie's breakfast and a smaller plate piled up with Bizzy's world-famous hush puppies. "Heard what happened. You need to stoke up. Nothing like hush puppies to give you a foundation for the day you're going to have."

*   *   *

Jolie had already paid her check and was waiting outside by the time Amy walked out of Bizzy's. She caught up with Amy quietly and fast. "Amy Perdue?"

Perdue spun around and stared at her, eyes wide with recognition.

"Can we talk a minute?"

Perdue looked like she wanted to bolt. An elderly couple in a big car bore down on them and managed to steer past. Amy kept her eyes on them as if they were the most fascinating elderly couple in the world.

Jolie said, "I'd like to ask you about Maddy Akers."

"Maddy?"

"Mrs. Akers. The police chief's wife."

Amy bit her lip. "You know? I'm late for an appointment. Can we do this later?"

Jolie heard the crunch of car tires again and automatically stepped back to get out of the way. A GMC Yukon came toward them between the two rows of parked cars. When it drew even, the window buzzed down and a dark-haired woman peered out. "Amy?"

Amy had gone from nervous to terrified.

The woman hopped down from the Yukon. She wore jeans. A simple top hugged a lean, strong body. Her sunglasses and the haircut and color looked like they cost a tidy sum.

The Yukon was silver. Maddy Akers owned a silver Yukon.

The woman said to Amy, "I'm glad I caught up with you." She swiped at a stray hair. "I can't make it in to the apartment today, so you'll have to handle the eviction yourself. You think you and Niraj can do that?"

Amy reminded Jolie of a rabbit standing up in the road, trying to figure out which way to run. Finally, she nodded.

"I have something to tell you…" The woman stopped. She looked at Jolie's shield and then at Amy. "Is something going on? Are you in trouble?"

Amy just stared at her.

The woman said, "Are you…?" Stopped, and tried again. "You're here because of my husband?"

Jolie introduced herself. In the corner of her eye, she saw Amy starting to back away. Jolie gave her a look that said, *Stay where you are.*

The woman said, "You're here to tell me about, um…" She stopped, took a breath. "You're assigned to my husband's case?"

"You know about your husband."

Maddy Akers nodded. Jolie couldn't see past the sunglasses, but the woman looked miserable. Like a sky as storm clouds moved in. She'd staved them off for a time, but now they were racing across the heavens until the whole sky was black. Jolie knew the feeling. She knew what Maddy Akers was going through. Disbelief had turned to stinging betrayal, the question running around and around in her head: *Why?* All this she felt coming from Maddy Akers in the fraction of a second before the woman started to cry.

She cried silently, tears running down her face. Pressed her manicured fingers against her cheeks, trying to stop them.

Jolie needed to talk to Maddy, now. Amy took advantage of her ambivalence. "Can I go now? I have to be somewhere."

Jolie nodded. She'd catch up with her later. Amy stormed toward her car with new purpose, shoulders pushing forward like a running back, bag crushed to her chest.

Maddy Akers looked at Jolie. The tear tracks were still on her face, but she seemed composed. "Can we get out of here?"

*　*　*

Maddy locked up her car and got into Jolie's. They drove in the direction of Gardenia PD, but Jolie made sure the Starliner Motel was on the way. Maddy Akers asked to stop there, which was what Jolie had in mind. Jolie had no plans to take her to the Gardenia PD, where her husband had been the chief, where all manner of emotions would be swirling around and there would be factions and allies and plenty of kid gloves. But she didn't want to go directly to the Palm County Sheriff's Office, either. That might make Maddy suspicious. Jolie wanted this to be between the two of them.

They parked outside room nine. Everyone was gone now. They couldn't go in, but that didn't seem to bother Maddy. They sat in the car, and the two of them stared at the yellow tape stretched across the open doorway. On the way over, Maddy'd told her she'd been driving around since she heard the news from her husband's second in command early this morning. Jolie asked her where she went, but Maddy couldn't remember all the places. "I just drove," she said. Meridian Beach, Port St. Joe, up to Wewahitchka and back. She turned off her phone because she didn't want to hear from reporters.

Jolie didn't push her. She knew Maddy wouldn't need any prodding to unburden herself. Pushing might even cause her to pull away. The woman had questions of her own. Did anyone hear anything? Was he found right away? Who found him? Who would do this? All the questions an innocent victim of a senseless crime would ask as they tried to get their arms around the enormity of the death. As if the details would help them. Some questions Jolie could answer, which she did.

They both knew it was all prelude.

Maddy Akers stared at the windshield. "I just don't understand how he could—" She stopped herself.

Jolie waited, then asked, "Could what?"

Maddy swiped at her eyes under the dark glasses. "How he could let someone just walk up on him like that."

Jolie stayed quiet.

"I don't understand why he was here at all. Why would he come to a place like this? It wasn't like him. People will say it was some *woman*. I don't believe it."

"I don't either." Which was the truth.

"How could he *do* this to himself?"

"Do what?"

Maddy stared at her. "What do you mean?"

"You said, 'How could he do this to himself?'"

Maddy covered her mouth.

"How could he do what?"

Maddy turned in her seat and stared at Jolie. "You *wanted* us to stop here, didn't you?" She bent her head down, swiped at her eyes again. Bunched her fist and hit her thigh, twice, hard. "I can't do this," she said through a blur of tears. "I tried. I just wanted to—oh, shit. I couldn't let them—" She stopped, staring at Jolie clear-eyed. "I think you're getting the wrong impression here. Either that, or you're trying to put words in my mouth."

Jolie put the car in reverse and backed out of the parking space.

"Where are we going?" Maddy demanded.

"I need to take your statement."

"That's it? That's all?"

Jolie said, "What else is there?"

8
LANDRY
ARCADIA, CALIFORNIA

Landry turned onto his street, which looked like every other street in the housing division in which he lived. The division was called Orchard Commons, although there were no orchards, and he didn't know what a "commons" was. But Orchard Commons was ten minutes on the 210 from Santa Anita, one of the reasons he bought in here.

Landry felt dispossessed. His wife Cindi was out of town with her sister. Two days ago he'd dropped his kid off at camp near Lake Arrowhead. She'd be gone for two weeks.

Cindi would be back in three days, but Landry missed her already.

They had been childhood sweethearts. They grew up together. He had been away for most of their marriage. Bosnia in the nineties, two deployments in Afghanistan, three more deployments in Iraq, and eight months working security for Kellogg, Root & Brown. But in the last few years, he'd made sure he stayed home as much as possible, making up for the time they were apart. Even on overnight trips, he missed her. It was a physical ache that centered just under his navel, and if it could be given a name, that word would be "longing."

This was worse by far. He had never been the one left behind before.

It was comforting to drive through the maze of houses in the flat, hot, California sunlight. The place was familiar in its sameness, every house looking like every other house, with the exception of the cars parked out front and the configurations of the bushes and trees. Every house had a two-car garage. Every house had a peaked roof. All the houses were tan stucco. Nice and neat, no surprises, their shadows falling the same way on the same white concrete driveways lining up to the same clean black asphalt.

There were people who would call this subdivision "cookie-cutter." But Landry prized order. It was an American thing, miles and miles of houses that looked the same. Like McDonald's. When he thought of his country, he thought of McDonald's, shopping malls, and subdivisions like this, all of them uniquely American. It was the new way. It was the twenty-first century.

He parked out front and went inside. Cold—Cindi kept the air conditioner cranked up.

Shutting the door on the hot California light, Landry experienced a brief twinge of futility. It happened more and more as he got older, the feeling that he was dispossessed. Life didn't have much purpose other than the purpose he gave it—his family, the racetrack, his job. It was that feeling that had caused him to go back to Iraq.

Landry was good at one thing—he was a warrior.

With Cindi and Kristal gone and the house empty, the feeling came back in spades. He set his keys and wallet and change on the dresser and walked to the kitchen. Not having his girls with him made him restless. He took out the orange juice and drank it right from the carton.

Orange juice was starting to give him heartburn, but he ignored it. The same reason he wouldn't go to a doctor for any ache or pain or even the flu. Doctors only look for trouble, and when they find it, before you know it they put you in a hospital where a cold can turn into pneumonia and you're on life support.

Of course in his job, he had regular checkups. He didn't comply, he'd be out, and the only thing he loved more than his wife, his daughter, and the ponies was his job.

He did things for his government that no one talked about. The only difference, as far as Landry could see, was that in this job he'd never been face-to-face with his employer. In fact, he didn't even know the name of the company. Some operations, he knew, needed to be outsourced. But the job was the same: to protect and defend the United States of America against all enemies, foreign and domestic.

Landry couldn't stand being in this empty house. He decided to go to his brother's barn at Hollywood Park and check on their Derby hopeful, see if the quarter crack on his foot was any better. He headed back to the bedroom to get his wallet and keys, stopping by the open doorway to Kristal's room.

Cool air came from inside, scented with strawberries. His daughter's lair. A Keep Out sign had been tacked to the door, but she left it open all the time—mixed signals. Kids, he found, *wanted* their parents to interfere. They craved structure. They knew that life was hard and scary and treacherous, so they wanted someone to protect them. Even when Kristal protested, it was halfhearted.

Landry rarely crossed the threshold into her room, however, because he trusted her. She knew damn well she'd better do the right thing, and therein lay the trust.

He was about to start down the hallway again, but his eye caught the poster on Kristal's wall.

Brienne Cross.

He'd glanced at the poster a few times on his trips down the hallway to the bedroom, even though he didn't like the way it made him feel.

But *this* time, he found himself unable to turn away.

It was as if he were in a forest, and something caught his eye, and he'd looked away and then back again, and saw an exotic bird in the branches where none existed before. He thought Kristal had taken the poster down. It had been well over a month since Brienne Cross died. He'd read Kristal's raw grief on Facebook, the childlike grief of losing an idol, but he'd thought that was over.

And yet, the poster remained.

He shrugged. Turned away. Almost.

His neck creaked as he looked back. Something compelled him. It felt as if he were in a long tunnel, and the only way out was to look at Brienne Cross.

Brienne lay in an infinity pool. Everything was completely still around her. Her face rose partway out of the water, long hair like golden seaweed spread out in a fan. She wore a skimpy blue bikini top. Her breasts rose up, droplets of water on satin flesh, surrounded by a deep, saturated blue. As if she had been a sculpture partially poured into a mold, or had been formed by an upheaval in smooth, pale rock. Her eyes wide open and startled, her lashes beaded with water. Her lips—

Her lips were parted. He recognized her expression. Surprise. His fingers closed around the crucifix on the chain around his neck. The silver filigree felt warm—alive to his touch.

He went back to that moment. Suspended on a breath Brienne Cross never got to finish, the moment she looked up into his eyes.

He saw those eyes, blue orbs filled with light. He saw them change from surprise to trust.

She had accepted that he knew what was best. She knew she was in good hands, even as he extinguished the light in her eyes and stopped her heart.

His heart wrenched inside him, as if it had been torn loose of its moorings. The feeling went away almost immediately. It was not physical pain. It was emotional. He could not turn away. He could not move. All he could do was stare at the poster.

He had shared something with her nobody else would. In that moment, he had known her better than anyone could have ever hoped to. He had held her with his eyes, he had told her without words it was all right, and she had submitted.

It was a communion they shared.

He realized he had never known a more emotional moment, or conversely, a moment so completely devoid of worldly passion.

He'd been raised Catholic. He didn't give a damn about that mumbo jumbo, the rosary, the confession, the standing up and kneeling down and repeating phrases over and over—as if those phrases would somehow take, somehow transform. They were just words sent into a void. That was what he'd always thought.

But now he knew that religion was real, and that transformation was possible.

All in a rush, he knew the truth. The world fell away, and it was just the two of them. There was no Cindi, there was no Kristal, just the two of them, Brienne Cross and himself, inextricably bound together.

He had never questioned a mission. In fact, he tried to know as little about the people he was charged to kill as possible.

But this was different.

Landry had carried out his mission. He had killed Brienne Cross.

Now he needed to know *why*.

9

Maddy Akers said to Jolie, "Did you know Kathy Westbrook had an eight-year-old son?"

Jolie and Maddy were in the new interview room at the Palm County Sheriff's substation in Meridian Beach. So new you could smell the white paint on the walls. They sat catty-corner at the small table pushed up against the wall, close enough to touch.

"Kathy's son," Maddy continued. "That's what bothered him the most. He couldn't stand the thought of that little boy out there somewhere without his mother. You know what happened?"

"Why don't you tell me?"

"Jim was primary on the hostage negotiation; he had an FBI agent for his secondary. Jim spent *hours* talking to Luke Perdue."

Jolie knew the story well. A few hours into the hostage situation, Chief Akers had persuaded Luke Perdue to throw out his gun. Luke must have seen one of the snipers and panicked. Standing in the doorway, he'd held Kathy Westbrook in the crook of his arm to use her as a human shield.

Both snipers fired simultaneously. Luke Perdue took a round dead center in the shallow triangle of eyes and nose. That bullet came from the sniper on top of Stearing Automotive. The other sniper, the one on the railroad car, missed his shot. His bullet took a downward trajectory through Perdue's jaw and obliterated Kathy Westbrook's frontal lobe.

"Jim yelled for them to hold their fire, but they didn't listen. Poor woman—he said she was there in the wrong place at the wrong time."

The Starliner Motel was a regular stop on Kathy Westbrook's medical sales route. She was headed to her room when Luke Perdue popped up out of nowhere, put a gun to her head, and forced her inside.

Nobody knew why he did it.

"You don't know what Jim went through the last month. He blamed himself for that woman's death. Even though he knew he did everything right. But late at night, you know? It creeps back in. He shot himself last night, but he was dead before that. He couldn't live with what happened."

"You say he shot himself?"

"That was a mistake. What I meant to say was someone shot *him*."

"Oh. I guess I misheard. Still. I can see why he might do that. Kill himself. You yourself said how depressed he was. If he *did* kill himself, it would be so unfair. To you, to your children. You have kids, right? They're both grown?"

She nodded.

"Can you talk for the mic?"

"Okay. Yes, I have two kids."

"You know what? If my husband killed himself, I know what I'd do." *If? God, you're such a liar.* "I'd make it look like something else, like somebody killed him. I wouldn't hesitate for one minute. I don't have kids, but if I did, I'd do it for their sake."

Jolie could see the wheels turning. Cagey. Then Maddy surprised her. "You're damn right I did it. And I'd do it again."

*   *   *

Maddy gave her statement.

Once she'd made her decision, Maddy was anxious to explain.

Her husband had called her from the Starliner Motel. He'd told her he was going to kill himself, and she pleaded with him not to. She heard the sound of the gunshot. She raced over, running two red lights to get there.

Maddy told Jolie she'd made up her mind standing in the doorway of room nine. Nobody else was around. Nobody heard the shot. She was alone with her husband of twenty-four years, except it wasn't her husband lying on the bed anymore.

She thought about her two adult children, what they'd think. She thought about the funeral, law enforcement coming from all over the state—the hero's funeral for a fallen cop. And yes, she thought about his life insurance policy. She thought about how she'd meet her bills now that her husband was gone.

She sat on the one chair in the room and cried. And then she went to work.

A cop's wife, Maddy knew all about gunshot residue. Jim Akers had shot himself in the temple—not through the mouth. Already it looked like a homicide. She cleaned up the gunshot residue on his hands with a moist towelette from her purse—the sharp alcohol-and-perfume scent Jolie had smelled in the bathroom wastebasket. Maddy took his gun because he'd shot himself with it. She took his backup gun because she might as well make a clean sweep. She took his phone to be on the safe side.

Maddy stared into the middle distance, her eyes filling with tears. "Now everyone will know."

Jolie held out a box of tissues. Maddy waved it away, visibly panicked. "I need to call my kids. I need to tell them before they find out some other way."

"Just a few more questions," Jolie said soothingly, "and we can wrap this up. You want something to drink?"

Maddy Akers nodded. Her pretty face showed the strain. "Coffee? With some cream?"

Jolie went back to the coffee machine and poured her a cup. She reached for the packets of cream in the jar by the coffeemaker, then thought better of it and pulled out her own stash of Shamrock half-and-half. She felt for Maddy. She understood what Maddy was going through, as few others could.

A cop's suicide, and the anguish of the wife he left behind.

In this one way, they were sisters.

10
LANDRY

A baby boomer, Landry grew up with television. He had two brothers and a sister who fought over what to watch. They were raised together in a fifth-wheel trailer, living on or near the back side of horse racing tracks all over the west. Not a lot to do in downtimes, so his siblings fought over the TV remote. To Landry, it was just so much white noise, but he'd grown accustomed to the space it filled up.

After Kristal was born, he became more particular about what they watched as a family—the History Channel or Discovery mostly.

Today, the TV was turned to National Geographic while Landry went through the tabloids.

He knew a lot more about Brienne Cross now. She was unknown until she appeared on *America's Newest Star*, which helped her single, "Stealthy Lovin'," make it to the top of the country charts. She appeared in some movies and released a Grammy-winning country album, *Marfa Lights*. When she became a judge on *America's Newest Star*, Brienne became an even bigger celebrity. Eventually this led to her own reality show, *Soul Mate*.

Landry had gone out and bought up every celebrity magazine with Brienne Cross on the cover. He'd printed up reams of information from TMZ and sites like it. Her death still generated publicity all these weeks later. The family had yet to arrange for a burial; for some reason there had been a holdup at the medical examiner's office in LA. This created a great deal of hysteria. People wanted to see America's Princess squared away. They wanted a big funeral they could all participate in from their living rooms. Half the tabloids hinted at a conspiracy theory.

He read about the lone survivor, Nick Holloway. Landry had been briefed about the survivor one day later, after he had gone to Salida, Colorado, to carry out the rest of the mission. The sheriff's cars racing by on Castle Creek Road had distracted them from going back into the house and checking everywhere.

A black mark on Landry's once-pristine record.

But lucky for Nick Holloway.

They'd let it go. A reporter for *Esquire* wasn't important in the scheme of things.

Nick Holloway was a lucky man.

Back to Brienne Cross. The Internet generated lots of stories, but most of them harped on the same themes. They concentrated either on her extreme behavior, or the idea that in most ways she was just like regular people. For example, she liked Burger King. Apparently, the idea that she was just like a regular person was very important to the people who read the fan magazines.

There was little point in reading this garbage, so he just looked at the photos—inhaled them. Even the ones where Brienne was featured as the "worst dressed" celeb for the week. In fact, he liked these photos best because he could see a little more of her as a person. Her inner conflict showed on her face; she knew she was dressed like a trailer park hooker. He wondered why she did it. In the photos she would look at turns tentative, defiant, and worried. Sometimes, it was clear she'd made a clothing mistake but was going out there anyway.

He admired that.

"Anyone who has ever had a personal encounter with a Florida cottonmouth knows where it got its name," the announcer on National Geographic said.

Landry looked at the television. He'd encountered a cottonmouth once, when he was at SDV school outside Panama City, Florida.

Landry opened to the article in *US Weekly* magazine. There she was with her golden retriever, Charlie, and her teacup Chihuahua, Spike.

"Contrary to popular belief, a venomous snake's bite is rarely life-threatening..."

Landry knew of people who had been bitten by venomous snakes. Most of them did fine because there was so little snake venom actually injected into their wounds. This was because snakes had only so much venom, and they used it to paralyze prey. They didn't like to waste it.

Landry turned the page. There was a story about the reality show, *Soul Mate*. Below were the photos of the four remaining contestants. He remembered them in a different context. He read their stories, seeing them for the first time as human beings with petty problems and lofty aspirations. He read each of their names aloud—the show producer, Justin Balough, Brendan Shayles, Amber Redmond, Connor Fallon, and Tanya Williams.

Brendan Shayles was the kid who looked at the stars. Turned out Brendan was one of the last two finalists chosen earlier that day. No wonder he was happy.

Poor kid. Brendan Shayles was in the wrong place at the wrong time.

Landry looked back at the television. There was the cottonmouth, coiled up, its mouth wide open and showing white—white like cotton. Showing his mouth as a warning, because snakes didn't use their venom indiscriminately.

He looked back at Brendan Shayles. The question remained: Why kill a bunch of kids from a television show? Why kill a celebrity like Brienne Cross? Were the kids collateral damage, or were they also the targets?

There would be a pattern. The Aspen killings weren't random, any more than mathematics was random. It would have its own logic.

The snake documentary was over, and now *The Dog Whisperer* was on. Landry switched the TV off.

He had undergone a battery of psychological tests for his current job—thoroughly profiled. He knew he'd been chosen for the job because he did his work without question. He saw his job in terms of mission only.

When he was working with the team, he answered to "Peters." There were four of them: Peters, Jackson, Davis, and Green. Peters had no connection to the life he had with his wife, his daughter, his brothers, and the racetrack.

Because he compartmentalized so well—it was an absolute necessity for him to do so—Landry had never looked for patterns in the missions he was given. He took each job as it came. He stayed away from the news and didn't read any paper except for the *Daily Racing Form*. He'd built a wall around the job, because the job defined him and he refused to look at it in any other light. The job was who he *was*. He carried out the missions that had to be done to keep this country safe and her people unaware. Blissfully unaware. He shouldered that burden for them.

But Brienne Cross?

Landry thought about some of "the Shop" missions, the ones that fit a similar profile to the Aspen killings. They had seemed unusual at the time, but Landry had lived long enough to know that danger could come from unusual sources.

There was the blonde Mexican woman in Malibu. She'd looked familiar. He'd dispatched her one twilight as she jogged alone down Serra Road near her rented house. His orders were to stab her in the heart and leave her there, exposed.

The Egyptian professor at Berkley. Landry could see a reason for this man's death. He could have been a radical Islamist.

But he didn't know for sure, did he? Because he didn't read the papers or watch the news.

The wealthy couple in Montana. The man had looked familiar.

He Googled them.

The Mexican woman was Jacinta Rivera, a Mexican pop star. She was very popular in the United States, but a superstar in Mexico. There had been a national day of mourning for her.

The Egyptian professor was a well-known political pundit and author. He had a show on CNN.

The husband and wife in Montana were both actors. The husband was an up-and-coming star, widely hailed to be "the next Brad Pitt." They had just bought the ranch and retreated there between films.

Landry stared at the crime scene photos of the ranch, remembering the mission. He and his team had been swift and merciless. That was a year and a half ago, during the hostage crisis at the U.S. embassy in Yemen. The U.S. government had botched the hostage situation, and both U.S. soldiers and American civilians had been killed and dragged through the streets.

He counted them on his fingers. A Mexican pop star. An Egyptian professor with a show on CNN. The famous actor who was the next Brad Pitt.

He found himself thinking about poisonous snakes, how they knew when to strike and why. And he thought: *What strange places to use your venom.*

11

"Stop!" Maddy shouted. "That's it. I'm sure this time."

In the last two hours, Jolie and Maddy had driven all over Palm County looking for Chief Akers's guns and phone, finally narrowing it down to a stretch of road between Gardenia and Port St. Joe. Dade Ford Road ran along an area punctuated by a dozen small sloughs and ponds. Maddy claimed she'd thrown the guns in one of them and the phone in another. But it was dark when she did it, with only a few stars to see by. She couldn't tell one place from another.

Three or four times now they'd pulled off to the side of the road, Maddy squinting through the windshield. Then she'd say, "No, this isn't it."

On the drive, Maddy told Jolie about her adult children. One girl had two children, a boy and a girl, and the younger girl was a theater major at FSU. In close quarters, Maddy's voice seemed very bright and loud—almost manic. Jolie felt increasingly uncomfortable, but it wasn't just Maddy's voice. She knew that at some point, she would have to get out of the car and walk out to one of these ponds.

Jolie wondered if this...*phobia* could affect her job. Nobody wanted a phobic cop, especially a water-phobic cop in a county where there was so much water.

Maddy said, "You know, I really think this is it. Up a little farther. Off that little road."

Jolie drove along the road's shoulder and turned onto the crushed shell two-track in the direction of the trees. She parked. Maddy got out, but Jolie remained in the car.

It was hot with the air off. Like an oven. Beads of sweat prickled her scalp.

Maddy waded through the brush a ways and turned back. "You coming?"

"In a minute," Jolie said. "You go ahead." She took the clipboard off the dash. She stared at it without seeing and made a notation—her initials. The heat buzzed at the edge of her nostrils, making it hard to breathe. She glanced at her computer. Looked through the windshield at Maddy, who was walking along the edge of the trees.

All right.

She pushed open the heavy car door and stepped out. Adrenaline rushed to her hands and feet, leaving her center cold. The buzz in her gut grew louder.

She watched Maddy push through the undergrowth. Lots of low vegetation and tall trees. Kudzu vine, too. Jolie stared at the kudzu. It was a special color green. She knew the color. What was it? Kelly. Kelly green. It was so bright, so luridly green, she had to look away.

Maddy called out to her. "I really think this is the place."

Jolie straightened and took a breath. Pushed off with her left foot. Kept on walking, right foot, left foot. She'd walk until she had to stop. Through the brush, she caught glimpses of the water, stained to a tea color by the tannin from the cypress trees.

And she surprised herself. Before she knew it, Jolie had reached the bank. Stood at the edge, looking down at the water.

And she felt nothing.

No dark, buzzing cloud of unreasoning fear. No feeling that she would die any minute. None of that.

She did experience a thrill. Pure, like salvation.

12

Nick thought: *This book will sell itself.*

He loved the idea, his agent loved it, and the publisher loved it. Why not? Something like that happens to you, why not use it? He'd be a fool not to.

Someone murders a bunch of people in an upscale house in Aspen, kills a big star like Brienne Cross, and you're the sole survivor? It's like the gods came down from Mount Olympus and said, "What the hell are you waiting for?"

His agent and his publisher wanted the book soon. Even before the ink was dry on the contract, they suggested he get out there and hype it. And so he did. He gave interviews to news organizations, tabloids, magazines, radio, and the bloggers. He always held something back, though, giving every one of them the same canned story. He needed to keep his powder dry for the book.

When he and his publisher were tossing around ideas, they fell into calling it "The Aspen Project." They all agreed he had a special perspective, having written the series of essays on Brienne's reality show for *Vanity Fair*. Nick had been embedded with the *Soul Mate* cast and crew, had been there for every flare-up, every temper tantrum, every romance, every act of subterfuge and double-dealing.

He would follow the lives of those who were killed—the four finalists, the producer, and Brienne Cross herself—and propel them to their moment with destiny. At the same time, he would tell his own story.

He had eight-thousand-plus followers on Twitter, and over five thousand on his Facebook author page.

He announced: "By the end of this week, I'll be living in Aspen for the summer. I'll be in and out, because I plan to meet with the families of the dead. I'm going to tell their story because until now, they've had no voice."

A follower asked if he had contacted the family members. "Yes I have, and I will be interviewing all of them for the book."

More questions: "Who was the guy you talked to out on the deck? Was he the one who saved you?"

Nick said, "He said his name was Mars. Weird name—maybe I dreamed it."

"Are you going to thank him?"

"If I can find him."

"Is that going to be hard?"

"I think he said his dad is a congressman from Colorado. I'll start there. Nick Holloway, intrepid reporter! Seriously, I have no idea how Mars knew what was going to happen, or why he saved me, but you can bet it'll be in my book. I'll keep you posted. Ciao for now!"

13

They didn't find the guns or the cell phone, and probably never would. No money in the budget to drag ponds, even if Maddy could remember where she'd been.

It was late afternoon by the time Jolie drove into Meridian Beach.

The town still had the ability to charm. The sand was white as sugar. The Gulf changed color according to its mood—olive-green, jade, dark blue, gray, and gold at sunset. Gift shops were strung along the two-lane highway. The locally owned supermarket sold groceries, sunscreen, beach towels, and beer. But every day, more pine forests went under the bulldozer and another multiple-family rental went up on the beach. It was starting to get giddy here, and Jolie wasn't surprised that her estranged family had gotten on board in a big way.

The first thing she did was run a bath. Interrogating Maddy had taken its toll. It took her back in time to the day she got the call from her supervisor, breaking the news. Earlier in the day she'd heard about a man shooting himself in a cabin in the Apalachicola National Forest, but she would never have made the connection. Life was good. She and Danny were happy. He was a cop, she was a cop. They understood each other.

When someone you loved committed suicide, there was no refuge from it. You couldn't help but take it personally. It was as if someone threw acid on you, and the acid stayed, eating its way through your soul.

It shamed you.

If you only did this, if you only did that. You played that game over and over until you thought you'd go mad.

The phone rang. Kay McPeek's name showed up on the read-out—her cousin.

Kay came with a very large string attached. She was a Haddox. True, Kay led a relatively normal lifestyle—she didn't live on Indigo, for one thing—but she'd managed to drag Jolie to the Haddox compound not once, but twice. Jolie had mixed feelings about that.

It was hard not to be impressed by all that power and ostentatious wealth. The family lived on a private island. Jolie found herself wondering what her life would have been like if she'd been part of the family. But when her mother married her father, a working man and artist with little money and fewer prospects, the family turned their backs on her. These were difficult thoughts to entertain, because Jolie couldn't help feeling she was being untrue to her father's memory.

Jolie answered, and Kay said, "Forty-eight days and counting."

The goal was for her daughter Zoe to reach the first day of classes at Brown University. "Just hope she doesn't get knocked up before then."

"You don't honestly think that would happen."

"No. Zoe's a cool kid—waaaaay too smart for that. But I'll feel a hell of a lot better when she's in the dorm. I'll finally be able to breathe."

Kay wasn't happy that her daughter was spending the summer at Indigo. She was sure Zoe's cousin Riley was a bad influence. But Zoe had lobbied so hard, wanted it so badly, that Kay had given in. It was only for the summer. After that, Zoe would be safely in Rhode Island.

"So did you go see the house?" Kay asked.

"I did." Jolie went to turn off the tap. She felt dirty and tired, and hoped the bathwater wouldn't cool off too quickly.

"I was right, wasn't I? Depressing."

"A little," Jolie said. "But maybe it wasn't back then. I remember my first apartment—what a dump that was. But I was too young to know any better. I can see a young couple just starting out being happy there."

"Young people in love," Kay said. "They'll live anywhere. You remember anything?"

"How could I? I wasn't even two years old. I took some pics, though."

"Well, good, you have a record of it, then. I'm glad it's not listed with us—that place is going to be a hard sell, even if it is the ancestral home of the Petal Soft Soap Baby."

Jolie smiled. Her big claim to fame.

Kay had made no bones about it; she wasn't thrilled about the idea of Jolie going back to her parents' house. She'd warned Jolie it would be disappointing. And it was. Jolie had hoped for some resonance, something that connected her to her parents during a happy time in their lives. But there was nothing.

They talked for a while longer, mostly about Zoe and her cousin Riley, Franklin Haddox's daughter. Riley was spoiled, and Kay suspected she was sexually active. "I wish I hadn't let Zoe stay with her."

"She's got common sense," Jolie said. "She'll be all right."

"Easy for you to say."

*   *   *

The water in the tub was cold. Jolie drained it and started filling it up again. In the meantime, she clicked through her photos of the house. A saltbox cottage, faded yellow. Sunny kitchen, linoleum floors, tiny nursery. The pocket yard, the canal out back. The canal looked a lot like the canal behind the house she lived in now.

Home of the Petal Soft Soap Baby.

Jolie clicked through the photos and tried to picture her parents living as newlyweds there.

As Kay said, they were young and in love. They didn't have much money. They were about to have their first and only child. But the place was too old. The story was too old. Whatever had breathed life into the love story between her mother and father was gone.

*   *   *

She must have dozed off, because the bathwater was stone cold. Jolie hitched herself up a little; she'd slipped down so her chin was almost in the water. The candle had burned low.

She looked across the tub at her knees, rising up like islands. That was when it hit. A hurtling torrent of stark, raving fear. Her heart wanted to burst. Heat suffused her face. The fight-or-flight mechanism kicked in. She couldn't stand to be in the tub another minute. She grabbed the sides and hoisted herself up. Her shin bumped and scraped the side as she scrambled out of the tub. Slipping, almost going down.

She grabbed the towel from the rack. Made it out the doorway. Shaking so hard she could barely work her legs. Her brain buzzed and stuttered. She couldn't think.

The chasm opened. She felt the pull. Step in and disappear for good.

Go! One foot after the other.

She made it to the kitchen. Shivered in the sun streaming through the window.

Twenty minutes later, she went back in the bathroom. The sight of the full tub threw her heart into overdrive. She punched the drain fixture and retreated to the kitchen.

Something was very wrong with her. Mental-illness wrong. First the pond, scaring her for no reason. And now the tub. Jolie knew she would not fill that tub again. Forget the lighted candles, the bath salts. She hoped she wouldn't react to taking showers, because then she'd really be in trouble.

After spending an hour Googling panic attacks and water phobias, she came to a conclusion. Panic attacks, it appeared, were tricks. Something unknown triggered the fight-or-flight reaction, and the body reacted, fooling a person into thinking he was in mortal danger. So the next time it happened, she would tell herself, calmly, that she wasn't in danger.

Mind over matter.

Right now she had two choices. She could sit here frozen in fear. Or she could work the case.

The case seemed to be wrapping up in a satisfactory way. Maddy's confession had sealed it.

But there were still things about the case that didn't add up. Amy Perdue, for instance. Amy was Maddy's employee—she worked at one of the apartment buildings Maddy owned. And Jolie was about eighty percent certain that Amy knew of Maddy's cover-up of her husband's suicide. That could be the reason for Amy's fearful behavior in Bizzy's parking lot, and the reason she'd driven to Maddy's house at seven in the morning on the day Maddy's husband died.

But Amy Perdue was also Luke Perdue's sister.

Luke died in room nine. Chief Jim Akers died in room nine.

For the first time, she wondered if she'd got it right. The coincidences piled up, yes, but all of them led to the same place. They led to a case solved. They led to a solid confession.

But why did she feel as if she were missing something?

Jolie went over the facts of the case in her mind. They seemed solid. But...

She needed to make sure.

It was time to talk to Amy.

14

First thing you saw when you reached the outskirts of Gardenia was the pulp mill, which looked like a giant scorched shuttlecock. Beyond the pulp mill was a labyrinth of gray buildings and industrial pipes. Sometime in the late nineteenth century, the sign "Iolanthe Paper Company" had been affixed to a trestle above the main building. The sign, lit by two dim lamps from above, featured a beauty with long flowing hair and tiny wings—Iolanthe, Queen of the Fairies.

Iolanthe was Big Paper in the Land of Big Paper. Jolie's family, the Haddoxes, sold out in the early seventies, laying the groundwork for two Haddox senators and a plum cabinet job, culminating in regular visits by the vice president.

Hard to be unmoved by such grandeur, but Jolie managed to keep a sense of perspective.

The Royal Court Apartments weren't royal at all, but just a regular stucco rectangle two stories high. Cramped little balconies fronted sliding glass doors.

Jolie didn't turn in the first time, but drove around the block and came back up the side street. On that first pass, she spotted a car parked alongside the outer wall of the apartments next to the office. A 1960s-era convertible. Cherry red, cherry condition. The writing on the trunk said *Ford Starliner*. A U-Haul truck was parked nose-out from the apartment closest to the office.

The sky was baleful red, the last light of day. As Jolie drove in from the right side of the parking lot, a wind blew in all the way from the Gulf, hot and pregnant with rain and dust, foul-smelling from the paper mill. An ill wind, rattling the tall palms out front like sabers. It buffeted the car as she slowed. The door to the office was wide open, and the wind caught angry voices and kited them into the ether.

A dark shape materialized in the doorway. As Jolie watched, it bent into a lurching run toward the U-Haul—a tall man, awkward running style, one arm folded across the other.

Hurt.

Young.

He could have been hit, knifed, or shot. She would assume whoever was inside had a gun, or a knife, or both.

Jolie stopped the car on a diagonal partway between the office and the U-Haul. Got out, crab-walked her way around the open door, and crouched behind the engine block. From there she could see both the office doorway and the U-Haul.

Glad she'd thought to wear her vest.

Another gust of wind and the office door blew shut. The angry diatribe continued.

She concentrated on the wounded man, now hunkered down by the front right tire of the box truck.

She identified herself and shouted, "You by the U-Haul truck. Sit down. Sit down now."

The man complied, trying to keep his hands out toward Jolie despite the injured arm.

"Cross your legs. Do it now."

He did.

"Put your good hand on top of your head. Do it now."

He did it—painfully.

"Do not move." She keyed the mic and got the Palm County dispatcher—Lonnie—and blurted out the code for officer needing assistance. She told Lonnie the subject inside had a weapon and asked for paramedics. Keeping her SIG trained on the man sitting by the U-Haul, Jolie also kept an eye on the office door. On the radio she heard distant chattering sounds—Palm County on another frequency. Another voice, another code. That would be the Gardenia PD. They'd be closer, even though technically it was not their jurisdiction. On her drive over, Jolie had checked to see if the Royal Court Apartments was inside or outside the Gardenia city limits. They were outside.

Which made this hers.

Lonnie said, "Palm County and Gardenia PD are on their way. What are you wearing?"

Lonnie was asking so they wouldn't mistake Jolie for the bad guy. "Jeans, a white tee, navy windbreaker."

"All units are responding."

The guy sat on the asphalt Indian-style as Jolie had instructed him. In the sodium arc lights she could see his dark blood, slick and shiny, where his shoulder met his forearm. She worried he would bleed out. She wanted to instruct him to take his hand off his head and stanch the wound as hard as he could with the palm of his hand, but she couldn't do that. The units would be here in minutes, but Jolie found herself counting down the seconds. One-one-thousand, two-one-thousand.

Time stretched. Adrenaline, at first quicksilver running to her extremities, started to recede. She had to be sure her strength and resolve wouldn't go along with it. Hoped she wouldn't be here alone long enough for her body to let down completely and start shaking.

But her bigger problem was the guy on the ground. Jolie didn't want him dying on her watch.

Inside the office, the shouting continued, riddled with expletives. Jolie worried that whoever had the gun might shoot someone else. But there was nothing she could do about that. All she could do was maintain the status quo.

Ten-one-thousand, eleven-one-thousand.

Jolie kept her eyes on the man by the U-Haul. It was as if he'd been preserved in amber. His hand remained on top of his head, and Jolie saw no weakness there. He'd probably be all right. He wore cargo shorts, a surfer's shirt, and boat shoes. In the yellow light, his face was stamped with his heritage along with his pain. Pakistani or Indian. Even sitting down he was amazingly tall. A beanpole.

The yelling turned up a notch. "I can't believe this. You sneak off with your boyfriend, and I get left behind to deal with the cops?"

The yelling man must have moved closer to the window, because now she heard whole sentences. The voice was familiar.

She heard a woman's voice but couldn't make out the words.

"How do you know?" the man demanded.

The female mumbled something unintelligible.

"How do you *know*? They aren't dumb. One thing's for sure—I'm not going down for this. I didn't do anything!"

The woman spoke, her voice barely there. If cringing was a tone of voice, this was it. "…be all right. You just… "

"So what happened? The three of you got together and said, 'Let's get Royce in on this, string him along, and *let him take the fall*'?"

Royce Brady. The owner of the Starliner Motel.

"…wasn't like…"

"Screw the old guy, huh? Like you really had the hots for me. How could I be so stupid? You guys having a threesome? Is that it? Are you and your boyfriend meeting that lying bitch somewhere while I sit here waiting for a knock on the door?"

"You shot Niraj. He'll go to the cops—"

"I don't give a shit. The way I feel right now, I might just call them myself. All I did was look the other way. That's all I did, but you...*you*. You set the poor fucker *up!*"

What Jolie was hearing was an impromptu confession. She saw it as a gift.

"Poor bastard...poor fucking fool didn't know he was sleeping with a goddamn viper!"

The woman said something else Jolie couldn't catch.

The man again: "I come here, thinking you and I had a thing, and there's this fucking *camel jockey*—" A pause. "It was all a lie, wasn't it? He didn't beat his wife."

The girl, whimpering now. "Please..."

He mimicked a female voice. "*Oh, Royce, she's scared to death he's going to kill her!* That was bullshit, wasn't it, Amy? Like everything else—just something you two girls cooked up to get me on your side."

Amy and Maddy.

Jolie realized that something had been bothering her all along, but she'd ignored it. Now, though, it all became clear. She recalled the sequence of events—Amy Perdue driving up Chief Akers's street this morning. An hour later, Maddy Akers drove into Bizzy's parking lot, just as Jolie caught up with Amy.

Just happened to show up.

Jolie flashed on the interrogation. The way Maddy gave it up so quickly. Jolie had thought at the time how it was like pushing over a domino.

We suicide widows have to stick together.

Maddy Akers had played her.

15

Before going in to interrogate Amy Perdue, Jolie found a quiet spot and tried to put herself in Amy's place. On a notepad, she wrote four reasons why Amy might have helped Maddy Akers set up Chief Akers's murder. Jolie would try one rationale after another, until one of them worked.

All you did was arrange to meet Chief Akers at the motel?
Did you think you'd lose your job if you didn't help your boss?
Was Maddy afraid of Chief Akers?
Did Chief Akers threaten to kill Maddy?

Amy wasn't the prime target here. Maddy was. Jolie wanted to make it easy for Amy to give up Maddy Akers. Her job was to find the right lever to pull.

To keep Amy around, Jolie was holding her on a domestic violence charge—Royce Brady claimed she'd hit him—but in a few minutes, she would tell Amy she was no longer under arrest. She would tell Amy that her only goal was to take Amy's statement and get her side of the story.

She'd already interviewed the gunshot victim, Niraj Bandhu, at the medical center in Panama City, and Royce Brady. Brady corroborated what Jolie had already surmised: that Maddy Akers had made her husband's death look like a covered-up suicide, when in actuality it was a homicide.

Interesting how it unraveled. Royce had thought he and Amy had a thing going, but when he dropped in on her unexpectedly at the Royal Court Apartments, he found out about Niraj, Amy's boyfriend.

"She set me up," Royce told Jolie. "I didn't even know what they were doing until I got to the room and saw him lying there dead."

He told her Maddy was desperate to escape her bad marriage, that her husband had threatened to kill her.

The gunshot victim, Niraj, had known nothing about the scheme, but he did fill in a few blanks. He told Jolie about the five thousand dollars Amy said she'd be getting soon. Amy told him it was money from a dead uncle. She told Niraj that as soon as she got the money, she'd move in with her cousin in Baton Rouge. He could stay or go—up to him. When she got the money, she'd be gone. She'd rented a U-Haul and had started to move the furniture.

*　　*　　*

The image of Maddy Akers searching the brush at pond after pond looking for guns and cell phones made Jolie laugh out loud. Despite the fact she'd been fooled, she couldn't help but admire the way Maddy's mind worked.

The two of them, beating their way through the bushes—what a show. Wherever Maddy had thrown the weapons, she would never have taken Jolie to the spot.

It was clear Maddy knew about Danny's suicide. It was common knowledge. She'd used Jolie's own feelings about her husband's suicide against her.

The theory was this: Amy lured Chief Akers to the motel, and Maddy snuck up on him and shot him point-blank. In one inspired stroke, Maddy deflected attention away from the act of homicide by making it appear to be a covered-up suicide, eliminating the spouse as primary suspect in the bargain. Not only that, but she'd provided a viable explanation for any trace evidence she might have left at the scene.

It was a brilliant, audacious plan.

But Maddy's scheme fell apart, as brilliant schemes often did, when she relied on the wrong people.

*   *   *

Amy Perdue looked small and childlike, her limp red hair concealing half her face.

Jolie led her through the confrontation with Royce Brady. As the injured party, Amy was cooperative. She was the wronged woman, a victim of domestic violence.

"No idea why he was so angry?"

"No. It was like he had a crush on me or something. It was crazy. He said really crazy things."

"Like what?"

"I don't know, just crazy stuff. He was paranoid. Like a paranoid schizophrenic. Why? What did you hear?"

"You work for Maddy, right?"

"Uh-huh. Did—" She stopped.

"Did what?"

"Nothing. Can I go now?"

"Just a few questions and we're through." Jolie smiled.

"Okay. It's just, I'm really tired and it's been so scary and I want to see Niraj. I want to see if he's okay. Is he all right?"

"Niraj is fine." Jolie leaned forward so their legs were almost touching. "Amy, was Maddy afraid of her husband?"

Jolie noticed that every time Amy got nervous, the leg crossed over her knee bounced. Right now Amy's legs were going like a jackhammer. "How would I know?"

"Royce said you were worried about Maddy Akers because her husband beat her. He even threatened to kill her."

"Is that what Royce said? She did mention something about that."

"So Maddy thought he was going to kill her?"

"That's what she told me."

"Thing is," Jolie said, "Royce said that you and Maddy planned to kill Chief Akers and make it look like a suicide. He said you asked him for help because the chief was beating his wife and he threatened to kill her."

"That's bullshit!" Her legs shook so much, the one on top slid off, hitting the floor with a smack.

"Is it? He went into a lot of detail."

Amy kept quiet, but Jolie saw something in her eyes. More than worry—the beginnings of panic.

"You know what I think?" Jolie said. "Maddy's a bad influence on people. Telling Royce that her husband wanted to kill her. That wasn't even true, was it?"

Amy concentrated on the table.

"Maddy lied to Royce. I bet she lied to you, too. It sounds to me like she used you. She told you she was afraid for her life. I can understand you'd be sympathetic—it's not easy being a woman. Domestic violence isn't taken seriously, is it? Men threaten their wives, and you just know some day they're going to do it. It happens all the time. So I can see how you'd believe her. Why *wouldn't* you believe her?"

Amy opened her mouth to say something. Stopped.

Jolie said, "To me, that's just plain self-defense. If my husband told me he was going to kill me, I surely would try to kill him first. I'm not going to wait there like a sitting duck."

Amy took a deep breath. Said in a small voice: "She told me he hired a hit man to kill her. He said it could happen any time. She was terrified."

"And you believed her. Who wouldn't?"

"If I told you what she did, what would happen to me? I mean, what kind of deal would I get? Would I have to do jail time?"

"Amy, if Maddy lied to you about her husband wanting to kill her, if she used you, that would be a mitigating circumstance. If you're forthcoming about this, I could talk to the state attorney, see what he thinks…"

She looked relieved. She wanted to talk.

Here we go.

"What if I had something to trade?"

"Trade?"

"So I wouldn't have to do jail time."

"That's up to the state attorney."

"What if I knew about something…" She twisted her hair. "You know, something bigger?"

Jolie stared at her.

"Something really huge."

Jolie said, "You're going to have to tell me more about it."

"If we can work out a deal, if you can promise me I won't go to jail, I'll tell you."

"I can't make that promise."

"Then I'm not telling."

"Amy—"

"Do you have a safe house?"

A safe house. Jolie realized something big was happening. It was time to talk to the state attorney. She stood up. "I've got to go to the little girl's room. I'll be back in a minute."

She opened the door and collided with her detective sergeant, Skeet.

It was not a pleasant experience. He shoved her back a little, hands clamped on her forearms, his bovine face blocking out the fluorescents above like a Macy's Thanksgiving Day balloon. "Whoa there, you in a hurry?"

He looked beyond her. "That Amy Perdue you got in there?" He leaned in through the doorway and spoke directly to Amy. "Ma'am? Amy Perdue? Your lawyer said to tell you he's on his way."

Jolie's disbelief turned quickly to anger as she realized what had happened. She looked back at Amy—who was as surprised as she was.

Amy didn't have a lawyer. Correction: she didn't *know* she had a lawyer. Jolie stepped out of the room, shutting the door behind her, and said to Skeet, "What are you doing?" She didn't know whether he understood the ramifications of his action or not. Skeet was dumb, but he also had a perverse streak.

Skeet's mouth turned up slightly at the corner. It made him look even dumber. "You're going to have to be clearer than that."

"How's this for clear?" Jolie said. "You just shut my interrogation down."

*　*　*

Jolie left Amy in the interview room to wait for her lawyer. From the moment Skeet poked his head in, Amy was off-limits—it was as if Amy's fairy godmother had come in and waved a magic wand. While she waited, Jolie called Sheriff Johnson at home and asked for a surveillance team on Maddy Akers. She didn't mention Skeet's blunder or her reaction to it. There was no point. Tim Johnson was a good sheriff in a lot of ways, but he let Skeet do what he pleased. The reason Tim didn't do anything about Skeet was because Skeet was married to the mayor's cousin.

"Surveillance? What are they looking for?" the sheriff said.

"Anything out of the ordinary. If she goes anywhere, I want them to follow her. They'll need two cars. I want to know right away if Amy goes by to see her."

She was thinking about the five thousand dollars Amy had coming. Jolie thought it was from Maddy for services rendered. "I'm asking for a warrant, for her financial dealings and also her house."

"You think you have probable cause?"

"Don't know unless I try. I'm thinking Doug Sharpe." Doug Sharpe was a judge who was known to be supportive of law enforcement.

"His wife is in a bridge club with Mrs. Akers."

"I'll have to take my chances."

*　　*　　*

The ringing phone woke Jolie. The clock said eight fifteen. Jolie'd had about six hours of sleep after being up thirty-eight hours. Typical, when a homicide was going. She lay in bed, let the answering machine pick it up.

A woman's voice drifted in from the other room—agitated.

Jolie ran for the phone.

"Amy?"

"Oh. You're there." She paused. "My lawyer said I shouldn't talk to you. I shouldn't be doing this."

"Then why are you?"

"Because…I think they're after me." She blurted it out.

"Who's after you?"

"It's…there was this car outside my place."

"A car?"

"Maybe I'm just…I don't know." She stopped.

"What can I do for you?"

"Do you have a safe house?"

Jolie was pretty sure they didn't have a safe house; the subject had never come up before. The FBI might. "I could probably arrange that," Jolie said. "But you're going to have to give me more information. We could meet—"

"I didn't hire that lawyer."

"Who did?"

"I don't know. But I didn't hire him. I think they wanted to make sure I didn't end up in jail. I think." She paused. Jolie could hear her swallow. "I think they want to get to me."

"Who wants to get to you?"

There was silence. Then: "You know what? This isn't a good idea."

"If you could just give me some idea who they are—"

"You think I'm crazy." Jolie could hear her breathing, ragged and fast.

"Amy—"

"I've got another call."

"Amy—"

"Okay. Why don't you check this out? See if I'm telling the truth, okay? And I can call you back. You have missing persons, right? You're police, you do missing persons. Was there anything like that? On Memorial Day weekend?"

Jolie was completely at sea. "A missing person?"

"I've got another call. This is *not* a good idea. Forget I said anything."

Then she disconnected.

*   *   *

71

Jolie sat in the kitchen, looking past the screened porch to the trees beyond. She could just make out the pond between the trees. Her stomach tightened.

She'd put it off long enough. She went into the bathroom and looked at the shower. Sunlight arrowed off the chrome nozzle. She took a deep breath and turned on the faucet. To her surprise, she was okay. She pulled the lever that started the shower. The spray hit the bottom of the tub. She undressed. Pretend it was just like any one of the thousands of times she'd taken a shower in her life. Nervous, yes. Terrified? No. Like her trip to the ponds with Maddy yesterday, nothing bad materialized. No big thunderclap. No crushing darkness.

She was fine.

16

Nick arrived in Aspen late in the afternoon. He got settled into his condo on Durant and went out to grab dinner. Saturday night, he couldn't get into Cache Cache. There was a line on the sidewalk outside Locust, so he left his name with the maître d' and took a short walk, watching the people on the street and window-shopping.

As he passed the newspaper vending machines, the front page of the *Aspen News* caught his eye. He fumbled with his change, dropping it on the sidewalk, all the while staring at the headline. Pulled out the paper and dropped *that*, too. Stared at it hard, his heart going hammer and tongs, heat suffusing his face.

"Aspen Man Found Dead in Starwood Home."

It wasn't the headline so much, but the photo on the right.

Mars.

In the photo Mars wore a heavy cable-knit sweater, his arm wrapped around a ski bunny at a local bar. His flared nostrils gave him a spoiled rich-boy look. He *was* spoiled—a congressman's son. Nick knew for a fact he was rich. When he'd seen Mars last, the guy was offering him a ride in his yellow Lamborghini. In hindsight, Nick knew Mars was trying to get him out of there before the killing started.

He swallowed, but his mouth stayed dry.

Please let the cause of death be cancer.

Someone on the sidewalk brushed by him, and he jumped a foot.

"Excuse me," the man said, and Nick muttered, "'S okay."

Please let it be something he's had for a while.

But Mars had looked pretty healthy that night.

Heart drumming, Nick read the story fast, then read it again, slower this time. His appetite gone.

Mars's real name was a mouthful: Frederick Cable Hollister III. Reading between the lines, Nick got the impression Mars was a rich ski bum who liked prescription drugs. In fact, he liked prescription drugs so much he died from an overdose of them in his fancy wood-and-stone house in Starwood.

Kid was a druggie. He probably came close a dozen times.

Maybe.

Or maybe there was a connection to the Aspen murders.

Maybe Brienne's killers found Mars and killed him to keep him quiet.

Maybe whoever killed Mars would come for him, too.

17
ZOE AND RILEY

Riley Haddox sat up. "Oh. My. God."

Zoe McPeek knew that tone. She heard her mom's voice: *Uh-oh. Riley's gone into crisis mode.*

They'd been sunning on the dock since noon. Zoe wasn't nuts about getting a tan; she knew all about melanoma and how sunning damaged your skin, but Riley was a tanning *freak*, so if Zoe wanted to hang with her, it was kind of required. She thought it was boring, though, and uncomfortably hot and sweaty. She could almost feel her skin turning into leather like Riley's mom, who rode horses and looked like them, too.

Riley was busy scrolling through her midnight-blue Sidekick LX. "How could I forget *that*?"

"What?"

"The *video*!" Riley cast her an impatient look, as if Zoe should know what she was talking about.

Zoe came this close to asking, "What video?" but she didn't dare. She rummaged through her memory bank, trying to figure out what Riley was talking about.

Mr. Clean, far enough away to give them some privacy, looked over at them. He wore swim trunks, but that didn't fool anybody; he still looked like a bodyguard. Scary looking, with his shaved head, dark glasses, and huge muscles—the reason Riley had nicknamed him Mr. Clean. Riley was no stranger to bodyguards—when

her dad was attorney general, they'd had a security detail that
went everywhere with all members of the immediate family.
Riley's dad told them two weeks ago he'd decided they should
have more security, citing an incident where a high school girl
in Panama City was kidnapped by a sexual predator. Mr. Haddox
said it was better to be safe than sorry.

Riley took it all in stride, but Zoe saw it as an invasion of her
privacy. Riley, who never saw a man she didn't like, flirted with all
three of the guys, even Mr. Clean.

Zoe just couldn't see why they needed security when all they
were doing was sunbathing on a private island.

"Earth to Zoe! You're not listening!"

Zoe looked up. "What's going on?"

"My whole life's going down the tubes, that's what's going on!
You see this?" She held up the phone, tapping one of the thumbnail photos. "See that red S? That means *sent.*"

"Sent?"

"Oh for fuck's sake, Zoe, you can be so dense! Somebody sent
a whole bunch of pictures from my phone, and I don't know who!"

"I don't see…"

"The video! It was sent from my phone to someone else." She
stood up, pulled her shorts on over her swimsuit, and reached for
her shoes.

"Maybe we can figure out where it went. Who touched your
phone?"

"I don't know!"

"You've only had the phone for a couple months," Zoe said.
"Has anybody else used it?"

"No, nobody…except Luke. He was the only one who got
near it."

76

Zoe watched as Riley teared up again.

"I miss him so much!" Riley grabbed herself around the middle, as if she had a stomachache. Zoe was used to Riley's breakdowns. She didn't blame her. Riley's boyfriend, Luke, was dead. He'd been shot after taking a woman hostage at a motel in Gardenia. Only the fact that Riley and Luke had kept their love affair secret had spared Riley from becoming a household name.

Zoe said, "You're sure he was the only one?"

Riley stared daggers at her. "Yes, I'm sure! We were in love. We shared everything!"

"Then the video is probably still on his phone."

"We've got to go over there right now."

"Where?"

"Luke's. Aren't you listening? What if he sent it to someone? Oh my God, what if it's on YouTube?"

Zoe said, "I think you're blowing this thing out of—"

"It wasn't just any video! Luke and I *taped* ourselves. You know, doing it. We used my phone."

Zoe felt bad for Riley, but she was also curious how that worked—just how they had managed to have sex and take pictures at the same time. Although she had never had actual *sex*, she'd seen porn on the Internet and thought the mechanics of filming yourself on a cell phone would be hard to do.

"What are you looking at?" Riley was still standing on one foot, still battling with one sandal. She threw it down on the deck and started to cry.

"It's okay," Zoe said. "We'll just go over there and get his phone. It'll be all right."

"You sure?"

Zoe didn't have an answer to that.

*　　*　　*

They took Riley's Boxster Spyder because Riley didn't like Zoe's Miata.

Speeding down the two-lane highway, top down, music loud, hair blowing in the wind, Riley freaking. She must have asked Zoe a dozen times if it would turn out okay. Zoe always said yes.

"You're sure?"

"Positive." Although Zoe had her doubts. She imagined Luke's family would have cleaned out the house by now. It had been over a month since Luke died.

Riley tried Luke's number. It went to voice mail. Zoe said she thought it was a good sign.

"You think so?"

"It's out there somewhere."

"God, I miss him!"

For the first time, Zoe began to believe Riley actually *did* love Luke. It didn't seem like it when they were hooking up, but now Riley seemed genuinely wounded.

Riley honked her horn at the black SUV ahead of them. "Can't he go any faster? He's driving under the speed limit."

The man holding the sharpshooter rifle in the open back of the SUV lifted a hand in a friendly wave. Riley returned his gesture by flipping the bird.

Behind them, Mr. Clean stuck close to their back bumper. He looked like an egg with sunglasses.

Riley glanced in the rearview mirror. "When we get there, make sure they stay far enough away, okay? I don't want them hearing anything and telling tales."

"Okay."

Riley parked in front of a junky-looking green house. Two little kids sat in a kiddie pool out front. A chunky woman in a striped tube top, cutoffs, and flip-flops watched them from the porch, her face impassive.

"Mrs. Frawley? I'm Riley Haddox—"

"I know who you are." She leaned forward in her lawn chair. The webbing looked like it would go any minute. "What do you want?"

"There are some things that Luke said I could have. Can you let me in so I can get them?"

"And exack'ly what kind of legal standing does a chippie have?"

"Ex*cuse* me?"

She pointed to the younger girl. "My neighbor's little girl is on'y three years old, but she's smart enough to look up your skirt. I know loose morals when I see it, and you can bet Luke did, too."

Zoe looked at Luke's landlady in her tube top over a pouchy brown midriff ribboned with scars.

"So I guess you didn't know we were engaged," Riley said. She held up her hand. Zoe knew for a fact that Riley had bought the ring herself and wore it on the occasions she didn't want to be hit on. Rare, but it happened.

"You think Luke would marry someone like you? For your money, maybe. I know all about you. I know about the times you drove by here and spied on him after he called it quits. Somehow I don't think he'd want you pawing through his things now."

Riley's face had gone slack with disbelief. For once, she had nothing to say. Zoe found her own voice. "Mrs. Frawley, Luke had something of Riley's she really needs back. If you could just let us in for a minute, we could be out of your way."

"You her attorney? You sure sound like one." She heaved to her feet and walked in the direction of the converted garage in back. "There's nothing left. Cops took everything. But I suppose you won't go away until you see for yourself. Watch Charly and the little one while I go get the key."

*   *   *

"Told you."

The blinds were pulled and the room was dark and sour-smelling, but the only thing that remained was the cheap furniture. Zoe cringed at the thought of living here, something Riley had retroactively fantasized about, after Luke died "an outlaw." Zoe had to wonder how long Riley would have wanted to live here after growing up on the Haddox compound, love or no love.

"When did the cops come?" Zoe asked.

"Later that day. Put up yellow tape for everyone to see, which sure hasn't helped me get a new tenant. Stuff like that gets around. They took out a bunch of stuff then, came back later that day to get the rest."

"Everything?" Riley's voice was bleak.

"It's all evidence now, I reckon."

Riley went to the dresser, pulled open the top drawer.

"Hey! I didn't say you could do that."

Riley ignored her. She opened another drawer, went to the kitchen and opened cabinets. Crashed around the apartment, looking more and more scared—scared and desperate. Zoe just stood on the stoop, wishing they could get out of here.

Mrs. Frawley looked at Zoe. "You look like a sensible girl. Not so caught up in your looks you can't listen to reason. If she's your friend, you ought to tell her she pushed Luke away with both hands."

"What do you mean?"

"Chasing after him like that, once he'd had enough. One thing I've learned, chasing never makes it better. It only makes a man so desperate he'll chew his foot off to get away."

"She loved him."

"She'll get over it."

Riley came out of the bathroom. "The police have *everything*?"

"Yup," Mrs. Frawley said. "Impounded his car, too. That's what happens when you take a woman hostage and get yourself shot up in a cheap motel."

* * *

Back in the car, Riley slumped against the wheel. "Oh, God. I am so screwed."

She looked shaken. Scared. Nothing like the Riley Zoe knew. It scared her. Zoe wanted to say something comforting, but the words stuck in her throat.

Riley started to cry.

Then Zoe had an idea. "Maybe Aunt Jolie can help us."

"Aunt Jolie? You mean the cop?"

"She's a detective. Jolie's a good friend of Mom's. Maybe she could find out who has the phone and see if she can get it back."

Riley wiped her nose and looked over at Zoe. "You think she could do that?"

"I bet she could pull some strings." Although suddenly, she wasn't so sure.

"Call her," Riley said.

18

Jim Akers wasn't the family man Jolie assumed him to be.

Nobody at the Gardenia PD was surprised that Maddy Akers had killed her husband.

"Did you ever know him to threaten anybody?" Jolie asked Acting Chief McClelland.

McClelland sighed. "I saw him threaten a confidential informant once, back when he was a deputy. Going on fifteen years ago. Said if the guy didn't stop torquing him around, he'd kill him."

"*Kill* him?"

"A lot of people say that. Like, if you do that again, I'm gonna kill you. Hell, *I've* said it. But he meant it."

He was clearly uncomfortable with the conversation. "Couple of weeks later, the CI went missing. Found him in a canal not far from here. His head bashed in."

"You think it was Chief Akers?"

"Well, that's open to conjecture. But I do think Jim was capable."

"Would he ever threaten his wife?"

"Now, *that* I don't know. He never talked about her. I don't want to speak ill of the dead, but Jim acted like he wasn't married. Once in a while he'd bring her to a cookout. I'm sure she talked to the ladies, but I don't recall ever having a conversation with her. Whether that was her fault or his, I don't know. But it kind of felt like he was hiding her."

Jolie had bought it—Akers as the quintessential small-town police chief.

Maybe Maddy, manipulative as she was, really believed her husband planned to kill her.

* * *

Jolie went looking for Davy Crockett. She had a number of questions about the motel standoff, and she could trust Davy to be straight with her. They'd worked together many times over the past few years on cases that required interagency cooperation.

And Zoe's call earlier today was on her mind—Davy was the only guy at the Gardenia PD who might help her.

Davy Crockett was a giant black man with a bullet-shaped head he shaved every morning. In deference to the name his parents gave him, Davy had a moth-eaten coonskin cap tacked up on the wall above his desk. Davy was the PD's only detective, what was known as a "generalist." He worked homicide, but he also worked auto theft, smash-and-grabs, and domestics. Davy had been a good friend of Dan's when they were both deputies with the sheriff's office. They grew up together, kind of (Davy lived in the black neighborhood in Port St. Joe), and played on the same football team in high school.

When they were through with official business, Jolie said, "Would it be out of line if I asked to see an evidence list?"

"For who?"

"Luke Perdue. I'm looking for his phone."

"You want to tell me why?"

Davy had three daughters. She thought he'd sympathize. "There's a teenage girl who's worried about some photos of her on his phone. Sexting."

"That ain't good. Tell you what, I'll go check the list. As I recall, that whole thing went down a week after Memorial Day?"

"June eighth."

"Don't seem like it was that long ago. Time sure flies in this business. If and when they release the phone, I'll let you know. Who they releasing it to?"

"Next of kin would be his sister, Amy Perdue."

Davy shook his head. "Kids. It sure was a lot tamer when I was growing up."

"You ever take naked pictures of your girlfriend?" Jolie asked.

"Sure. And hid 'em away in a drawer. But these days…" He tapped the folder he'd been carrying against his leg. "Doesn't she know she's gonna end up on the Internet?"

*   *   *

Davy came back to the break room ten minutes later with a printout of the evidence list for Luke Perdue. "Talk about a wild-goose chase," he said.

Jolie took the pages from him. There were a number of pieces of evidence the police had confiscated from Luke Perdue's apartment. "No cell."

"Nope. Thought that was kind of strange myself."

"It wasn't on him when he was killed?"

"Doesn't look like it."

"Well, I know he had one. The girlfriend was very clear about that. Do you know who went to his place that day?"

"Crowley and LeFave. Just before noon on the day."

Jolie checked her watch. She wanted to call Judge Sharpe and see about the search warrants. She worried Maddy would have already destroyed whatever evidence remained. As Davy walked her out, she asked the same question she'd asked Acting Chief McClelland. "Do you think Chief Akers would threaten his wife? Threaten to kill her?"

Davy said, "He was into control, I know for a fact. Secretive, too. He didn't share what he was thinking with anybody else. The truth is, I have no idea what he would do and what he wouldn't do."

"Most people, you have a general idea," Jolie said.

He nodded. "Not the chief, though. He kept himself to himself." He added, "He had one hell of a temper. It was like a nasty storm brewing—everyone could feel it coming, and nobody would know what would touch it off."

19

ASPEN, COLORADO

This RadioShack was like RadioShacks anywhere, Landry thought. The interior was one long oval connected to a smaller oval, like a child's drawing of a cat. Fluorescent lights in boxes were set into the ceiling, the lighting harsh and muted at the same time. Sparse shelves. A quiet atmosphere. Only two men in the store, a clerk and a customer discussing iPod models.

The RadioShack was the same, but the shops around it were upscale. The scenery was spectacular.

Landry bought two wireless lapel microphones, $49.95 each. Inside each box was a single-channel mic, built-in compander noise reduction, with a two-hundred-foot operational range. Each box contained a lapel microphone transmitter, a receiver, and a 9-volt AC adapter. He bought four sets of AA batteries for the transmitters (two extra) just to make sure. The microphones were cheap, but that didn't matter. For certain occasions, you could get just as good stuff at RadioShack as you could going high-end. In the military they even had an acronym for it: COTS—commercial off-the-shelf. And Landry liked a bargain.

Stepping outside into the diamond-hard sunshine, holding the RadioShack bag with the boxed microphones inside, Landry looked in the shop window next door. He gathered the store sold clothing for the new generation, casual stuff you could wear to class or on a skateboard. Navy hoodies were displayed in the window, a photo above showing an unshaven twenty-something rappelling down from a helicopter. The clothing line was called "SEALS."

"If you only knew," he said to the display. The kid in the ad would likely want no part of SEALs training he'd endured at the Naval Amphibious Base on Coronado.

*   *   *

That evolution of BUD/S training was to keep him from drowning by making it a working proposition. He, along with the other trainees, was thrown into the water bound hand and foot. Hands behind the back. Normally, he was pretty tough. He liked to train— no, make that, he loved to train—and he was strong. Stronger than the guys who quit. Stronger than the guys who stayed. He was bigger than most, but he was able to keep up with the little guys, the compact guys who excelled in SEALs training. He was near the cutoff at the top of the age range, but he was as good any of them and smarter than most. Invincible. But when he plunged into the nine-foot-deep pool, something inside him broke loose. It was mortifying, this rebellion at the idea of drowning, apparently hardwired into him. There was yelling, there was berating, there was the water closing over his head as he sank. There were other bodies in the water, wires of refracted light cutting their bodies into pieces.

Commotion at three o'clock. Guy flipping out. Had to be taken out of the pool. Thrashing like a fish on a hook. Landry felt like flipping out too, felt like he really was *drowning, even though he wasn't. Straining to breathe. Chest burning. The first time his feet touched bottom he had forced himself to stay under, using what little breath he had, holding it for the required minute before shooting up to the surface like a cannon. He was expected to bob on the surface for five minutes. Any way he could, but ideally, he* should conserve energy. There was some fuck with a watch. Yelling at him. That fuck was his BUD/S indoc instructor, a real hard-ass named Keogh, a man he admired. No, make that a man he worshipped. But right now he was just the fuck who was stretching the time out, way past five minutes. Fifteen minutes, maybe. How could he get away with that? It was blatantly unfair, but that was something Landry'd learned first thing: the SEALs were not about fairness. They were about unfairness. He could feel himself slipping under the water. Blow it out. Grab a breath. Chin up. His body bucked, got torqued around. He looked like a prisoner and he felt like a prisoner. At this moment, he was less than a human being.

He was less than nothing and more than everything, because if he made it through, he truly would be invincible.

This was how you were forged.

This was what made you a warrior.

His swim buddy was having trouble. He couldn't let that happen. His bond with his swim buddy was greater than his bond with his wife. They did everything together. They never left each other's side. They even went to the head together. He managed to get closer, managed to throw him some confidence. At least he thought that's what happened, because they both made it. Float, bob, swim, forward and back flips. Other stuff. Interminable.

They called it drown-proofing. It was the worst thing he had to do, the one thing where he thought he would break, where he thought he would give up the dream and admit defeat.

But he didn't break that day. He didn't quit like some of the others.

He didn't have quit in him.

*　　*　　*

Landry stared at the mountain above town, thinking about last night.

Mars cooperated as much as he could, but he didn't really know anything. He said his father kept him on a tight budget. He needed money, and when some guy approached him at J-Bar with a proposition, he was happy to oblige. What it came down to was babysitting some guy and making sure he left the party at the house on Castle Creek Road by a certain time. Mars said he tried everything, even enticing Nick Holloway with a ride in his Lamborghini. As time grew short, he got Nick to walk down the hill toward the street to get some air, and "just sort of pushed him over the edge" into the garage, which was cut into the hill below the house. But Mars had no real information on the guy who hired him—it was a cash transaction.

Mars died hard, from a combination of opiates and Valium. His choice. But he had a seizure. His feet drummed on the polished pine floor of his Starwood condo.

It looked like an accidental drug overdose, which was what it should look like, but the whole thing bothered Landry. It was not his style to let someone suffer.

If Mars had not glanced out the window and seen Landry without his ski mask, Landry would have let him live. But once that happened, Mars was doomed.

And now Landry was no closer to finding out who ordered Brienne Cross's death, or the deaths of the others.

He worked for a shadow company that worked for a shadow government, and up until now he thought he was on the right side.

Now he knew better.

He walked. It was a nice day. Clear. Lots of people on the street; he was just one of them. Thinking about how he got here.

He'd started out pure. Like white socks, straight from the department store. You wore them once and they got a little worn. The threads stretched, almost imperceptibly. There was the slightest discolor. Enough so that you cared about them a little less. They were no longer white and new, fresh off the cardboard. They'd been in your shoe. By the end of the week, after a washing, they weren't new in any way. Then you got careless. One day you wore them to mow the lawn. You got grass seeds in there and sweat from your feet, and they started to yellow. Before you knew it, they were just old socks.

He was a warrior. He'd stood up for his country. He did good and bad things, but they were all for his country. And when he felt he couldn't go on—when he realized that he was pushing his luck and five tours were enough—he returned stateside and became an instructor at BUD/S. They say a racehorse has only so many times he can run down the track. That was the way Landry felt when he returned from active duty. He'd run his requisite number of times, and after that, he was through. But then he wanted to go back, he was restless, and he had a way to make a lot of money. Warfare and money together: the best of both worlds. That was when he took the sock out of the cardboard. Eight months working for Kellogg, Root & Brown. Making money hand over fist. Feeling the resentment of the soldiers. Their eyes on him: *You sold out.*

That's how he came to kill a bunch of kids in Aspen, Colorado.

He arrived at his destination and waited. It didn't seem like a long time.

He saw Nick Holloway leave his condo and drive away. He watched the car get smaller as it proceeded down the street. He watched until it turned the corner and was lost from view.

He bugged the condo. In and out in five minutes.

20

Long ago in a galaxy far away, Jolie was a sharpshooter. She'd earned three sharpshooting medals, attaining the designation "Expert." Her instructor had a saying. Miss one day of practice, you know it. Miss two days of practice, your instructor knows it. Miss three days of practice, *everyone* knows it. Running wasn't the same as shooting, but Jolie felt rusty when she started out on the street outside her house. It was still dark. Misty halos wrapped the streetlamps. Dew glittered on the grass. She smelled bacon and eggs coming from the bungalow on the corner of Conch and Highway 98. Crossed the deserted two-lane highway and took the easement through to the beach. Once on the sand, she picked up the pace. The regular sand, not the hard-packed. The scene before her grooved into her memory. The beach, the slow-heaving blackness beyond, the constantly rearranging fringe of surf in between. The rumble and sigh. Her calves felt like heavy bags of sand, hard to move. Being rusty bothered her, but only a little. The job got in the way, and since the job was her life, that was okay.

She got into a rhythm. Not the one she was accustomed to. Harder won, as if the sand she ran on sapped the blood straight out of her legs. She thought about going over to the hard-packed sand. On her left, buttoned up, were Cockatoo's Fine Seafood and Beach Ware Gifts. The Quik Mart across the highway. She came to the place where she had to jump a rivulet of brackish water. Shoes hitting the sand, one-two, one-two, one-two. New construction.

Space. More new construction. The little park. Her mind going back to Amy, asking for a safe house. Amy was going to run. She might have taken off already. Jolie ran past more new construction, just a frame and poured foundation. Amy's boyfriend, Niraj Bandhu, had been released from the hospital. Maybe Amy was there, or maybe she'd packed up the rest of the U-Haul and taken off. Jamaican Pete's ahead, kayaks stacked on their sides. A surge of water crawled up the sand in a long curve. Jolie ran around it. The other night, she'd observed the way men reacted to Amy—like they wanted to eat her up. They'd acted guilty and embarrassed about their behavior, reminding her of her dad's old dog when he peed on the carpet. Guilt didn't stop the dog, and it didn't stop them. The dog couldn't help his incontinence. The men were helpless, too, in their way. All of them, Skeet included. The deputies who were there that night—smitten.

Jolie couldn't see it, herself. Amy Perdue was no bigger than a flea. She had freckles and weak eyes. Her eyes were pale green and dull as grapes—nothing to them. Limp red hair parted in the middle. No boobs whatsoever. But she had something. It came off her person, silent as a dog whistle. Pheromones?

Amy's talk of "something bigger." Her belief that someone had hired a lawyer just to get her back out on the street. Maybe Amy was paranoid, but it was clear she was in *some* kind of trouble. Jolie didn't know what it was, but she knew Amy was in way over her head. It didn't take much of a leap to think it might involve her brother Luke and the standoff at the Starliner Motel. That was the biggest thing to happen around here in a long time.

Jolie turned around and ran back, reviewing the events at the Starliner Motel. Luke taking the woman hostage, Chief Akers trying to talk him out, the FBI sharpshooter's bad shot.

Did Amy really think the FBI shot Luke on purpose? But Amy wouldn't be in a position to know about that. No one would. It wasn't like she could phone the FBI and ask. Try talking to the FBI! Impossible.

Amy might be prone to conspiracy theories. Her brother was killed, the FBI shot him, she didn't want to blame her brother, so she conjured up a scenario wherein the FBI shot Luke to…what? That's where it all broke down.

Over the little rivulet. Past the Quick Mart, the incandescent light white against the indigo sky. And Riley—Riley had Jolie on her speed dial, constantly calling and texting about her boyfriend's missing phone. Strange, Gardenia PD having no record of a phone. But Davy'd told her that the FBI was involved, which made sense. They had the snipers. So maybe the FBI had the phone. *Probably* the FBI. She jogged across Highway 98. Slowed to a walk on Conch. Home. The cat in the window, his cries silenced by the glass. Leaning with her hands on her knees, Jolie's breath came in sharp gasps.

The FBI.

First thing she'd do today: go and talk to Luke's landlady, Mrs. Frawley.

As Jolie unlocked the front door, she thought of something else.

As far as she knew, even in all the media coverage of the standoff at the Starliner Motel, nobody had come up with a reason why Luke Perdue had taken Kathy Westbrook hostage.

Most everyone she'd talked to had thought he'd "just snapped."

But no one, it seemed, wondered *why*.

* * *

"All I know is there was two sets of police that came here that day," Mrs. Frawley said. They were standing on the porch outside her house. Mrs. Frawley rolled a stroller with a baby in it, back and forth. The doors to Mrs. Frawley's Saturn were open, a child's car seat on the walk. The little girl was skipping back and forth across the driveway. "I'm on disability, and with Luke gone, that's seven hundred dollars less I get a month. These are supposed to be my golden years, and *this* is what I'm doing when I should be on a Caribbean cruise, meeting the man of my dreams. Babysitting."

"I'm sorry about that," Jolie said. "There were two sets of investigators? Are you sure?"

"Yup. And they came in twos. Two plus two."

"Two plus two equals four!" called out Charly, who was now pushing the car seat down the walkway.

Jolie asked, "Did they identify themselves?"

"They said police. But they didn't have to—I knew it by looking at 'em. All that black Velcro stuff they wear."

"Did they give you their names and badge numbers?"

"Two of 'em did. Those were the regular cops. The first set, they were FBI."

"Did they say FBI?"

"Can't remember if they did or not."

"You know what the FBI looks like?"

"Of course I do. I watch *NUMB3RS*, all those shows. Char, come here!" she bellowed. Charly came hopping up and turned her back so Mrs. Frawley could help her with her My Little Pony backpack. Little kid wasn't seven years old, and already in a harness.

Jolie asked, "When did they come?"

"Mid morning? The first set. The FBI agents."

"Did they have a warrant?"

"Didn't ask 'em. Just handed them the key and stayed out of the way."

"They say anything to you?"

"They said Luke was in trouble, he was a danger to himself and others. I heard it on the news right before they got here, someone taking that lady hostage. At the time I didn't make the connection because I couldn't see Luke doing something like that."

"Did they take evidence?"

"Both batches of 'em did. Walked out with bags of stuff."

"Did you see what they took?"

"I was in the middle of dyeing my hair. I didn't want to leave it on too long."

"Did they take a cell phone?"

"Could've been in one of them bags."

"Granny?" Charly said, tugging on her grandmother's sleeve. "When's Luke coming home?"

"Sorry, baby, he's moved on to a better place." Mrs. Frawley rolled her eyes.

"Why doesn't he come back? He just went on a playdate."

Jolie hunkered down on her heels. "He went on a playdate? When was this, sweetheart?"

Charly chose that moment to turn shy. She pushed herself behind her grandmother and stared up at the trees.

"Charly!"

"It's okay," Jolie said.

Mrs. Frawley's voice softened. "Sweet pea, answer the nice lady."

"Do you know when Luke went on the playdate?"

"When he went away with that man."

"What man?" Jolie asked gently.

"The one that…" She stopped, looking confused. "The one in the black car."

"You mean the FBI car, honey?" Mrs. Frawley said. "Those men weren't here then."

"It was like a movie."

"Movie's her favorite word. Everything's a movie."

Jolie said, "Did Luke get in the car with him?"

"Uh-huh." She nodded, fidgeting with the straps of her backpack.

"When was this?"

"*Jeremy* just came on."

"Honey, that's early," said Mrs. Frawley. "There were two men, Charly. They came here later. Luke wasn't here then."

"What time does *Jeremy* come on?" Jolie asked Mrs. Frawley.

"Ten in the morning on Disney."

"But you didn't see anything."

"I was busy. I work from home, doing mailers."

"You didn't hear a car?"

"My printer's really noisy. Plus, I never miss *The Today Show*. Have to turn it up because I'm deaf in one ear."

Jolie bent back down so she was face-to-face with Charly.

"You said you asked Luke where he was going?"

The little girl squirmed. "I called to him. I was in the door."

"What did he say?"

"He said he was going with Will."

"Will?"

Mrs. Frawley shrugged. "She's got Will Smith on the brain. I have all the *Men in Black* DVDs."

"Did he say anything else?"

"No."

"Then what happened?"

"The man got out."

"Got out? Of the car, you mean?"

She nodded gravely. "He scared me."

"Why?"

"Because he looked like a bad guy in the movies."

"Movies again!" Mrs. Frawley snorted.

Charly said, "When he lifted his arms, I could see a *gun*."

"Where was the gun?"

"It was under his arm."

"Do you remember what color his hair was?"

"It was yellow, like Granny's. Only real short."

"Anything else you can remember?"

"He stood like this." She spread her legs slightly and put her hands on her hips. "He was right over there." She pointed to where the walk met the driveway. "I asked him if Luke was going to be in a movie, and he said yes. It was a secret, and I couldn't tell anybody."

Then her face lit up. "Is Luke going to be in *Men in Black*?"

*   *   *

Davy Crockett met Jolie at Bizzy's Diner. He sat down, placing his hat with deliberation on the table. The top of his skull gleamed in the low lights of the diner. When he turned to look for the waitress, Jolie noted the shar-pei folds where his head met his neck. Despite his massive proportions, his bare head made him seem vulnerable, like a newborn. "What's so important you had to interrupt me in the middle of my Lean Cuisine?" he asked her.

"Sorry about that."

"Don't be. I didn't plan to eat out, but now I'm here, I believe I'll have the Manhandler Breakfast. They're still serving breakfast, aren't they?"

"Far as I know. But what are you going to tell your wife?"

"What she doesn't know won't hurt her. A man's got to have some kind of life. It's not like I'm sleeping around or anything. So what's up?"

"It's about Luke Perdue."

He frowned. "The one-man wrecking ball. Yup, he sure did raise our profile at the Gardenia PD. Made us look like a bunch of clowns. FBI didn't come off looking too good, either."

Jolie told him about the man she believed picked up Luke Perdue on the morning of the standoff. "It was right before ten a.m. What time was the call-out?"

Davy thought about it. "Between ten a.m. and eleven. If you pushed me, I'd guess right around ten thirty. You're saying just before Luke showed up at the Starliner Motel, he left with an FBI agent?"

"That's what the little girl said. The FBI showed up at Luke's apartment around ten forty. I know that's true because Mrs. Frawley was looking at the clock. She was dyeing her hair."

"Jesus, that's fast."

"Around ten, some guy—Frawley thinks FBI—picks Luke up. At ten thirty you get the call-out to the Starliner Motel—"

"And fifteen minutes later, the FBI's searching the premises."

"Without a warrant," Jolie said. "I'm sure they'd claim 'exigent circumstances,' if Mrs. Frawley had asked."

"Which she didn't," Davy said.

"When did the standoff end?"

"Around dinnertime. I remember seeing the chief when he came in." He shook his head. "The man was shell-shocked."

"Do you know when Gardenia PD was dispatched to Luke's place?"

"It wasn't at ten forty, I can tell you that much." He leaned forward. "What does all this mean?"

"I have no idea."

"It was FBI shooters who took him out. Her too. You have any ideas?"

Jolie had been thinking about it since she left Mrs. Frawley's. "Maybe he was scared."

"So he holds a woman at gunpoint?"

"If he was scared enough. If he got away from the blond guy? The man Charly saw? He might have seen that as an option." Jolie realized how weird this sounded. "You think the FBI picked him up for some reason and he escaped?"

"Neat trick if you can do it. Why are you dumping all this on me? Luke's Most Excellent Adventure is the Florida Department of Law Enforcement's headache. They're the ones who're investigating the Starliner Motel shooting now."

"Then you'll have something you can give the FDLE."

He ran a palm over his clean skull. "Tell you what. Y'all give me Mrs. Frawley's contact info, I'll see it gets to the right people. Then it'll be their headache."

From his solemn expression, Jolie could see it sinking in. And there was a lot more to this story. Jolie saw her uneasiness reflected back to her in Davy Crockett's eyes. They both felt the same way.

Jolie said, "The little girl—Charly—said Luke was going with Will. She thought it had something to do with Will Smith, the actor. But maybe Luke told her he was going *against* his will."

"Could be. Looks like the FDLE's gonna have their work cut out for them."

The waitress came and took their orders. After she left, Davy said, "Now I've got something for you."

21

Davy knew a guy who knew a guy. The second guy did some work on Chief Akers's house. Davy thought it was under the table. But the thing was, this guy—his name was James Dooley—used to get drunk up in a bar in Wewahitchka, where he lived, and claim he had "offed thirteen people." He would tell anyone who listened he was a hit man in another life, but now he'd gone straight, although he still did favors from time to time.

"Do real hit men boast?" Jolie asked.

"How would I know? But you might want to check him out just the same."

After they parted ways, Jolie tried Amy's cell again. This time Amy's mailbox was full. The Royal Court Apartments were only a couple of blocks from Bizzy's, so Jolie drove by. The U-Haul was still out in front. As Jolie walked across the parking lot, she heard a thump and a scrape. She came around to the end of the U-Haul and saw Niraj Bandhu and another guy carrying a table into the apartment. Niraj struggled, his arm in a sling.

Jolie followed them in. Niraj's face looked pale and sweat popped out on his forehead. He sat on the couch.

"You probably shouldn't be doing that," Jolie said.

The other guy, a skinny Southern rocker type, took one look at Jolie and said "Hey, man, I gotta go."

When he was gone, Niraj said to Jolie, "She's not here. She never came back. They replaced her at the office."

"Maddy replaced her?"

"I guess so. I haven't seen her, either."

"You're staying?" Jolie motioned to the coffee table and the other furniture.

"I didn't know what else to do, and I have to get that U-Haul back or it's going to cost me another day."

Jolie asked, "Do you know a man named James Dooley?"

"I don't think so."

"Did Amy ever say anything about Chief Akers threatening his wife?"

"We didn't talk about things like that. I knew she and Maddy were good friends, but it wasn't really my business. She had her relationships and I had mine. Kind of hard to explain."

"Did you ever talk to Chief Akers?"

"I don't think I ever met him."

Jolie asked if Niraj had ever met Amy's brother, Luke.

"I met him a few times. Man, he was antsy."

"Antsy?"

Niraj shifted on the couch and winced. "He had all this energy. Like he was going somewhere in a hurry."

"He was ambitious?"

He laughed. "No, he just talked big. He's like those people who think they're gonna win the lottery. Always talking about how he'd strike it rich. Amy, she liked to burst his bubble. He'd be boasting about some new can't-miss scheme, and she'd just blow him out of the water. She could be very cruel."

Jolie didn't doubt it. "When was the last time you saw him?"

"It's been months."

"What did Luke do for a living?"

"Worked for a landscaper. Blowing leaves, trimming hedges, that kind of stuff."

"I take it he didn't want to be a leaf blower forever."

"No kidding. He talked about getting his own tree-trimming business and stealing his boss's main client."

"Main client?"

"The attorney general of the United States, you believe that? Luke thought he could shut out his employer, offer him a better deal." He let out a short laugh. "Quintessential Luke. He knew nothing about running a company—totally out of touch with reality."

"Did you know about his underage girlfriend?"

"Riley? That was one of his plans. He said he was going to knock her up and marry into all that money." He grinned. "If Luke owned a store, it'd be called Schemes 'R' Us."

Jolie asked him if he was surprised Luke had taken the woman at the motel hostage.

He thought about it. "I was and I wasn't. Luke wasn't the violent type."

He scratched his arm. The sleeve of his T-shirt rode up, revealing a peacock tattoo. "One thing I wasn't surprised about, though—he sure got himself into a shitload of trouble."

* * *

Jolie was about to run an NCIC search on James Dooley when Skeet came by her desk. "I need to talk to you," he said.

"Okay."

He had a weird smile on his face. "How about we go to my office?"

Jolie pushed her chair back to get up. Just then she heard a voice out front and recognized it immediately. Riley Haddox. "I need to do one thing first."

Skeet said, "That's fine."

"You sure?" Jolie glanced in the direction of the front room.

"It's been waiting all day. It can wait a little bit longer."

He had some kind of secret. Jolie knew from experience it didn't bode well for her.

"Anytime in the next couple hours." He rapped his knuckles twice on her desk before walking down the hallway to his office.

Jolie went out to meet Riley.

Zoe was with her. Did Riley take Zoe with her everywhere?

The contrast between the two girls was dramatic. Riley was beautiful. Blonde hair, lithe body, the works. Zoe, on the other hand, was just pretty. There were some people you pegged as likeable before they opened their mouths, and Zoe was one of them. She was shorter than Riley and heavier, but, taken altogether, attractive. Jolie found her attention going to Zoe, which Riley clearly sensed and didn't like.

Riley took back the spotlight. "Do you know if the police have the phone? Can you get them to give it back?"

"Why don't we go to my desk?" Jolie couldn't say "go to my office" because she didn't have one, just the desk pushed face-to-face with Louis's desk. But since Louis was taking vacation time, they'd have a modicum of privacy.

Riley clacked behind her.

Jolie motioned to one chair and pulled another from around Louis's desk.

Riley sat down, then Zoe. Riley said, "Why didn't you call me back?"

"Because I didn't have anything until just a while ago."

"You *were* going to call me, weren't you?"

This girl needed a good talking to. Through Kay, Jolie knew that Riley's father was at his wits' end with her. He couldn't control her and apparently didn't even try. At this point, she wasn't even going to college—any college. "If I'd had anything, I would have."

Riley's eyes narrowed.

Clutching her purse to her chest, Zoe leaned forward. "It's been so good of you to help us. Riley's just so scared—"

"I can't imagine if those photos got out!" Riley said. "What would I do? It could hurt us—hurt my family. It would be humiliating!"

Jolie didn't think it would be any more humiliating than being forced to resign as head of the DOJ after he was charged with failure to report a substantial amount of income on his tax returns. But she didn't say that. Her own daddy had brought her up to be better than that. "I wish I could help you, Riley, I really do. But there's some question where the phone is. It was not put into evidence by the Gardenia PD. It's not with the FBI, either."

Riley's mouth dropped open in shock. "Are you serious? What am I going to *do*?"

"I don't know."

"*No one* knows where the phone is? How can that be? Mrs. Frawley said—"

"Mrs. Frawley said the police searched Luke's apartment, but she didn't see what they took."

"But what do I do *now*?"

The phone's GPS could be tracked, but all Jolie's requests to date on tracking phones had been denied due to privacy issues. Law enforcement agencies big and small didn't want to touch that hot potato unless it was absolutely necessary. "I don't think there's anything you *can* do."

Riley stood up. "Well, thanks," she said, her voice like ice. "I guess I should've expected you wouldn't help me."

"Could you sit down for a moment?" Jolie said

Riley sighed. "What now?"

"How close were you to Luke?"

"We were going to get married."

Jolie looked for an engagement ring, but didn't see any.

"We were keeping it a secret."

Because he was eight years older than you? Jolie thought. *Or because he worked for a landscaper blowing leaves?*

Riley said, "I need to be somewhere."

"Just a couple more questions. Do you have any idea why Luke would take that woman hostage at that motel?"

Riley stared at her.

She looked stricken.

"Riley?" Jolie asked gently. "You must have wondered about that."

"They framed him. He wouldn't do something like that. Why would he?"

"Who framed him? The FBI? The police?"

Riley said nothing.

"How do you think that happened?"

"They framed him. They made it up." She stood up. "I've got to go."

Jolie said, "You must have thought about this. If they framed him, you must have a theory how they did it?"

"I don't know how they did it. That's your job. We loved each other, and now he's gone—why can't you just leave me alone?"

"Was he afraid of someone? Did he ever mention that someone was after him?"

"Am I under arrest? Because if I'm not, I'm going. Come on, Zoe!"

She walked out the door—clack, clack, clack.

Zoe rose, purse clutched to her stomach. "I'm sorry, Aunt Jolie. She doesn't mean to be rude. She's just upset. She…"

Jolie stood up too. "Do you think Luke was framed?"

Zoe looked miserable. "All I know is something was going on."

"Something?"

"What I meant was…" She looked around for help, but there was none.

"Zoe, if you know anything, you owe it to your friend to tell me. Does Riley know why he went to the motel?"

"No! There's no way she'd know."

"Why is that?"

Zoe looked miserable. "Because they broke up Memorial Day weekend."

*   *   *

When Jolie got to Skeet's office, he was standing by the window. "Look at that," he said. "You'd think the president was just here."

Jolie saw the two black SUVs follow Riley's Boxster Spyder out of the parking lot.

"Is it true you're related to those people?"

"Tangentially."

He stuck his hands in his pockets and gazed at the solar system poster that took up one wall of his office. "Hope you're not planning on getting a security detail for yourself," he said. "We'd have to move Louis into the cleaning closet just to accommodate them." He nodded to a chair. He had his copy of Chief Akers's case file in front of him on the desk.

"You know we've been having budget cutbacks," Skeet said. "We're shorthanded. Everybody is, but with Louis out…Tim and

I talked early this morning. We agreed that we just don't have the manpower to keep up surveillance on Maddy Akers."

In a way she'd been expecting it. Maddy had done nothing except go to places like the Piggly Wiggly and the car wash for three days. Jolie was disappointed, but it had not been out of the realm of possibility. Jolie wasn't ready to bring Maddy in for questioning yet—she needed more evidence to make an interview worthwhile. She needed something that would rattle Maddy, trap her into giving something away. But now Skeet had taken away Jolie's ace in the hole.

Skeet stood. "I hope this doesn't put a crimp in your investigation."

"Life goes on."

Skeet nodded sagely. "Life *does* go on."

Jolie thought of Chief Akers lying on the bed in a hotsheet motel, blood soaking into the mattress underneath his head. *Life goes on,* she thought.

Sometimes.

22
ASPEN, COLORADO

When Nick Holloway came back from laying in supplies, the first thing he did was turn on Fox News. He was unloading groceries into the refrigerator when he heard the words, "Brienne Cross." He looked up in time to see two scruffy men shuffling into the Pitkin County Courthouse in manacles and leg chains. The Pitkin County Courthouse was one block away from where he was staying.

The Aspen killers had been caught.

Just like that, Nick's fear that someone was out there lying in wait for him evaporated.

Their names were Donny Lee Odell and Ray Marquette, and they were about to be arraigned for the murders of Brienne Cross, Justin Balough, Tanya Williams, Brendan Shayles, Amber Redmond, and Connor Fallon.

No mention of Mars's death, but that would probably be tacked on later.

Donny was the younger one. He had that country-peach face peculiar to Southern white boys and the wispy beginnings of a Fu Manchu. He had long, limp hair and spaced-out eyes. Two tats Nick could see—a teardrop tat in the corner of one eye, and barbed wire wrapped around one stringy bicep. The orange jumpsuit made him look jaundiced. Nick imagined Donny's growing up years: a single-wide with plenty of siblings. He had no doubt they'd have the same blank look Donny had, as if life had whacked them hard in the face. He'd drive a seventies-era GMC truck with a Confederate flag in the back window and do the majority of his shopping at a convenience store—cigarettes, Slim Jims, and six-packs of beer that would cost twice as much as they would at a grocery store.

Ray was older and meaner. His eyes weren't passive like Donny's. In fact, he had the evil eye thing going on, thought he was Manson. His head was shaved, and a thatch of hair jutted out from his chin, somewhere between a soul patch and the beard on a Civil War general. No mustache. Scars on the face, as if he'd grown up in an era of smallpox outbreaks. Tats crawled across his shoulders and arms, and he had one hoop earring. He was bulky enough to overturn a car, and his jailhouse muscles stretched his sleeveless orange jumpsuit to the breaking point. Nick pegged him as the instigator and Donny as the follower.

Now he could put faces to the killers who haunted his dreams. A couple of white supremacist types with obviously low IQs.

All his worries had been for nothing. Now he could move on.

He wondered if, down the road, he could interview Donny and Ray. Unlikely, but he'd discuss it with his agent.

But first, he walked down to the courthouse and became part of the crowd. Not much to see. Satellite news vans, reporters, cameras, even a staging area where the Pitkin County sheriff gave his press conference. The sheriff had a good time giving the press conference, too—his time in the sun. Nick liked being part of the crowd. Anonymous. He noticed a couple of celebrities behind dark glasses and under ball caps, and felt a kinship with them. *No one knows who we really are.*

*　　*　　*

On his way back from the courthouse, Nick picked up a sandwich for lunch, went home, and called his agent.

"Let me get this straight," Roger said. "You want to expand the story to include this guy Mars?"

"Come on, Roger, he saved my life."

"You *think* he saved your life. But is there any proof of that?"

Nick sighed. His agent never really trusted him, despite the fact that he'd delivered a bestseller that had surprised everyone. "I'll find the link. All it will take is a little investigative reporting."

"I don't know," Roger said. "Sounds like mission creep to me. The story about those kids in the house, as told by the sole survivor—I thought that was what this book was about."

"But Mars is the reason I survived."

"You don't know that."

"But I can find out, can't I?"

"That's what I mean. Mission creep. This thing is becoming amorphous. And that means it's going to take longer to write. We talked about this. The sooner we can get this book out the better."

"Don't worry so much. I've written on deadline all my life." He looked out the window at the beautiful day and felt energized. "I'm going out to the house later—I really want to see it again. Now that it's empty, it might be a good way to start the book. But first, I'm going back to see if I can talk to someone in the sheriff's office."

Roger said, "Think about what I said, okay? Don't lose focus."

"Oh, I won't, Roger. Don't you worry about that."

*　　*　　*

As Nick crossed the street to his car, he noticed a man on the sidewalk, his face tipped up to the sun in appreciation of the day. Nick shared his appreciation of the pure blue sky, benign sunshine, and cool shadows. It was as if his life had been handed back to him. He'd been in three narrow scrapes in his life, and he'd come out of them in one piece every single time. The child-killer who tried to get him in his car when he was nine. Nick got away, but another kid wasn't so lucky—his body was found the following spring in a wilderness area. Then his near-miraculous survival of the Aspen massacre.

And now Donny Lee and Ray were safely locked up. They couldn't come after him now.

The biggest dividend from the Aspen massacre had been completely unexpected: Nick was now magically free from fear. The idea that death was out there waiting for him, waiting for one slipup, one lapse in judgment or awareness—that was gone. Just like that.

The reaper had three cracks at him and couldn't get it done. He was pretty sure there wouldn't be another, not for a long time. The ultimate irony? If he died in his sleep at a hundred and three.

Nick got the runaround at the sheriff's office. After an hour of waiting, he went back to the officer behind the Plexiglas window and told her he was the sole survivor of the Aspen massacre and needed to talk to Detective Sloan. But the woman must have been in the job for a long time, because she just blinked at him and looked bored. "You'll have to wait your turn, sir. There's a lot going on today and everyone is out."

So he gave up and drove to the Aspen house.

He didn't expect to see a realtor's sign outside. And he *really* didn't expect to see the "SOLD" panel hanging from two short chains underneath.

The house looked like something out of a magazine—the stacked stone entrance and solid pine construction, the mowed lawn, the flowers nodding in their beds. Under the peaked roof, the massive expanse of glass was dark, reflecting only a couple of clouds in the deep blue sky.

He knew nobody lived here—at least not yet. And the house *looked* empty.

What he'd really like to do was get in and look around. Photograph it for his book. See if there were any traces of the mass murder. Of course there wouldn't be—not if the place was already sold. The heavy-duty cleaners would have come in and hosed the place down and replaced what needed replacing. They'd make it sterile and generic again. As if they could wipe out the house's psychic history.

He wondered who had bought it so quickly. There were always the nuts out there who wanted to live in a murder house, people who got off on it. Like those women who wrote to Charlie Manson or the Night Stalker.

The smell of cut grass took the edge off his nerves, reminding him of baseball games when he was a kid. Through the trees he could see Castle Creek, gold in the shallows, dark under the trees and undergrowth. A couple of hundred yards downstream, a fly fisherman cast his line backwards and forwards like a coach whip before settling it on the water in a bright line.

Hands in his pockets, looking more casual than he felt, Nick walked down the driveway to the empty garage.

He saw right away how the guy had stashed him there. The garage was a sub-story, cut into the hill. A flagstone walkway ran down the hill alongside. It would have been easy for Mars to roll him down the walkway and push him over the lip of the retaining wall into the garage. There was a three-foot drop to the plastic garbage and recycle containers, which would have broken his fall.

From there it would be a simple thing to shove him under Brienne's black Escalade.

What he didn't understand, though, was why. *Why me?*

He stood in the coolness, staring down at the immaculate concrete. Not one oil spot marred the garage floor.

Why was *I* spared?

Nothing came to him.

Finally, Nick walked back up the walkway to the deck above. The deck cantilevered out over the rushing water. He remembered drinking beer that night—quite a lot of it—and the incredible feeling of well-being it generated. A warm, rosy feeling.

"Hey there."

He looked around. A man climbed the steps from the creek below, the fisherman he'd seen earlier. Tan vest and waders, aviator sunglasses, fly rod, and an old-fashioned wicker creel with a trout tail sticking out. He couldn't say for sure, but everything looked top-of-the-line—even the trout.

Abruptly, Nick felt foolish. The guy must live here. He'd been wrong that the house was still empty. He put on his best smile. Inclusive, winning, the way he greeted people on tour. Stepped forward and held out a hand, even though the man had his hands full.

As he framed his welcoming sentence, the man said, "You're Nick Holloway."

He found himself grinning foolishly. Had the guy read his book?

"You're the survivor. I saw you on the news." The man set his creel down. "I can't believe it. The sole survivor."

"Guilty," Nick said. "This your place now?"

"Name's Cyril," the man said. "Just closed on it a week ago yesterday, as a matter of fact. Thought I'd kick things off with a fish supper. So how did you get so lucky?"

"I have no idea."

"You must have friends in high places, that's for sure."

"Wish I knew who they were. I'd hit them up for a loan."

"No idea? That seems strange."

Nick shrugged. Nick had made the decision to keep whatever he learned about Mars to himself. It was his story, his exclusive, and you never knew who might try to capitalize on his hard work. He'd been the one shoved under the Escalade, and he was going to be the one to write the story.

"Nice day, isn't it?" The man pushed his baseball cap back. The cap was tan, too, like the rest of his clothing. The words *Chernobyl Ant* were written across the front.

"Chernobyl Ant? What's that?"

"A fishing fly—a terrestrial." The man told Nick that he tied his own flies, went on to explain what a terrestrial was, and then gave him a list of the places he'd caught fish with the fly. Went into too much detail for Nick's taste. Then he nodded toward the garage. "That's where they found you, right? Hey, if you've got time, I'd like to hear your story. I've got Rolling Rock in the house, and I can cook up this trout. Care to join me?"

Nick realized he was famished. It was the mountain air. Guy seemed a little anal-retentive, but what the hell. There were worse ways to spend an afternoon. This was his opportunity to get into the house again. If the fisherman wanted to hear the story about his brush with death, if he wanted a vicarious thrill—fine with him. "A beer would be nice," he said.

They stayed out on the deck. The water rushed underneath. The sunshine at this high altitude felt good but was probably deadly. Nick wished he had sunscreen, but he put it out of his mind.

The conversation turned—as it always did—to Brienne Cross. Nick was bored with Brienne Cross, but he understood the interest. She was a big star.

"What was she really like?"

"To be honest? She was boring."

"Boring?" Cyril straightened. "I would have never guessed that."

"You're right, it doesn't quite do her justice. Let's see…she was also shallow, vapid, and dull. But incredibly good-looking."

Cyril stood up. "You want a margarita? I made a pitcher earlier today."

They went into the house. Cyril suggested Nick dice some tomatoes, avocado, and scallions for guacamole.

The kitchen was the same as Nick remembered. Cyril said he'd bought the place lock, stock, and barrel. Nick looked into the big living area. The same furnishings he remembered, maybe a couple of them conspicuous by their absence. Brienne Cross was found lying on the couch. That was gone. The other furniture was sheathed in opaque plastic. It gave the place an otherworldly feel, as if it was not quite there. *He had escaped.* The gratitude he felt was overwhelming; it sang through him like a tuning fork, reverberations running through his soul.

He was *alive.* They were dead, the people from this room, but he was still here. Still here to walk along the Aspen Mall lined with trendy shops, still here to appreciate the aspens and the sunshine and the good food and his chance encounter with the know-it-all fly fisherman.

He wanted to photograph the big room. He liked the idea of the indifferent plastic, the understated quality to a place where four people had been murdered. Patience, he reminded himself.

He started cutting vegetables while Cyril grilled him about the show, *Soul Mate*. So he went into it: How Brienne would sneak her boyfriend in, even though there was a rule against that. How reality shows were really scripted, which was why there was so much narrative tension and outright fights among the players.

He talked about the little field trips to Nobu's, to J-Bar, to Caribou. Picking out jewelry, clothes, dining out, clubbing, all of those kids trying to prove they were most like Brienne. That they could be her soul mate. All the hoops the young people jumped through to be Brienne's best friend.

Nick felt a twinge of regret. He realized he'd been uncharitable. Brienne was just muddling through life like anybody else, even if the cross she had to bear was gold-plated. Conscience made him say, "She was nice enough, don't get me wrong. But the business turned her into a shark."

"A shark?"

"You stop moving, you die. If you're a celeb in this day and age, you can't just tread water and expect to remain viable."

Cyril looked confused. Apparently, he didn't know *everything*.

"Stardom today has to be maintained. If you're not in the headlines, the public forgets about you. So you have to work harder—incredible pressure. That's why she took drugs."

"She took drugs?"

"Hell yes. Oxycontin and hydrocodone, stuff like that. If those two dickheads hadn't broken in here and killed her, I would have bet she'd be dead in a year."

"That's hard to believe."

"Oh, believe it."

He told Cyril these kids weren't prepared for fame. They were thrown into the deep end and they had to perform. It changed them. They became tough, greedy, and hard nosed. They had only one job: to stay in the public eye any way they could. Drive over a paparazzo's foot? Good. Have a baby? Great, especially if it broke up someone else's marriage. Split up with your boyfriend? Make sure it's messy. Get into a public fight with another woman? If you grabbed her hair in your fist and knocked her off her Manolo Blahniks—fabulous.

If all else failed, go commando.

"Why can't people just let their children grow up and be normal?" Cyril said.

*　　*　　*

Cyril expertly brushed the fish with beaten egg whites, coated it with salt, pepper, and cornmeal, and placed it in tinfoil before carrying the platter out to the deck. He started the grill, then regarded the trout with a frown. He opened the foil, added some beer from his own bottle, and closed it back up. The shadows were longer now. Nick excused himself and went into the house. He really did have to take a leak, but first he took a dozen photos with his phone. Quietly, he made his way upstairs, worried about creaking floorboards. There were none.

He knew Ray and Donny Lee, those knuckle-dragging white supremacists, had done their worst work up in the back bedroom. It was vicious—the pictures posted on the Internet. Disgusting photos, so bad you didn't even know what you were looking at. Whatever it was, it looked like raw, bloody beef sliced from a gnawed T-bone. Apparently, the idea that a white kid and a black kid were sleeping together unhinged Donny and Ray. The interracial romance, which had been developed (cynically, by the producers) over a period of weeks, might have been the reason Donny and Ray targeted the house in the first place.

The door to the room was closed.

He turned the knob. Unlocked. Good.

He was surprised to see that ground sheets covered the floor. And that wasn't all.

On the wall behind where the bed had been, Nick saw the ghosts of bloodstains. Someone had slapped on a coat of paint, but it didn't completely cover them. Like a Rorschach test.

Weird, the guy buying the house in this condition.

It sort of shocked him, but not so much he forgot to take pictures.

23

Landry unpacked his groceries on the small table by the honor bar. Although his purchases were representative of the items the hotel sold at a premium, they were much cheaper at the grocery store. With his savings, he was able to buy Carr's water crackers instead of Cheez-Its, Pepperidge Farm Milano cookies instead of Oreos. He lined his remaining purchases up on the table: brie, smoky sharp cheese, pickled artichoke hearts, and a half bottle of Penfolds red—a nice meal.

He sat down on the king-sized bed and took off his shoes. He liked the room, which was done in a generic Spanish style. The coverlet was floral, the colors burnt umber and burnt sienna. The walls were clean white. A carved cabinet concealed the TV—the usual.

He turned on the TV and channel-surfed.

CNN had a special on Afghanistan. He clicked right past it.

Afghanistan, in his opinion, was the nut that could not be cracked. Far worse than Iraq on its worst day. The terrain was impossible. The little villages in the mountains were the same now as they were a thousand years ago. Like some of the cliff-dwelling ruins you'd see in New Mexico.

His platoon, in joint operations with the CIA, had gone after terrorist cells and the Taliban along the border with Pakistan. They'd been given an intelligence package regarding a man named Matteen Wahidi. Landry thought it was pretty thin. They went in at the optimum time, three a.m., rousting the target and his family in the rabbit warren where they lived. The family consisted of Wahidi, his wife, his children, his father, his mother, and his grandfather. Landry had his doubts Matteen Wahidi was working with Al Qaeda. The problem involved his accusers, the two men who spoke up against him. Landry knew they had been paid for their help. They say you can't buy an Afghan, but you can rent one. The accusers gave it away in their shifty eyes, the holes in their stories, the cues they took from each other, and in the rank stink of their sweat. The smell of fear rolled off them. Landry realized they were afraid of Wahidi in a deep, atavistic way that inferior men always feel in the presence of the genuine article. Wahidi spoke in his own defense, then stood silent, his family behind him. "Matteen" in Pashto meant "well-mannered" or "disciplined one." His wife was in tears, a two-year-old boy clinging to her leg and screaming. But Wahidi's other children were stoic, like their father. Matteen Wahidi looked each of his captors in the eye, one by one. When his gaze reached Landry, they took each other's measure. Wahidi knew what was in store for him. He knew—and his family knew—he would not be coming back.

It was the way of the world. Landry had learned early on that things like this happened. When he was eight years old, Landry had watched his favorite racehorse, a gelding who had dropped down the claiming ranks, be led onto a van that would take him away. He ran to the fifth wheel and put his head under the pillow so he would not hear the van pull away. His mom came in to comfort him. She told him the horse was going to a farm, but Landry had seen the van on the backstretch before. He'd heard people talking. The horse wasn't going to a farm.

Like the horse, Matteen Wahidi was taken away. The horse's death had been horrifying but short. Wahidi would dwell in the terrible twilight between life and death, sanity and insanity, desperation and hope. They would break him. No ifs, ands, or buts. He would eventually talk—be eager to talk—and tell them what they wanted to hear, whether it was true or not. The disciplined one, the well-mannered one, would babble about anything and everything to get some respite.

Landry couldn't have done anything, and anyway, he had long ago hardened himself to injustice. People lived and people died, and nothing in life was fair. Wahidi would have to find his reward in paradise.

Landry shifted through the channels and landed on E! There was more on Brienne Cross, six weeks after her death. They interviewed her sister, who looked exactly like her. Sabrina. He spread a towel on the bed and ate there, watching television. This was something he'd never do at home, eating on his bed. But he was in a hotel, so anything went.

After eating, he powered up the Hewlett Packard laptop to see what he could find. The answers could be on Holloway's computer. Nick himself had been disappointing. He really didn't know who had spared him.

As expected, the security was minimal. You just needed a password to get in—the family pet, your sister's name, your favorite baseball team. From the suitcase crammed full of records and written correspondence he'd brought with him, he'd mined a list of words. He tried one after the other, and got in on the third try.

He loaded Outlook Express. Landry knew what to look for. He'd downloaded a list of names and numbers from the cell phone, but he didn't see any that would tell him what he wanted to know. But looking through the e-mails, he recognized one name immediately. The man had been all over the TV in the last couple of years. He fit the criteria—the only real link Landry could see.

There were two e-mails. He read them both. Reread them. Read the responses. He selected "Reply" to the original message, wrote his own response, and hit "Send."

Then he went to Orbitz.com to make his reservations. He spread the plastic out on the bed. Visa Card, Discover Card, Amex, driver's license—an old picture, unflattering in the way driver's license photos usually are. It looked nothing like him. Amazing how people changed in looks from age thirty to age forty. He could write a thesis about it.

He selected the Visa card and typed in the numbers. Expiration date, 3/13. Hooked up the portable printer, printed up his ticket, folded it in eighths, and put it in his wallet. He heard thumping sounds outside his window, kids running on the walkway.

He would miss this place, but there was always another room, another adventure.

24

By the time Jolie got home, it was going on dark. She fed the cat, made a sandwich, and took Madeleine Akers's case file out onto the porch.

The pond was out there in the darkness, but she couldn't see it—the moon wasn't up yet. There was a nice breeze tonight, cutting the sticky heat.

Jolie had a decision to make. Either she took over surveillance on Maddy Akers herself, or gave up on the idea entirely. She was sure Amy would come for her money—if she hadn't already.

Jolie's first instinct was to ask Skeet if she could continue watching Maddy Akers on her own, off the clock. But she knew he would turn her down.

Skeet didn't have a suggestion box on his door.

Another option: ask for time off for personal reasons and do it on her own. But if Skeet found out what she was doing, she'd be fired. Sheriff Johnson would stand for a lot of things, but that kind of insubordination wasn't one of them.

Chief Akers might have been a bad guy. He might have mistreated his wife, although the jury was out on that. But Jolie had taken his case, and she was dedicated to finding his killer.

So there was no other option.

She'd keep tabs on Maddy herself.

She reread the two surveillance log sheets. Maddy's actions were about what you'd expect in the aftermath of a loved one's death. She went to the grocery store twice and the Gardenia Police Department once, stopping to gas up the car on the way home. She went once to Babbitt's Funeral Home and once to the Royal Court Apartments, working in the office for about twenty-five minutes. Jolie supposed Maddy could have met up with Amy there, but Deputy Wade didn't see her. A few neighbors dropped by Maddy's house with covered dishes. One daughter spent the night. Two delivery vans dropped off flowers.

Jolie was beginning to doubt the hit man theory. She'd checked out James Dooley. He had a record, but it was small stuff. There was an outstanding warrant, which she made note of—she might want to use it sometime. It did cross her mind that someone delivering flowers could have gotten up close enough to deliver the coup de grâce.

She didn't think a guy like James Dooley could pull it off, though.

* * *

As Jolie went into the bedroom to change clothes, she found herself looking at Danny's official portrait.

It occurred to her that she hadn't actually *seen* that photo in a long time, even though it was prominently displayed. She picked up the framed portrait and looked into Danny's eyes. Well, she tried to. But there was nothing there. No secrets revealed, no answers at all. It was just a photo.

Jolie set the portrait back on the dresser. Carrying her clothes, she turned away, then back. Dumped the clothes on the bed. She took the photo off the dresser, folded the cardboard stand against the frame, opened the bottom drawer, and put the photograph inside.

*　　*　　*

Jolie drove into Gardenia just past ten p.m. Ed, her next door neighbor, had lent her his Dodge Ram. Ed was a veteran of the Korean War—a tough old bird. He'd lived next door to her father for twenty years, spent most of that time arguing politics on her dad's porch over a couple of beers. When Danny died, Jolie took her dad's house off the market and sold the house she had with Danny. It had been a good move.

Ed's Ram was hardly unobtrusive, but there were a lot of Dodge Rams in Gardenia. Plenty of working men, hunters, and fishermen lived out here.

An added bonus: Ed's truck had dark tinted windows.

One the way out of town, she stopped at the grocery store and bought energy bars, nuts, and juice. She took along plenty of water and a pot to piss in, just in case.

Then she settled in for the duration.

Nothing happened.

*　　*　　*

Back in the office by eight a.m., she picked up a message from Judge Sharpe's clerk, asking her to call him. After a short wait, the clerk put her through to the judge.

"I'm sorry," Judge Sharpe said. "I'm denying a search warrant at this time. You just don't have probable cause. I'll need more than the word of an alcoholic paranoid like Royce Brady."

*　　*　　*

The second night showed a steep decrease in her enthusiasm. At least she'd squeezed in a nap before driving out to Maddy's just before dark.

The Akers house was halfway down Jackson Street, which dead-ended at a park. A narrow alley fronted the park and ran perpendicular to Jackson, forming a T. An all-night convenience store sat on the west corner of Kelso and Jackson, separated from the neighborhood by a low fence and some weedy elms. It was an ideal place for Jolie to watch Maddy's house. She could see every car that turned onto Jackson from Kelso. And she had a clear shot of Maddy's front door.

So she glassed Maddy Akers's front porch. Like watching a pot boil. There was nothing—just the street, the streetlamps, the house with a light on in back.

She switched from binoculars to her camera with the telephoto lens. Started to drift off, catching herself. The camera, suspended by a strap around her neck, rested on her chest.

She woke to the sound of a whining transmission as it accelerated out of the corner—

Amy's car.

Twenty past three in the morning.

Jolie had waited so long to see that car, that when it finally showed up the whole thing felt like a dream. Jolie was slumped down below the dash of the Ram, her eyes following the play of headlights as they passed over her truck and moved on. She scooched up a little bit and looked through the telephoto in time to see the taillights blink out in front of Maddy Akers's house.

Amy got out of the car and strode up to the front porch, standing under the light. She knocked on the door. No answer. She knocked harder. Still no answer. Then she started pounding. "Maddy? Maddy! I know you're in there! Wake up!"

Jolie felt as if she were frozen in amber, still sleepy. An image bloomed in her mind's eye—a ridiculous image—of Maddy answering the door and Amy pulling out a gun and popping her.

She stamped her feet—one foot had gone to sleep—and eased the Ram's door open. The interior light stayed off; she'd turned the switch off last night.

Amy was pounding on the door and screaming. Lights came on in a house across the street.

Jolie slid out and touched her feet to the asphalt. Gently closed the door to the Ram.

"Maddy! You'd better come to the door! I mean it!"

Crouched low, Jolie crab-walked to the corner, using bushes and trees for concealment. The camera hanging from the strap looped around her neck, Jolie was glad for the telephoto lens. The plan was to take photos of the two of them out front, then tail Amy. Amy would be the one with the money.

The door opened and Maddy stepped outside. Jolie was concentrating so hard on getting a good shot, she didn't hear the truck turn onto the street until it accelerated past her in a pall of blue smoke.

She would think afterward that it was like watching a movie. It happened that fast.

The truck slowed to a stop in front of Maddy's house, idling rough. Both women turned to look. Jolie let the camera fall to her chest and reached for her weapon. There were two loud cracks. Maddy bent down as if to pick something up from the porch floor.

Jolie brought up her weapon. Shouted, "Police!"

Three more cracks, rapid succession. The shriek of tires. Both women down, pushed over like dominos.

Something whizzed past Jolie's ear. She heard the crack, like firewood exploding. Was she hit?

No time.

Get into a shooting stance. Double-grip, slow it down, *breathe!* Aim for the tire, squeeze off the shot.

She missed. Heart racing in overdrive. Ear stinging like a son of a bitch. Blood trickling down into her collar.

A light snapped on in the house across the street, a man in pajamas running outside. She couldn't risk the shot. "Police!" she yelled. "Go inside! Go inside now! Call 911!"

The truck accelerated. The passenger banged the side of the truck, yelling, "Go-go-go-*go!*"

Man in his pajamas, just staring at her, in the line of fire.

"Police! Inside, *now!*"

The man backed toward the door. Still didn't have a clear shot. *Switch gears.* Pointing the camera one-handed, she clicked a photo just as the truck hit the corner to the alley. The truck skewed sideways, back panel whacking a reflective pole hard.

Accelerated in a funnel of dust.

Gone.

Jolie sprinted toward the Akers house. Both victims on the ground. They looked like discarded clothing under the porch light. She punched 911 into her cell. Identified herself as police, gave the code for officer needs assistance, and told them to send an ambulance.

Description? *Truck. Concealed license plate.* Color? *Muddy under the streetlights—maybe red. Or brown. Seventies GMC or Chevy. Two men with a rifle.*

A rifle?

Yes, a rifle. Driving north, alley off Jackson.

The phone dangled from her hand. The next thing she knew, she was standing over Maddy Akers as if she'd been teleported there. Maddy appeared to be dead. Her neck and jaw had been taken out, one large clot, shiny black in the lamplight. Amy was dead too—shot to pieces.

Sirens.

CPR. Not Maddy, her neck was blown out. Amy. As she stepped in Amy's direction, her foot almost skated out from under her.

The porch was slick with blood.

25
FRANKLIN
PANAMA CITY, FLORIDA

The former attorney general of the United States, Franklin Haddox, throttled back the twin Yanmar 480 HP diesels and piloted his boat, *Judicial Restraint*, through the pass into St. Andrews Bay.

Today was the one bright spot in an otherwise miserable week. He would finally meet his distant cousin, the author Nick Holloway, for the first time—just the lift he needed.

The vague worry that had plagued him since Memorial Day weekend had hardened into dread in the last couple of days. But he wouldn't give in to it. He couldn't. You needed a steady hand on the tiller in situations like this. Frank knew Mike, and even his own wife thought he was weak. Both of them confused weakness with caution.

In truth, Mike Cardamone was the loose cannon. He was the one who didn't think things through. Maybe it was because he'd been in the CIA for so long. Mike thought like a spook. That incessant desire to snip every loose end, even if doing so could lead to a complete unraveling.

Frank didn't want to think about it, but it kept digging its way into his thoughts. Where would Mike stop? For God's sake, was he going to go after *everybody*?

The thought chilled him.

Frank was fairly certain Mike didn't know about Riley and that crazy, hostage-taking asshole, Luke Perdue. Mike lived in DC. He hadn't been down here in months. Still, he had an uncanny way of finding out things.

There had been no hint of anything like that in their phone conversations. Mike *did* talk about the standoff at the Starliner Motel. He talked about the surveillance they'd put on Luke's sister Amy, but he never mentioned Riley.

Frank's gut clenched. Mike was a spook at heart. He wouldn't tip his hand. If he knew that Luke Perdue and Riley were sleeping together, he would have logically made another assumption: that Luke could have showed Riley the photos.

A couple of days ago, Frank had taken Riley out on the boat— just the two of them, on the pretext of a day out together. Riley'd acted like it was a big drag to go out with her dad, but Frank knew she was actually happy about it. That was the thing about Riley. Every emotion showed on her face.

He told her he knew about Luke. As always, she was defiant. "He was *my* choice! We loved each other! You don't even know what real love is."

Riley had a point there. Sometimes he and Grace seemed more like co-conspirators than man and wife. They spun scenarios, talked tactics well into the night, didn't touch one another in public. But there was another side to their marriage.

"It was over, okay?" Riley said, her face stormy. "He broke up with me. And now he's dead! *That* should make you happy!"

It was embarrassing. His daughter making a fool of herself over a pot-smoking loser. Frank managed to get the truth out of her: Luke told Riley he was going to get some pot from his truck, and then snuck off into the night. Probably couldn't stand all the drama—Frank could relate to that.

But the thing was, it happened that night. The night in question. Frank could not let that go. But Riley wouldn't—or couldn't—tell him anything more. She did manage to rub Frank's nose in it about the pot. "Yes, Daddy, we smoked pot. We had sex, too. Lots of sex—I could tell you the positions, all the things we did."

He almost slapped her, but didn't. She was still the fruit of his loins, and he owed it to her to protect her. Even if she was dumber than Pontoon, their goofy Irish setter.

Riley had to make everything a fight. She thought her behavior was shocking. But she couldn't even be shocking consistently. Riley had always lacked focus. It was difficult to take her tantrums seriously.

She was needy, and that kind of neediness made him recoil—the reason he avoided her as much as possible.

He was sure Riley had not seen the photos from that night. It wasn't just wishful thinking on his part. There was a certain logic at work here. If Luke left and never came back, if he refused to see her, then he didn't get a chance to show her the photos.

The problem was, so much was open to conjecture. When they recovered Luke's phone, the first thing Mike did was have forensics done. Turned out to be a throwaway phone. There was nothing on it. The phone had never been programmed, which meant they'd been outwitted by a meth-using, leaf-blowing redneck.

Luke's real phone was still out there somewhere. Frank knew it and Mike knew it, and all this uncertainty could lead Mike to think of Riley.

Mike didn't know Riley the way Frank did.

Riley couldn't keep a secret. She would have told Frank about the photos long before now. She would do anything for attention, and if she knew about those incriminating photos on Luke's phone, it would have come out already.

He'd just have to put it out of his mind.

Today he needed a distraction, and he'd found it.

Franklin still marveled that his cousin, four times removed, was a bestselling author. Frank had written his own book, but it had sat in a drawer for three years because his writing teacher said it needed work.

It had been a fluke, how Nick ended up on his radar screen. Lifeline DNA Genetic Testing offered to trace Frank's ancestry back four generations. They'd offered the service for free, in gratitude for a favor Frank had done for them in his previous life as a congressman. Since it was a freebie, he took it. All he had to do was supply his DNA, wait for the report to come back, and voilà, turned out he was related to a bestselling author.

When Frank e-mailed Holloway in May, Nick told him he wasn't really looking for long-lost relatives. He'd had his DNA tested because he was writing an article about genetic testing companies for *Esquire*, but added, "If I ever get out to your neck of the woods, we should get together."

And now Nick was here, doing research for his new book.

Frank hoped Nick would take a look at his manuscript. He had little doubt he'd find a publisher—he was, after all, famous in his way—but he wanted the book to be *good*.

And although Nick didn't know it, he owed Frank. Big time.

He took the Hinckley under the drawbridge and aimed for Bayou Joe's. Idling into the Massalina Bayou, watching a pod of dolphins at play in the sequined water, he felt his usual sunny optimism sweep over him. Life was good. He could handle whatever came his way. There had been some rough seas, but it would all turn out all right.

The restaurant straddled a small dock where boaters could tie up on three sides, a maritime spin on the old-fashioned drive-in. It was one of Frank's favorite places.

A man detached himself from the shade of the overhang, walked down the dock, and helped him tie up. He wore a ball cap, sunglasses, a khaki-colored shirt, and Army-green cargo shorts. Muscular calves, no socks, boat shoes, duffle at his feet, and what looked like an expensive saltwater fly rod case propped up against the wall of the restaurant. Franklin knew immediately it was Nick. Taller than he'd expected, and the stubble from a couple days growth of beard made him look more rugged than both his book photo and the television interview he'd given to Larry King after the Aspen bloodbath. One word came to mind: manly.

Nick Holloway could be a Haddox.

Frank took pretty good care of himself, watched what he ate, worked out every day in his home gym. Pretty decent shape for a man of fifty-five, but he was nothing like this man.

The guy said, "Nick—"

"Holloway. I know. Franklin. But you can call me Frank."

They shook. Good strong hand. "Nice boat," Nick said.

"The Hinckley T44 FB. I wanted a sports fisher, but I love the Hinckley, so I had this one modified. Downriggers, live bait wells, all that good stuff. You know your way around a boat?"

"I've been on one or two in my time."

They followed the waitress to a small table on the covered dock and sat down.

"So," Frank said.

"So."

"We finally meet face-to-face. Cousin."

"Cousin." Nick grinned.

"What made you change your mind?"

The waitress came. Frank didn't need to consult a menu. He ordered a Trash Burger and a Heineken. Nick ordered a grouper sandwich and water, no ice, lemon.

Nick said, "Nearly getting killed has a wonderful way of sorting out your priorities. To be honest, I didn't think I needed any more family, but after I got a second chance, I decided I should look you up."

"I'm glad you did." Frank leaned forward, elbows on the table. The smell of french fries and battered fish floated on the air along with the subtler smell of the bayou—decaying plants, feeding fish, a hint of petroleum. Waves lapped gently against the dock. Frank said, "I've been reading your book. It's thrilling."

"Good. It's a thriller."

The food came.

"What was it like? Waking up under that Navigator in the garage?"

"Escalade."

"Oh, it was an Escalade?"

Nick nodded. "Before I even opened my eyes, I smelled motor oil. It was like an out-of-body experience."

"How did you find out everybody else was dead?"

"A detective told me. For a while, he even suspected me."

For one dizzying moment, Frank thought about telling Nick the truth, that Nick had him to thank for being here now, eating a grouper sandwich at Joe's. But as a man once said, that wouldn't be prudent. It was something he could never tell anyone. "You ready for some fishing?"

That slow grin again. Guy had a way about him. "Absolutely."

"I think you're going to like the boat. Kings are running just offshore. Or, if you want, we could go for grouper, you want to go farther out." The two beers were making him feel benign, expansive. The sun was shining, and the fears he'd had earlier seemed to dissipate into the air. He nodded at Nick's baseball cap. "What *is* that, anyway?"

Nick looked confused. "What?"

"A band or a boat?" Feeling jocular. Good food, good company.

Nick looked at him, sunglasses catching the light and bouncing it back.

"The writing on your *cap*. Chernobyl Ant. Is it a band or a boat?"

"Oh, this?" Nick gestured to his cap. Smiled.

"Neither," he said. "It's a racehorse."

26

Brown water spilled out of the spaces between the tailgate and the truck body as it was raised from the pond outside Gardenia.

It was late morning, not two full days after the drive-by shooting at Maddy Akers's house.

An hour before, a man walking his dog along his usual route by the highway spotted something in the pond. The something he spotted was the juncture where the top of the tailgate met the side panel of a late-seventies GMC Silverado, two-tone burgundy. The color of a Dr. Pepper can.

This could be the truck the shooters drove.

But it wasn't Jolie's case now. She was here as a witness, at her fellow detective Louis Gatrell's behest. He wanted to see if she could identify the truck.

Jolie had not been in to work since the night of the shooting. She'd meant to drive to Weems Memorial in Tallahassee, had planned to be there in case Amy Perdue regained consciousness. But as soon as the scene at Maddy's house was secured and Jolie had been tended to by the paramedic, Sheriff Johnson sent a car to transport Jolie back to the Palm County Sheriff's Office, where she had been relieved of her firearm. She was told to hire an attorney, which she did. Yesterday, Jolie spent the morning answering questions in the officer-involved shooting hearing.

Jolie would not be going to Tallahassee. She would not be allowed to follow any of the leads she had developed. She was on paid leave pending a final report on her disposition as a detective with the Palm County Sheriff's Office.

It didn't look good.

But then, nothing looked good. She couldn't sleep, could barely make herself eat. As much as she needed to make up for all the sleep she'd already missed, Jolie found her mind playing the scene out over and over as she lay in bed at night. She felt lost without something constructive to do to get her mind off the carnage. Jolie couldn't help but feel she should have been able to stop the shooting. If she had acted sooner—

Going down that road was madness, she knew. But she wanted to do something. Wanted to at least be at the hospital where Amy was.

Jolie had been questioned, somewhat harshly, about her use of deadly force in a city neighborhood. Her lawyer told her not to admit to going there on her own—even though it was clear to everyone that was precisely what she'd done. Jolie did admit to firing her weapon.

As she left, Skeet called out to her, "Hope you have another job lined up. If I have anything to say about it, you're toast."

"The way you run things, we're all toast," she muttered under her breath. The lawyer, a tight-faced woman from Panama City, poked her in the ribs.

* * *

Jolie was pleasantly surprised that her proximity to this pond didn't bother her at all. It was possible that her fear of the pond behind her house—and her fear of the bathtub—were momentary glitches. Whatever they were, she seemed all right now. This left her free to think about how much trouble she was in.

She'd seen Sheriff Tim Johnson's face at the station earlier. He wouldn't even look in her direction. His disappointment was heavy in his features, his eyes. He seemed tired and sad. Sad was an expression people adopted when they looked back. When there was something to regret.

He'd looked like a man who was preparing to give a good friend some very bad news.

"What do you think?" Louis asked her as the truck was winched onto the flatbed tow truck that would take it to "The Barn."

Jolie squinted against the sunlight, trying to concentrate. "It *could* be."

Louis sighed. He looked weary, too. He'd been brought off the bench, and now he would be working the Maddy Akers homicide around the clock. "Could be? Can't you do any better than that?"

"It was dark."

Louis shrugged. "Guess that's the way this is gonna go."

"I'm just not sure, all right?"

"I wasn't saying anything against you," Louis said. "I was talking generally."

"I know. I'm sorry."

"Hey, it's a bitch."

* * *

Over lunch at the Jack in the Box, Louis caught Jolie up. Amy Perdue was on life support and was unlikely to regain consciousness. There had also been a development regarding James Dooley.

The Strange Case of the Boastful Hit Man, was the way Louis described it.

According to Louis, Dooley hadn't been home for two or three days. This morning, unable to get a warrant, Skeet made the call—exigent circumstances—and sent a team in to breach Dooley's house. Inside, the trash stank to high heaven. The man's two dogs, kept in the backyard, had gone through all their water and food and were now with animal control. James Dooley appeared to have absconded. It bothered Louis that he'd left the dogs. There was a BOLO on both James Dooley and his 1985 brown Chevy truck.

Turned out they didn't have to go far to find him. He was in their own jail. Dooley had been incarcerated for three days at the Palm County Sheriff's Office jail in Palmetto after committing a minor traffic violation. An enterprising deputy ran him for wants and warrants, arresting him on the spot for a broken taillight.

Skeet found out about Dooley's incarceration when he put the BOLO out and got the call from the Palmetto deputy who arrested him.

His Chevy Fleetside had been sitting in the impound lot in Palmetto for three days.

Louis told Jolie that Skeet went to Palmetto and interrogated Dooley himself. Of course he knew it was a wild-goose chase. Dooley couldn't be in two places at once. According to Louis, it left Skeet in a foul temper.

There was no evidence that Chief Akers had ever hired someone to kill his wife.

In the aftershock of the drive-by, Jolie's mind had fallen into certain lines. She was sure Maddy was the target, that Amy was collateral damage. But what if it was the other way around?

Jolie was beginning to believe there never was a hit man.

Maybe this was about *Amy*.

Jolie said, "Louis, you recovered Amy's phone after the shooting, right?"

"Sure did, and put it into evidence, just like it says in 'The Big-Boy-Pants Detectives' Handbook.'"

"Have you done forensics yet?"

"We've been busy with other things."

"There might be evidence on that phone."

"Evidence?"

Jolie had to frame this carefully. "I think she and her brother Luke were into something bad. There might be information on her phone about that."

"And you know this because?"

"She said something about it when we talked," Jolie lied. "She said there were photos."

"Photos."

"That's what she said."

"Photos of what?"

"She didn't say. But she said I'd know 'em when I saw them."

*　　*　　*

Elbows on the table, Nick Holloway leaned forward and smiled at Frank Haddox. "Ever hear of Giant's Causeway?"

A gull hovered like a baby's mobile just beyond the rafters of Bayou Joe's, its bright eyes on the last of Frank's onion rings. Frank thought the bird looked alternately clownish and homicidal.

"Giant's Causeway?"

"The racehorse. Nearly won the Breeder's Cup in 2000. I own one of his offspring."

"You own one of his offspring?"

"Actually, in partnership. We drew straws to name him and I won. I named him after my favorite fishing fly."

"Oh. Well that's interesting."

"You know what one of my partners wanted to call him? Spotcheck Billy. Guy's a Little Feat fan, Spotcheck Billy's in one of their songs. I don't think that's an appropriate name for a Kentucky Derby hopeful, do you? It lacks…"

"Gravitas?"

"That's the word exactly. Gravitas."

With that, their conversation petered out. Frank began to wonder if this was such a good idea. He didn't know the guy. In fact, Holloway seemed a little…off. Maybe bestselling authors were like that. All that time alone inside their own heads—maybe they weren't adept, socially.

He could feel the guy scrutinizing him from behind his dark glasses. The way the light bounced off them—Frank couldn't see the man's eyes. For the first time, Frank questioned his decision to leave his security detail behind.

Frank decided right then this would be a short day. They'd go out a ways, do a little fishing, and be done by early afternoon. He wouldn't call off the fishing trip altogether though. Something told him not to piss this guy off. Go out for an hour—they wouldn't even have to talk—then leave him back at the dock. That decided, he stood up. "What do you say we go get us some kings?"

Just as he said it, a shadow crossed over them—a pelican landing on a nearby piling. A storm was coming later this week, but today was beautiful. A beautiful sunny day, but Frank felt goose bumps crawl across his shoulders as the man smiled.

Dark glasses and excellent teeth.

"Sounds like a plan," Nick Holloway said.

27

As Jolie and Louis walked back to their cars, Louis's phone rang.

After disconnecting, he said, "We got an owner for the truck—matched the VIN number. It was stolen from an auto body shop in Panama City. Guy dropped it off three days ago—was gonna restore it to its original condition. Bad deal, huh? Now his vintage truck's got a big dent in the rear quarter panel, and I'm sure two days in the pond didn't do it any good."

"It could be where he hit the post in the alley."

"That's what I was thinking. We'll go on that assumption. Guess I'd better get back."

"Guess so."

"I'll, uh, keep you apprised."

"It's okay, Louis."

"Hey, just occurred to me. You asked me if there were any missing persons reported on Memorial Day weekend, remember? Palm County didn't have a missing person, but Bay County did. Panama City Beach—a friend of mine took the info. There was someone—a young guy named Nathan Dial." He gave her the contact info for the Panama City Beach PD.

"Thanks, Louis."

"No prob."

"Be sure to check out Amy's phone. It could solve the case for you."

"Okay."

* * *

Back at home, Jolie called the Panama City Beach detective, Craig Jeter, who had taken the missing persons report on Nathan Dial. "Kid left his car at the bar, must've hopped a ride with somebody," he said. "To tell the truth, I'm surprised he didn't show up after a day or two."

"What do you think happened?"

"Could be a number of things. Maybe he found himself a new relationship. He disappeared from a gay bar."

"You think he'd just up and go? Leave all his stuff?"

"I've seen weirder. But he could just as easily have gotten into some big trouble. I wish you good luck." He gave her what he had, which wasn't much. Jolie got the feeling he didn't take Dial's disappearance seriously. Kids "took off." She got the impression that he thought gay kids in particular could fall off the face of the earth and nobody would know where they went. Or care.

Her second call was to Scott Emerson, Nathan's roommate. He suggested they meet at the Waffle House on Thomas Drive in Panama City Beach.

Jolie had to decide which weapon to take. She felt naked without one. Although the Palm County Sheriff's Office had given her a replacement firearm for the SIG Sauer P226, she decided to leave it at home. It would be best to take her own weapon. She had four handguns to choose from—she chose the other SIG.

The badge, she took.

As Jolie crossed the Grand Lagoon, she saw high-rise hotels lined up along the beach like dominoes. It was bright and sunny, the sky a diaphanous blue—a beautiful day to play hooky.

Stopped at Cove Bar on the way in.

Cove Bar dated back to the early sixties, a low brick structure painted dark purple. A round sign loomed at a forty-five-degree angle above the door. According to Detective Jeter, Nathan told his roommate he planned to meet a guy named Rick at the bar on Friday night of Memorial Day weekend. From there they would go to a party.

He was never seen again.

The bar was closed. Jolie took a couple of photos of the bar and the parking lot where Nathan's car had been left behind, then drove a mile west to the Waffle House.

She scanned the parking lot, wondering what kind of car Scott Emerson would drive. He was a college kid. It was likely he'd use cheap transportation. She thought he'd drive the Chevy Cavalier without hubcaps.

Inside, she sat at the counter, ordered a Coke, and waited. The cook in her white paper hat glanced at her inquiringly, and Jolie shook her head. The cook turned back to the griddle and didn't look at her again.

Jolie knew she was skating right on the edge—first talking to the PCB detective, and now meeting with Scott Emerson. If Skeet found out, she had no doubt he'd use it against her. But nobody at the Palm County Sheriff's Office knew about Nathan Dial except for Louis. And Louis was a little busy right now, trying to solve her case.

By a quarter past two, Jolie realized Scott Emerson wasn't coming.

She called and got his voice mail. She'd wait another ten minutes and then give it up. A young woman went by and sat on the stool at the end of the counter. The girl could have been sashaying down a runway. She made a big production of setting her rose-pink alligator bag down on the stool next to her and checking her phone. Jolie caught the potent combination of perfume, tanning oil, and beach sand—a Panama City Beach girl. Long blonde mane—Jolie guessed, hair extensions. Makeup troweled on, but she was still beautiful. Halter top that matched the bag, bare brown midriff, tiny short-shorts, stork legs ending in translucent sandals on five-inch heels. Fiddling with her bejeweled cell phone, every gesture over the top. A girly-girl.

Jolie had never looked that good. Didn't think she'd want to. She liked to watch other people, but didn't like them watching her.

The beach girl ordered lunch, flirting with the heavyset female cook, speaking in a high baby voice, ordering waffles, cheese eggs, and hash browns, "scattered, smothered, covered, and chunked."

Little girl with a big appetite.

Jolie tried Emerson again.

Christina Aguilera's "Can't Hold Us Down" blared down the counter. The beach girl consulted her phone—she made a big production of it.

Jolie punched in Emerson's number again.

"Can't Hold Us Down" sounded again. The girl looked at her phone again and dropped it in her purse. She got up, paid the cashier, and walked out the door.

Jolie watched through the window as the beach girl walked right past the red Miata, straight to the white Cavalier. Bent from the waist to unlock the door, her rear end pushed out and up, showing off the beautiful line of her tanned legs.

Her tiny, compact butt.

Hair shiny in the sunlight.

Too shiny. And her butt—too small. The only part of her shape that didn't look right. She sat in the car and folded her perfect legs in.

Jolie dropped a five on the counter and hustled outside to her own car just as the Cavalier turned right on Thomas. She followed, staying back a car or two. Wondering: Why the elaborate *La Cage aux Folles* show? Was it just a lark, for her benefit? Or to make a point?

If there was a point, Jolie couldn't see it.

They went up over the Grand Lagoon. Turned right on Albatross and left onto a dead-end road called Coleridge Lane. A right into the newly resurfaced parking lot of the Harbor Village Apartments. Blue-gray siding, white trim, nautical theme, including a ship's wheel on the sign.

Scott Emerson and Nathan Dial lived at the Harbor Village Apartments.

She waited, parked behind a banana tree. From here she could see the girl take the walkway to building C.

Five minutes later, Jolie knocked on the door of 23C.

28

They were just beyond the channel markers when Nick Holloway said, "Let's try the grouper."

Frank said, "The grouper?"

"I've never fished for grouper. It'll be a challenge."

"You wouldn't rather troll for kings? We could put a line in the water right now."

"No. I'd like to go for grouper if it's all the same to you." That blinding smile again.

"But it's going to take longer to get out there. We'd have to use the downriggers…" Frank paused. Trolling for kings would be faster—they'd be closer to shore, and he wanted this to be quick and painless. He supposed they could go to the nearest artificial reef, drop anchor, and hope for the best. Maybe the man would get tired of waiting, or maybe he'd get lucky. Still, Frank had to try one more time. "King mackerel's running right now. If it was me…"

Holloway shrugged. "It's your boat."

A muscle in Frank's jaw flinched. There was, implicit in Holloway's reply, the notion that Franklin Haddox, former attorney general of the United States, was an imperfect host. "Grouper it is, then."

Frank heard the strain in his own voice, the false cheeriness. He knew he'd been pushed into a corner. In a lifetime of politics, Frank had run into plenty of alpha dogs—especially in the White

House—and he knew when someone was trying to crowd him. It felt like Holloway had Frank's neck between his jaws and was pressing ever so slightly to make his point.

Frank had a lot of practice backing down and saving face. He thought it was wise not to fight every battle. He may have lost a few skirmishes, but he'd managed to push the president's agenda through with virtually no compromise. Frank Haddox had met plenty of Holloways, and in the end, he'd always managed to beat them.

Frank knew this guy would zero in on any weakness and use it for his own ends, and he wouldn't give him any ammunition. "Well, it's a nice day for it," he said.

Striking just the right note. He sounded like a host who was fine with anything as long as his guest was happy.

They headed into the Gulf, both of them on the flying bridge. Frank kept an eagle eye on the GPS, looking for Cap Martin's Reef, a cluster of reef balls off Meridian Beach, but also keeping his eye on Holloway. The man scanned the Gulf. He looked like he lived on a boat. This was not the impression Frank had gotten from his book, although to be fair, there had been no mention of fishing or boats.

Holloway leaned over Frank's shoulder. Frank could feel his cousin's breath on his neck. He turned. "What?"

Holloway said, "We're three miles out. International waters."

"So?" Just then he glanced back at the GPS. "We're over the reef," he announced. "Let me get you rigged up."

Too cheerful. He'd have to watch that.

*　　*　　*

An hour later and not a bite. Holloway didn't seem concerned. Frank tried small talk, but the guy wasn't very forthcoming.

Frank thought about his manuscript down below. He'd already decided not to mention it. He just wanted to take the man back to the dock and get away from him.

Being around Nick Holloway was unsettling. It got worse as the day went on. Frank felt absolutely nothing coming from him, like he was a hole in the air, a dead zone. Guy was a cipher, with his baseball cap pulled low, the sunglasses, the Croakie. The sun became increasingly oppressive, nailing them under its glare. Too bright, the light bouncing off the dark blue water, hurting Frank's eyes. The uneasiness in his gut settled in. Whenever his mind wandered, it went to disturbing images, like the report of a grisly homicide he'd seen on Fox News last night, or Somalian pirates seizing a cruise ship.

It was lonely out here today. He saw only one other boat, at least a mile away. This shouldn't bother him, but it did. It added to the bad feeling in his gut.

Frank didn't dare look at the guy head-on. He had no doubt Holloway could read his mind. So he busied himself with lures, drink and snack offerings, frequently checking his own lines, all the while tracking Holloway from the corner of his eye.

Then it came to him that the guy didn't just seem alien. He looked *different*. Different from the man he'd expected.

He had Holloway's book, *Hype*, down below. Planned to ask Nick to sign it, but that wasn't an option now. He wanted to divest himself of the book as quickly as he was going to divest himself of its author.

"Can I get you something stronger?" he asked. Cheerful—too cheerful.

"No, thanks."

"I think I'll get something for myself then."

He ducked into the cabin, went to the cupboard above the galley, and pulled out the book. Closed his eyes for a moment, his heart thumping hard.

Opened the book to the photo on the back flap.

He wasn't surprised.

Could have been him—there was a passing resemblance—but Frank knew the Nick Holloway he was hosting right now was not the Nick Holloway on the book cover. The jawline in the photo was too soft. The shape of the face too wide. The eyes…well, he hadn't seen the man's eyes since they'd met, but he doubted the man fishing from his boat had ever looked anxious.

Even in a headshot, the author didn't look like a big man.

And the way the author was dressed—as if he'd pulled his clothes out of a trash bag.

Okay, if the guy up on deck wasn't Nick Holloway, who was he?

A thrill of fear went through him—it was the feeling he'd always imagined people in a jetliner felt when the plane went down fast. Pure terror.

The man out there fishing from his boat was the reason he'd hired a new security detail. The reason he had three bodyguards, none of whom was on this boat right now—

Cardamone.

There was buzzing in his ears. He couldn't feel his hands. The screaming jetliner was gaining speed, the fear stark and real, adrenaline hurtling through him.

The man was here to kill him.

He needed a plan. A plan, a plan. *Concentrate!*

Here he was in the cabin of his beautiful boat, and he could barely register what he was looking at. The air seethed with visible molecules—the cabin seemed to swim before his eyes.

A shadow filled the narrow doorway, blocking the sun. He started to turn in Holloway's direction, but he didn't make it all the way.

The next thing he knew, something stung his neck. A wasp maybe.

After that, nothing.

29

Scott Emerson suggested to Jolie that they take a walk around Harbor Village. "It's too nice to be inside."

"Don't you want to change clothes first?" Jolie asked.

"No, this is fun. I don't dress up all that often, believe it or not—too much hassle. You're probably wondering why I got so elaborate." He spoke in his normal voice, a honking tenor. That voice coming out of the Barbie doll face was disconcerting.

Jolie waited.

"I wanted to see how smart you were. Well, actually, I wanted to see if you were as dumb as Detective Jeter. Completely clueless, not to mention deeply prejudiced."

"You think he didn't do enough?"

"Honey, he didn't do *anything*! You have no idea what it's like to be a second-class citizen. How did you figure out who I was?"

"It was the hair."

"Looks kind of fake, doesn't it? It's real human hair, but it still doesn't look right. Especially under those lights. Eating at the Waffle House is like eating under klieg lights. Anything else give me away?"

"Your car."

He smiled and his Adam's apple bobbed. She wished she'd noticed that earlier. "You're right. No self-respecting girl would drive around without hubcaps." He cradled his boobs for emphasis.

"And then there's your ass."

"My—?" His hand flew to his lips. "Oh, honey, *that* is just plain junkyard dog *cruel!*"

Jolie struggled not to laugh.

"I'm getting to you, Mrs. Policeman. I can tell. So why is the PCB police department suddenly interested in a missing faggot?"

They took a walk, following in the direction of the pool.

Jolie said, "I'm not with Panama City Beach PD."

"You're not?" For the first time, Scott looked nonplussed. "You said you were a detective."

"Palm County Sheriff's Office."

He stopped walking and looked at her. "Is he dead? You're not notifying me because I'm the closest thing to a next-of-kin, are you?"

"I don't know if he's alive or dead," Jolie said.

"Then why are you here?"

"We're working in conjunction with Panama City Beach PD. Could you tell me what happened the last night you saw him?"

He told her that Nathan left the apartment around eight o'clock at night. The night before, he'd met a guy, "Rick," at Cove Bar. Rick invited Nathan to go with him to a party Friday night.

Jolie asked Scott what the man looked like.

"He said he was a big guy. Not his type—he prefers someone who's willowy, like me—and by the way, we're just roommates. You have to understand Nathan. He's always been a climber. Impressed by wealth, power, that kind of thing. He said that he had a feeling this was going to be a real power party."

"Power party. Did he say where this power party was?"

"Didn't Jeter tell you? You didn't see his report?"

Guy was smart. "I'd like to hear your story, from you. No filters."

"Okay, he said San Blas. That's really it."

"He didn't say anything else?"

"He said I wasn't invited."

"You asked to go with him?"

"Oh no. I'm not the *least* bit interested in that kind of scene. He volunteered that little piece of information. Let me know that this was an exclusive party. He wanted me to be impressed that he was something special."

"Was he? Special?"

"He was—is—a good person. Too impressed by people with money, but he grew up poor in Alabama. Father was a steel worker or a drywall installer or a tire-banger, I forget exactly what. Nate was obsessed with 'making it.'"

Jolie asked him how he planned to do that.

"He was looking for a sugar daddy. He said he wanted to be someone's little pet. A 'beloved, cosseted pet,' he said. He wanted someone to take care of him."

"Did he ever mention a man named Luke Perdue?"

"Never heard of him."

"Amy Perdue?"

"Wait a minute. Luke Perdue does sound familiar. Oh, I know. That was the guy who got shot up in that motel room, took the woman hostage, am I right?" He shook his head. "No, I don't think Nathan would have ever met that guy. Different circles *entirely*."

Jolie tried him on Riley Haddox. Threw in Zoe Haddox. Nothing.

"What do you think happened to him?" Jolie asked.

"You really want to know? I think that big guy, the one who lured him to that party? I think he had his way with him—then killed him."

*　　*　　*

Later that day, Scott took Jolie on a guided tour of Cove Bar. He insisted. She understood why. He wanted to be part of it, because he cared about his roommate, because he wanted to do the right thing, or just because he just wanted in. Jolie understood his need to do *something*. Jolie was like that, and she recognized a kindred soul in Scott Emerson, hair extensions notwithstanding.

She wanted to find out who killed Maddy and nearly killed Amy. This was the only way she could see to move the ball down the field. So in a way, she and Scott were on the same mission.

Cove Bar was as retro inside as out. A low white ceiling with mica-sparkles, black walls, black lights, a neon martini glass above the George Jetson bar. Pulsing alternative rock at odds with the time warp decor.

They must have rounded up every Formica chrome dinette set in the twenty counties.

"Technically, those tables and chairs are from the fifties," Scott said. "But why quibble?"

He'd scrubbed off the makeup and transformed himself into a very good-looking man. Maybe a little slender, but if Jolie was fourteen, she would have had a crush on him. He wore a madras shirt, cargo shorts, boat shoes without socks: "My *Two and a Half Men* Charlie look." His fashion statement didn't quite fit with this crowd (not a lot of this crowd appreciated Charlie Sheen), but clearly, he didn't care. "I hate this place," he said.

"Well, try to hide it."

"My mama always said, you get more flies with honey than vinegar. But I always asked her, 'Why would you want flies?'"

They sat at the bar and ordered drinks, a shot and a beer for Scott, a Diet Coke for Jolie. She paid.

The bartender had a salt-and-pepper crew cut and the physique of a dead lifter. He said to Jolie, "I don't drink either. Eighteen years sober, how about you?"

"Thirty-three years."

"But when she was a baby she could really put it away," said Scott. "You remember me?"

"How could I forget? Take it Nate still hasn't made it home?"

"I don't think he will, do you?"

The bartender wiped a glass and set it in the rack. "Nope." He looked at Jolie, saw the shield on her belt. "Why don't we go on in back? Wait here."

"Wow," Jolie said. "He's cooperative."

"He's good people."

A woman took over the bar, and the man with the crew cut, Darrell, led them to a tiny room off the back. He prefaced their conversation by saying, "I don't want any trouble."

Jolie introduced herself. "Just a few questions."

"Okay." Darrell turned to Scott. "I'm sincerely hoping this will be the last time." He looked at Jolie, leaned back, and lit a cigarette. "All's I can do is tell you what I know. Nate was kind of a regular here. Enough so I knew what he liked to drink. He was hot for older men, especially if they looked like they had money. I've heard some stories, but I won't bore you with them. Let's just say Nate had a healthy view of sexuality. A very healthy view. You could say he was inclusive. You with me so far?"

"We're good."

"That's pretty much all I know personally about him. This place is a rumor mill—you don't see a lot of gay bars in the south—and the general consensus seemed to be that Nate was pretty hot. Appealed to a certain type, the kind who wants promiscuous but vulnerable. I don't spend a lot of my time babysitting customers, so a lot of this stuff I heard secondhand." He leaned back and folded his arms.

"That's it?" Scott asked. "I thought you said he talked to a guy named Rick."

"That's what I heard. I didn't actually see them talking."

Jolie asked, "You didn't see this guy Rick?"

"I didn't see them together. Heard later that this guy, Rick, picked Nate up. And I thought, *Good for him.*"

"Did you see them together at all?"

"Might have. But it's hard to remember. I see a lot of stuff. This bar is a hotbed of horny young guys looking for other horny young guys. That's the clientele." He looked at Scott. "Most of what I know about Rick and Nate, I heard from Scott in our numerous conversations."

Jolie ignored this. "What about his car?"

"Didn't know it was his. I don't sell a lot of drinks in the parking lot."

"Did you call to have it towed?"

"The owner did. He's out of the country at the moment. Mexico. I can give you his cell, but he'll just tell you what I'm telling you. The car was out there for three days, so he had it towed."

Jolie said, "What does Rick look like?"

"Big guy. Short hair. Very butch. He wore nice clothes, but you could see he was ripped."

"Have you seen him since?"

"No. Only saw him that weekend. I'd remember a big guy like him."

"You're sure?"

"Pretty sure. He looked kind of out of place, like he wasn't from around here. Just an impression I got." He added, "Blazer, slacks, nice shoes. You know what he reminded me of? A bodyguard."

"Anything else you can remember?" Jolie asked.

He thought about it. "Only that he kind of worked the room. He was everywhere. Hung out with a lot of guys. Come to think of it, they were all pretty boys. I think he was trolling for a young one."

"Did he give you his name?"

"No. But I heard someone call him Rick."

"You think he was looking for a boy—a particular type?"

"Looked that way to me." He added, "I guess he found one."

30

Cyril Landry was ninety-eight percent certain Franklin Haddox would tell him the truth. Landry had five IV bags of triptascoline—what Dennis Ngo at the Shop lab termed "scopolamine on steroids." Like scopolamine, triptascoline was an anesthetic. Like scopolamine, it was an amnesic drug, only more so. Three times more so. It had been used effectively around the world as an interrogation tool. Landry had complete confidence in the drug. His only concern was the man's fear level. Excessive adrenaline could burn the drug up in a hurry, so Landry wanted Franklin calm, happy, and stoned. It would take a minimum of forty-five minutes to get a baseline. Forty-five minutes at least before he could start the actual interrogation.

At the moment, Franklin was regaining consciousness. Landry adjusted the petcock on the IV upward just a tick. This was tricky. How would Franklin react when he realized where he was?

Franklin was propped up against stacked pillows in the forward stateroom. Landry sat beside him, his long legs stretched out past the foot of the bed. They could have been a married couple watching the evening news. Only way he could do it—even luxury cruisers like the Hinckley were tight on space. The cherry wood and teak of the cabin was mellow and, Landry hoped, soothing. The bedspread and cushions were deep blue. Restful. Franklin stirred. His expression was amiable. So far, so good.

"Hey," Franklin said, his voice woozy. His eyes widened when he saw Landry—a small shine of fear.

"That was a nasty fall," Landry said.

"Fall?"

"You don't remember?"

"Not really." Bleary smile. "You're Nick, right?"

"Right."

A shadow seemed to pass across Haddox's face. Uncertainty. Landry opened the petcock a little more.

Goofy grin. "Hey! You're my cousin!"

"That's right. Remember I was going to interview you?"

"You were?"

"Uh-huh, for *Esquire*."

"Oh." His hand rose and pulled on the IV tube. "Wass that?"

"It's nothing."

"You sure?"

"I'm sure. Let's get to the interview, shall we?" Landry adjusted the drip and waited for it to take effect.

*   *   *

"What is your name?"

"Franklin Edison Haddox the Third."

"What is your wife's name?"

"Grace. Goodnight Gracie." Smile.

"Do you have children?"

"Yes."

"How many?"

"One. No, two. Does Frank the Fourth count?"

"Sure."

"Frank the Fourth died." He stopped, bemused.

Landry waited.

A tear squeezed out of Haddox's eye. "That wasn't fair."

Landry didn't want to push any emotional buttons yet. He adjusted the IV up another tick.

"What were we talking about?" Haddox asked. "Hey, are we on the boat?"

Landry said, "Where do you live?"

"That's easy. Indigo."

"What is Indigo?"

"It's an island. Off Cape San Blas. My family's version of a gated community. Haven't you seen it?" He sat up straighter. "Is your magazine going to take photos? You know we have an octagon house that was built in 1849 by Orson Fowler." He spoke like a drunk, carefully enunciating the numbers.

"Oh. What kind of boat do you have?"

"A Hinckley T44 FB. Have you seen it?"

Loopy smile.

*　　*　　*

Landry had established Franklin's truthfulness and willingness to talk with the control questions, leading Haddox through his occupation (attorney general); his hobbies (fishing and hunting); his daughter's name and age (Riley, seventeen). Two sisters, one deceased. Two nieces, Kay the real estate agent and Jolie the cop; his grand-niece, Zoe, currently staying with his daughter in the guest house. He went into depth here, explaining that although Riley and Zoe were the same age, Riley was actually Zoe's aunt. He found this endlessly entertaining. Landry pushed him—gently—to move on. Franklin told Landry his mother was long dead and his father, Franklin II, was a former senator and was once "very powerful." Landry caught some emotion there and quickly moved to safer ground. "What's the best fishing day you ever had?"

"Oh, that's easy." He gave the date, the location, the catch, and the weather conditions.

Landry wrote everything in a small spiral notebook. Even though these were throwaway questions used to establish a baseline, they could be important in putting together a picture of the man.

Landry led the attorney general into phase II. This was where he asked "reactor" questions meant to elicit emotion. He wanted to prod Haddox into reacting viscerally. He wanted to see how the man handled questions that might threaten him.

This was what he learned:

Haddox's daughter Riley would never amount to anything. She was the biggest disappointment of his life.

His son, the apple of his eye (he actually said this), died in a drag-racing accident his senior year in high school, eight years ago.

His wife was his best friend. He was guarded about her. Landry tried to find out why, but ran into a brick wall. Franklin said twice, "She's the best thing that ever happened to me."

He did, however, resent the time she spent with her horses.

His father was a "great man," but he was stubborn, arrogant, and dismissive. "I'm the attorney general of the United States of America, and he still treats me like a child. I got farther up the ladder than *he* ever did."

Franklin added, "Now he's got dementia, he's still stubborn and dismissive, but he's nuts, too. Living with him is like *Groundhog Day*—he can blame me for the same thing over and over."

Franklin hated celebrities, especially Hollywood liberals. "They're what's wrong with America. They're bringing us down. They have no morals, but God, are they self-righteous! What an example to set for Riley—you can see why she's so messed up."

A diatribe followed, morphing into how President Stephen Baird had kept the country safe. He "almost eradicated terrorism in our time," but then he died and now "that woman," nothing but a placeholder, was the president of the United States.

"You can't work with her. You wouldn't believe what a fucking hillbilly she is. She doesn't know what the hell she's doing, she should be running bake sales for the PTA, and here she is, the most powerful person in the world. And she has no idea how to use that power. Grace defends her. I guess women stick together, am I right?"

He rambled on. Landry let him.

Now he knew the former attorney general's sticking points. He knew just how Haddox reacted when threatened. Franklin was a master of righteous indignation. He bridled at "the ingratitude of people." His sense of entitlement was astounding.

Landry adjusted the IV down a notch. He had to achieve just the right balance, and the triptascoline was very strong.

Landry went back to the initial questions, staying away from anything controversial. He asked Franklin his name, his age, favorite color, hobbies, what the island was like. Haddox became genial again, forthcoming. A happy drunk.

He was primed.

Now the interrogation would begin.

31

Cove Bar was heating up. Scott pushed through the crush, Jolie in his wake, and called out over the thumping bass to a man in a white tee and jeans. "Brock?"

The man moved slightly, under the arm of his taller boyfriend. Pantomimed: "Me?"

Scott said to Jolie, "Brock attracts men like flies. If Blazer Man was trolling, trust me, he'd start with Brock."

Jolie motioned toward the door. "Can we talk outside for a minute?"

"Sure thing, hon." They filed out into daylight, Brock's lover holding on to his belt like the caboose on a choo-choo train.

The sun hit them, bright and hot. But at least they could talk out here. They stood in the shade of the sign's big round shadow sprawled on the sidewalk like a reverse spotlight.

Jolie described the guy, Rick. Asked if he had tried to pick Brock up. Brock's boyfriend, Roger, straightened, glared at her.

Brock said to Roger, "You remember, I told you about him."

Roger glowered.

Brock said, "He's mad because when he was visiting his sister in Tampa, I went to the bar. I mean, where else would I go? These are my *friends.*"

"You could have stayed home. I was only gone three days."

"The guy," Jolie reminded them. "Rick."

"Ah, yes, I remember him. He seemed dangerous." Gave a delicious shudder, and Jolie thought Roger was about to deck him. "Oh, come on, Roger! Don't hate me because I'm beautiful."

"Dangerous how?"

"Just kind of...he had a vibe. I got the feeling he could be brutal."

A feeling. Great. "What specifically made you think he could be brutal?"

"His eyes. They were like stones. Nothing in them."

"How did he approach you?"

"He just came up and started talking. Not flirting, he wasn't even all that friendly. He might as well have been picking a lobster out of a tank." He put his hand in Roger's back jeans pocket.

"What did he say?"

"He told me he liked the bar, asked if I came here a lot. He said he was new in town, and he was going to a party and asked me if I was interested."

"He came *on* to you!" Roger said.

"Oh, don't be such a bitch. I didn't go, did I? Guy gave me the creeps. It was like, I said no, and he just crossed me off his list and went on to the next one."

"The next one?"

"There's this blonde Adonis, his name is Jimmy, but he's taken, big-time. This guy, Rick, saw him across the bar and made a beeline straight for him."

Jolie asked, "Did he tell you where the party was?"

"Cape San Blas. I think it was a club."

"A club?"

"I don't know Cape San Blas that well, but it sounded like a club, or maybe a gated community."

"How did you get that impression?"

"Because I overheard him talking on his cell a little later. He said something about 'Indigo.' I thought it was a club."

Jolie stared at him. "Indigo?"

"I think that's what he said."

Jolie thanked him and started for her car. The sun seemed to bear down on her, crushing in its intensity. She heard Scott behind her. "You going to drop me off?"

"Sure."

"Well, thanks."

Jolie registered the sarcastic tone, but her mind wasn't on Scott Emerson or his hurt feelings. Her mind was on Indigo. Maybe there was a bar or a club or a gated community on San Blas named Indigo. Maybe.

But in her heart, Jolie knew the truth: there was only one Indigo.

32

Cyril Landry said to Frank Haddox, "If you'll forgive me for saying so, it sounds like your father was threatened by you."

The attorney general snorted. "You've got that right."

"As you said, he was a senator. But you were in the cabinet, the inner circle."

Lazy grin. "You know what they call the attorney general? America's Top Cop. That's what I was. I still am. When you address me, you call me the attorney general."

"Top Cop. Imagine. All that power in one man's hands. I wish I knew what that felt like."

"It's…like a drug. You're flying so high…you never want to die." He seemed to lose focus, rubbed at the tube in his arm.

Landry adjusted the drip upward. "No one understands what it takes to protect this country."

"That's certainly true. Most people don't know half of what it takes. Not a *quarter* of what it takes."

Landry said, "You know what my dad's favorite Bible quotation was? The Lord is my shepherd, I shall not want. You're like that shepherd."

Haddox pointed at Landry. "Exactly! That's it, exactly!"

Too much triptascoline. The man would be singing beer hall songs if Landry kept it up. He dialed it back.

"The scope of what you're doing," said Landry. "It's breathtaking."

"You know about it?"

Landry shook his head in admiration. "Brilliantly audacious."

Haddox winked. "No one's supposed to know about it. It's our little secret."

"No one does. Just you, me..." Landry ticked their names off on his fingers as Haddox watched.

"The executive director of the CIA," Haddox said, then frowned. "He's not executive director anymore. He left, and then I left later, almost two years to the day."

"A lot of money to be made," Landry said. "But that's not the reason."

Haddox nodded sagely. "That's not the reason. But you're right, a *lot* of money. This kind of thing is expensive—specialized—and there aren't many people in the world who can do it. But it's worth it! To protect this country, to make sure we're free."

"So the executive director—help me out here—what's his name again?"

"Cardamone." He spat the name. An adrenaline spike. Landry turned down the juice, jotted down the name, and led Haddox away from that subject and back to safer ground. "What did you say the name of your island was?"

"Indigo. It was named after a plantation we had in East Florida back in the early eighteen hundreds. Before my great-great-grandfather made his fortune in paper, our family grew indigo. Stinking stuff, killed everybody. The slaves—killed 'em in five years, on average. Not the proudest moment in Haddox history."

Now that Haddox had calmed down a bit, Landry led him back to where he wanted to go. "But *this*. The scope of the operation, it's breathtaking. How did you do it?"

"What?"

"How did you stay under the radar?"

"You mean what I think you mean? We're not supposed to talk about that. I told Grace— "

He stopped. His eyes fearful. "Oh God."

Landry remained stock-still.

"Nobody knows Grace knows."

"It's our secret," Landry said.

For the first time, Franklin Haddox started to struggle. "What's this in my *arm*?"

"It's the cord to the blind, see?" Landry said quickly, turning up the drip. *Talk him down.* "What's it like, living in an octagon house?"

"We don't *live* there."

Testy.

"My mother wanted it kept a certain way, *preserved*. No kids playing cowboys and Indians on her expensive old moth-eaten oriental carpets. She and my father built two freestanding houses to *live in*, back in the fifties. Painted 'em yellow to match the Wedding Cake. That's what we call the…octa." He paused. "Octagon… al. House." He looked up at Landry, seeking approval. "I bet you don't know about the secret passageway."

"Secret passageway?"

"It was built in the twenties, during Prohibition. Those were wild days—my great-grandfather knew a lot of movie stars, had an affair with one of them. Can't remember who. Mary Pickford and Douglas Fairbanks came down here for R and R. Lot of people came down here to let off steam. Valentino. Clark Gable, in the thirties. They wanted to get away from all that *scrutiny*."

"Tell me about the passageway."

"It's a secret." He winked, a broad stage wink. Landry didn't like the wink, and he didn't like Haddox.

"Passageway?" Landry reminded him.

"Goes from the Wedding Cake to the cabanas and comes out by the old boathouse. The pool was built in, oh, 1922? They'd bring the booze out on boats and take it through the tunnel. Just a precaution—my great-grandfather bought off the local constabulary, used to hunt 'gators with the sheriff. Ironic, huh? Sheriff probably enjoyed Great-Granddad's bootleg booze on a number of occasions. Now one of the family's in the sheriff's office, did I tell you that?"

"Your niece?"

"Don't really know her—long story. Her only claim to fame was being the Petal Soft Soap Baby. Her mother—" He stopped himself. Got that sly look in his eye. Something there. Landry doubted it was relevant to what he needed to know, but he asked anyway. "Her mother?"

"She's dead." He focused on Landry. "Long, long story. Her daughter... Did I tell you we have a cop in the family? A *detective*. Real small potatoes—my guess is she spends all her time investigating bicycle thefts, things like that."

Landry turned the subject to security. Specifically, what kind of security they had on the island.

"You won't believe this, but when I left? They said I was on my own—no more security detail. Just like that."

"But you have security now?"

"Rent-a-cops. But the place is secure, you'd better believe it. The VP comes down here a lot, so everything's in place, paid for by the U.S. government—motion sensors, cameras, all sorts of stuff. You should see it when Owen comes. Snipers on the roofs, Coast Guard, one if by land, two if by sea. It's like a traveling circus, only real buttoned-down, you know? All those guys in suits talking into their wrists. Reminds me of when I had my own motorcade. Nobody appreciates how important I was to this country."

Diatribe time. Landry let him ramble. Finally he wound down. "I did a lot for the people of the United States."

Landry held Frank's wrist up and checked his pulse rate. He said, "I know you did. The average American Joe doesn't understand that, but I do. I admire you."

"You admire me?"

"I like the way your mind works. But I'm curious. What gave you the idea?"

"The idea?" Haddox looked at him, confused.

"Aspen. Brienne Cross. It was brilliant."

"Oh, that. Aspen wasn't the first, and it won't be the last, either. You remember the Mexican singer? What's her name? And a bunch of others—you wouldn't believe how easy it was—how well it's worked. Talk about 'thinking outside the box.' Simple but brilliant. Brienne Cross is just the tip of the iceberg." He smiled.

Landry smiled, too.

33

On the way out of Panama City, just before Tyndall Air Force Base, there was a little hole-in-the-wall flower shop called Sweetheart's. Jolie bought white roses there. She slid open the frosted glass door and picked out the bouquet, not the most expensive but not the least expensive either, and inhaled the damp sweet smell of the flowers, beaded with moisture.

She paid the clerk, a woman she recognized but did not know by name, a big woman in a flowered smock with dozens of rings on her fingers that matched her barrettes. The woman beamed, her cheeks exactly like round apples, and asked Jolie if she wanted a card to write her sentiments on.

"No thanks," Jolie said. "He knows what I think."

"That's the best kind of relationship," the woman said.

Jolie drove into the cemetery off Palmetto Road and walked to the headstone set into the grass like a paving stone. The stone was polished granite. She couldn't really afford it, but felt she had to give him the best. He'd been denied the big send-off, with cops from all over Florida, spit-shined and stoic, tears in their eyes. The fired salute, the folded flag, Jolie in a black dress and veil. None of that. She tried to make up for it with the gold engraving of a badge cut into the stone. The dark gray granite shimmered in and out of a lone pine's shadow, declaring itself bravely: this was a person somebody lavished money on.

Jolie set the flowers in the cup and glanced at her watch. Every month, sixteen of them, she'd come here on or around the anniversary of Danny's death. Lately, the date seemed to slip by and she'd make it sometime during the week. Her devotion had stayed the same—forced. First it was stunned and forced. Then it was raw and forced. Then it was angry and forced. Now it was just forced. She'd skipped right past grief, and she felt guilty about that. There was nothing left to her presence here except her need to show the world that Dan Tybee was not forgotten.

Her father had taught her about solidarity early on. Hold up your side. Danny was a good cop, and he deserved a cop's funeral. If they didn't give him the send-off, she would. Whether or not she loved him, she would damn well give him that.

The really bad thing? She *had* loved him. She'd loved him unreservedly, up to the moment the gunshot reverberated through the air of that deserted cabin.

Kay told her to let it go. "It's time you stopped being a widow." "You need to move on." "Don't be a martyr."

She wasn't a martyr.

Truth to tell, being a widow made things a whole hell of a lot easier. She didn't have to even think of finding another man. That was off the table for now—no way she was ready for that. She wore the ring and she visited the grave and she refused to talk about it and that pretty much did the trick. But coming to his grave had become a chore, something she did for the sake of doing. When she stood at his grave, Jolie felt nothing but impatience. Her mind filled with other things she had to do.

But she'd keep him here. Keep his memory. He'd slipped away from her in every other way, but here, under her feet, she finally had his attention.

34

Landry went online to look for an off-track betting parlor. He found one—a ten-minute taxi ride away from Frank's slip in the Emerald Bay Marina in Panama City, where they were currently moored.

Frank kept the slip so he could entertain guests or play golf at the Marriott.

Landry's older brother called him early this morning with the news that Chernobyl Ant would finally run today at Hollywood Park. It would be his first race. The colt had the recurring quarter crack, but the patch on his hoof was solid and the track conditions were good, so it was a go. Earlier, Landry had clicked through the channels on Franklin's satellite TV and discovered that Frank's service didn't subscribe to the racing channels.

Landry made sure the attorney general was secured in the bed—trussed up like a Thanksgiving Day turkey—and raised the level of the triptascoline drip. He closed the blinds and locked everything up tight. He had Frank's card to get in and out of the gated marina.

The OTB was in a bar, smoky and dark and anonymous. Lots of characters. They looked as if their lives had been drifting out of them, like a slow leak in a tire. Too many beers over a lifetime, too many cigarettes. But then the horses came on simulcast and life came back to their eyes, as if these people remembered who they were. The racetrack could do that.

He took a place at the bar and looked up at the monitor. There was one race before Chernobyl Ant's. Landry watched the horses parade down the track at Hollywood Park. Bright green grass. Palms. The California haze. Landry loved the backstretch, loved the action there. It would always be inside him. The only thing more important to him at the moment was taking care of business for Brienne and the others.

Now he knew why they died. All of them: the Egyptian professor, the Mexican pop star, the actor and his wife in Montana.

It was the result of Franklin's "audacious plan." "So simple," he'd told Landry, the triptascoline working just like a truth serum.

"It didn't bother you that they were innocent people? That you just picked them off a list and killed them for the hell of it?"

"Not for the hell of it," Franklin said. "They were important. They were a distraction."

A distraction.

And Landry had followed orders, blindly. He'd had no idea he was working for private interests, not for his country. He couldn't bring Brienne Cross back, but he could avenge her death. Her death, and the others.

The race was coming up. He picked a powerful gray colt, and the gray won. His jockey expertly flipped his whip around and wriggled it—his version of celebrating in the end zone.

Landry knew what it was like, that feeling of athleticism, the rocking action in the stirrups as you balanced above the horse's back, the ground rushing underneath. Pushing with his wrists on the animal's neck, the horse quickening. The feeling when you crossed the wire in first.

He'd ridden twenty-six races as a bug boy. Then he shot up into the giant he was now.

When it was over for him, he'd closed the door. When he closed a door in his life, that was it.

Finally, it was jockeys up. The colt looked good. A flashy chestnut like his daddy. He moved with confidence, interested in his surroundings. No fear in him. He broke a step slow, but caught up fast. Too fast? Landry felt his heart thump hard. Was the jock screwing up? Bejarano—he had to know what he was doing! They'd sweated blood to get him.

Settling into a good rhythm going down the backstretch, three from the rail, the colt moving up. Well within himself. You could tell by Bejarano's arms, following the reins in a subtle rocking rhythm, steady and relaxed, but there was coiled strength underneath. Plenty of horse. And then, right before the turn, Rafael shook the reins and Chernobyl Ant took off.

Landry didn't know when he realized it would be a rout.

First he was ahead by a length, then widened to four, five, six, his lead growing with every stride.

Eleven and a half lengths at the wire!

The feeling bubbled up inside him. A deep and satisfying smile warmed him like a rising sun. He ignored the cigarette smoke, the dank smell of whiskey, the crowd jabbering. Walked out into the sunset, appreciating the palms fluttering against the lurid red-and-plum sky.

Eleven and a half lengths.

35

A man stood under the overhang of the gift store and bait shop, eating a candy bar. Landry had been on his way back to the boat when he spotted him.

The man was easy to make. He pretended to look at the bulletin board by the door, which was cluttered with business cards and photos of tourists holding up big fish. It was dusk, gloomy, but he could tell the man kept one eye on the AG's boat. He looked casual, but wasn't. For one thing, he wasn't really looking at the photos. Landry could tell by the inclination of his head, by the small movements he made, shifting slightly to the left and then turning back. His cap pulled down too low.

Landry walked down the other dock to a slip holding a sports fisher and stepped aboard. Walked around the outside of the cabin as if he owned it. Bent down to work the line.

He did this for maybe a minute. Darkness closing in. He slipped into the water, swam under the dock, and came up on the other side. Got his bearings and swam to the other dock, right to where Frank's boat, *Judicial Restraint*, was tied up.

He had not lost his ability to board a boat silently. It was like riding a bicycle; you never forgot.

He slid sideways through the narrow doorway to the galley, looking toward the stateroom doorway. He'd memorized the layout. He saw the edge of something black—a man's leg, clad in cargo pants. Knife in a scabbard. Soft-soled shoes.

Another man.

The watcher by the bait shop must be a lookout. He could be one of Frank's people, but Landry doubted that. He was pretty sure that someone besides him was interested in Frank's business.

The man on the boat must have just gotten here. He was bent over the bed, looking at the bag of triptascoline, trying to figure out what it was.

The entry to the stateroom was extremely narrow. Landry sidled in, then moved quickly.

The man sensed something and stiffened. Landry had seen this in a rabbit just before a hawk bolted out of the sky—a sixth sense. But the man wasn't a pro. It took him a second to believe his senses, and by that time it was too late. Landry held his head in a vise, hands on either side of the head. He jerked backwards, wrenching the neck sideways at the same time. Heard the pop as the neck snapped, severing the spinal cord: instant unconsciousness, followed by death.

He allowed the body to fall back against him, then lowered it to the sole. The smell of feces was overpowering.

Landry found a roll of paper towels and a bottle of Fantastic. He cleaned the body up and dragged it to one of the bench storage seats in the galley. Lifted the hinged seat. Empty. He heaved the body inside and closed the lid.

More cleanup. There wasn't much. Urine trailing to the bench seat, pulled along by the man's heels. Landry worked efficiently and quietly in the light of the dim lamp from the stateroom. He wet a towel to get rid of the Fantastic smell, wiped the galley sole dry. Admiring the satin finish of the cherry wood sheen.

Twenty minutes later, he felt the boat rock as the lookout stepped aboard.

The man was quiet and careful, but eventually he would have to come through the doorway.

When he did, Landry shot him.

36

Jolie thought: *Memorial Day weekend.*

Something had gone on at Cape San Blas that weekend. A party, a gathering—something. She remembered Kay mentioning it. Kay was always mentioning parties and galas and barbecues and visiting dignitaries, and Jolie was always tuning her out. Now she wished she'd listened better.

She almost called Kay, but decided not to. As much as she liked her cousin, this time she would keep her in the dark.

She Googled Memorial Day and Indigo. Memorial Day and Frank Haddox, Memorial Day and attorney general and "party." And so on.

Zip.

Jolie thought about Zoe and Riley, the day they visited the sheriff's office. Riley worried about the nude pictures on Luke's cell phone. Zoe telling Jolie that Riley and Luke broke up that weekend.

Jolie didn't like coincidences, but she couldn't see how these pieces fit. What did Riley's and Luke's breakup have to do with a missing gay man? Luke and Riley's breakup seemed straight-forward and self-contained: Luke had broken up with Riley, and Riley was worried that Luke had a sex video of her on his phone. The phone was probably with the FBI—swallowed up into a black hole.

So Jolie tried it from the other end. The man named Rick had come to Cove Bar looking for a young man to take to a party on San Blas. A certain type. *Like picking a lobster out of a tank.* Technically a man, but slim, young-looking, boyish.

A memory poked up.

It was just a piece of gossip, something her cousin Kay had told her when they were alone together on a shopping trip in Tallahassee. Kay looked around at the few oblivious shoppers in the mall before saying anything. "The veep's coming this weekend."

"The veep?"

"The vice president? Owen Pintek? Remember him?" As if Jolie should know everything she did about the goings-on at Indigo Island. "I know I told you this. He's always coming down here—it's private and he can have a good time."

"I like his wife." The vice president's wife worked tirelessly for the women of Afghanistan. She'd used the bully pulpit, and used it well. A beautiful, charming woman. Genuine.

"Merle doesn't come down here much."

"Why not?"

"They have separate lives." Kay lowered her voice. "Between you and me? He likes boys."

* * *

Jolie Googled Vice President Pintek, plus visit, plus Cape San Blas. The first two of seven hits were from the *National Enquirer*. The other four looked like blogs, each one referencing the *Enquirer*'s headline: "Veep's Secret Gay Hideaway."

The article about the vice president was the cover story for the April 3 edition of the *Enquirer*, accompanied by a telephoto shot of Indigo Island.

"After months of playing hide-and-seek at Washington's toniest gay underground love nests, Vice President Owen Pintek has moved operations to a private Florida island more suitable to hedonistic fun and games, insiders say. 'He can't get out and about the way he used to since he became vice president,' says one staffer close to the VP. 'Too many people know about him—and his unusual appetites.'"

Jolie had never paid attention to the *National Enquirer*. It wasn't on her radar at all. She'd walk right past it in the supermarket, never even register its existence. So she had no idea that the vice president of the United States would be on the cover. She opened up the cached webpage and scanned the article from over two months before. It was mostly innuendo with no real facts—enough journalistic leeway to drive a truck through.

The whole case hinged on the word of an unnamed staffer, as well as "sources close to the vice president." According to the staffer and the sources, Pintek not only liked boys, but he liked rough sex. He liked sex games, he liked bondage. He liked being choked, and he liked choking. And his favorite place to blow off steam was Indigo Island, the home of the former attorney general of the United States.

Jolie went back to Google. There were no references to Owen Pintek and his sexual preferences other than this *Enquirer* article and another in the same tabloid—a rehash. Jolie often watched CNN on the nights she was home. She'd never seen any reference to Pintek's homosexuality. She'd never read about it in the paper. She doubted this story had made the mainstream media. It was all innuendo.

She went back to the Google search, looking for other references to the VP, and found the important one, halfway down the third page. Just a small snippet, a quote from the *Port St. Joe Star*.

Owen Pintek was in town on Memorial Day weekend.

He was at Indigo.

* * *

Jolie drove into the empty parking lot of the Starliner Motel. The neon sign was dark. She remembered that first night, remembered the way the sign buzzed and blinked: N- VACA-CY. The office door was locked. She walked around the side of the office, which also served as Royce Brady's living quarters, but the shades were pulled and no light seeped out. She knocked on the door out of practice, but she knew the place was empty.

There is always a feeling to a place that has been abandoned. Even if it's only been a day or two, everyone knows. The animals know and move in. People driving by sense the place isn't lived-in anymore.

Jolie tried Brady's number, got his voice mail. She should know the disposition of the case against him, but didn't. Was he incarcerated? Doubtful. She was sure he'd have been able to make bail. In fact, it could be that he wasn't even charged.

She could ask Skeet, and he'd probably tell her. But then he'd want to know why.

She ran through the sequence of events on the day of the standoff. According to Mrs. Frawley's granddaughter, Charly, Luke Perdue left with a man on the morning of the standoff. An hour later he took Kathy Westbrook hostage and holed up in the motel room. Chief Akers negotiated with him for several hours, and it looked as if it would turn out all right. Then Luke brought his hostage to the door, and that was when it went wrong. The FBI sniper killed them both.

Which led to the question, did the FBI have anything to do with his? Could it have been a setup?

If it was a setup, there would have to be a reason. Jolie couldn't think of any, except a tenuous relationship between Luke and Riley's breakup and the vice president acting on his predilection for young men. Both happened on the same night, on the same weekend.

It all became clear. Luke didn't just go out to get some pot and then left. He left because he saw something. Something that scared him.

Scared or not, Luke had told Amy. He'd involved her in it somehow. Jolie was sure of it.

She took the walkway that ran along the front of the units. She came to the oleanders and looked through a gap in the hedge at the railroad tracks beyond. The streetlight shone on them. The rails glimmered like a broken silver necklace.

Jolie could guess the location of the shooter's railcar by the trajectory of the bullet that crashed through Perdue's throat. She pictured the FBI sniper and his spotter lying belly-down on the railcar's roof.

What happened that day? What made Luke take that woman hostage?

A road paralleled the railroad tracks.

Jolie pushed through the break in the oleanders, crossed the tracks, and stepped onto the road. The street followed a slight grade to a shallow basin. Jolie saw houses and trees along the road, the glow of their windows.

She started down the hill.

37

The CO2 Dan-Inject JM Standard, extremely compact and with a total length no longer than its barrel, was made for precision shooting, although Landry hardly worried about it from ten feet away. The lookout's body had blocked the entrance to the galley—it would have been impossible to miss him. Landry broke the tranquilizer rifle down and cleaned it while he waited for the triptascoline to take effect, taking his time and admiring the sleek efficiency of this model and its weather-resistant anodized aluminum parts.

When he was done, he gently laid the JM Standard in its soft-sided case and turned his attention to the lookout. He removed the dart from the lookout's neck, dragged him to the other bench seat in the galley, and propped him up. He started the IV drip and adjusted it downward.

Next, Landry walked Frank to the radio and had him call his security detail. Frank told the head of security he was having too much fun out here, and he would be back home in the morning. The head of his security detail believed him. In fact, the man's voice betrayed the fact that this had happened many times. The head of security made the same weak arguments he must have made before. But Frank, drugged as he was, could be headstrong. And Landry had primed the pump, telling Frank he was cooking sea bass accompanied by a very nice Pouilly-Fuissé. They were old friends by this time—blood cousins. So

Frank sounded three sheets to the wind but happy, which was exactly what Landry wanted. Afterwards, he led Frank back to bed and let him sleep.

Landry took the boat out into the bay. It was going on dark, but that was fine. His attention turned to his captive, the lookout. He knew he would have to be patient with this man.

Turned out, it didn't take long to break him. The man, an FBI agent named Eric Salter, was ambivalent, angry, and riddled with guilt. Once he started talking, he didn't stop.

Eric Salter told Landry that he and his partner had been sent to monitor the former attorney general's actions. Salter admitted that the surveillance wasn't officially sanctioned by the FBI. He and the other guy, the dead man currently residing in the Hinckley's bench seat, were "on their own."

"What's your partner's name?"

"He's not my partner. He's a private investigator named Bakus. Some investigator. He doesn't know his ass from a hole in the ground."

The reason Salter was here at all was because of a mistake he'd made in Iraq. He'd killed innocent civilians. Someone in the U.S. knew what he'd done and held it over his head.

Salter told Landry he'd been en route to a hostage situation four weeks ago when he received a call on a secure line.

The caller told him to shoot the man in the motel room.

Eric Salter was a sniper with the FBI.

He said no, of course. But then they put his eight-year-old daughter on the line. She'd been picked up on her way to school.

"So now it wasn't just about ruining my career," Eric Salter said. "They would have killed her."

Landry thought about how he would feel if someone had picked up Kristal. His reaction would have been different. He would have found the abductor and killed him slowly. He asked, "So you shot this man when you didn't need to?"

"Yes. It was clear he was going to surrender."

Landry stared at the man until he squirmed. In that moment he seemed truly lucid, the self-hatred in his eyes shining through. "I thought I had a clean shot, thought I could take him out, but… he moved."

"He moved?"

"Just a quarter of an inch, but it rattled me."

"It rattled you because you didn't want to do it?"

"Roger that." Vituperative.

"Then what happened?" Landry asked, although he wasn't particularly interested in a hostage situation at a motel.

"I had the shot. I was sure I had the shot."

"But you didn't?"

"I got him. But I got the hostage, too."

*   *   *

When they were done talking, Landry turned up the triptascoline until Eric the FBI agent drifted off into the netherworld. Landry found his carotid artery and injected air from an empty syringe just below the jawline. The resulting embolism was quick, pain-less, and hard to trace. That done, he deposited the body in the other bench seat compartment.

The FBI agent hadn't been much help. He was too consumed by guilt and self-loathing. He didn't know who ordered the hit. It was all pretty much a wash.

Clearly, the agent's fear had affected his aim at the motel. He wasn't choosing his shot. He was *forcing* his shot.

Eric Salter had failed as a sniper. It was probably just as well he was dead.

38

Jolie went to seven houses and asked about the standoff at the Starliner Motel. Nobody saw anything. Or didn't remember seeing anything, which was the same. Kids played in the street. One of them, harnessed to an iPod, zoomed his bike up and down the road in the dark.

Jolie started back up the road. She heard the hum of bike tires, and the boy skidded to a stop right in front of her. He let the earbuds drop. "You asked my mom about the standoff?"

"Why, did she see something?"

"No, but I did."

"What did you see?"

"I saw a guy."

He was walking the bike now, the two of them side by side, heading up the low incline. "What guy?"

Kid shrugged. "Never saw him before."

"Can you describe him?"

"Kinda hard to see. He kept to the shadows."

"Where'd you see him?"

He pointed back the way they'd come. "See that first house on the left side? See the boat?"

Jolie could barely make out an aluminum boat lying face-down on some blocks.

"I saw him crawl out of there."

"Anything about him stand out?" she asked.

"He had long hair. Didn't have a shirt on."

"Pants?"

"Jeans. They were kind of low. Not like they were supposed to be, just they were big on him, like he was starved skinny."

"Sounds like you saw a lot."

He shrugged.

"Then what?"

"I was on my bike. When I came back, he was gone. But a few minutes later, I saw him in the Frohmans' backyard."

"What was he doing?"

The boy paused, looked at her. "He pointed his gun at me."

"His gun?"

"He said, 'Get the fuck out of here or you'll be sorry.'"

"He yelled at you in broad daylight?"

"You think I'm lying?"

"No."

"You're thinking, how come nobody saw anything? Because everyone was inside. Or in school. That's why I never said anything to my dad, 'cause I cut school."

"You cut school?"

"I pretended I had a stomachache. Mom works, so I went home and snuck in and got my tackle and went fishing at the Ghost Lakes."

"How was the fishing?"

"Crappie."

Jolie smiled—kid had a way about him. "What did you do when he waved the gun at you?"

"Are you kidding? I took off! Mama didn't raise no fools." He was good with accents. Sounded like that black kid who had a TV show when Jolie was a child. "You gonna tell me what's going on? Was he the guy who took that lady hostage?"

"Could be."

"Then I'm a hero." He held his hand out. "So where's my reward?"

"I guess I could talk to your mom."

He sighed. "Didn't think I'd get anything."

"You mind if I record your statement?"

"Nope."

Jolie pulled out her microcassette recorder, and they went through it again. After they were done, it was full dark. "You going to be all right riding back?"

"Are you kidding?" He got on his bike. "You don't want to hear about the car?"

Jolie stared at him. "Car?"

39

As she walked back up the road toward the motel, Jolie thought about the description of the car Mark Armstrong had given her. Dark blue, "official-looking, like the Secret Service, only older."

Jolie asked him if he saw who was driving. It was just one guy. He had a buzz cut, wore a dark jacket. Close to Charly's description of the man at her house. Jolie asked him how many times the car went by.

Four times, he said. Cruising, real slow—it spooked him.

Before or after the man hid under the boat?

After.

Anything else?

"The front was crushed in. The bumper was dragging, like he'd just been in an accident."

It appeared that someone, someone "official," had picked up Luke Perdue. Luke managed to get away, maybe by causing an accident? Then he hid under a boat, went into the Frohmans' backyard, and threatened a boy with a gun. It would have taken him only a few minutes to get from the Frohmans' backyard to the Starliner Motel.

Jolie didn't have any more facts, but she could guess what happened from there. Luke Perdue must have spotted Kathy Westbrook and forced his way into her room. He'd been described as desperate. Desperate and scared?

Running away from Buzz Cut? Did he somehow get Buzz Cut's gun?

The gun Luke had used that day had been a "throwdown"—the serial numbers had been filed off. It was untraceable. That would fit with a rogue FBI agent, or even a regular cop. Some cops were known to have an extra, untraceable weapon on them, in case a situation went bad and they needed to point to another suspect.

Be prepared. The motto wasn't just for Boy Scouts.

She could ask Louis to put a BOLO on the car. Dark blue, smashed right quarter panel. But it all happened a month ago. The car was probably long gone. She could only ask Louis for so many favors before wearing out her welcome.

She took out her phone and called Zoe.

Zoe answered on the first ring.

"Did Riley tell you why Luke broke up with her?"

"Why he broke up with her?" Zoe sounded confused. "I don't think she knows."

"He never told her?"

"She couldn't reach him. He wouldn't answer the phone. He hid out from her."

"Hid out?"

"I shouldn't have said that."

"Why not?"

"Because that wasn't fair. They were in love."

She was trying to sound like a caring friend.

"He didn't really love her, did he?"

"I don't know." Her voice was faint, as if she'd pushed the phone away from her mouth. "I guess, I don't know, maybe he was using her."

"Why do you think that?"

"I don't know. Honest."

"What did Luke look like?"

"He was skinny."

Jolie vaguely remembered his picture in the paper. "He had long hair and a mustache?"

"Uh-huh."

"Zoe, did Riley tell you what happened that night?"

"He just…left. At first she thought it was a joke. I was gone that weekend with my mom, but she called me a bunch of times. She was so upset. She couldn't reach him, and it drove her crazy. She tried *everything*. She drove over to his house, but either he was out or he wasn't answering."

"Did she tell you what happened right before he left?"

"Just what I told you—he said he was going to his truck to get more pot."

"So there was no hint that he was going to leave? She thought he would be back?"

"Of course she did! That was why she was so upset."

"Did he meet the vice president?"

"What?"

"The vice president. He was there that weekend."

"I don't think so. There's no way her mom and dad would introduce Luke to the vice president. We had our orders."

"Orders?"

"Like, if anybody important came, we were supposed to stay at the bungalow. We weren't supposed to leave, because they had to have their privacy. They didn't want us spying on them."

"Could you spy on them?"

She didn't answer.

"Zoe?"

"Look, I…"

"Zoe, this is important. I'm not out to bust you. I just want to know if you've ever spied on any of Riley's parents' guests. Have you?"

"Riley's gonna *kill* me!"

"This is important, Zoe. It might have to do with what happened to Luke."

"You mean, why he *died*?"

Jolie didn't answer.

"Uh, well, there's this old tunnel—it comes out by the pool, like there's a backdoor to the cabanas. On hot nights sometimes, we sneak out there and have a smoke—sometimes we raid the liquor cabinet—and if anybody comes we're, like, *gone*."

"Did Luke know about it?"

"Uh…"

"Did Luke know about it?"

Her answer was meek. "Yes."

*   *   *

Jolie called Royce Brady again. This time she got him. She told him to meet her at the motel.

"Now?"

"Now."

He showed up ten minutes later and let her into room nine. She did a thorough search. Opened the toilet tank, ran her hand behind it. Reached under the bed, especially around the casters. Checked between the bedspring and the mattress. She looked in every nook and cranny that could hold a cell phone, but there was nothing.

"Are we done here?" Royce said.

"Looks like."

"Good." He locked the door behind them. He didn't bother to ask her what she was looking for, just stalked to his car. He had his own troubles.

Full dark now. Jolie went behind room nine, shined her Mag Lite up at the narrow bathroom window, which cranked outward. Nothing on the ledge. Nothing on the ground below, except for weeds and trash. She walked alongside the oleanders, shining her light through the leaves.

Forget it.

He probably stashed the phone in his apartment, and whoever came to the house that day found it.

Jolie opened her car door. She stared down the road at the neighborhood where Mark Armstrong lived. There *was* one more place to look. The boat. The upside-down boat on cinder blocks that Luke hid under.

This time the street was quiet when Jolie parked at the top and walked down to the house with the boat.

The boat was in the third yard down close to the street. Jolie got on her hands and knees on the springy grass and looked under the boat. Played her Mag Lite over the cinder blocks, felt along their exposed edges. No cell phone. He could have hidden it anywhere. Maybe the FBI really *did* have it. One thing for sure: it wasn't here. The only objects she found were three empty beer bottles and a snuff can—kids must use the boat as a place to party.

She heard a door open and peered out. Someone came out onto the porch of the house two yards down. Jolie stayed under the boat, hoping they'd go back in.

When the neighbor went back inside, she slid out and walked back up the road to her car.

40

Franklin Haddox tried to focus on the man sitting on the bench seat opposite him. They were still on the boat. The guy looked familiar—Frank thought he might be his cousin. Nick, the writer. But the man didn't act like a cousin. He wasn't dressed like a writer, either. He wore a dark blue cap pulled low over his forehead and a windbreaker. He looked deadly serious, as if something terrible had happened. Lines of disapproval bracketed his mouth. He reminded Frank of his security detail back when he was in the cabinet. Much more professional than the buffoons he had now.

Frank understood this was official business. He decided not to say anything—he wanted to see where this was going. Plus, he had a massive headache and no memory of what he'd been doing before he found himself sitting in the galley, resting his head on his arms on the dinette table. Sleeping it off, maybe.

The man opposite him leaned forward so their arms were touching. He smiled, which made Frank feel better. There was something confidential in the smile, as if they shared a common goal. It put him at ease immediately.

"What do you know about the man under this seat?"

"Seat?" The feeling that they shared a common goal vanished. Frank felt something move in his chest. He realized what it was: fear, a clump of it, dissolving quickly and shooting into this system.

The man said, "Do you need a refresher course?"

"Refresher course?"

The man sighed and rose to his feet. He looked saddened, as if he carried the weight of the world on his back. He pushed the seat cushion to the floor and with one swift move opened the storage compartment. Quick—then let the lid slam back down.

But Frank saw it all right. Mashed into the small space, fetal position, neck at an impossible angle, a human pretzel—it would be impossibly painful if the contents inside the box were still alive. But they weren't. Even with the lid down, Frank could see the eye, fixed upward like the eye of a gaffed tarpon.

The realization slammed down on him with its full weight. His face radiated heat. "You don't think *I* would…I couldn't do something like that." But he knew people who could. Surely there was a way to sort this out.

The man stood over him like a stern father.

Frank's vocal cords barely gained purchase, and his question came out in a squeak. "Who are you?"

"Special Agent Eric Salter."

"FBI?" A fresh bolt of terror shot through him.

"Correct."

Stall him. "Can I see some ID?"

Salter reached into his trouser pocket, pulled out his wallet badge, and flipped it open—he was FBI, all right. He put it back, plucked at the dark slacks above his knees, hunkered down beside the offending bench seat, and looked into Frank's eyes. "What do you know about this?"

"Nothing!"

"There's a dead man in your bench seat. You've been lying here with your head on your arms for approximately—" he stared at his expensive diver's watch, "—twenty minutes. Sleeping it off?"

"No—I mean yes."

"Do you know this man?"

"No. I don't think so."

He reached for the lid. "Refresh your memory?"

"*No!* Please, no!"

"What did you do?"

"Nothing! I swear! I couldn't..." He stopped. Knew full well he could order someone killed. Order it and sit on his boat and clink glasses as it was carried out. But it was for a good reason—

Special Agent Salter slammed his hand down on the dinette. Nonsensically, Frank thought: *Careful of the wood!*

"Did you kill this man?"

"No!"

"Did you kill this man?"

"No! Are you crazy? I couldn't, I can't. Someone must have—"

"What? Sneaked in here while you were sleeping? Right here, with your head on the table?"

Then he hammered Frank with questions. Where was he going? Who was on board? Did he know this man? The questions came in a rapid-fire sequence, like a drill sergeant. Frank didn't have a chance to answer them fully.

Finally he managed to say, "I want my lawyer."

The agent rose to his feet and stood over him. His face stormy, the anger building up in his chest, his shoulders. He was massive, like a boulder about to roll downhill and crush whatever lay underneath. "Get up."

"Up?"

"Get up now."

Frank started sliding across the seat.

"Do it *now!*"

He scrambled out so quickly he banged his knee on the bench. He registered the throbbing pain, but it was second to the pure adrenaline of his fear, hurtling through his veins. He stood back. Legs shaking.

The agent shoved the cushion to the galley sole and flung open the lid.

The burst of adrenaline was so hard, so explosive, that Frank felt his heart seize. He stared down at another man, this one mercifully head-down, pressed into the box like a broken toy.

41

"So you're saying they're Cardamone's people?" Frank asked. He'd recovered nicely, after a glass of Remy, especially after Agent Salter told him he knew Frank wasn't responsible for the dead men in the bench seats.

"If we're correct, their allegiance is to Mike Cardamone."

"And Cardamone's people are watching me? And Grace?"

He nodded to a bench seat. "There's your proof."

"But they weren't here to hurt me?"

"We don't believe so, no. Not at this juncture. But that could change."

Frank ducked his nose into the snifter and inhaled. Swirled the glass, took a small sip. He still had the headache, but the Remy seemed to have quieted it somewhat. "So you're saying if I fired my security, I'd have less people to worry about."

"Fewer."

"Fewer?"

"Fewer people to worry about."

"Oh. Right. Sorry, grammar was never my strong suit. I can't believe you know all this."

"We're the FBI."

"Well, that explains it. Mike was number three at the CIA, you know. He thought the Fibbies were like the Keystone Cops. But now I'm getting the idea it's the CIA that's incompetent."

"That would be a dangerous assumption to make," Special Agent in Charge Salter said.

"So the whole cousin thing—you made it up? You posed as Nick Holloway to get on this boat? So Nick Holloway isn't my cousin after all?"

"Oh, he's your cousin, all right. We intercepted your e-mails."

"You can do that? Wait, of course you can." Talk about irony. "Our lawyers had to construct new language to make that happen—it was pretty fancy footwork, let me tell you—a real bitch to do. Jesus, that's ironic. So Nick meant it when he said he was busy. When he first wrote me back."

"That's what it looks like."

"Why the charade? I don't understand—"

"We wanted to see if Cardamone was keeping tabs on you. As it turns out, he is. It's clear he sent these two men to keep an eye on you."

"Whatever he's involved in, I have nothing to do with it. We're friends, and that's the extent of it."

"You're more than that. We have the wiretaps to prove it. We've been monitoring Cardamone for some time."

Franklin had been a prosecutor for a long time. He knew the outlines of a potential plea bargain when he heard it. Time to lay the groundwork. "You know none of this was my idea—what Cardamone and the president were doing."

"I didn't think it was. So to review, it was just you three who knew about the program. Cardamone, President Baird, and yourself."

"That's right. Just the two of us now that Baird is dead."

"Then it comes down to you or Cardamone."

"That's right."

Special Agent Salter let it sit there between them for a minute. Then he said, "You could be a big help to us."

"Turning state's evidence, right?"

"It's a good deal."

"But there's my reputation to think of. I was the Top Cop. The attorney general of the United States of America. It would kill Grace."

"Better than the alternative."

"What alternative?"

The special agent said nothing.

Frank shuddered. "He'd kill all of us."

"You're the only witnesses. You and Grace."

"But Riley's innocent. And my dad—"

"You know Cardamone. You think that will stop him?"

All of a sudden, the Remy didn't taste so good. Frank swirled the glass again, his heart speeding up. He did know Cardamone. He knew what the man was capable of. The hairs on the back of his neck stood up. They'd been standing up, off and on, for the last week. But still, it was impossible for him to grasp this concept completely. "How would he get away with it?"

"How did you get away with Brienne Cross?" Salter looked down at his notes. "The Egyptian professor from Berkeley—?"

"Okay, okay, I see your point. But won't Cardamone suspect something if I fire all my security?"

Salter said, "I'm sure you can finesse it. This is going to happen fast. If you can get him to come down here—"

"I can get him to come down here, don't you worry about that."

"*If* you can get him to come down here," he repeated, "we'll take it from there."

"You'd be putting my family in danger."

Salter just stared at him.

"My family's already in danger."

"Correct."

"You have people there now?"

"We have the island under surveillance."

Frank sighed. "Any way you look at this, I'm lucky if I escape jail time."

Salter's face was impassive.

"I don't want Grace exposed."

"I can't promise anything. You know that. But if we can get Cardamone to admit what he's done...we may not need her."

Frank had a truly lucid moment. He looked straight at Agent Salter. "That's bullshit."

Salter stood. "Your choice. Somebody's going to pay for all those deaths. Conspiracy's a federal crime, and the death penalty *will be enforced*. We'd rather it be Cardamone."

Frank's future was bleak, any way you looked at it. There was very little wriggle room. He would have to convince Cardamone to come down here. He would have to get him to talk. Never easy—the guy was wary as an ibex.

Maybe there was a way out of this, but right now he couldn't think of one. There were two dead bodies aboard, and the FBI knew about it. He didn't think he could have killed them—that just wasn't part of his makeup—but he couldn't account for a few hours. He'd had something to drink, and he supposed he *could* have blacked out. It was within the realm of possibility.

At any rate, they were here, on his boat.

For a while now he'd been afraid that Cardamone would come after him, and worse, he'd come after his family. Special Agent Salter offered a way out, and he'd damn well take it.

For now.

42

By the time Landry and Franklin were through with their talk, it was going on eleven p.m., and Landry had some things to do. He decided to anchor out in the bay just off Panama City and put in to Cape San Blas early in the morning. One reason for this, Landry anticipated trouble when Franklin fired his security team. There might be unpleasantness. No one enjoyed losing a lucrative contract. Unlikely it would come to anything, but the one important lesson Landry had taken from his Boy Scout years was the motto, "Be prepared."

He wasn't tired, but he wasn't at his best, either.

Franklin was still feeling the effects of the drug. The triptascoline, in combination with the Remy Martin, rendered him incoherent. He seemed content to drift off. Good for him and good for Landry.

Landry went up on deck and made his nightly phone call. For the call he used a throwaway cell phone he'd bought at Target for $29.95 plus tax—it didn't have to be expensive to preserve his anonymity. A friend of his, a fellow racehorse owner who was also a tech genius (he'd named one of his horses Phreaker), had created an invisible voice mailbox for him. The mailbox was situated inside a major phone system, but no one knew of its existence. Landry's contact number remained the same, but the box had been designed to erase itself every twenty-four hours, then migrate to a different location. Even Landry had no clue where the voice mail was. It could be in Vegas. It could be in Keokuk. All he knew was that it worked. It was the perfect way for him to contact the Shop every night without revealing his location.

Usually, he received an automated response. "There is nothing at this time. Please check back tomorrow. Thank you, and have a nice day."

The "have a nice day" line was a little over the top in Landry's opinion.

But tonight, he did not receive that message. Tonight, the message was different.

He closed the phone and thought about it for a minute. It was a beautiful night. Warm, but there was a breeze. Panama City stretched out before him like a diamond-studded crescent. He looked east, toward Cape San Blas, a black spit of land that jackknifed out into the Gulf and created the bay. He could see a smattering of lights there too, up to where St. Joseph State Park started and the private houses ended.

He didn't spend time pondering the deeper meaning of the message. Right now he needed to make arrangements. He opened the phone and called his younger brother.

Gary answered on the second ring. "Did you *see* him? Eleven and a half lengths! Jesus! Rafael was wrapping up on him at the end. Could have been twelve, thirteen lengths if he'd let him go."

"The foot okay?"

"Colder than Cruella De Vil's titties. Did you see the way he exploded when Rafael asked him? Did you *see that*? Holy Jesus take-me-to-the-ballgame-and-buy-me-a-fucking-hotdog *Christ*, he's the real thing. The Kentucky Derby, man. The First Saturday in May."

For a moment, Landry let that hang in the air. It was like the notes of a distant trumpet calling soldiers to battle, sweet and pure.

A thrumming started up in his gut, a combination of excitement, anguish, and desire. The First Saturday in May was like the Holy Grail, except the Holy Grail wasn't anywhere near as good.

He tried not to think about it. "Hey. You like Ocala?"

"Ocala?"

"You want to go to Ocala and check out the stud farms? All expenses paid?"

Skepticism crept into his brother's voice. "What are we talking here?"

"All you have to do is fly in to Panama City and rent a car."

It took him a moment, but then he said, "Sure, I can do that."

"Use the Amex. Try Orbitz first. You have to be in Panama City by four p.m. tomorrow at the latest. Don't forget to use—"

"Your driver's license, gotcha."

"The one for Peters. That's important, it's got to be under that name."

"Hey, bro, haven't I done this before? I know what I'm doing." A pause. "So, what kind of car? It's a long drive to Ocala."

His brother. Always pushing the envelope. "Anything you want."

"A Hummer?"

"Almost anything you want. I'm paying for the gas, so be considerate."

"A Caddy, then. I guess I could get away. A week?"

"If you want."

"Shandra won't be happy."

"Take her with you. All I'm saying, use a different card for her."

"Nah, she's got something going. It'll be just myself, I guess."

*　　*　　*

They had breakfast at anchor in the bay. Franklin cooked—eggs Benedict, chopped red potatoes with onions, and a garnish of fresh fruit. Frank took his breakfast cooking seriously. He wore a barbecue chef's apron with a drawing of a spatula and a barbecue fork.

Landry was impressed by Frank's resilience. In fact, he enjoyed Frank's company, once the unpleasantness was out of the way. Landry was surprised by this. As one of the architects of the Shop, Franklin would pay the ultimate price. It was clear Frank thought he was going to ace this, that he would come out unscathed, once he delivered Mike Cardamone to the FBI. Landry let him think that. It made for an interesting hour of wide-ranging conversation, not to mention delicious victuals.

Frank stood over him in his chef's apron, holding a real spatula, which looked a lot like the one emblazoned on his chest. "You like the eggs?"

"I love the eggs."

"There's more. Want another?"

"Absolutely."

"The hollandaise is an old family secret. That lemony zing? Do you taste it?"

"I like the zing."

"Thought you would." Franklin replaced Landry's plate with a fresh one filled with more eggs Benedict and cottage potatoes, and sat opposite him. He leaned forward, elbows on the table. Landry's mother would call that bad manners, but times had changed and even Landry put an elbow on the table now and then.

"You really think this is going to work?" Frank asked.

"If you can get Cardamone here." The hollandaise really was zingy. He'd have to remember to get the recipe.

"And he'll end up in supermax?"

"That's my guess."

"Good. He's a dangerous guy. Not only is he a spook, but he was special forces. You know how those guys are. They're nothing but glorified assassins. I've heard that once they get a taste for it, they can never go back."

Landry shrugged.

"What I'm really worried about is Grace. She's not part of this."

"I'll do what I can."

"You see, she was just being supportive. You know how husbands and wives talk about everything? It was like that. Are you married?"

"I have a wife and a daughter."

"Then you know what I'm talking about. I'd really like to keep her out of this." He paused. "You know what it's like to love someone, really love someone? That's how I feel about Grace. I imagine that's how you feel about your wife. More strawberries? There's plenty."

"No, thanks. But I like this hollandaise."

"It's good, isn't it? But you see, Grace, she's the love of my life. I don't know about what it's like, your marriage, but with Grace it was always me wanting her. Even though I was the attorney general of the United States, even though I have a law degree from Yale and she was just a local girl who only went to two years of junior college, I think—I'm pretty sure—I love her more than she loves me. Not that that's a bad thing. Every marriage is a balancing act, right? Kind of like a teeter-totter."

Landry wasn't sure why Franklin was telling him this. It didn't seem important in the scheme of things. But Franklin's time was growing short, so Landry decided to be polite and listen. Plus, Frank was a tremendous cook. And he had a way about him. Charming at times. He liked the fact that Franklin remained upbeat in the face of adversity. A glass-half-full kind of person. The eternal optimist.

Frank licked his lips. "Thing is, what I'm worried about, is she's got this connection to a church. The Victorious Redemption Spiritual Church. Have you heard of it? It's been in the news a lot."

Until recently, Landry had paid no attention to the news. But when he became interested in Frank, he had researched him on the Internet—be prepared. He knew where Frank was going with this. Grace's association with the church had taken up the whole first page of Google. Since talking about it was clearly cathartic for Frank, Landry pretended interest. It was the least he could do.

"The reverend there is…well, he's kind of off-the-wall. He's a…ah, I don't know quite how to put this—he's sticking his pecker in a lot of hornet's nests. I know there have been death threats. And there's at least two investigations into his dealings—"

"There are."

"There are?"

"There are two investigations. There *are*."

"This is the second time you've corrected my grammar. You used to be an English teacher before you joined the FBI?"

"Let's get on with the story. What kind of investigations?"

"Bribery. Money laundering. Something hinky going on there. Gunrunning, maybe, to the Congo. The minister, his name is Mister Wembi, and that's what they call him, with the Mister always before the name, like it's a second language or something. He's white, but he spent a lot of time in Africa hunting witches—can you believe it? He was a 'witch identifier.' Even took the African name, which I think is weird. Probably a marketing ploy. Grace has donated a lot of money to the church, and she's on the board—she's, well, religious. It's the one thing I don't like about her. Well, that, and all the money she spends on the horses."

"What kind of horses?" Landry asked, suddenly interested.

"Arabians. And Hackneys. She drives them."

Hackneys. Some people.

"We're not as rich as we used to be," Frank mused. "I'd say we've lost about thirty percent of our wealth, which, when you think about it, isn't too bad. But Grace doesn't like the way we look to outsiders. Like we're obscenely rich. She wants me to get rid of this boat, but I won't. This is my baby. She's got her horses and her church, and I've got the Hinckley."

"Understandable," Landry murmured.

Frank took both ends of his linen napkin and began twisting it in his fingers—an annoying distraction.

Landry said, "So what do you want from me?"

"I'd just like to keep that aspect—the church—quiet. It has nothing to do with any of this. The Shop. Nothing at all. I'm worried that if this guy, this reverend, gets wind of it, he'll set her up to take the fall."

"For the gunrunning and money laundering? How deep is she into this? It doesn't sound like she's just on the board."

"It's…the church is an obsession. I just don't want her hurt. Those people—on some level, I think they're dangerous. He is. He's scary. A charismatic leader, kind of like the guy with the Kool-Aid, Jim Jones."

Landry had had enough of this conversation. "Consider it done. We'll keep that under our hat."

"Good." He was back to cheerful again. "That's a big load off my mind."

"No problem."

"I was wondering…"

"What were you wondering?"

"Are those two men—the ones who were killed—are they still on board?"

Landry nodded. "I put them on ice, though, that's why there's no smell."

"Ah, I see." He thought about it. "The ice from the bait well?"

"Yes."

"Do you really need them? Couldn't we weigh them down and throw them overboard?"

"You know I can't do that. That would be tampering with evidence. Besides," he added, "they're not eating anything."

"I guess," he said at last. "I just thought I'd give it a shot."

Landry nodded, then got up and started clearing the table. "Can you write out that recipe for me?" he asked.

* * *

"Tell me about Danehill Security," Landry said as they approached Indigo Island.

Franklin shrugged. "Not much to tell. I hired them a month ago when the shit started hitting the fan. Grace wanted me to go the cut-rate route, so we compared prices. They're not exactly the A-Team. I'd say they're more like the E-Team. Or even worse than that."

"Oh?"

"These guys don't have any discipline. It's just a job to them. But you have to understand—I'm spoiled. As the attorney general, I had a topflight security detail."

They came in on the leeward side, rounding the spit of land that ended St. Joseph Peninsula. Motored past the state park— white beaches, marshy areas, trees noisy with birds, wildlife, and campers. Next were the expensive houses and private docks. Up ahead, in the crook of the peninsula's elbow, Landry saw two islands.

"Opal Island," said Franklin, motioning to the smaller one. "It's a resort. Very exclusive."

Gated. Palm trees. Golf courses. A complex of buildings. All very high-toned, pristine. But the island had almost a plastic patina to it, like Saran Wrap. More Disney World than Florida panhandle. It didn't look real.

Indigo Island looked real.

There were similar palms. There was a small golf course, but it appeared shoddy and neglected in the bright morning sunlight, like a paint-by-numbers set. The trees encroached. A very tall wrought iron fence made a sporadic and halfhearted ring of the island, punctuated by No Trespassing signs.

Landry squinted past the black bars of the fence. He spotted stables and a good-sized riding ring through the trees. The octagonal house Franklin had told him about looked like a wedding cake. It reminded Landry of Dickens's *Great Expectations*, a book he'd read in high school and one that had fascinated him by its pure weirdness. The house looked like something Miss Havisham would have kept in her refrigerator—if they'd had refrigerators in her day.

The other three structures were painted to match the octagon house, yellow with white trim. Rectangular swimming pool, chaise lounges lined up razor-straight facing the pool, like you'd find at a high-class hotel. Three permanent cabanas. Golf cart paths ran through the compound like ant trails. Plenty of parking.

Landry noted a causeway, maybe two hundred and fifty meters long, linking Indigo Island to the mainland. Narrow. Landry guessed the causeway had been built early in the last century—the only way onto the island by land. There was a guardhouse situated on the small spit of land that led onto the causeway. Dark uniforms, ball caps. The security company. The E-Team.

They tied up at the dock opposite an ancient, beat-up skiff—had to be twenty years old. Landry thought it must have sentimental value. In his travels, he'd noticed that rich people didn't seem to throw away their old possessions. He'd seen plenty of stud farms breathtaking in beauty but still containing the odd rusty pickup or old shed.

The boathouse, a real antique, was empty. Frank had mentioned they'd sold a lot of their toys recently. The jet. The expensive cars. The picnic boat. The only thing they hadn't cut back on, according to Frank, was Grace's Hackneys. She still had plenty, and they were eating him out of house and home.

"Where are your agents again?" Franklin asked.

Landry motioned to the houses and the boats tied up to the long docks on the peninsula, and to the trees and bushes onshore.

Franklin nodded. "And why do we need to get rid of my security people?"

"This is an FBI operation. Your people would only get in the way. They're the E-Team, remember?"

Franklin nodded again. "The Keystone Cops, only dumber."

Franklin handed over control of the boat to Landry. Landry enjoyed the docking procedure on the Hinckley. He'd done it before, but of course Franklin didn't remember that. The jetstick was a lot like the joystick on the video games Landry grew up with. Docking the Hinckley was just like parallel parking.

The morning was sunny, but there had been some chop in the open bay. Weather reports did not lie.

A storm was coming.

43

As they tied up, Landry spotted a girl lying on the other dock. She looked exactly like a Barbie doll. Tanned Barbie, maybe. She was lying on a chaise cushion that had been dragged out to the dock, talking to a member of Franklin's security detail. Big guy, biceps that only came from hours in the gym, his Danehill Security cap sitting atop a bulging shaved neck like a child's beanie. He dangled his feet in the water. Landry could hear hip-hop music coming from somewhere. He detested hip-hop music. He glanced at Franklin. The man's face was grim.

"That Riley?" Landry asked him.

"Uh-huh." The way he said it showed he was simmering. "She's after the help again."

The help, Landry thought. Like Luke Perdue. He hopped down from the boat to the dock and started walking in their direction.

Franklin rushed up behind him, trying to keep up. "What are you doing?"

"You'll see." He crossed to the other dock and strode toward the two people at the end. He didn't pause when he reached them but let the momentum carry him right up to the moment he pushed his foot into the security man's back, toppling him into the water.

The man had time to say "Hey!" before he hit. He made a big splash—probably weighed 240.

The guy stood up in the waist-high water. His face was red, either from the sun or from anger, except for the white triangle of zinc oxide on his nose. "You mother fucker, what'd you do that for?" he yelled, trying to get up on the dock. He had to pull with his arms and hands.

Landry stepped on one of the hands. "You know what my wife's favorite TV show is?"

The guy just stared at him.

"*Celebrity Apprentice*. You ever watch *Celebrity Apprentice*?'"

"What the fuck? What are you talking about? Get off my fucking hand!"

"Donald Trump? Remember the part where he says, 'You're fired'? Well, that's what you are, chum. You're fired."

"Get your foot off my hand!" The guy looked at Franklin. "Who the fuck is this fucker?"

Franklin looked nervous, but said, "He's my new security."

Landry was really starting to like Franklin.

"You can't fire me. We've got a contract—"

Landry's foot came off the man's hand and toed into his larynx. You could overdo it, so Landry pulled back at the last moment and tipped up the chin, just enough pressure to send the man back into the water.

"Daddy!" screamed Riley.

The guy stood up again. He looked up at Landry and let out another string of profanities laced with obscenities. Landry felt uncomfortable with that. He was raised the old-fashioned way, and you didn't curse in front of a lady. But a glance at Riley told him she wasn't one, so he let it go.

She looked avid. Like a cat waiting for a mouse's next move.

Landry returned his attention to the security guy. For a moment Landry thought the guy would lunge at him, but then he thought better of it and waded to shore. He emptied his cap into the water and slapped it against the dock, then glared at Franklin. Franklin took a step back.

"You don't have to fire me. I quit!"

"Daddy, what are you doing?" demanded Riley.

Franklin glanced at her and then back at the security guard. "I want all of you off-property ASAP. I'll settle up with your boss."

"Fuck you."

The E-Team.

*   *   *

Riley tagged along as they went to the security center situated in a metal outbuilding not far from the main house. She wasn't the only one who tagged along. A pack of dogs joined them, mostly terrier types. Yapping and snapping, making Landry wonder how thick his socks were.

In the security center, Frank reiterated his position, this time to the chief of security, whose name was Melvin Graus. He told Graus that Danehill was no longer providing protection for the island. The chief was understandably upset. First he tried intimidation, then he tried logic, then wheedling, and back to intimidation. To his credit, Franklin stood firm.

"You know there's a provision in here about premature termination of the contract," said Graus. "You're going to have to pay us a substantial amount in penalties."

"You can talk to my accountant about that."

"I've never heard of Salter Security." He glared at Landry. "Are you sure of this guy's bona fides?"

"His bona fides are fine," Franklin said.

Landry liked Franklin better all the time.

"Okay then. You'll be hearing from our attorney."

Franklin said to Graus, "I want you off the property by noon today."

Landry leaned near Franklin's ear and said, "Eleven."

"Eleven today. Eleven sharp."

"But we have equipment to move, electronics—we can't just pack up like we're in the circus."

"You'd better get to it then."

Landry said to Franklin, "Boss?"

"Yes?" He sounded slightly bemused at Landry calling him boss.

"Do you want me to escort Mr. Graus out?"

"Yes, you do that."

"I can find my own way out," Graus said stiffly.

Landry stood over Graus and held his eyes. "I'll want to see your inventory."

"That's bullshit."

Landry said to Franklin, "It's a precaution. We wouldn't want him walking off with any equipment he doesn't own."

Franklin said, "I hardly think he would do that—"

Landry ignored him and remained where he was—towering over Graus. He felt Graus's confusion, calculated the moment the smaller man would take a step backward. He was off by about two seconds.

"All right, if that's what you want," Graus said to Franklin.

"Good, I'll meet you—all of you—by the guard's gate at eleven hundred hours," Landry said. He held Graus's eyes until the man looked away.

After Graus was gone, Frank said, "I need to practice what I'm going to say to Cardamone. Mike is a smart guy. He'll know something's up if I don't sound convincing."

Landry was sure Franklin would be convincing, but he said, "Okay. But I'm going to need to see the grounds."

Frank led the way out of the security center. He seemed pleased with himself. Standing up to someone was probably a rare occurrence for him. Landry noticed Riley looking at her dad in a new way. She was looking at Landry, too, but her look for Landry was different.

As they walked in the direction of the octagon house, Franklin took the lead, pointing out hidden cameras and infrared sensor grids. "A lot of the equipment was installed by the Secret Service for Owen's visits," Franklin said. He added for Landry's edification, "The veep. This stuff is all inactive right now. Some of the equipment is Danehill's, but not much. Are you sure you guys have it covered?"

"You're covered. You can't see our people, but they're there."

"When I was in the DOJ, I had a very good relationship with the FBI."

"That's good to know," Landry said.

They continued on. Franklin walked on ahead, rehearsing his lines for his upcoming conversation with Cardamone. He was far enough ahead so they couldn't hear what he was saying. Riley moved closer to Landry and said, "Why do you keep looking around like that?" she asked.

"Like what?"

"Back and forth."

"Looking for threats."

"But you said the FBI has it covered."

"Ever heard of measure twice, cut once?"

"What?"

"Never mind."

"I can't believe Daddy stood up to Graus that way."

"Why?"

"It's just not like him. He lets things slide."

"What else does he let slide? You?"

"Oh, I get away with stuff."

"Are you sure you're getting away with anything?"

"What do you mean by that?"

"Children need guidance. Didn't anyone ever tell you that? For your emotional well-being, you need someone to set the parameters every once in a while."

"That's fine for a child, but I'm seventeen."

He said nothing.

"Can a child give you a blowjob that will set your hair on fire?"

All this acting out—he found it disturbing. "You're a regular little potty-mouth. If my daughter said that to a stranger—"

"You'd what? Give her a spanking?"

"Take away her iPod, her iPhone, her television, her bed, her furniture, and make her stay in her room for a month."

"That doesn't sound so bad. What if she did it again?'"

"I'd flush her hamster down the toilet."

"You wouldn't do that!"

"You have a hamster?"

"No."

"Then you're not in a position to know, are you?"

*   *   *

Frank stopped on the oyster-shell path by the maintenance shed and looked back at them. "Do you want to go with me in the golf cart?" he asked Landry.

"I'd rather walk."

"Okay." He sounded perturbed, but by the time he took off in the golf cart, his lips were moving and he was once again practicing his speech for Cardamone.

"Is your mother here?" Landry asked Riley. "Grace?"

"She's either shopping or she went to Tallahassee."

"Tallahassee?"

"To her church. She spends half her time there."

"You know when she'll be back?"

"If she's shopping, maybe late this afternoon. There's not a whole hell of a lot to shop for around here. Now it's Kohl's instead of Bergdorf's. She used to fly to Atlanta to do her shopping, when we had the jet. That's all over now. This place is so *lame*. I was born here, and I can't wait to get voted off this island, you know what I mean? What a *back*water. There is nothing to do! And now you got rid of Mr. Clean."

"Mr. Clean?"

"The guy you pushed into the water. I used to think he was hot."

"He didn't look so hot to me."

She giggled. "That was funny, the way he sputtered like a wet cat! He was, like, so surprised! He told me he has a really big dick, but we didn't get that far."

Again with the provocative statements. He knew she did it just for its shock value.

"So your family's cutting back?"

"Oh, you wouldn't believe. Mommy didn't even want the veep to come here the last time, thought it was too *ostentatious*. That's her favorite word now. She's afraid the peasants'll storm the castle or something." She told him about the "ratty old oriental carpets" and the fact that her mother kept her saddles and bridles in her bedroom, which was a huge mess and smelled of dirt and horse hide. The way they used things over and over, all the equipment breaking down. The heater for the pool. The air-conditioning in the octagon house. "Which is, by the way, falling apart! It looks good from the outside, but it smells. Those old walls, I bet there's mold. That's where we keep *the senator*."

"The senator?"

"My grandfather. Dad calls him the senator. As if he's still the senator. He's got round-the-clock nursing care. Dementia."

Landry nodded. His mother-in-law suffered from dementia. It was a terrible disease.

"But he gets around. He's always in the hothouse playing with his roses—thinks he's gardening, but he's actually making them worse, touching them so much. He used to raise champion roses."

Landry ticked the family off on his fingers. "Your mom, your dad, the senator, and you. Have I got that right?"

"My cousin Zoe lived here until last night."

"Oh?"

"We got in a fight and she moved out. She's a pain in the ass, but in another way, she's really amusing. God, was she upset when I threw her out."

"You threw her out?"

"Uh-huh. She said bad things about my boyfriend."

"You have a boyfriend?"

Riley told him about her boyfriend, Luke. He'd worked for the tree and lawn service that kept the grounds neat. She told Landry that she and Luke had been in love and were planning to run away together, like Romeo and Juliet. But then he died.

"How'd he die?"

"In a shoot-out with the police." She told him the story, portraying Luke as an outlaw. "He wasn't going to let anyone take him—he wasn't going to go without a fight."

Landry thought that kind of logic was the ultimate in stupidity. "Why did he take that woman hostage?"

Riley didn't have an answer to that—it didn't fit with Luke's heroic image. She had no idea why Luke Perdue would take a woman hostage in a motel. None at all. So she glossed over it with proof that he loved her, then went back to blaming Zoe for saying bad things about him.

"What did she say?"

"She said he was sneaking around spying on the vice president. She was lying."

Landry thought this was an interesting side trip. He didn't know if it had any bearing on his own investigation. He'd have to ask Franklin about it. It was an interesting coincidence that Luke Perdue got himself killed in a motel holding a woman hostage.

Was this the hostage Special Agent Eric Salter shot? Eric Salter, the FBI agent he was currently impersonating.

Eric Salter had been consumed with guilt because his shot had taken out both the bad guy and the female hostage. Someone—Cardamone, probably—blackmailed Salter into doing jobs for him. He had been one of the two men keeping track of Franklin Haddox.

Small world.

*　　*　　*

The dogs accompanied them to the octagon house. They'd run ahead, then circle back. Always watching Landry and Riley to gauge their reactions. Outside the octagon house, Riley turned into a tour director. She gave Landry a canned speech she must have repeated a hundred times. There were two stories, a basement, and a cupola, she said. The low hill it sat on was man-made, she said. You could see the whole island from the cupola, she said.

Close up, the octagon house looked smaller than he'd expected. Riley told him the island had been built almost from scratch in the twenties—the reason it could accommodate a basement and the tunnels in an area where you normally wouldn't find basements or tunnels. The tunnel, she said, was considered a "structural marvel"—those were the words she used—and had been designed in such a way that it would not flood during storms. She also told him her grandfather was sensitive to sunlight, so he had a room in the basement. Stairs from the outside led down to the basement. Landry noted that the steps had once been wide but were now narrow, to make room for the wheelchair ramp running alongside.

They went up the steps into the house, the dogs' toenails clicking on the hardwood floor. The ankle-biters had given up trying to penetrate Landry's desert boots.

The floor was empty of furniture. The room partitions had been taken out, except for what appeared to be a kitchen and a bathroom by the stairwell along the far wall. The windows let in plenty of sunlight. You would be able to see someone coming from all eight windows.

"What do you use this place for?" Landry asked.

"Mostly press conferences, when the veep is here. We rent this floor out for parties and weddings. We don't really need the money, but Mommy thinks the place should be used. Once a month, some wildlife group meets here. Upstairs is storage."

"May I look around?"

She shrugged. "Sure."

She'd clearly lost interest in him. The novelty had worn off. It was heartbreaking. He would need years of therapy to recover from such a devastating blow. As he went up the stairs, he heard her talking on her cell phone.

The upstairs was as advertised. Jumbles of old furniture, some of which might be antique—Landry wouldn't know. Ranks of folding chairs and long folding tables, school cafeteria-type stuff. The door to the cupola was locked. He came back down the stairs, his shoes echoing in the empty space. The dogs funneled down behind him and followed as he stepped into the sunlight.

Riley was outside, texting.

Frank drove up in his golf cart. "Don't you think we should get this show on the road?"

"We're just getting to know each other," Riley said between text messages. By now it was a symbolic fight, not a real one.

"Scoot."

"Daddy—"

"I mean it."

"Fine." She didn't stomp off, but it was close.

Frank patted the passenger seat of the golf cart. Landry got in.

"I thought we'd go to the cabanas," Frank said as they zipped down the path. "It's private, so no one will overhear."

"Are you nervous?"

"Nope. Just cautious. This guy has antennae like a lobster."

"He won't be able to bother anybody when he's in supermax."

"That's what I'm counting on."

As Landry had surmised, the cabanas were really bungalows, tastefully done up in what Landry thought was a cross between art deco and beach cottage. "Before we get started," Landry said, "I'd like to see the passageway."

"Sure thing." Franklin led him outside and around to a small structure, a pool shed set flush to their cabana. Inside, pool equipment was hung neatly. There was a narrow space to the right, and beyond that a small closet—a restroom for the landscapers, Frank said. He opened the door to what looked like basement steps in a regular house. The steps and walls were concrete. The workmanship was nothing to write home about, but the tunnel had lasted since the twenties—not bad. Frank pulled the string to the overhead lightbulb and they started down, their footsteps echoing on the walls. It got damper and cooler as they went down, seven steps. The steps opened onto a narrow passageway stretching into the darkness. The tunnel reminded Landry of a mineshaft, timbered at intervals. He had to hunch his shoulders and pull his head in like a turtle to go through. Overhead bulbs lit the way. You had to pull each one on as you went—very low-tech. Three of them were out. About thirty yards in, they came to a T. Franklin explained that the tunnel on the left led to the octagon house. They took the tunnel on the right. At the end of the passageway, they reached another door, also without a lock. Approximately fifty-five yards in. The steps up were wooden and led to a structure similar to the pool shed. Wood-planked and cramped. They emerged out onto one of the docks inside the cavernous boathouse.

"Pretty neat, eh?" Franklin said. "They had wheelbarrows they'd trundle the bootleg whiskey in. It's also how my great-grandfather smuggled in his girlfriend."

"His girlfriend?"

"An actress called Ariel Sawyer. She was big early on in the silent era. She was the girlfriend of a notorious gangster named Hugh Gant. Great-granddad was seeing her on the sly. That's what the tunnel was for—not the booze. The booze came in by boat, and they could have just as easily carted it along the paths. It's a private island—who'd see them? But he couldn't take a chance with Ariel.

"The tunnel looks jerry-rigged, but it's not. There's actually a sophisticated construction, the way the floors are slanted, places to catch runoff—architecturally, it's quite brilliant. When you consider that this is an island in Florida, built-up or not. We don't use these tunnels now, except as an alternate escape route for the president or vice president when they're staying here."

Landry eyeballed the boathouse, in case he needed to come here again. He did not have a photographic memory, but he'd trained himself to observe quickly and thoroughly. He looked for places where he could ambush someone or places where someone could ambush him, places where he could see and yet not be seen. He looked for cover. He looked for concealment. He looked for places to escape if he had to. And here it was: an official escape route for the president.

The boathouse had an old fish camp feel. Distinctly Southern. "Let's go back," he said.

When they got back to the pool shed, Franklin said, "Wait until you see this." He motioned Landry over to a shelf which held more pool accessories and pushed aside a case of shock treatment bags. Set into the wood at the back of the shelf was a window. Landry looked in at the cabana they'd just left. From this vantage point he could see the bed, the small dinette, the couches covered with throw pillows.

"One-way glass," Frank said. "Like the cops use. Used to be just a little hole, discreetly placed. But somewhere along the line came the upgrade. No one's supposed to know about this," he added.

"No one?"

"Actually, I'm pretty sure everyone knows. At least the immediate family." Franklin looked at his watch. "Time to rock and roll."

44

As Jolie entered the house after her run, she spotted the light blinking on her phone. It was Kevin Moran, the FBI special agent she'd worked with on a kidnapping a few years ago. Another friend of Danny's. Kevin was an ideal special agent; he was eminently self-contained. She wondered, though, how much he liked working this area, where very little happened.

Of course, plenty was happening now. Jolie had a feeling it would only get worse, not better. Whatever she was stuck into, it was like swimming in the pond. You had no idea what else was in there with you.

When she reached him she said, "So, you think you can help me?"

"Probably not."

"I heard the FBI was investigating Luke Perdue even before the Starliner Motel."

"Chilly this morning, don't you think?"

It was nothing of the kind. "Okay, so maybe that's not true about the FBI watching Luke. But it *would* stand to reason, since the FBI was involved in the hostage situation, there would be an investigation after the standoff at the Starliner Motel."

"Then again, we do live in a tropical climate."

"In fact, if you guys were any good, you'd dispatch someone immediately to his home address."

"Warmer. Let me go turn the fan on."

"Did the FBI go to Luke's house?"

"It's possible. Probable, even."

"To interview Mrs. Frawley?"

"You'd think."

"Did they collect evidence?"

"That would be a negative."

"So you're saying it was just Gardenia PD? They were the only ones who collected evidence?"

"You have any idea how hot it is here? I'm loosening my tie as we speak."

"So the FBI has no evidence from Luke Perdue? Not even, say, a cell phone?"

"Gotta open a window. It's like an oven in here."

"No cell phone? You sure? You talked to the agents involved?"

"Look, I've got an appointment in a couple of minutes."

Jolie pushed through. "I understand that Special Agent Belvedere was the secondary during the hostage negotiation."

"Not my jurisdiction. Sorry."

"Special Agent Frederick Belvedere—that's what I hear. He worked with Chief Akers."

He said nothing.

"I wish I could talk to him. Clear up a couple of things."

"Well, what do you know? They finally put the air-conditioning on in here."

"Just a couple of things. Yes or no. We could even play twenty questions."

"It's getting *frigid* in here."

"Couldn't you ask him, just in case he's feeling talkative?"

A pause. And then, "No promises."

"Sounds like a warm front's coming in."

"Time will tell," he said, and hung up.

The phone rang again immediately. Jolie thought it was Agent Moran calling back. But it was Skeet.

"What are you doing today?"

"Not much."

"Then why don't you come down to the office? Say, half an hour."

*　*　*

Skeet Mullins asked, "What the hell do you think you're doing?"

He sat at his desk, feet up, and swiveled on his office chair, back and forth, squeak-squeak-squeak. Annoying as hell, but Jolie was used to it. "What do I think I'm doing?"

"You're telling me you don't know what I'm talking about?"

On the drive over, Jolie had tried to figure out how much Skeet knew about her activities, and she came to the conclusion that Detective Jeter of Panama City Beach PD might have called and left a message with Louis. That was the logical assumption, so she went with it. She gave him her most mystified look. "Do you mean going to Panama City? I didn't know going to Panama City was a problem."

"Panama City?"

"I was there yesterday. Is that a problem?"

Now Skeet was the one to look mystified. His mystification was a lot more convincing than hers. Either he was acting, or he didn't know about Detective Jeter or the missing Nathan Dial.

"Are you moonlighting for the state police?"

"No."

"Well, you act like it. Last I heard, the hostage situation at the Starliner Motel was the FDLE's case. So what were you doing questioning anyone, period? What part of 'paid leave' don't you understand?"

So that was it? When she'd gone into the neighborhood behind the Starliner Motel, she must have offended someone with her questions. Maybe Mark's parents didn't like her talking to him.

Skeet dropped his feet and leaned forward. "You're on leave pending the conclusion of an investigation into an officer-involved shooting concerning a reckless discharge of a firearm. You cannot represent this department, you cannot go out there playing detective like you're Nancy Drew."

That hurt. When Jolie was a stars-in-her-eyes rookie in the sheriff's office, she had expressed her desire to become a detective. Skeet started referring to her as Nancy Drew. Behind her back, but she'd heard about it.

"You are to cease and desist until the officer-involved shooting investigation is over. Am I clear?"

"Yessir."

"Because if you keep it up, if you continue to flaunt this department's regulations, the *state's* regulations, you *will* be summarily fired."

Just then—of course—her phone chirped.

"What's that?" demanded Skeet.

Jolie checked the readout. "It's my neighbor. I bet you my cat got out again."

"Well, now you'll have plenty of time to take care of things like that," Skeet said.

* * *

The minute Jolie was outside the building, she took out her phone. She punched in the number of her caller as she walked to the car.

"This is Special Agent Belvedere," he said without preamble. "You wanted to talk to me?"

Jolie told him what she wanted to know. It didn't take long, because she knew she wouldn't get much.

"I can't talk about that."

"I don't mean specifically. Just generally. Your general impression."

Silence. At least he didn't hang up. Jolie added quickly, "As little or as much as you would like. I just want to know your observations regarding the subject, Luke Perdue."

"This is part of your investigation into Chief Akers's death? That's a little far afield, isn't it?"

As her Irish grandmother would say, in for a penny, in for a pound. "I know, but it's important to know what his state of mind was."

"The chief's, or Luke Perdue's?"

"Both."

Another pause. Then Special Agent Belvedere said, "If you're talking about Chief Akers, I heard suicide was ruled out."

"It hasn't been ruled out." Another lie. For a brief crystallizing moment, Jolie realized just how far off the reservation she'd strayed. "You can see why Chief Akers's state of mind would be affected by the outcome of the hostage negotiation."

"Damn rumor mill. Okay, I'll only say this once, just to characterize the situation. And I insist you *do not* repeat this. The subject—Perdue—gave us all the signals that he would surrender."

"Surrender? You sure of that?"

"I've been in hostage negotiation for fifteen years. It was only a matter of time."

"Are you saying he wanted to be taken into custody?"

"No. I'm saying he was *desperate* to be taken into custody."

"You were pretty sure he would have released Kathy Westbrook and surrendered himself to the authorities?"

"Not pretty sure. Positive. I hope this helps." Jolie could almost hear him check his watch. "I'm late for an appointment. Are we through here?"

"Yes, we're through."

He said, "It's too bad."

"Too bad?"

"I know how I felt when it ended the way it did. You can bet Chief Akers felt the same. It could have affected his state of mind."

"That's what we think," Jolie lied.

"Good talking to you, and now I really have to go."

As she closed the phone, Jolie heard a car door slam and footsteps approaching. She looked up and there was Kay.

Kay crossed her arms over her chest. "I want to show you something."

Her voice was too high, and her face looked pinched.

"Is something wrong?"

"Wrong?" Her nostrils flared, and white lines bracketed her mouth. "Oh, you could say that."

"Kay—"

"Would you *come* with me?"

"Is Zoe all right?"

"Like you care."

"What's this about?"

"It won't take up much of your time. I *promise*." Kay stalked to her Navigator, her shoes ticking on the pavement. Turned back when Jolie didn't follow. "If you were ever my friend, ever my friend at *all*, you'd come with me."

No choice. Jolie got in and Kay swerved out of the parking lot.

On the road Jolie asked, "You want to tell me where we're going?"

"It's a surprise."

They went east on Highway 98. Jolie tried to figure out what had Kay up in arms, but the only thing she could think of was her talk with Zoe. Would Zoe go running to her mother, just because Jolie asked her about Luke's last night with Riley?

Unlikely. Zoe would have to be a real pushover to tell her mother every little thing. But something had made Kay like this. The tight lips, the whiteness around her nose and mouth, her designer sunglasses blocking Jolie out.

In Port St. Joe, they turned onto Fifth Street and Jolie guessed where they were headed. Her parents' house. The one that was on the market. Jolie had no idea why, but she could feel the tension, feel the anger about to spill over. It scared her. She thought that maybe Kay was this close to flying into a rage.

In front of the house, Kay slammed the car into park. The air conditioner was like a fog, clinging to Jolie's face as she looked past the windshield at the shabby yellow cottage. "Would you mind telling me what this is about?"

Kay turned to look at her. Unseeable behind the large Dolce & Gabbanas. "I should have known better. You spoil everything you touch. You use people, Jolie. I tried to build a relationship with you, and you just used me to get what you wanted."

"What are you talking about?" But Jolie knew that on some level what Kay said was true. She did use people. That was part of her job, and she was good at it. But always it was for a righteous cause. She'd been right to browbeat Zoe. That was what this was about. She'd hurt Zoe's feelings. Zoe had run to her mother. But what hung in the balance? The death of a young man. A cover-up. The potential abuse of power going to the highest levels of the United States government. Her family's complicity—

"My own daughter won't speak to me."

"Why? Because I asked her a few questions?"

"Riley kicked her out last night. She cut her dead."

"I'm sorry."

"You're *sorry*! Like that means anything. Zoe's heartbroken. This was her *best friend*! She was escorted off the property like a common criminal, all because of you!"

Wait a minute. There were a lot of things wrong here. Jolie wanted to defend herself. Why had Zoe told Riley anything at all, if she knew it would upset her? Why was Riley so angry? Surely Kay could see the relationship was abusive, if Riley could go off the deep end like that. All sorts of thoughts crowded through her mind. But what she said was, "Why are we here?"

"Because it's time you knew the truth."

"The truth?"

Kay pulled the keys out of the ignition. "Yes, the truth."

Jolie followed Kay up the walk to the house. There had been a garden, but no one had kept it up and the plants were yellowed and sickly. A squat garden gnome stood by the door, jolly and sinister at the same time. Jolie remembered the long crack in the front window, like a graph line. "Kay, I came here already."

Kay punched a code into the Realtor's lock on the front door, and they went inside. "You go ahead," Kay said.

At that moment, Jolie felt she could be in danger. As a cop, she had a sense for that moment when things changed, and this was one of those moments. "No, you go ahead."

Kay did.

When Skeet summoned her to his office this morning, Jolie had left her replacement firearm behind. She didn't want to get into a fight with him over it, in light of the fact that her service weapon had been confiscated. But she still had her Walther PPK .380 in an ankle holster. It would be a little harder to access, but she was glad for the backup.

They went through the house. Jolie doubted Kay was capable of violence, but it was second nature for Jolie to question assumptions. Wary, she kept her eye on Kay's purse. She knew Kay carried. She had a small snub-nosed revolver, a "girl's gun." Kay moved with jittery purpose. They landed in the kitchen, the old round-shouldered refrigerator humming. A card from the realty office sat on the round table. Kay picked up the card, which had been folded in half so it stood up in a triangle. She took out a McPeek Realty pen and scribbled something on the card.

Kay finished writing and looked at Jolie, her breath coming quickly. Her arm draped over the shoulder bag, which rested high on her body.

Jolie looking for a quick move.

"Zoe told me she's not going to Brown."

"Why not?"

"She told me she doesn't want to go, and I can't make her."

"What does she plan to do?"

"The big thing? The most important thing? Get back in Riley's good graces. Be best friends again. She cried for an hour *straight* last night. All because of you. She...she threatened suicide."

The thunder in Jolie's chest grew. She saw Kay's hand inch toward the clasp of her bag. "Do you believe her?"

"I don't know. She was destroyed. What did you say to her?"

Jolie told her the truth. Eye on the shoulder bag, she told her that she asked if Luke knew about the passageway. If they had been spying on people at the cabanas. Thinking, it wasn't that important. Thinking, Riley was overreacting. Thinking, you were a kid once, too.

"Are you investigating my family? Is that it? You befriend me, worm your way into my family, and then try to gin up something against us? Is this all revenge?"

"Revenge?"

She swept her arm out. "For *this*! For the squalid, stupid lives your mother and father led, all because she wouldn't listen to reason? And now you've spoiled everything for my daughter. Just what do you want to know about my family?"

Jolie stuck with what she knew to be true. "I did not try to worm my way into your family. If you recall, I never even wanted to set foot on Indigo. I was not interested. And my parents loved each other—"

"Loved each other! You don't know the first damn thing about their relationship."

Kay held out the card, and Jolie took it. Kay had written "Belle Oaks," on it, and underneath, "Tallahassee."

"Belle Oaks?"

"Yes, Belle Oaks."

"What is it?"

But Kay didn't appear to be listening. She stared into middle space, in her own world—unaware of Jolie. She was working something out behind her eyes. Then her expression cleared, as if she'd decided on something. "Did you see the bathroom?"

"The bathroom?"

"Miss Baby Soap—did you see the bathroom?"

"Yes I saw it, the last time I was here."

Kay said nothing. Went back into that middle space. Jolie could almost feel the electricity in the air between them. Kay was like an exposed wire. Jolie had the feeling that if they touched, she would get a shock.

Then Kay came out of it again. When she spoke, her voice sounded neutral, almost dead.

"Right now, the way I'm feeling, I could do you real harm. You know why I brought you here? No, you don't." She stopped. The air seemed to go out of her. "This is fucked."

Jolie had never heard Kay use that word. "Kay? What's this about?"

"I can't. You deserve it for what you did, but I'm not like you. I'm not going to be the one to tell you. I can't."

"What are you talking about?"

"You're the detective. You figure it out." She hitched her bag higher on her shoulder. "This is the end, though. We're not friends anymore." She turned and walked to the front door, opened it, and was gone.

Jolie's ears burned. What was Kay talking about?

I'm not going to be the one to tell you.

Kay brought her here to show her something. Something that would hurt her.

Jolie couldn't fathom what she could have asked Zoe that would upset Riley so much. It was clear Zoe wanted to be Riley's friend in the worst way. Kids, these days especially, could be devastated by bullying. They could think the whole world was falling apart, that their lives were worthless. Yes, Zoe could quit college over this. Yes, Zoe could contemplate suicide. Maybe Jolie had been so intent on the prize, she had forgotten that.

She looked at the Realtor's card. It was made of good stock. Pleasant to the touch, excellent production values. Jolie looked at the inside again. *Belle Oaks. Tallahassee.* It meant nothing to her.

The bathroom. Jolie walked down the short hall to the open doorway. Kay had used the word squalid, but that description didn't quite fit. The place was gloomy, sad, and small. Jolie had a hard time picturing young love flourishing here.

Loved each other! Kay had said it with such contempt. Jolie looked in at the bathroom, glimpsed the cheap aqua tile she remembered from last time, when she took a cursory look through the house. The place had been cleaned, but she sensed an underlying grunge beneath the surface.

This was the real home of the Petal Soft Soap Baby. Her mother had bathed her in this bathtub. This room was nothing like the photo spread in the magazine—everything fresh and clean and white. This was the reality. Just two young people who loved each other and their baby—

She heard Kay's scornful voice again. *Loved each other!*

Jolie pushed the door open further, thinking of her small family, "just the three of us" as her dad liked to say. She thought about what little childhood she'd had here. The Soap Baby's house. No memories. The card Kay had given her pricked against her palm—Belle Oaks. A bad feeling welled up inside, and her hand clenched, crushing the card. Something hot and hard as iron clamped around her chest, making it hard to breathe.

Then came the thunderclap, the chasm yawning underneath her feet. The feeling she was being crushed to death, blackness dropping like a curtain over her eyes. Her heart rate jumped into the red zone, fear hurtling through every synapse and nerve.

45

MIKE CARDAMONE
WASHINGTON, DC

As he approached his building on F Street, Mike Cardamone glanced at the American flag flying above the mansard roof. It never failed to inspire him. He loved this country—its strength, its resilience, the fact that it was a beacon of light to the world—even if the world didn't appreciate it. He climbed the steps briskly to the back entrance, glancing at the gold plaque by the door. Whitbread Associates, LLC. Suites 201 A-E. Discreet, not showy. Old Washington—exclusive.

He'd come a long way from trading fire with Iraqis in the heat and sand of Desert Storm. Even his stint at the CIA seemed like a century ago. He was where he wanted to be—the CEO of an up-and-coming security firm in DC.

His Jamaican administrative assistant told him the new advertising material was on his desk. Her name was Filigree, no kidding, and she wore bright colors, bracelets, and scarves; she gave everybody in the building the willies, but she was the best assistant he'd ever had.

He walked into his inner office and set his briefcase down on the chair by his massive mahogany desk. He could look out the bay window and see the Old Executive Office Building from here, but today he barely noticed it. He had a lot on his mind.

Two boxes sat on the desk. He opened one of them and took a promotional booklet off the top of the stack.

"Whitbread Associates LLC is uniquely positioned to address the challenges of a perilous world, drawing on experience, ingenuity and versatility to meet the global problems of the twenty-first century. We offer a roster of incisive strategies that transcend the traditional values of the past, forging a new order in an increasingly uncertain world.

"Whether you wish to open new markets in out-of-the-way places, require due diligence on recent acquisitions, or seek new strategies for old problems, Whitbread Associates LLC offers a full roster of services."

Then the bullet points:

"When a Dallas CFO was kidnapped and held for ransom, a Whitbread team was sent to recover him, with a net result of two dead kidnappers and a fortune saved.

"When a foreign minister of an oil-rich country needed counterterrorism experts to protect their oil fields, Whitbread Associates LLC stood guard."

"When a well-regarded pharmaceutical company fell prey to product tampering, Whitbread Associates LLC tracked down the culprit, who is currently serving a lifetime sentence in a federal prison.

"If you have a problem, we can solve it."

He read it over, smiling. They'd managed to squeeze everything into this striking six-page booklet: risk assessment; providing due diligence on prospective mergers; personal protection for foreign and domestic executives; stolen asset recovery; and protection of prominent individuals and companies from media attacks.

Only one thing bothered him. If the actions of one unit ever saw daylight, he might as well take these boxes of slick booklets and chuck them in a landfill.

One small division, burrowed deep within Whitbread LLC like the smallest Russian nesting doll, could bring down the whole company. Whitbread Associates did many things, every one of them at a high level. But one division—a paramilitary unit, a domestic version of the Joint Special Operations Command— had become a liability.

Business was good. Mike was poised to reap the rewards of a decade of war, individual freedom, and intense paranoia. But the pet project they'd come up with during one of those fishing trips off Cape San Blas was outdated, and worse, dangerous. There was a new administration now, and that bitch with the Texas twang must have been a bookkeeper before she became the president of the United States. She had unloosed the bean-counters, and pretty soon they would get to Whitbread's place on the ledger, and someone would start asking questions. Like: Just what do you do? What exactly are you outsourcing? At the very least, they'd cut Whitbread loose. At worst, they might start an internal investigation inside the DOJ.

The big money was overseas. Face it: the unit had outlived its usefulness.

Mike stared out the window at the sullen summer sky.

Times had changed. Celebrities weren't the draw they once were. It used to be the media flocked to a Paris Hilton, or a Britney Spears, or a Lindsay Lohan. If one of them stubbed a toe, it was big news. But with all the troubles the country had suffered lately, there seemed to be a change of tone. People were preoccupied with their own problems, not personalities.

One thing the American people *weren't* interested in: how the U.S. government did its business—even its dirty business. They were interested only when the government raised taxes. Then it was Katie Bar the Door. Nothing else mattered to them. They were too busy trying to hold on to their mortgages or keep their kids in college.

Frankly, the program he'd thought up along with the (now deceased) president and the attorney general wasn't necessary anymore.

Although you have to admit, it did come in handy when the veep killed that boy.

* * *

Filigree brought in a contract for him to sign. Today she wore a saffron peasant blouse, a purple and green print skirt, and a red sash.

Moments after the boy's body hit the water miles off Cape San Blas, the operation was a go. Doubtful anyone would have raised a stink about a promiscuous gay kid, but the vice president's sexual proclivities had made the cover of the *Enquirer* twice. Even though it was the kind of sensational stuff the voting public as a whole ignored, the story had been released into the ether, like an invisible gas waiting for a lit match.

The lit match couldn't have come at a worse time.

The day of the VP's trip down to Indigo, Owen Pintek's chief of staff received a call from a writer with *People* magazine concerning their upcoming article on Owen and a male prostitute.

People wasn't the *Enquirer*. This would be believable. In the interview, the prostitute, who was amazingly photogenic, said he feared Pintek.

And where was Owen? Down in Florida, choking the life out of a young man as if nothing had happened.

And so Whitbread deployed its A-Team to Aspen before the *People* article hit.

Mike was stationed in Kuwait during Desert Storm. He saw his share of oil rig fires, and he saw how KBR dealt with them—by setting off massive explosions that sucked the oxygen from the fire, thereby giving it nothing to feed on. Fight fire with something bigger—an explosion.

They'd needed to manufacture a virtual explosion to take up all the media's considerable resources, something that would suck the air out of everything else in the news—

And it worked. The media always chased the Next Big Thing— one bright shiny object after another. The murders in Aspen swallowed the news week whole, like a python swallows a pig.

One thing Mike took away from it, though, was the realization that Indigo was bad mojo. Place was like a black hole, swallowing up all the good they had done, almost as if it were cursed. When you thought about it, where did the veep get carried away and actually *kill* a young man? On Indigo Island.

Franklin was a liability. Mike was sure Grace knew about the unit. Right there, that was enough. Not only that, but you couldn't rely on Frank in any way. He'd turn on you as easily as he'd turn on his worst enemy. He was kind of endearing in a bumbling way. But the man had nothing inside him that was constant or reliable. It was all about self-preservation with Frank—he went on pure instinct. Like a cockroach.

*   *   *

Mike took his lunch at his desk, a chicken Caesar sandwich from Cosi. Outside, the traffic was picking up. Horns honking. Cars whooshing by after the light. Mike could smell Filigree's perfume—patchouli oil mixed with the scent of sandalwood. He'd told her to stop burning that fucking incense! The last thing he wanted to do was make the place smell like there were foreigners doing business with his firm, even if Whitbread worked mostly with foreign governments now.

He wondered for the thousandth time why he put up with her. Realized that if he ever fired her, she'd probably lay a curse on him.

But nothing could spoil today. He was relieved to have finally made the decision. It would be easy to erase all traces of the Shop. He'd set the unit up so there would be no blowback. From the beginning, the operatives had been kept in the dark. They didn't know exactly where their paychecks were coming from. They only knew their employer was associated in some way with the United States government, that they were working for God and country. But they didn't know the who or the how or the why. The company was concealed—again, like the Russian dolls, dummy company inside dummy company.

Long ago, Mike had drawn up a cover story in case he ever needed it, revolving around Grace Haddox's church. The weird but charismatic minister, speaking in tongues and making the news regularly with his antics. He fit the mold—the Jim Jones/David Koresh mold. There was even a rival Congolese church with ties to human trafficking and money laundering—a group that would be easy to blame.

One last black op for the unit, and they would be disbanded and sent to one of the foreign divisions.

Keep it simple. Use both teams. Two targets—the cultist church and the attorney general's compound. Take care of everything in one swift motion. The result would be a dangerous cult consumed by a cleansing fire. By sunrise, he would have wiped out every trace of the Shop.

The phone rang. Filigree came on the line. "Franklin Haddox, sir. Do you want to talk to him or should I make an excuse?"

Franklin? Was he a mind reader?

Keep your friends close and your enemies closer. "It's okay, Fil, put him through."

Frank's voice came on the line. "Mike."

"How are you doing, Frank?"

"Not so good."

"What do you mean, not so good?"

"I think the FBI is onto us."

"Calm down. What makes you think the FBI could possibly know anything about what we're doing?"

"I think…I think they're watching me."

"You're paranoid."

"Someone followed Grace home last weekend, from Tallahassee."

"From the church?"

"What does it matter where she was? Jesus! You need to come down here. We need to have an emergency meeting."

"I can't come now. I'm in the middle of—"

"Right now, Mike. I'm this close to calling my lawyer and seeing what kind of a deal I can get."

"For Christ's sake, man, get a grip! No one can prove anything."

"For all I know they're tapping us right now."

"This is a secure line, remember?"

"It's time to pull the plug."

"Well, we're going to need to talk about—"

"You need to come down here, Mike."

"No can do, Franklin."

"There's a jet waiting for you."

"I thought you sold your jet."

"Netjets. You'd better be on that plane, or you just might be the last man standing. If you're not here by five p.m., I'm calling my lawyer. And we're going to throw you to the wolves."

"Frank—"

"Be on the plane, Mike. If you aren't, if you aren't here at Indigo by five p.m., you can kiss your ass goodbye."

He hung up.

Mike looked at the phone in his hand. He had never heard Franklin Haddox talk that way.

He had no illusions. Frank meant every word he said. He was probably speed-dialing his lawyer right now.

Mike thought maybe he *should* go. It wouldn't be a bad idea to get down there where the action was, but he'd prefer to maintain control by taking his own jet.

Unfortunately, both of Whitbread's jets were already in Florida, one in Tallahassee, the other at a private airfield near Port St. Joe. They would stay there until early tomorrow morning. The jets were on standby. They would be used to get his teams out of harm's way as soon as possible.

Both operations were scheduled for the small hours of the morning. Ultimately, it would be up to the teams when to go in and what resources they would use to complete the mission. He didn't want to second-guess them. But now Mike was worried.

Clearly, Frank had some kind of sixth sense. Like a cockroach, scuttling out of the light just before you bring down your shoe.

* * *

Eight hundred miles away, Frank breathed in and out, trying not to hyperventilate. He'd taken the big step—no going back now. Mike Cardamone was ruthless. If he hadn't been coming for them before, he was coming for them now.

Frank had enjoyed playing him like a fish on the line. But now it was over, it wasn't so much fun anymore.

Frank looked at Salter. "You're sure all your men are in place?"

"We've got them positioned on the island and on San Blas, but you'd never know they were here."

"Because I'm telling you, this guy doesn't fool around."

"See that fishing boat out there?"

Frank nodded. He felt queasy.

"Our best snipers are on that boat. So, do you think it worked?"

"It worked," Frank said.

"How do you know?"

"I just know." He looked down at the phone tucked into his palm. His hand was shaking.

Landry said, "Tell me everything you know about Mike Cardamone."

"W-what do you mean?"

"His attitude toward warfare. Would he send someone after you or come himself?"

Frank thought about it. Finally, he said, "He's pretty hands-on. He was in special forces, and he's always boasting about that. He…he has a cruel streak."

Special Agent Salter nodded. Smiled. "Good," he said.

46

Landry left Indigo shortly after Frank finished his call to Cardamone. He told no one he was going. He made only one quick side trip, to the boat. The dock was so wide you could drive on it.

He'd chosen the maid's sedan, a seventies-era Pontiac, for the spacious trunk. He needed every bit of it.

Before leaving, Landry had laid it all out for Frank. Landry told him he would be nearby, concealed, watching and waiting along with his team for the first sight of Mike Cardamone. He told Frank that Cardamone would be coming in the early hours of the morning with his team. Frank believed him. Frank was not to answer the phone if Cardamone called—anything else he said might make the man suspicious. The AG was to sit tight and wait, stay with his routine. Play a round of golf, have lunch, work in his office—but stay on the island. As long as he remained at Indigo, he would be under the FBI's protection.

Landry didn't completely trust him, but it was the best he could do. He had more important business to attend to, and there was no choice in the matter.

Landry drove seventy miles out of his way to Llewellyn, Alabama, a town with little to recommend itself except for a bank, a smattering of small businesses, a Sonic, and a gun shop. He had lunch at the Sonic, enjoying the old-fashioned car-hop experience, then drove two doors down to the gun shop set back from the road.

A yellow plastic sign stood out on the grass, the stick-on letters proclaiming, "CHUCK'S GUNS AND BAIT – Ammo All Kinds – Smith & Wesson Special Ask Within – We Have Wigglers." Behind the grimy store window, backed by a sun-faded panorama of a woodsy fishing scene, rifles and handguns shared space with an umbrella stand holding cane fishing poles.

Landry had to duck to get through the door. Chuck's was small inside, too, like a sod house on the prairie. The owner sat on a stool behind the cash register. Late fifties, Harley cap, ponytail, a complexion like the deli meat mortadella.

"Good day, sir."

Landry nodded toward the window. "You know you misspelled wigglers?"

"Wigglers?"

"On the sign. There's an 'r' in it. After the 'w.'"

He thought about it. "That don't sound right. If it was, it'd be pronounced 'rigglers.'"

Landry removed the packet from his hunting vest and laid it on the glass counter.

"And what is that, sir?"

Landry undid the flap and laid out three thousand dollars in cash.

The owner looked at the money, then at Landry. "What's this for, sir?"

Landry nodded to the clock. "Almost lunchtime. You could go for a coffee while I take a look around."

The man stared at the money. "How do I know it's real?"

"There's a bank two doors down. Why don't you deposit it?"

"You're just looking, right?"

"I promise I won't steal anything."

"Doesn't appear that you would. Thank you, sir." He took the packet and stuffed it in his own vest. "But you're wrong about wigglers. I grew up around here, and it's always been wigglers."

Landry watched him walk down to the curve in the road where the one-story red-brick bank stood in a patch of mowed lawn. He watched as the man went inside. Then he started shopping.

Before long, the box he'd brought in with him was full. He pulled a bag of Pemmican off the rack by the cash register and put it on top, just as Harley came back. Harley scrupulously avoided looking at the box and its contents.

Landry laid out another three thousand dollars. "You have some nice weaponry here. I like your sound suppressors."

"Yes, they're the best. Expensive, too." Looked ruminatively at the three thousand dollars. "So nothing struck your fancy?"

"Maybe next time. Where's the nearest liquor store?"

"Sir, guns and liquor don't mix."

"Tell you what, you give me back the six thousand, and I'll put everything back."

"There's a liquor store on the way out of town, on 71."

"Thanks." He looked out the window again. "I really think you should change that sign."

"I'm not changing that sign, sir. You can forget about that. It's still a free country, last I heard."

Landry nodded, picked up his box, and walked out to the car. The maid's car fit right in around here. He loaded the box into the backseat. He would have liked to put the box in the trunk, but the trunk was taken. He covered the box with an army blanket.

At the liquor store, Landry bought three ice picks and four bags of ice from a sullen kid with a faceful of acne and a mullet.

He was surprised anybody still wore mullets, even in the deep South.

He drove to a Dumpster hidden from view by a strip mall, opened the trunk, and replaced the melting bags of ice under and around the bodies of Special Agent Eric Salter and the "piss-poor" private investigator, Ted Bakus. Salter had told him Bakus was in way over his head. This turned out to be true.

Landry threw the old ice bags in the Dumpster.

Back inside the car, he loosened the handles on the ice picks. Just a couple of threads; he didn't want them too loose. Then he stopped for pie and coffee at a diner called Sandie's in Wewahitchka, Florida. He hated secondhand smoke, and the fifteen minutes in the diner irritated his eyes, but on the up side, the pie was good.

* * *

From the post office box in Port St. Joe, he picked up the key to the safe house. The safe house was on the outskirts of Port St. Joe, in a recently built subdivision. A third of the subdivision was unoccupied.

A foreclosure sign stood outside the safe house. The house next door was empty. A cloud of mosquitoes dogged him to the house. He looked over the fence to the neighbor's yard. The pool was olive-green. Algae floated on top.

He went in through the kitchen. A list of instructions had been left on the counter. He read them through, paying particular attention to the detailed schematic of the target area, which included aerial photos and blueprints.

He was right about the target.

Landry looked at his watch. His brother Gary would have landed by now, probably already on the road, visions of stud farms dancing in his head. If someone with the Shop checked, they would see that Bill Peters had departed LAX at six thirty this morning, changed planes in Dallas and Atlanta, and arrived in Panama City at four fifteen this afternoon. A check with the car rental desk at the Bay County International Airport would show that Bill Peters had rented a car from Avis. No one would know that Landry had been in Florida for the last two and a half days.

Landry divided up the handguns, ammo, knives, rifles, sights, infrared scopes, night vision goggles, and suppressors, then stashed them in three of the house's four bedrooms—one for Jackson, one for Davis, and one for Green. There would be three bags of goodies, and three closets. The walk-in closet he saved for Jackson.

Every time they met, they spent time getting acquainted with their weaponry. Broke the firearms down, cleaned them, put them back together. Checked the sights. So many weapons for them to look at.

It would be like Christmas morning.

As Landry decided which guns would go where, he flashed on the Aspen massacre. That one, they'd kept simple—just three Bowie knives. Two were destroyed afterwards, but the last one they left in the possession of a white supremacist gas station attendant named Donny Lee Odell.

Acting on an anonymous tip, the local police, the ATF, and the FBI converged on Bud's Texaco in Colorado. Landry had watched it on television. The local cops paraded Donny Lee out before the cameras, a jacket draped over his manacled hands. He looked a lot like the poor mope with the mullet at the liquor store in Llewellyn—the same kind of stupid. Donny was a natural because he was weak. He had been jailed twice for the possession and sale of crystal meth.

The plan had been to set him up and then widen the circle to his friends, the white supremacists he hung with. From what Landry had seen on the television, that plan seemed to have worked. Donny Lee insisted he spent the night playing pool at a Salida tavern, but it appeared there was no one to corroborate his story. Donny Lee Odell had been on the wrong path long before the knife was discovered in his car.

Landry knew about Odell from an incident in Iraq four years ago. Donny Lee Odell's lack of caution and subsequent cowardice had been responsible for the death of another soldier. Everyone in the armed services who was in Iraq then knew about it. Odell had received a dishonorable discharge, but he had returned stateside to continue on with his life.

Until Landry found him.

If Odell was executed, or if he spent the rest of his life in prison, Landry wouldn't lose sleep over it.

If he was going to lose sleep, it would have been over Nick Holloway, ignominiously wrapped in plastic and stashed in the Aspen murder house. But if you looked at it from a karmic standpoint, Nick had cheated death once already. He couldn't stave it off forever; Landry was merely the instrument of his fate.

He sat on his heels and regarded the weapons in the closet Jackson would be using. Jackson was the strongest. He was smart and skilled. Levelheaded—not easily distracted. A professional. No hesitation in him.

Green was like his name. Green. He was somebody's cousin. He'd never been in the military, never known hand-to-hand combat. He did have a black belt, but his black belt was earned in a Bushido storefront at a strip mall in El Cajon.

Davis was a hothead. When he was angry, he had the strength of three men. Not ten men, not two men. Three. He was dangerous the way a wounded bull in the bullring is dangerous. Unpredictable. Like Landry, he was a SERE graduate.

Still, Jackson was the most like Landry.

Jackson would go first.

47

Jolie sat at a table at the Burger King in Port St. Joe. Her neighbor Ed was on his way to pick her up. She fiddled with the realty card with the words "Belle Oaks" scribbled on it, now crushed into bad origami, her mind going back to the interminable time she'd spent in her parents' house.

Jolie thought she'd had it all figured out. She could take a shower but not a bath. Needed to be careful around ponds. But this time, there was no water involved at all.

But something must have happened there, in the bathroom of their little house. *Just the three of us.*

It had taken her an hour to get to the Burger King, mainly because she didn't go in a straight line. She'd managed to get out of the house and then walked for miles, forcing herself to keep from breaking into a run. After putting block after city block between herself and the house, Jolie began to feel better. The feeling of doom finally dissipated.

She must look like a crazy person.

This is your life. You're about to be fired from your job. You are rendered completely helpless by panic attacks that can come on at any time without any warning. You're willfully disregarding orders and planning on investigating a sitting vice president of the United States. You've alienated your closest friend.

That alone was a revelation. Kay *was* her closest friend. If you went further, you might say Kay was her *only* friend. The only friend who had stuck around to get past her defenses, if you didn't count her father's pal Ed, whom she'd known since she was in high school. Jolie realized she'd changed since Danny's death. She'd withdrawn from people. Okay, big revelation. Who wouldn't change after someone you love commits suicide? But Kay had managed to break through.

And this is how I reward her.

But there was no going back now. Jolie was sure Nathan Dial had been lured to Indigo. She was sure he'd been killed there. She was almost sure that the vice president of the United States had something to do with it. Think about that. The vice president of the United States.

Kay's own words: *He likes boys.*

Jolie doubted Owen Pintek had planned to kill a young man. Maybe it was a choking game that went too far.

And then there was the cover-up.

She uncrumpled Kay's card and looked at it again. Belle Oaks was a place in Tallahassee. She could go look it up right now on her phone, but she had a feeling—and this was all it was, a feeling—that doing so would derail her investigation.

Kay was angry with her, and she'd lashed out. She'd never once mentioned a place called Belle Oaks. Never said anything bad about Jolie's parents, either. But Kay knew something, and whatever it was, it couldn't be good.

Loved each other! The contempt in her voice.

Jolie itched to look it up. She wanted to know what Kay meant.

Outside, she heard a big diesel engine as the black Dodge Ram rumbled into the parking lot.

Ed was here.

48

Jackson, Davis, and Green all came in together, which surprised Landry. For one second, he felt he was on the outs. As if they had all lined up against him, as if they knew what he was planning.

But logic won the day. There weren't that many flights into Panama City. It was likely they would have all arrived on the same puddle-jumper from Atlanta, since Atlanta was the closest hub. The Panama City airport was small and never crowded, so common sense would dictate they'd end up at the same place, the rental car desk, at about the same time.

Of course Jackson, Davis, and Green didn't drive up in the car. The rental car was parked somewhere in the neighborhood, many streets away. They had walked in, separately, from different directions. But all of them arrived about the same time, so he knew they'd come together.

They went through the instructions on the kitchen table and gamed a few scenarios, landing on the simplest. Come in quietly by boat. Put someone on the road, command and control. The presence of a vehicle would also provide a second means of escape if the first was blocked.

Set up before midnight, come in around four a.m. Everyone asleep, probably in a deep sleep. This mission would be close-up work—knives—with automatic rifles afterward for window dressing. A fire. Make it look like Congolese rebels. Landry told them he had already rented the boat and laid in the necessary materials.

But they would never get a chance to accomplish their mission. Landry knew that if they reached the island, they would carry out their orders or die trying, as they had been trained to do. But Jackson, Davis, and Green would never get a chance.

The first rule of warfare: kill the enemy before he kills you.

In this case, he would kill the team before they had a chance to massacre the people on Indigo. Landry felt responsible for them—everyone with the exception of Franklin Haddox was innocent. If they died, they would be collateral damage and he could live with that. But he would do his best to make sure that didn't happen.

Franklin Haddox's days were numbered, but Landry would not kill him yet. He still needed the former attorney general.

And so Landry and his team went over the probable number of people on the island, including the help and the security team the Haddoxes had hired, and where they would be.

On paper, the raid would be simple and clean. Nobody anticipated any trouble. Jackson, Davis, and Green for one reason, and Landry for another.

When they were through planning the raid, Jackson, Davis, and Green got settled in their rooms, and Landry went to his. After ten minutes, Landry walked to the kitchen. His room was at the back of the house, at the end of the hallway. Jackson's room was on his right, and Davis's was on the left. Also on the left, closest to the living room, was Green's room. Landry walked past the open doors to the other rooms. All three men were preoccupied with their weapons. In the kitchen, he opened the refrigerator, took a drink from a bottle of water, returned it to the refrigerator, and walked back. He glanced in at Jackson. Jackson was on one knee, breaking down an AR-15. The rifle would be no use to him except as a club, but there were plenty of other firearms lying within arm's reach. Landry didn't expect it to get to that point. He gave the doorjamb a quick tap with his knuckles, and Jackson, instantly alert, looked up. Smiled.

"What do you think?" Landry asked.

"Good stuff." Jackson was not a man given to hyperbole.

Landry stayed by the door, and they talked. Mostly about weaponry, but a little about the mission. Landry walked casually to the window, lifted one of the blinds, and looked out. Mentioned the number of foreclosures. They talked about that. Got into a rhythm. It was an interesting conversation. He kept the conversation going even as he stepped away from the window and came up behind Jackson. He clapped his hand hard to Jackson's forehead to steady him, then drove the ice pick deep into the soft hollow where the skull met the neck.

Immediately, Jackson crumpled. When the ice pick punctured his brain stem, his fuse box was blown. Death was instantaneous. Landry eased him down to the floor. He pulled gently on the handle and it disengaged, leaving only the eight-inch steel spike in the base of Jackson's skull. He dragged Jackson into the walk-in closet and closed the door.

Landry listened for noise in the house. But he heard only the sounds he expected: men breaking down their weapons.

Landry tapped on Davis's door next. His door was ajar. Davis said, "Come in."

Inside, Davis knelt over his cache of weapons. He looked up for one second but then looked back down at the weapon he was disassembling. Landry talked about their plan for Indigo as he walked in. Fewer than two seconds to reach Davis—keep walking and keep talking. But then Davis half turned, sensing what was about to happen. Landry's hand made a claw as he walked and talked, and he shoved the claw hard into Davis's throat, temporarily paralyzing him. Landry whipped him around, steadied the forehead with one hand and planted the ice pick in the brain stem with the other.

As Davis began to topple, Landry caught him under the arms and gently let him down.

Davis's boot thumped against the closet door on the way down.

Landry froze. He listened—nothing. Green was in the next room. Landry wriggled the handle on the second ice pick, but he had trouble getting it to come off. He could just as well leave the handle in—by the time the evidence was sorted out, he'd be long gone. This wasn't the time to get anal-retentive about it. He left the handle on.

Landry heard Green's voice behind him. "You guys—"

Then an intake of breath. Then nothing. Landry looked at Green.

Green stood in the open doorway, black cargo pants and vest, nylon and Velcro—bulky. Peeling sunburn, yellow buzz cut. He looked like a dandelion.

Hands empty.

Realization came to Green's eyes as Landry launched into him, another claw to the throat, but at the last moment Green twisted. Landry was put off balance, and his hand thwacked hard against the wall.

His wrist might be broken.

He got Green in a half nelson with his right arm, and with his left he dug into his vest and found the last ice pick. Kid's hands prying at his elbow, Landry clamping the kid hard against his body, the kid kicking out in a panic, no martial arts stuff but pure adrenaline, Landry letting go and shoving Green to his knees, shoving downward, downward, so the kid's nose was in the carpet, the ice pick slipping in Landry's hands as he pushed it in hard.

But he missed the hollow, the soft place. The pick dug in and then stuttered sideways, nicking the carotid, blood spouting, the pick pinging to the floor, the kid fighting like a tiger for his life.

Landry flashed on one of his dad's colts. The colt's leg had snapped, and they were waiting for the vet. The colt thrashed in agony, the shine of confusion in his eyes when he realized he could no longer run. That was the look in Green's eyes, even as he fought on. His arms and legs not working the way they should be.

Green was dying, but it would take time. Landry couldn't let him suffer. He still remembered the relief he'd felt when the colt was finally euthanized. Ten years old, and he desperately wanted that horse to die. He stepped in close, ignoring the manic blows, many of which connected. Maneuvering behind Green, he clasped his hands on either side of the kid's head. He dug his nails in, his fingers slipping in the cascading blood before gaining purchase. He wrenched Green's head sideways, jerking back at the same time. Heard the audible *chuck* as the neck snapped and the kid dropped.

Landry looked down at Green, then at his own wrist. The pain radiating from his wrist could no longer be ignored. A hairline fracture, probably. He might have done the wrist even more damage in the few seconds it took to put Green out of his misery.

But it was worth it.

49

The house felt stale, as if Jolie had been away for a month. It felt empty, too. She turned on CNN, went to the kitchen, and poured herself a Coke. Hot outside, hot inside.

The cat came in and looked at her. He wanted something. She dug around in the refrigerator and gave him the last of the deli chicken. "You're not supposed to have scraps," she said, but he ignored her.

She hadn't told Ed specifically why she was stranded at the Burger King in Port St. Joe, just that it was job-related. Which was pretty much the truth. Jolie liked it that Ed was happy to drop everything and come and get her. She had to listen to some war stories on the way back—the same ones she'd heard probably seven or eight times now—but that was fine with her. Ed telling her his war stories and Jolie listening was a big part of their relationship.

Jolie tried Kay but got her voice mail. It was the third time she'd tried to reach her, and it was clear Kay had decided to ignore her calls.

Jolie had always been sure about the story of her life. Her mother died when she was a baby, leaving her dad to raise her on his own. A father and mother who loved each other, both of them doting on their baby girl. Their happy future cut short by the ticking time bomb in her mother's head—the aneurysm that took Dorie Burke's life.

That was gospel.

But maybe Kay was right. Maybe her parents *didn't* love each other. Maybe they were on the verge of a divorce. Maybe one of them committed adultery. Maybe even domestic violence.

Jolie couldn't believe that. Not her father. He was a gentle, loving man. A hopeless romantic. A tilter at windmills—a liberal Democrat in a right-wing county.

She couldn't picture her father hurting her mother. Not beating her, not sleeping around. It wasn't in him.

Her phone rang. It was Louis. "Just wanted you to know we looked at Amy Perdue's phone and didn't find anything substantial."

"You looked at her photos?'"

"We looked at everything. There was nothing I would call incriminating—not in her e-mails, anything like that."

"What kind of photos did she have?'"

"Usual stuff—lots of photos of her and her boyfriend, parties, the beach. Stuff like that."

"Her brother Luke worked for a tree service on Indigo—the attorney general's place on Cape San Blas. Were there any pictures there?"

For a moment there was quiet. Then Louis asked, "Why would you want to know that?"

How much should she tell him? "This is something I was working on before Amy was shot. Luke might have seen something illegal going on there. He might have taken photos and shared them with Amy."

"Illegal? What are you talking about?"

"Sex stuff."

"You mean wild parties?"

"Yes, wild parties."

"The kids or the adults?"

"The people in the house, Louis."

There was a pause. "What are we talking about here?"

"Have Ted do forensics, will you do that? Maybe he could recover data that's been erased."

"What would he look for?"

"Evidence that Luke sent her photos. Evidence that photos were erased. I don't know what those guys can do. It's possible she downloaded them to a disk, something like that."

"I don't see probable cause here."

"Somebody *shot* her, Louis. There's your PC."

"Okay, okay, I'll see what I can do."

But she had the feeling he wouldn't. Not if he knew the caliber of people who might be taking part in wild parties on Indigo Island.

Few people would touch something that radioactive.

*　　*　　*

Jolie drove to the neighborhood down the hill from the Starliner Motel and parked outside the house with the boat on blocks. A barechested man in baggy shorts answered her ring. Sixty or so, uniformly tanned from the sun and water, had wild gray hair that made him look like Nick Nolte in his booking photo. He wore a choker around his neck with a shark's tooth tied into the leather cord.

"Help you?"

Jolie saw him looking at the gold shield on her belt. She gave him her spiel, that she was a detective with Palm County Sheriff's, that she had two kids in custody whom she believed were committing burglaries in the neighborhood. She told him a neighbor had seen kids crawling out from under his boat, and asked if she could look under there for evidence.

He regarded her skeptically. Jolie wondered if her lying skills had gone downhill. Lying was like that cartoon coyote running off the cliff into thin air. You were fine unless you looked down.

"What are you expecting to find there?"

"Fingerprints."

He nodded. "Let me get my sandals on, and we'll go take a look."

They went out to the boat. The man lifted the edge of the boat so Jolie could see under. There were the beer bottles. There was the snuff can.

This time she had evidence bags and gloves with her. She donned the gloves and bagged each bottle and the snuff can.

*   *   *

Back at home, she pried the lid off the snuff can—Copenhagen Wintergreen. The rich tobacco smell wafted out at her with its twin siren promises of comfort and death.

Inside, surprise, surprise—snuff. The can was about half full. She touched her finger to the snuff and pushed it around. And there it was. Wedged crosswise across the bottom of the can, packed in cellophane and previously hidden by plugs of chew, was what could have been the tiniest cigarette lighter in the world.

Only it wasn't a cigarette lighter. It was a USB flash drive. Using gloves, Jolie carefully extracted the flash drive from the can and plugged it into the USB port on her laptop. And waited.

She got impatient, her heart thumping hard. Electricity running through her veins as the computer took a couple of seconds to digest the information. Then the window came up. She clicked past the window, and the data on the flash drive came up.

There was only one file on the drive: "Photos."

She clicked on it, and up they came. Five thumbnail photos.

At first glance, four of the photos were broken up into light and dark space. The dark spaces formed a V shape in two of the photos. The last photo showed a crowd—men in dark slacks and mostly dark polo shirts, and something white. Very white.

She started at the beginning and clicked on the first photo. There were three sets of dark trousers. Two of them standing, forming the V of light area she'd seen. One set of legs kneeling on the floor—she could see the bottoms of the man's shoes. He was on his hands and knees, the bottom of a tan polo shirt pulling from belted trousers. Beyond the kneeler, between the trousered legs of the standers, Jolie saw what looked like another leg. A naked leg, stretched out on what looked like gleaming tile. Saltillo tile.

She clicked on the next thumbnail. The picture was out of frame, as if Luke had been too excited and had clicked it hastily. But still, Jolie could see the kneeler better. He'd moved a little, so she could see his shaved head. Big guy, *massive*, his face turned away. He wore an earpiece. The kind worn by the Secret Service.

She saw more of the naked leg between the trousered legs. Men bent forward. One of the leaning men stretched out an arm, reaching toward something Jolie couldn't identify.

In the next photo the angle was different, and Jolie could see the unidentifiable thing a little better. Red as a beet against the tile.

Mashed, pulpy.

Jolie had seen photos like this before, in crime scene pictures. She'd seen them in person, too. People who had been beaten beyond recognition.

Her stomach recoiled. She knew the man lying on the floor was Nathan Dial, although he would be impossible to identify.

Once again, she was amazed at what one person could do to another. Fourth photo: the man in the tan polo shirt bent over the supine man, administering CPR.

Fifth photo: the men in the polo shirts and slacks and earpieces hustled another man away from the man on the floor. The tableau had the quality of a medieval painting, soldiers ushering someone away to safety—or to his doom. The man they were hustling was pale and clearly bewildered. His gray hair stuck out from his head. She couldn't see his face. Every line of his body told Jolie he was stunned, that he had difficulty moving under his own power.

A thick white terrycloth towel was wrapped around his waist.

*   *   *

Now what?

She'd been vindicated. Great. But now what?

This was proof, but it *wasn't* proof.

Chain of evidence.

There was none.

Maybe if Luke had been arrested before and he had fingerprints on file—this could link him to the flash drive.

It would be helpful. And Jolie bet he had been arrested before.

But was this the vice president? She couldn't tell. Was this Nathan Dial? She doubted his own mother would know him. The man with the shaved head giving CPR—perhaps he could be identified.

There was the Saltillo tile. Jolie hadn't spent very much time at Indigo. She guessed the tile belonged to one of the cabanas, but since she'd never been to the cabanas she wouldn't know.

There were other furnishings, but they were a blur. Something that could be a wall sconce. What looked like the edge of a bed—a bedspread, just one corner. Pale green, a striped design.

*　　*　　*

Louis met her at the JB's in Gardenia. JB's was filled to the gills with the lunch crowd, and the babble covered anything they might say. The waitress was harried, banging down ceramic coffee cups and a carafe, taking their order quickly. She returned in ten minutes with Louis's food, and Jolie knew from experience she wouldn't be back for a long time. Jolie had coffee but nothing else; she opened her laptop on her side of the table.

Louis said, "You said something about photos?"

Jolie pushed the laptop across to him.

"What are these?"

"What does it look like to you?"

"Somebody got beat up bad. Where'd you get this?"

Jolie told him about her search for Luke's missing phone. "No one has his phone—not Gardenia PD or the FBI or you guys."

You guys. Jolie realized what she'd just said, and she understood then that she didn't feel part of the Palm County Sheriff's Office anymore.

"This is what you wanted me to look for on Amy's phone? What do you want me to do with it?"

"Investigate. It's part of your case."

"Where do I start? There's no chain of custody. I can't use this."

"I suggest you start at the beginning."

"What's the beginning?"

"The standoff at the Starliner Motel on Memorial Day weekend. That was the same weekend the vice president was here—at Indigo."

She filled him in on what she'd learned from Nathan Dial's roommate, Scott Emerson. Told him about the man, Rick, trolling for young men at Cove Bar. "That could have been a fake name. He could be the big guy giving the kid CPR in the photo."

Louis shook his head. "I don't think this is going to fly. Why don't *you* go to Skeet?"

"Because he'll listen to you."

Louis considered that. He motioned to the laptop. "It could get you fired."

"Right."

"So I can take this?"

"Go ahead. I've got it on my hard drive."

He removed the thumb drive and rose ponderously to his feet. "I don't think there's a snowball's chance in hell of doing anything about this. We're talking about the vice president of the United States."

"You've got a better chance than I do."

"Okay, lemme see where you found this thing."

She gave him the can of Copenhagen and the photos she'd taken of the boat and the grassy area where she'd picked up the can.

He sighed. "My wife's lawyer's got me jumping through all sorts of hoops—and now this."

50

Jolie had done what she could. Louis would have to go at it from another angle and come up with evidence of his own. He'd have to build a case; he was a talented detective. As long he could deal with his personal problems, Jolie had no doubt he'd find a way to connect the dots.

But she wouldn't leave it at that. She'd be riding herd on him, funneling information to him as it came up. She might have handed him the case, but this wasn't the end of her involvement.

Her first thought after seeing the photos was to get Kay to take her to the island. She wanted a look inside the cabanas. She wanted to look for the Saltillo tile, a pale green striped bedspread, the wall sconce.

Kay wasn't going to help her now, though.

Belle Oaks.

The words had been in the back of her mind all this time, nagging like an aching tooth. Maybe now was the time to address it. Back at home, she turned on CNN to see what was going on in the world—a habit she'd gotten from her dad. Then she sat down at the kitchen table and Googled "Belle Oaks" plus "Tallahassee."

There were a number of matches: the Belle Oaks Restaurant and Golf Club, the Belle Oaks Riding Academy, and a private health care facility. Jolie eliminated the riding academy immediately. There was a Belle Oaks Drive, too.

Again, Jolie wondered what Kay had been aiming at. Did her parents fight in the bathroom, and she'd somehow witnessed it? She was not even eighteen weeks old when her mother died, and she had no memories from that age. But perhaps she'd absorbed it in some way. Was that the reason for her panic attack at the house?

She thought she knew her father, but maybe—

No.

Maybe someone had broken into the house—a home invasion.

The CNN music for breaking news came on. Jolie ignored it. Since 9/11, these channels had "breaking news" on twenty times a day.

She clicked on the private health care facility. A photo of a red brick Federal-style mansion came up, framed by tall oaks draped with Spanish moss and a green lawn. Another photo at the side— two elderly women and an elderly man eating ice cream cones in the sunshine.

Jolie was still looking at the elderly man and the elderly women having the time of their lives, when she heard the words "Vice President Pintek."

She looked at the TV.

The screen was dominated by an aerial view of the vice president's residence, the Naval Observatory.

As a cop and a longtime watcher of CNN, Jolie knew aerial views seldom meant good news. Maybe someone had breached the grounds.

But it was worse than that.

The vice president of the United States, and Jolie's number one suspect in the death of Nathan Dial, wasn't the victim of breached security.

He was dead.

*　　*　　*

Whatever had been, whatever she had planned up to this moment was no more. The vice president was dead—no one could prosecute him now.

She needed to get away from the hot, muggy house. Needed to get away and think. She went for a drive.

Jolie didn't know how she felt about the VP's death. A number of things, actually. First, satisfaction. Payback. Owen Pintek was dead. Now she could leave it alone. Louis would drop it, and Jolie could stay on paid leave and forget about turning over any rocks or tweaking any noses. She wouldn't get into any further trouble with Skeet. She could keep her job without even trying. Jolie knew this. Skeet didn't have enough to fire her, not without her help. And now she wouldn't give him any more ammunition to use against her, because it was over.

Except there was one thing. Her family. It was possible—likely, in fact—that someone in her family knew about Nathan Dial's death. Uncle Frank, probably. He was the attorney general and a longtime friend of the VP's. They'd both been in President Baird's cabinet. Maybe Franklin had been part of the cover-up. And there was Luke's death. Who had he tried to blackmail with the images on his phone? The vice president of the United States, or the Haddoxes?

Jolie thought he'd go for the Haddoxes. Blackmailing them would be nowhere near as daunting. The Haddoxes were local. How would Luke get in touch with the vice president of the United States? The simple answer: he couldn't. But Luke worked for the tree service that took care of Franklin Haddox's grounds. In his ignorance, he'd think that would be the same as accessing the vice president.

She drove to Gardenia, past the Iolanthe Paper Company, past the shuttered Starliner Motel, then over to Panama City. All the time thinking about the people who had been killed. Luke and Amy died because of their blackmail scheme. Kathy Westbrook and Maddy Akers were collateral damage. Then there was Nathan Dial, whose death started everything.

Now the vice president was dead, too. According to the television reporter, there was no information other than the death appeared to be due to natural causes. His wife discovered him in their bedroom early this morning, "unresponsive." That was all the information available, although CNN played it over and over again in a loop and the experts had been brought on to make their guesses.

Jolie followed Route 30 into Panama City Beach. She drove past the Waffle House where she'd met Scott Emerson. Thought about Scott, how they worked the Cove Bar together.

He should know the truth.

Shouldn't do this. But Jolie was tired of all the things she shouldn't do, so she punched in his number. Almost gave up as the phone rang and rang. Thinking it was just as well he didn't answer. This could be a Pandora's box. And then he picked up.

"Have you seen the news?" she asked him.

"Is it Nathan? Did they find him?"

"No. Vice President Pintek is dead."

A pause. "What does that have to do with anything?" Another pause. She could almost hear him thinking—putting it together. "You think…" Then he said, "*Jesus.* You think that was the party? You have any proof? How…?"

"Listen," Jolie said. "It's common knowledge that the VP was into rough sex with young men." She did not tell him about the photos. About how much she really knew.

"Oh *God.* That guy Rick. Somebody said he looked like Secret Service. Are you sure? And now the vice president's dead?"

"Turn on the television."

She heard him do that. Jolie listened to the news in the background, but Scott Emerson said nothing.

Time stretched. She became aware of how hard the phone was pressed against her ear. "Scott?"

"Why are you telling me this?"

"Why?"

"Yes. Why?"

"I thought you'd want to know what happened to Nathan."

"I don't know anything, except who you think the guy was. I don't know how it happened or why it happened, I don't know how they disposed of him, I don't know anything. And now this man—the man you *think* did this—is dead and he'll never pay for what he did, and there's nothing I can do about it. Nothing!"

"I thought you'd want closure." She winced as she said it, because people had often used the same word with her, and she despised the word.

"Closure?" he said. "What the hell is that?"

51

When it was full dark, Landry walked the three blocks to the maid's car. He drove to the house, backed up into the garage, and opened the trunk. Getting Special Agent Salter out was a challenge, since Landry didn't have the use of his right hand and Salter was a big man like himself. But Landry had been trained to drag bodies, living or dead, in ridiculously impossible circumstances. By using his body as a brace, he was able to leverage Salter's body to the concrete floor. That was all he had to do—no need to get elaborate.

The private investigator, Ted Bakus, was easier. He weighed a little more than half what Salter did. Landry pushed Bakus's leg out of the way to make sure it cleared the back tires of the maid's car.

He rounded up the weapons from each of the rooms and put them in the trunk, then showered and changed into an extra set of clothes he'd brought with him.

On the way back to Indigo, Landry stopped at the Buy Rite drugstore in Port St. Joe where he bought a wrist brace, a large roll of duct tape, several rolls of packing tape, and an industrial-sized drum of Motrin. The Motrin he popped like candy.

The duct tape was for an emergency, in case he needed to reinforce the wrist brace and keep his arm steady.

He drove to a Dumpster behind a boarded-up restaurant and got out, leaned against the car, and made the call. The phone was answered on the first ring—a young man with an accent. India or Pakistan.

"I'm trying to reach the Realtor for the house on Island Lane."

"Let me look it up for you, sir." A short pause, then he rattled off the number. Landry disconnected and punched in the new number.

"Hello?"

Landry said, "Would it be possible to see the house tonight?"

"What time?"

"My friends and I can be there by eleven." Landry was telling the man that the team would be in place by eleven p.m.

"Why not in the morning? It can be as early as you want."

"I'm afraid by then it will be too late. I have a very early flight." This was Landry's way of saying that they would raid Indigo in the wee hours of the morning and would be flown out shortly afterwards.

"I'll check with my wife and call you back."

"Thanks." Landry disconnected, stomped the cheap cell phone into bits, and threw it into the Dumpster.

Landry was all for covering his tracks, but an enigmatic conversation like the one he'd just had seemed more like something out of *Mission Impossible* than real spycraft. But from what Landry had learned of Cardamone, the man was CIA all the way. If the CIA had a choice between doing something straightforwardly or in a sneaky way, they'd take sneaky every time.

When he got to the island, he went looking for Franklin. He needed to get some sleep and wanted a quiet room.

52

Jolie lay in bed, watching the numbers on her alarm clock roll over from 5:29 to 5:30 a.m.

The vice president of the United States is dead.

The world was completely out of whack.

She sat up.

All of this was much bigger than she'd thought. It had gone from scandal to the death of a sitting vice president. If the vice president of the United States died because he'd become a liability, the enormity of the crime was stunning.

Yesterday, Jolie had lowered the flag as she did every evening. Ed was outside puttering around, so he came by and stood with her. Jolie felt tears collect in her eyes and drain into her throat—she couldn't talk. Ed had been in the infantry and had seen so many kids his own age die right in front of him. He had accepted their deaths because of what the United States of America meant. Because dying for your country was worth it, if that country was the United States.

Jolie thought about her dad and his strong belief in this country. He knew it wasn't perfect and he was often on the wrong side of issues—at least that's how this town saw it—but he still had that belief. He'd loved his country probably more than any other single thing.

She got up and turned on CNN, expecting more coverage on the vice president's death, sure they'd run it into the ground. But they surprised her. There was another aerial view, this one of a burning building in Tallahassee.

Breaking news.

Jolie was about to switch channels when she heard the name of the building in question. The Victorious Redemption Spiritual Church.

Grace's church.

Goosebumps ran up her back and fanned out along her shoulders.

Oily black flames poured out of the roof, people running like ants along the sidewalk. Jolie sat down, stunned, and watched.

At least thirteen dead, but probably many more.

Gunmen had stormed the church compound in the early hours of the morning, shooting people in their beds, torching the church and the outbuildings.

The Reverend Wembi and his wife were unaccounted for and believed to be dead.

The fire in the church itself was still burning, but the police had secured all but one of the outbuildings, and the survivors had been taken either to a hospital for treatment or to a school nearby where contact could be made with loved ones.

Stunned, Jolie watched.

There was speculation who set the fire, but the general consensus was political. At least one terrorist group had claimed responsibility—a rival faction from the Congo.

Among the missing was Grace Haddox, wife of the former attorney general of the United States.

The phone rang.

Kay's voice—sounding lost. "Did you hear what happened?"

"I'm watching it now. Is there any word about Grace?"

"No, but I think she's dead. I had this feeling...it's..." She stopped. "I have to get out there."

"To the church?"

"No—I think we need to be there for Riley. Just in case. Zoe and me."

Jolie said, "Can I go with you?"

"I guess. Maybe that would be good—you deal with emergencies all the time, don't you?"

*   *   *

They were silent on the drive over. Zoe in the backseat. Jolie in the passenger seat.

Kay's knuckles tight on the wheel.

Jolie'd only met Grace once, for less than half an hour. Grace had been polite, but dismissive. *Look who Kay brought home.* But Jolie had had recent dealings with Riley. Riley was a frightened child. Behind all the attention-seeking, Jolie felt Riley's desperation. There was something she wasn't getting. And now her mother might be dead.

Jolie looked at Kay but Kay ignored her, her eyes on the road. Jolie could see Kay going through the contingencies, considering the alternatives, what she'd find, what she'd do. Jolie wondered if Kay was rethinking bringing her along.

Jolie knew everything had changed. Kay was still mad at her, but that didn't matter anymore. Kay had put that behind her for the moment. There was too much to deal with. Riley needed help, and Riley was family. Jolie marveled at how quickly Kay dropped what she'd thought was important before and focused only on her family and how she could help them. Kay had a strong bond with her family. Kay belonged, and she would always be there to help.

Kay had invited her to belong, too.

Jolie realized she *wanted* to belong. She wanted to have a family again. She prized her friendship with Kay. But something stood in the way. Her own small family. Her dad and herself. All her life her dad had told her to watch out for those less fortunate, to protect the weak. It had been ingrained in her. It was the reason she became a cop.

Nathan Dial had been treated like so much garbage. His body was disposed of and his death was covered up. He had no one to speak for him, no one to step up and bear witness to the atrocity of his death.

No one to give him justice.

No one but her.

53

Landry's watch alarm woke him at four a.m.

Franklin had given Landry a guest room in the main house. Nothing fancy, which surprised him, because these were rich people. The room was functional but not spectacular. The white jacquard bedspread was nice, though. Landry had slept well. His wrist throbbed, but as long as he wore the wrist brace, it was all right.

He made the bed, hospital corners as he had been trained to do, and sat on the jacquard bedspread. Thinking about Cardamone.

He didn't waste time wondering where Cardamone was. He knew Cardamone had flown to Panama City, but after that, he'd disappeared. If his thought processes were anything like Landry's, he would stay away from hotels and rental cars. He would not use credit cards. He would rent a house somewhere nearby, a cash transaction.

After Landry's phone call to the Indian man at "Gulf Homes" last night, Cardamone would think Landry's team was in place on Cape San Blas in preparation for an assault on the island in the small hours of the morning. If Cardamone didn't hear soon, he would begin to wonder. Before too long, he would become worried. He would check the news and see nothing. In addition, the two men who had been keeping track of Franklin's whereabouts— Agent Salter and Ted Bakus—had not reported in. Landry had

Bakus's phone. He'd expected to hear from Cardamone yesterday, but maybe the man was too cagey for that. Presumably, they would have called Cardamone if the attorney general did anything out of the ordinary.

Landry thought it doubtful they'd check in with Cardamone if Franklin kept to his routine. Cardamone was a busy man. So it was possible he thought everything was okay.

But when it dawned on Cardamone that there had been no assault on the island, he would send someone to the safe house on Sea Oats Lane.

He might expect to find four dead men—that was within the realm of possibility. But instead of Jackson, Davis, Green, and Peters, he would find Jackson, Davis, Green, Salter, and Bakus.

Landry thought he would be shocked by that. Cardamone would wonder: How did one-offs like Salter and Bakus meet up with his elite assassination team? And where was the fourth member of the team—the team leader?

He would want to know what happened to Landry.

Cardamone would run through a number of scenarios, the most likely being that Landry had killed the other five. But Cardamone wouldn't know for sure.

So what would he do next?

He would double down. He would send another team, if he had one. Landry suspected he had at least one other team, maybe more. But it would take time for them to get here.

Or, from what Franklin had told him about Cardamone, he would come himself. In an ideal world, that was what would happen. Cardamone would come alone, and Landry would be waiting for him. But Landry didn't think so. Cardamone would send the other team.

The question was, would Cardamone come along this time, to make sure?

Franklin had told him Cardamone was hands-on. The man was proud of his time in special forces. According to Franklin, he spent hours a week at the firing range and worked out six times a week. His favorite saying was, "You make your own luck."

He would consider the assault on his men an assault on him.

But he was smart. Had to be, to have survived this long. And the smart thing to do was stand back and let his team do their work.

A quick knock and his door opened. Franklin stood in the doorway. He looked stricken. "Grace is dead."

"Dead?"

"There was a fire at the church. A massacre." Franklin came in and sat down on the bed next to Landry. His movements were slow and wooden, like a zombie's. Shock.

"Are you sure she's dead?"

"I know it. I can feel it." Franklin looked at him. "She was the main target."

"Why was she the main target?"

"Grace was the chief fund-raiser for Wembi's church. She was in all the way. All the stuff they were doing, hiding assets, tax fraud. And she had friends at the capitol in Tallahassee. They were investigating the rival church for gunrunning and money laundering and their ties to dangerous groups in the Congo. It was all a competition between the two churches."

"A competition."

"Yes, but it got out of hand. The other reverend, Beebe, swore he'd wipe her out and all her family. It was probably just an empty threat to scare us." He sighed. "But you don't even know the half of it."

"What's the rest?"

"The vice president is dead."

Landry absorbed this. "You think Cardamone had him killed?"

Franklin nodded.

"How did he die?"

"They say cardiac arrest." Franklin rubbed the bridge of his nose, looking around as if he didn't recognize where he was. Then he teared up. "She's dead. The love of my life is dead, and it's all because of me." Then he reached around and grabbed Landry and held him in a sideways bear hug.

It wasn't a homosexual thing, Landry knew that. But he recoiled. More from the blatant show of emotion than anything else. But he let Franklin hang on to his neck, cry into his chest like a little boy—loud sobs. Embarrassingly loud sobs. After a decent interval, Landry patted him on the back and disengaged.

"Turn on the television," Frank said. "They might have news. Maybe she's not dead." His voice sounded hopeful but strangled by tears.

Just then Franklin's cell phone rang. He answered, stood up, and went to the open doorway. "You're sure?" he asked. "When did they—? They're sure? They've made an identification? You're sure?"

His footsteps echoed down the hallway.

When Franklin was gone, Landry turned on the TV. As Franklin had told him, there was a fire at the church.

Landry looked at his watch. It was now almost six a.m.

Decision time.

Now he knew for sure there was another team. It was the team Cardamone had sent to the church to kill Grace. Landry headed a team of four, so it was likely the other team had four members as well, although he would allow for more.

Landry changed channels to CNN. He kept the sound turned down. The screen was divided. One showed the church, the boiling smoke, the firemen. The other, the larger screen, showed a panel of doctors at a press conference, talking about the vice president's death.

Cardamone's other team was in Tallahassee. Tallahassee was two hours away by car, less than half that time by jet. The minute Cardamone knew about the safe house, the other team would be on its way to Indigo.

The wise choice would be for the team to set up and wait until the early hours of the morning, or at least until midnight, but Landry couldn't count on that. With the weather as cover, they could just as easily come in and take them out quietly, then wait until dark to do the second half of the job: to make it look like a Congolese uprising. Landry couldn't rule that scenario out. He had to plan for the possibility that they were two to three hours away at the latest.

It was even possible they could be here now.

Landry switched to the local channels to see if there was anything about the house on Sea Oats Lane. The only shows on were talk shows. The church fire in Tallahassee and the death of the vice president of the United States didn't make a dent in the talk show lineup, apparently.

Landry had no idea where Michael Cardamone was in the space-time continuum. So he decided to act as if Cardamone's other team was on their doorstep.

He made a check of the island, looking in the places he would hide his people if he'd been the team leader. Plenty of places to look. The island was a wonderland when it came to accessibility. It could be accessed by water almost all the way around, and by the causeway. There were secret passageways. Stables, boathouses, cabanas, lush vegetation. He couldn't cover it all, but after the seventh or eighth hiding place, he sensed the team wasn't here yet.

Then he went looking for Frank.

Frank sat at an umbrella table poolside. Riley was with him, dangling her legs in the pool.

If Landry was interrupting anything, it hadn't really gotten started yet. Franklin and his daughter were like two distinct pods, separated by a small space.

As Landry approached, Riley glared at him. Her eyes were red from crying. Franklin, on the other hand, looked distracted, almost thoughtful.

"Franklin," Landry said.

Franklin looked up. In another world. "What?"

"How many employees do you have right now? On the island."

"Employees?"

Riley said, "Why don't you go away?" She pulled her feet out of the pool, dripped her way across the tile, and reached awkwardly around to hug her father's neck from behind. Landry thought she'd need a lot more practice.

Franklin didn't seem to notice his grieving daughter was hugging him around the neck. "Employees?" he repeated.

"How many?"

Franklin closed his eyes, counting in his head. "Four, altogether. At the moment, because we hire out to a grounds crew. The maid, two kitchen help, and the senator's attendant, Jason."

That trued up with Landry's own count. "Are they the only people here, other than the family?"

"Other than the senator, yes."

"You sure?"

"Yes."

"They have to go."

"Go? Why?"

"Never mind why. You need to get them off the island."

"What will I tell them?"

"Tell them they have the day off. Tell them it's a free day. You're a good talker, Franklin. They'll believe you."

"Okay."

"Now."

Riley said, "Why don't you leave us alone? Can't you see we're in *mourning*?"

Franklin patted her on the shoulder. "He's trying to help us, puddin'."

Landry said, "Round them up and get them off the island. The three of us will meet at the octagon house in ten minutes."

"You can't order my daddy around like this!"

"Franklin? Do it now."

Franklin nodded, then walked to the golf cart. Riley dogged his steps, turning back twice to give Landry a furious glare and a few choice profanities. Franklin got into the golf cart and Riley shoved in beside him. She might as well have been a gnat for all the attention Franklin paid her.

Five minutes later, Landry watched through binoculars as the four employees trooped to their vehicles and drove out. Franklin had followed them to the edge of the island. He sat in the golf cart, watching as the cars filed across the narrow causeway and out past the empty gatehouse before turning on Cape San Blas Road.

Franklin started up the cart and made the U-turn. Abruptly, the cart jolted to a stop. Riley jumped out and ran out onto the road, waving her arms.

Landry saw what she was running at. An SUV had turned off Cape San Blas Road and was now bumping along the causeway.

* * *

"Mom, stop!" Zoe shouted. "Stop the car!"

As Kay hit the brakes, Zoe slithered out of her seat belt, shoved open the door, and ran out onto the causeway to meet her cousin.

They hugged. Riley was sobbing. Jolie could hear it even with the air-conditioning on and the windows rolled up.

Kay got out too, and Jolie followed suit. They all met halfway down the narrow road, the water lapping up on the rocks bordering the causeway. If Riley and Zoe had ever been in a fight, it was hard to believe it now. They were wrapped in each other's arms, holding tight, Riley's jagged sobs rending the air, Zoe saying over and over, "It's all right, it's all right."

Kay with them, one hand holding on to the loop at the back of Zoe's jeans.

A tableau. Jolie stood off to the side. She was the outsider, but that was okay. It reminded her what her job was.

A golf cart zipped up, and her uncle got out.

Jolie had never met him. She'd seen him on TV though, had watched him during the congressional hearings. He had been charged with criminal failure to report taxable income, although there had been more serious charges—bribery and tax fraud—that had been dismissed in favor of the one count. Mostly, she remembered, in answer to their questions, he'd said, "I don't recall."

He walked up but then hung back. Finally, he tapped Kay on the shoulder. "You have to go now."

Kay looked at him, incredulous. "What are you talking about, Frank?"

"You have to go. You'll have to go up to the gate and turn around. Why don't you take Riley?"

"Riley?"

"She can go with you."

"What are you talking about? We're here because—"

"You have to go, Kay! Now!"

Kay seemed to grow in stature, and she was pretty tall to begin with. "I will not. Riley needs us. *You* need us."

Riley and Zoe were walking toward the island, still hugging, Riley still crying, but she was talking in between sobs. Franklin Haddox looked in their direction. "Riley! Get over here right now!"

Kay shot a glance at Jolie, and Jolie understood exactly what it meant. *Get in the car.* She did. Kay climbed in, pulled the heavy door closed with a hard thump, belted herself in, and put the car in drive.

Franklin was yelling at the window. "Kay! Kay!"

She ignored him. He ran alongside, pounding on the door. "You have to go! You have to get out of here!"

She drove off the side and onto the rocks to get around the golf cart. The SUV canted sideways and the water lapped at the wheels, but they made it.

Franklin running after them. Pounding on the back window. They reached the island.

Music filled the car—Kay's ringtone. She answered but didn't take her foot off the accelerator. They were almost even with the girls. Kay dropped the phone, thrust the car door open, and yelled, "Get in!"

"We're not leaving!" Zoe shouted.

"Yeah, okay, we're not leaving," muttered Kay. Then she said into the phone, "Did you hear that, Franklin? We are not leaving—"

Kay turned to Jolie. "He hung up on me."

Franklin was now even with Riley and Zoe. Riley was yelling at him. Zoe was showing her solidarity. Franklin was thumbing his cell phone, and he seemed to be pleading with the girls. It looked to Jolie as if he was alternately talking on his cell phone and to the girls.

Kay tracked them in the SUV.

Music filled the car again.

Kay ignored it.

She drew even with the girls, buzzed down the window, and said "Get in."

"I'm not going home!" Zoe said.

"No, you're not. Just get in."

The girls piled into the car, and Kay accelerated past Franklin. Music filled the car again.

This time she answered. "What *is* it, Franklin?"

She listened. She snapped her phone closed and announced, "He wants us to meet him at the octagon house."

*　　*　　*

Landry knew how quickly things could go south. *Anything that can go wrong, will go wrong.* So it wasn't surprising when Franklin's extended family showed up. One of them was the sheriff's detective. The cousin, Jolie. Franklin seemed unable to deter them. Which was what you'd expect from someone like Franklin.

Bad enough. But that was only the first shoe to drop.

First thing, get the extended family out of the way. Landry called Frank and told him to send them to the octagon house. He also told him to keep them occupied.

Then he turned his attention to the other shoe: the sheriff's vehicle currently turning off Cape San Blas Road and approaching the gatehouse. Franklin, who had been driving his golf cart in the direction of the octagon house, answered Landry's call on the first ring.

"Why's the sheriff here?" Landry said. "Did you call him?"

"The sheriff?"

"Behind you."

The golf cart slewed to a stop. Franklin leaned out, craning his neck around to get a view of the gatehouse.

Landry asked him, "You didn't call the sheriff?"

"No. Why would I do that?"

Landry knew the ring of truth when he heard it. "What's he doing here?"

"I don't know."

Landry wondered if the sheriff had come to notify the attorney general about his wife's death. Probably. "Get rid of him, Franklin."

"What do I say? Anything about what you guys are doing?"

"No, don't mention us. The sheriff's office doesn't know about the FBI's involvement, and we're going to keep it that way. How many people in the patrol vehicle?"

"One."

"Do you recognize him?"

"It's the sheriff himself, Tim Johnson."

That sounded like a death notification. The sheriff would have come personally, especially for the attorney general. "If he is here to notify you, let him notify you. Then tell him you're grieving and you need some time to be alone with your family. You know how to do that. But get him out of here."

"Okay."

Landry watched Franklin get out of the golf cart and meet with the sheriff. He watched them talk. They talked only for three or four minutes. Then the sheriff climbed back into his SUV, made a K-turn, and drove away.

*　　*　　*

Kay drove to the octagon house and parked. They got out and Franklin led the way. The Haddox dogs appeared out of nowhere and followed them up the steps, but Franklin didn't let them come inside.

Kay had once showed her the house, just a quick glimpse of the first and second floor and the cupola. She noticed the wheelchair ramp for her grandfather, going down to the basement. The basement wasn't really a basement, but a half basement—there were half windows to the outside.

Her grandfather was in there, somewhere.

She'd never met him, either. The day she came, he had "taken a bad turn," and wasn't seeing visitors.

Jolie found herself amazed that she had spent most of her life not twenty miles away, and she had never met her grandfather or her uncle.

The first floor was as Jolie remembered it: a cleared space with a stairway to the back and an open kitchen and a closed bathroom. The windows, empty of window dressing. Franklin bustled past them, went to a closet under the staircase, and started pulling out folding chairs. He handed one to Kay and one to Jolie. Took his own chair to the center of room.

"What the hell are we doing?" Kay said.

Franklin stopped, mid-unfolding, and looked at her. Finally he said, "We're to wait here."

"Wait here for what?"

He looked at Kay again. Jolie could see him thinking. It put her in mind of her computer when it was trying to process a big file. Frank's disk was full. She sensed he had the answers just behind his tightly closed lips, but was afraid that it would be overwhelming, would shock them—so he said nothing at all.

"Franklin?"

He looked at Kay. "We just have to."

"That's no answer."

"Shut up, will you, Kay? I didn't ask for you to come here."

An argument ensued, all the old slights and hurts coming up. Jolie had been witness to and part of many family arguments in New Mexico, and she'd had plenty with her dad and with her husband. Years of intimate knowledge of one another, plenty of history, lots of cues that Jolie would miss. They sparred without really saying anything at all. "Why should I shut up?" "Because you don't know what you're talking about." "Then why don't you tell me what's going on?" "Look, it's complicated." And the kicker: "My wife just died, Riley's mother—can't you cut me some slack?"

Jolie sat and watched and listened. Franklin kept looking out the windows. Went from one to another to another. Nervous. Worse than nervous. Scared. He checked his watch. He used his cell phone, and even that was secretive, the way he held it, the way he turned away, his mouth pressed close to the phone. Agitated, arguing with whoever was on the other end. Slammed the phone shut. He looked at turns nervous, angry, impatient, terrified, annoyed, and resigned. Pacing the room, going to the windows, calling someone and getting no answer.

Jolie kept her eye on him because he was the only one who knew anything. His actions confirmed her suspicion that he was in over his head. She wondered where Franklin was in the food chain. Pretty low, judging from the way he was acting.

She knew two things: he was terrified of someone, and he was waiting for something to happen.

She'd left her primary weapon behind—it didn't seem appropriate, coming here. But she had the Walther PPK .380 concealed in an ankle holster. She needed to be ready for whatever happened. And something would happen, she was sure of it. She leaned forward so that her elbows rested on her knees. That way she could grab the Walther if she needed it.

Riley and Zoe had been sitting together, but now Riley got up and went to be near her dad. She hovered near him like a moon to a planet. When he went to one window and looked out, she hung back but shadowed him.

Franklin told Riley to go sit down. Riley reacted the way Jolie had always seen her react. She got into a snit, said a few belligerent things, and stalked back to her chair next to Zoe. Bounced back up and started shadowing her father again.

His moon. Smaller and weaker and left out in the cold and the dark.

Jolie felt sorry for her. The only thing that mattered in her life was the man who ignored her. He never once looked in her direction. He stared out the window, checked his cell phone, paced. He did everything but look at his daughter, the one person who shared his loss.

Jolie thought how sad this was.

Then a chair came flying through the window in an explosion of glass.

54

A figure stepped in through the window. Black clothing, face covered by a balaclava. What riveted Jolie's attention most was the rifle aimed at them. Aimed at *her*.

Quick calculation: no way could she grab the Walther before he shot her.

"Facedown on the floor! Do it *now*!"

Jolie dropped. There was nothing else to do. He had the rifle.

She heard the feet crunching on glass shards. The next thing she felt was the pressure of a rifle barrel against the back of her neck.

"*Do* not move!"

He jerked her arms behind her back and wrapped her wrists, once, twice, and then the sharp tearing sound of tape. She'd handcuffed bad guys a thousand times, but he was quicker. Much quicker. He frisked her equally as fast. Confiscated her purse, her cell, and her Walther PPK. He kept the Walther and tossed everything else out the broken window.

A ripping sound as he tore tape off the roll. It looked like packing tape. He wound the tape around her ankles, then rested the gun muzzle against the nape of her neck again and whispered, "Stay still."

She would. No question about that.

"Be quiet."

She would. You could hear a pin drop.

Then he was gone. She heard the tape ripping, again and again—everyone taped, wrists and ankles. She saw his boots go by—combat boots. And the rifle—she saw the long barrel when he hunkered down to tape Kay.

One arm was silver.

She realized the silver was duct tape. Wound all the way from the thumb and wrist up to the elbow.

An injury.

She felt the rifle muzzle again. "You a cop?"

"Yes."

"Sit up."

It was awkward, but she did. He aimed the rifle at her face—point-blank. For a moment, she believed this was it. Say your prayers. What would it feel like when the bullet hit? He would be good, so she would feel nothing at all. She usually tried not to think about death, but now it was all she thought about.

He pointed the rifle at the ground. "You do exactly as I say. You hear me? Exactly as I say."

She felt absurdly grateful. If he had a ring, she'd kiss it. Instant Stockholm syndrome.

"Daddy, why's he doing this?"

Riley.

"*Daddy!* You're not going to let him get *away* with this? Do something!"

The silence was resounding.

"You have to tell him to stop!"

"Puddin'—"

"*Quiet!*"

"Don't you tell me to—"

Their captor took a step in Franklin's direction and aimed the barrel at the attorney general's face.

His voice was low, but it sent chills up Jolie's spine. "Quiet," he said to Riley. "Last time."

*   *   *

"Stop here."

Jolie stood at the bottom of the shallow stairs into the basement, the last in line. Their captor touched her shoulder with his rifle muzzle. "In there."

He opened the door to a cramped room containing a hospital bed and an oxygen tank. Roses were everywhere. On the bed table, on the ledge by the window, in pots on the floor. The scent was heavy, cloying, and underneath there was the underlying medicinal smell you found in hospitals.

"What's all that noise? Who's there?" The bathroom door opened, and a man in pajamas shuffled in. A tall man, good-looking for a ninety-year-old. He was tanned, with white hair and a rugged face, marred only by the cannula for the massive oxygen tank parked by the bed.

He stopped and looked at them. "Who are you?" he asked.

"Dad—"

"Shut up, Frankie. Who are you?" he said to their captor. "Are you a ninja?"

Their captor lifted his rifle in reply.

Jolie said, "He's defenseless. You don't need to shoot him."

Their captor nodded toward the oxygen canister. "I wasn't going to shoot him. I was going to hit him." He said to Jolie's grandfather, "This is your lucky day. You've got company."

"I don't want company. I'm sick of company. Like that asshole Jason. What a sanctimonious little turd. He won't even let me have my one cigarette a day." He looked straight at Jolie. "Dorie, can you get me a cigarette?"

298

He'd mistaken her for her mother.

"Dorie, go get your dad a cigarette, will you?"

"I can't," she said. "Oxygen."

"You think I'll blow us to kingdom come, do you? That's an old wives' tale. I've smoked plenty of times and never had a problem." He squinted at her. "What's that getup? You used to dress so nice—you had *style*."

Jolie had no clue how to talk to a man with dementia. Disabuse him of the idea she was her mother? Humor him? She wasn't sure, so she kept silent.

"Dorie, is the kid all right?" Franklin Haddox II canted his head like a curious bird. "You should bring her here. I want to know for sure she's okay."

Jolie had no idea what he was talking about.

Her captor shifted his feet. Bored, but putting up with it. It came to her with clarity that he would not kill them—at least not now. Why would he herd them down here when he could have killed them all at any time before this?

Kay said, "Granddad, how are your roses?"

Her voice was too high and too bright.

"My roses are fine." He dismissed Kay with a look and turned to Jolie. "Dorie, you haven't seen my hothouse. Maybe *that* would get you over your funk. You never even asked to see the rose I named for my grandchild."

"Grandchild?" Kay asked.

"*Jolie!* Who did you think I meant?" The old man looked daggers at Kay. "Who did you think we were talking about? I named a rose for you too, so I don't see what all the fuss is all about."

Kay said, "Granddad, I think you're confusing Dorie with her—"

"No, no, no! She needs to hear this. Dorie, do you have any idea how much it cost to buy off all those people? Everybody and their brother. Cops, public records, the paramedics. I don't know what got into you! You were such a sweet, lovely child. Now look at you. I hear you're a cop."

"Granddad?" Kay said. "*Jolie's* the cop, remember? Not Dorie."

"I know it's Jolie. Are you trying to make me look bad? I know all about you," he said, looking at Jolie. "You're a detective, and you want nothing to do with your own family." He pointed a crooked finger at her. "I didn't like your father, but he and I saw eye to eye on this. We did the right thing. He might have been a goddamn fool, but he was smart enough to know who to come running to when he needed help. We did the right thing."

"Right thing?" Jolie asked.

The old man frowned at her.

"Who are *you*?"

*   *   *

Landry stayed in the old man's room longer than he'd planned to, drawn in by the strange conversation between the old man and the female cop. The dynamic intrigued him.

He went outside and took stock of the situation. First thing, he blocked the causeway west of the gatehouse by parking Frank's two Suburbans crosswise. That took care of land. But he still had to deal with air and sea.

He glassed the boats in the bay. A couple of fishermen were out early. The people he was worried about could be on those boats now, pretending to be fishermen. It was what he would do. There was no other sign of movement in the air, sea, or land, except for the dogs. They fell in with him as he scouted the island, following him back to the octagon house. He brought them inside and went to the kitchen on the first floor. There was some meat in the freezer. He defrosted it in the microwave, led the dogs outside, and fed them. He fed them a little at a time. He'd go back inside, get more meat, and call them with, "Come dogs!" By the third time they came running. By the fifth time, they were camped outside the front door.

The dogs would alert them if anyone came their way—an inexpensive alarm system.

Then he found the right spot in a lushly vegetated patch of garden with a good view of the water and the road. High enough to see the two obvious points of entry—a good place to set up as a sniper.

He settled on his stomach in the dark shade of a royal palm and looked through the sight once again at the boats. The fishermen, if they were fishermen, were fishing. But while it was still bright and sunny, he could see the chop on the water and clouds massing when he looked toward the Gulf. There were more boats when he looked again, drifting in, and he wondered if there were a lot more on Cardamone's team than just four.

55

Jolie tried to find a way out of her grandfather's room, but they were locked in. The basement windows were too narrow to get through. Whatever their captor had pushed up against the door was too heavy to move.

She wondered why he didn't just kill them.

She would have.

Jolie went through his actions so far. He had shocked them by throwing the chair through the window. He'd taped them up quickly, paying particular attention to her because he knew she was a cop.

Control and intimidation.

Everything he did from the moment he broke through the window had been calculated to keep them off balance, cowed. He wanted them to depend on him, and only him.

Which meant he wanted them for something.

Jolie glanced at Franklin, who sat against the wall, his feet out in front of him, his head pressed into the corner. Riley beside him. She'd stopped crying, stopped talking. Maybe she was in shock. As Jolie watched, Riley burrowed herself deeper into her father's body, so he had to raise his chin and rest it on the top of her head.

Jolie wondered if Franklin knew their captor. Something in his body language. A certain...familiarity. She thought back to the scene between Riley and the man in black, the way she talked to him.

There was something in her voice—resentment?

No. She was affronted.

Riley told her father to order their captor to leave, but Frank did nothing.

Could this have been planned? Done for their benefit? Like a play?

Ridiculous thought, but it nagged her. What if it was for their benefit, and then it went wrong?

She needed to get Frank talking. There was plenty to talk about, so she started with the subject that brought her here.

"Franklin, what happened to Nathan Dial?"

He didn't respond. But Riley glared at her.

"Franklin? Did the vice president kill Nathan Dial?"

"Leave my dad alone!"

"Franklin?"

He looked at Jolie with the eyes of a resentful child. "What do I care? My life is over. My wife is dead, I've failed my own family..." He stared at the floor, every line in his body saying, *I give up.*

"No, you haven't, Daddy. It's *her* fault."

Jolie would have loved to hear Riley's take on why it was her fault. "Just tell me, Franklin. For the family's sake. Did the vice president kill Nathan Dial?"

He gave her a look of annoyance. "What difference does it make now? That's all water under the bridge."

"Not for his family it isn't."

"Who cares? He was a godless homosexual."

"His family cares. Did it ever occur to you, Franklin, that all of this might be connected?"

Kay said, "Jolie, what are you talking about?"

"You heard him. The vice president killed a young man named Nathan Dial."

"Vice President Pintek? You can't be serious! I don't believe that for one minute. Is that why you came with me? You didn't want to help with Riley, you wanted to sneak in here and interrogate my uncle!"

Franklin said to Jolie, "What do you mean, connected?"

"The VP is dead, Frank. Grace is dead. Somebody wants to cover this up. More than you already did."

"You don't know what you're talking about." But there was something in his voice that told her she was close to the truth.

"What did you do, Franklin? Take your boat out in the middle of the night? Chain him to an anchor and dump him in the bay?"

Kay clapped her hands over her ears. "Shut up! Shut *up*!"

"Frank, is there more I don't know?"

"There's nothing."

"Why now? Why did the VP die now? You had it all covered up—"

"I'm not talking to you."

"You leave us alone!" Riley shouted. "You're just jealous because we never wanted you, we—"

Jolie tried to keep her voice level. "A boy was killed, Frank."

Kay glared at Jolie. "I don't believe you! Frank wouldn't do that."

"What about the guy who took us hostage, Franklin? Is he a part of the cover-up?"

"How would I know?"

"I think you know him. I think you planned this."

"You're crazy."

Something jabbed her shoulder. A crooked finger, ending in a yellowed nail.

Her grandfather, the senator. His hawk nose was inches from her face, eyes like shiny black beetles. "I've been stewing about this for a long time, and I just can't let this go."

Jolie opened her mouth to reply, but he was ahead of her. "How could you *do* it?"

"Granddad," Kay said, her voice unusually high. Alarmed. "Granddad, that's not Dorie, that's your granddaughter, Jolie, remember? She's grown up, she's a policewoman…"

He ignored Kay and grabbed Jolie's shoulders. He launched into a tirade, spittle flying from his mouth, a jumble of angry words. For a moment Jolie couldn't comprehend what she was hearing.

Then she understood.

"What kind of mother tries to kill her own child?"

56

Landry kept watch on the causeway and on the bay. Several cars went by on Route 30, but none slowed near the turnoff to the causeway. But when he looked into the bay again, there were more boats. A flotilla of them—and they weren't fishermen. They were photographers.

A car door slammed, the sound carrying across the water—a Channel 7 news van parked on Cape San Blas road just outside the gatehouse. More cars coming, a line of them, like cars let out of a stadium parking lot after a football game. Parking on both sides of the highway, cameras out, large and small. A Tallahassee network affiliate satellite truck, this one WCTV.

He looked back at the boats. Pleasure craft, jammed with people. Jammed with people with cameras. No helicopters, though. He doubted any city news affiliate within five hundred miles of here could afford a helicopter.

If this was the raid, it was elaborate—a cast of thousands.

This was a storm all right. A media storm.

*   *   *

Just the three of us.

Jolie sat with her back against the wall, her legs stretched out in front of her. She'd relocated to the bathroom, where she couldn't be watched. She felt like a traffic accident everyone had slowed down to see.

Jolie tried to put away her emotions, see it as a story that had happened to someone else. As a cop, she'd witnessed plenty of senseless carnage over the years. The sordid homicides, the lives turned upside down. A moment of blatant stupidity. An uncontrollable rage. If you looked at it as a cop would, you could be dispassionate about it. She should be dispassionate—it was a long time ago.

But she died of an aneurysm.

"No," Kay had told her. "There was no aneurysm. She didn't die. Not then."

Then there was the move to New Mexico. Jolie didn't remember the move to New Mexico, but she remembered the move back.

Her father had kept her away from them, the family. Only twenty miles away, but the gulf between them was immense. He didn't forbid her from seeing them, but Jolie felt as if an invisible fence had been built around her. She couldn't remember how she got the impression that the Haddoxes were wealthy and powerful and had no time for her. They couldn't accept that her mother had married her father. She didn't even know if her dad said these things, couldn't remember an instance when he did, but Jolie arrived at these conclusions nonetheless. Maybe she'd been the one to fill in the gaps. A child who loved her father. Adored her father. She knew they had rejected him, and she took it personally. She knew he was an outsider, so she'd stood with him.

"I wasn't going to tell you," Kay told her.

You *almost* did.

"I didn't think it would be something you'd want to know."

No, thought Jolie. Who'd want to hold *that* conversation?

"That's why I left yesterday. I couldn't say it."

But it was all out in the open now, wasn't it?

Belle Oaks wasn't a retirement facility. It was a home. Belle Oaks was an old mental hospital upgraded and changed to accommodate people with psychological and neurological problems. Schizophrenics and bipolars, people with Alzheimer's and dementia. The suicidal. Belle Oaks was a private hospital where the rich sent their family members to be warehoused.

Dorie had lived to be fifty-eight.

Fifty-eight.

Kay told her Jolie's mother died last year, of a heart attack. In Tallahassee, only a hundred miles away.

And Jolie never knew it.

"She didn't know who anybody was," Kay told her. "She suffered brain damage when she fell."

* * *

Jolie asked Kay for all of it, and Kay told her all of it.

Jolie's mother's instability and anger. How she'd fly into rages. How she'd become increasingly dissatisfied with her life. Her growing regret about everything she'd thrown away to marry Jolie's father.

Their side of the story.

According to Kay, the one thing that kept her going was the Petal Soft Baby Soap contest. The company flew mother and daughter to New York and shot the commercial there.

It was all Dorie could talk about. But more and more she confided in her older sister, Kay's mother. How she missed her family, how she missed Indigo. How disappointing her life was, except for the Soap Baby.

Then it ended. The baby soap people tried a different kind of advertising campaign, and life became unbearable again.

The rages started back up.

Jolie's mother hated her life. Maybe she hated Jolie's dad. Maybe she even hated Jolie.

*　　*　　*

Jolie's back was getting tired. She stood up, did some stretching even with her taped hands, and then leaned against the wall. The room smelled of bathroom cleanser, and underneath the cleanser smell was the faint odor of urine. The cloying smell of roses overlying all of it. In the other room, people talked in hushed tones. Jolie heard the word "she" a lot. She tuned them out.

The reason Jolie was still here, the reason she was alive, was because her father had lost his job at the ironworks factory. He came home in the middle of the day to find his wife sobbing and screaming as she held her baby underwater in the bathtub.

And Jolie wondered why she'd freaked out in the tub.

There was a struggle, and her dad saved her. In her thrashing, Dorie slipped on the tile, fell, and hit her head.

Emergency surgery and a coma followed.

Jolie closed her eyes. She could hear the murmuring in the other room. They were talking about it. Weighing every nuance, turning over every lie.

Dorie regained consciousness, but when she did, she had the intellectual ability of a seven-year-old. No more rages, though. Those were gone.

The rose smell got stronger, seemed to seep under the door along with the voices. A sickly sweet smell. *I named a rose for you.*

Jolie's dad called the only people who could really help him: the family. They sent a private ambulance. They got the best doctors. Had plenty of conferences in the waiting room, at the house on Indigo Island. A plan was made. Dorie Haddox Burke died of an aneurysm, sudden and heartbreaking for her family.

Jolie remembered the photo in their family album—a white coffin under a mound of white lilies.

Her father, who hated to see even a butterfly die, must have been relieved to spare her a story like that. The story that went like this: Your mother didn't want you. Your mother hated you so much she tried to kill you.

So instead he knitted the fabric of their lives together into a new story. A new story with a sad ending. It was always "just the three of us." A loving father, a loving mother, and the child they doted on.

Jolie left the bathroom and went up to Kay. "You knew it all this time, and you never told me?"

Kay looked helpless. One of the few times she was at a loss for words.

"All this time?"

Kay opened her mouth to speak, stopped.

"Save it," Jolie said, tired in her bones. "I can't think about this right now."

57

Mike Cardamone parked the old Subaru several blocks away from the safe house. The Subaru rattled and the oil light stayed on permanently, but he'd picked it up yesterday for cash from a man who was as secretive and paranoid as himself.

He put the sunscreen in the windshield, locked up, shouldered his duffle, and started walking.

The subdivision was empty in the steaming heat of summer. Blinds were closed. Cars locked up in garages. Abandoned houses on every street. It was not yet seven a.m., but the heat was already oppressive, and by the time he reached the house on Sea Oats, he was wringing wet.

He stared at the house, 8459 East Sea Oats, closed-up and blank-faced. It gave him a bad feeling. He continued around the block, went into the alley, and hopped the wall. After making sure the neighbors were nowhere in evidence, he unlocked the back door.

A fly zoomed out, clipping his cheek. And another, followed by the smell. Underlying the smell of the hot, closed-up house was the bloated stench of death.

He stepped back out into the yard. They'd need a cleanup crew pronto. But even as he punched in the number, Cardamone realized he had to go in.

He had to know what happened here.

The cleanup crew on the way, Cardamone reached into the duffle and pulled on a jumpsuit, plastic booties, a shower cap, and gloves.

He started with the hallway and checked the back rooms. The corpses were no shock; he'd expected to find them there. Jackson, Davis, and Green were recognizable from the photos he remembered. Professional job. He was only surprised by the third one, Green. Green, of all people, had put up a fight. Glued to the floor by his own gore. Arterial blood had arced up and out, spraying the walls.

Do not go gentle into that good night...

His mother's favorite poem.

He searched the rest of the house with mounting unease.

Where was Peters?

Another surprise—two bodies in the garage. Neither one of them was Peters.

With a shock, he recognized them: Salter and Bakus.

So where was Peters?

*   *   *

On his way back to the rental house, Cardamone's thoughts raced. He needed to discipline himself, think this through. The house would be wiped clean. No worries there.

But where was Peters?

A couple of phone calls confirmed what Cardamone already knew: there had been no raid on the compound off Cape San Blas.

Could Peters have done all this?

Cardamone searched his memory banks. Peters's real name was Cyril Landry. Had Landry connected up with Franklin somehow, or was there someone else?

He would have to call back the second team. It would take time to get them all back together, and an assault on the island right now would not be optimal. Not if Franklin knew about the raid. Not if there were hundreds of reporters with cameras roaming the island. Better hope the storm came in on time and chased the media away.

It all came down to this: was Franklin behind this? It seemed impossible. Franklin was such a screwup.

In fact, it was one of Frank's adventures that made Mike decide to pull the plug.

Franklin told him about his long-lost cousin, Nick Holloway, who was chronicling Brienne Cross's reality show for *Vanity Fair*. He told Mike he'd had no choice but to save Nick's life.

Frank knew a congressman from Colorado who had a son named Mars. Mars lived in Aspen, couldn't keep a job, and partied all the time. "Kid's a real sociopath," Franklin said. "Perfect for the job."

Frank had had to do it all on the fly, but Mars was easy to find. The kid liked the easy cash, thought it would be a lark. Mars tried to lure Nick away from the party, but that didn't work. Ultimately he put Rohypnol in Nick's drink, rolled him down the walkway, and pushed him into the garage and under Brienne's car.

When Mike found out about it, he sent one of his operatives to scrub Mars. That was how it was: Mike always had to clean up Franklin's messes.

Turned out Mars was already dead. Someone had gotten there ahead of him.

Or else the kid really did OD.

He needed to get the team back here. He might not use them, but at least he'd have them if he needed them. He called Gulf

Homes, his clearinghouse for sensitive communications, and set it up.

He discovered, miracles of miracles, that his jet wasn't en route to Atlanta, as had been planned. It was still in Tallahassee. A mechanical problem had kept it on the ground—a lucky break. The jet was ready to go, and presumably his team was still in Tallahassee.

It was meant to be.

And *this* time, he'd be with them, to make sure nothing went wrong.

Back at the house, he turned on the TV so he could follow the news while he waited for his team leader's call.

Something one of the anchors said caused him to look at the TV.

He saw an empty space, trees in the background, some wind. The camera swung to a familiar figure striding across a green lawn and onto a white shell road.

Staring at the television, Cardamone sat down on the bed, his heart rate increasing to jackhammer speed. His ears burned. He stared a hole in the TV set, but the image didn't change.

The attorney general had thrown down the gauntlet.

58

When their captor came for Jolie, her first emotion was gratitude. She'd wanted to get out of that room and away from those people in the worst way.

Inside the security center, he motioned her to a chair. Overhead was a bank of LCD screens, three vertical rows, six screens across, capturing images from remote cameras all over the island.

Bringing her out here, wanting her to watch the cameras—he must trust her on some level. Jolie could use this. "You want me to be a lookout."

"That's right."

"I should at least know your name."

"It's Cyril."

"The old man needs medical attention. He's confused, frightened. Terrified."

"That's a shame."

"He needs to get off the island."

"How would you do it?"

Jolie tried not to show too much eagerness. "We could take the Hinckley."

"No."

"But—"

"Do you know what the stakes are?"

"I know there's a terrified old man, innocent people are hostages—"

"That's nothing."

"*Nothing?* These people did nothing to you."

"Franklin did."

"Franklin? What did he do? If we're going to leave, we have to go now. The storm is—"

He slammed his hand on the desk. "You're not going anywhere."

She stared at him.

"You remember Michael Jackson?"

"Michael Jackson?"

"His death blotted out all the news—it was all Michael Jackson all the time. Remember? Nothing else could get through. Cable TV, radio, newspapers—it was all-consuming. Do you remember Iran?"

"Iran?"

"The riots? That girl, Neda, who was killed? All of that ended when Michael Jackson died."

She did remember, but she was confused. "What does that have to do with getting out of here?"

"*Listen to me.* That's what these guys did. Your uncle and Cardamone—Cardamone owns a security firm called Whitbread Associates. The government outsourced a program to Whitbread that would—every once in a while, not very often—take a high-profile celebrity out."

Jolie stared at him, unable to make sense of what he was saying.

"They killed celebs to cover up other stuff."

"That's crazy."

"Sure it's crazy. Doesn't mean they didn't do it. Governments act crazy all the time. Wiping out a whole people like the Nazis did? Crazy."

"What proof do you have?"

"I worked for them. I killed Brienne Cross."

Jolie heard the *whop-whop-whop* of a helicopter in the distance. The rain falling, dripping from the eaves. The cold air blowing in with the scent of magnolia through the open doorway.

Time seemed to stand still. *I killed Brienne Cross.* Did he really say that?

He held her eyes steady. She noticed the small scar, like a satin stitch, along his jaw. A strong jaw. Some would even say he was handsome.

I killed Brienne Cross.

She noticed his hand, complete with wedding ring, curling and uncurling. Pictured him—she'd seen the photo of the house—pictured him stabbing those people in the house.

A killer with a wedding ring...

The women screaming, dying. The young men...

He leaned toward her and she cringed. But all he did was remove the duct tape that bound her wrists. She rubbed her hands and looked at him.

Then he bent down and clamped a manacle around her ankle, wrapping the leg chain around the table legs and padlocking them together.

"I've got things to do." He instructed her on what to look for on the monitors, and left her there alone.

The rain came down harder now, but Jolie barely heard it. She was numb.

Cyril had said to her, *I killed Brienne Cross.*

Any hope she'd had that they'd get off the island alive vanished.

Cyril had told her, "Look for movement. Look for something different. If anything looks strange, unusual, let me know. Look at shadows, look at the vegetation, look at anything that would make a good hiding place." Jolie watched the monitors. Concentrated on them, looking from one to another. An hour went by.

The novelty of watching the cameras began to wear off. The recent hurt, which had been crouched outside her conscious mind while she studied the monitors, came closer. She pushed it away. The sky darkened outside the metal shed. The wind picked up. The air felt like electricity, and sure enough, soon she could hear thunder.

I killed Brienne Cross.

Something moved.

She flicked her eyes to the screen—it was the camera outside the security center shed.

The scrape of a shoe on concrete.

It was Cyril. "Turn on the TV." He nodded toward the corner of the room. The TV set rested in brackets like one you'd find in a motel. Jolie saw the remote on the desk and hit the power button.

"Cable news," he said.

Jolie turned to CNN.

As she did so, she caught movement on one of the screens. A figure in a suit and tie walked in the direction of the causeway.

Franklin.

She turned to tell Cyril, but he was gone.

Jolie watched as Franklin walked across the lawn, his face resolute. A wind came up and blew his white hair around his face. He carried something in one hand. A piece of paper.

Jolie could see the sky turning a mixture of gray and an aqueous blue-green. The storm was coming in fast now. Negative ions bounced around, an electric feeling. The smell of rain. And the sound of thunder. And the lightning.

Franklin appeared on the monitor focused on the gatehouse, set on the small spit of land coming out from the peninsula. The news vans and satellite trucks were parked beyond the empty gatehouse and along the road. Franklin made a beeline for the sea of telephoto lenses, booms, microphones, cameras, and reporters. He passed through the gatehouse, walked around the parked Suburbans blocking the causeway, and stood before the cameras, holding the piece of paper out in front of him. Far out in front of him, as if he'd forgotten his reading glasses.

"I'm here to give a statement regarding the death of my wife." Frank's hair feathered in the wind. "I will not be taking any questions."

He cleared his throat and launched into a rambling speech about his wife, the mother of his child, the love of his life. He asked the press to leave the family to share their grief in private.

The wind grew stronger, almost pushing him off his feet. The air darkened as he opened his mouth to speak again. "As I said, I will not be taking questions. But as the former attorney general of the United States and a proud citizen of this country, I feel I have to follow my conscience. As you know, I lost a good friend in the vice president of the United States, Owen Pintek. Because of our friendship, and against the advice of my attorney, I wish to make an additional statement."

Jolie heard the cameras click—dozens of them.

"As the attorney general of the United States, I sought to preserve the Constitution. I would be derelict in my duties to stay quiet, when I believe..." He stopped, and peered at the paper again. "When I'm *convinced*, that there must be a full and comprehensive investigation into the vice president's death."

There was a collective gasp from the news crews, just as a blast of wind shoved through the ranks and knocked a microphone from the hands of a female reporter.

Franklin continued speaking, his eyes never leaving the fluttering paper, his voice quavering. "Due to our long friendship, and the personal debt of gratitude I feel to my dear friend Owen Pintek, it is incumbent on me to state my belief that the possibility exists that his death was…unnatural."

The camera shutters started clicking again. He stared hard at the paper in his hands. "After certain legal issues have, er… been explored, I promise you I will call a press conference to fully answer your questions to the best of my ability. That is all I have to say at this time."

He turned, nearly bowled over by another gust of wind, and walked back through the gatehouse toward the main building. A chorus of reporters shouted questions.

Then the skies emptied, and the rain came rolling out in billows. Everyone was soaked. Thunder cracked and boomed, and lightning split the sky. The former attorney general of the United States disappeared into the octagon house, and the reporters ran for cover.

The rain blew in through the open doorway, and Jolie shivered.

59

Jolie's captor brought in a box of weapons and a duffle crammed with gear. Two-way radios, the latest generation of walkie-talkies—with earpieces. Maglites and a first aid kit, including packets of antibiotics. There were large-caliber handguns, semi-automatics, and a couple of sound suppressors. Edged weapons—Jolie recognized a Ka-Bar knife. There was also a sniper rifle.

Cyril checked the sight on the Heckler & Koch .45. "Question for you. Why are you here?"

"Why?"

"Family, or police business?"

She told him about her role in the family drama. Her friendship with Kay and her daughter Zoe.

"Is that it?"

"I want to know for sure what happened to Nathan Dial."

"The kid the vice president killed."

"You know about it?"

"Franklin told me."

"Why would he tell you *that*?"

"He was under the influence at the time. Ever heard of scopolamine?"

"What?"

"It's not important. So what are you going to do? Arrest your own uncle?"

"I can't arrest him now. I need evidence."

"The kid was gay, right?"

"So?"

"You his mother?"

"No. But someone should have been."

"He was a throwaway."

"To them."

"You'll never find him—Dial. He's long gone."

"I know that." She could have told him that you could convict someone without a body, but didn't.

He said, "The vice president's dead. He's out of it. Nobody's going to prosecute him now. You think you can nail your uncle for covering it up?"

"I have no idea." She nodded to his arsenal. "You going to use all of those yourself?"

He looked at her but said nothing.

"If you let me go, I could protect my family."

"You're more good to me here."

She tried again. "Can't we get them off the island?"

"No."

"*Why?*"

"You don't know what you're up against. A team of operatives is coming—killers."

"All the more reason to let us get out now."

His lips tightened in a thin line. "When Cardamone and his crew get here, I'll let all of you go."

"*If* Cardamone comes. There's no guarantee he's coming."

"He's coming."

"You're going to leave me chained like this?"

When he didn't answer, she said, "I have to be able to protect myself."

Shadows from the raindrops on the window crawled down the side of his face like ants. His expression was unreadable. Dark in here, even though it was midday. Half his face was in shadow.

"You were wrong when you said you didn't need me," she said. "I was a sharpshooter champion."

He motioned to the gear bag. "If you can get yourself out of here, you'll have all the firepower you need."

And he left her there.

* * *

It seemed as if hours went by, but when Jolie looked at her watch, it had only been forty-five minutes.

Staring at the image on the monitor so long it was a blur.

Trying not to think about Brienne Cross and those kids killed in Aspen. Hard to believe what Cyril had told her.

But she *did* believe him.

Her eye caught movement in the bay. She realized now that most of the boats were gone. Now there was just a steady curtain of rain and gray-green mist, the rain so thick it washed away the shadows. But she saw at least one boat out there. She couldn't tell distance, but it was beyond the waves coming in on the little beach, just a smudge, a shadow. There one moment, and then the waves moved and she wondered if it was her imagination.

She caught something else, the screen that showed the causeway. A man walking toward the mainland. It could be Cyril, or it could be someone else.

She looked at the place where the boat was—what she thought was a boat.

Couldn't see it now.

Then the room went dark.

*   *   *

Staying under cover, Landry made his way toward the gatehouse. The media was gone. In just ten minutes, it had gone from dozens of cars and news vans to a couple of stragglers on Cape San Blas Road.

He entered the gatehouse and, concealed from view, waited. It wasn't long before an SUV on the mainland slowed down on Route 30, stopping less than an eighth of a mile away. The headlights shone through needles of rain as it pulled off onto a cleared space and engineered a K-turn. The vehicle moved slowly, as if the driver was worried about getting stuck in the mud. The SUV backed up almost to the water, blocking Landry's view. Then it pulled back out onto the road, going in the other direction.

Landry had gamed this scenario himself, with Jackson, Davis, and Green. They'd gone over the schematic showing the landline and utility power running along the causeway in a flexible conduit, connecting to the mainland, how they could cut the power at its source, a junction box just above the water line. The box was concealed by bushes for aesthetic effect.

It would take a while for the op—possibly a former Navy SEAL like himself—to make it to the cable running along the causeway. Landry stayed in the gatehouse and scanned the water, looking for one of three things. Rising bubbles from SCUBA gear. He saw none; if the swimmer used SCUBA gear, he would have to ditch it before he reached the shallower water near the causeway. Landry looked for a snorkel, or perhaps a floating plastic bottle hiding a snorkel. He saw nothing like that. Then he looked for the man's forehead and nose to come up very briefly in the wave troughs. There was a large expanse of water along the causeway, a continual pattern of wavelets cresting and disappearing, some dark, some white. All running together. Landry concentrated on the water and waited.

He almost missed him—a small movement, disappearing almost instantly. His eye followed the trajectory, and after a very long time, he saw the tip of the man's nose again. At the same moment he heard the *whop-whop-whop* of helicopter rotors in the distance. He wondered if the local news affiliate had a helicopter, or if the helo belonged to Cardamone.

No time to wonder—here was his chance. He kept low to the other side of the causeway, walking along riprap, his eye on the water, and hid opposite the junction box behind the rocks at the edge of the causeway. The swimmer would have a cable cutter and a knife—possibly two. But Landry had surprise, and he also had a knife.

His quarry came out of the water, hugging low to the rocks and slipping into the concealment of the bushes. Before he could hack all the way through the cable, Landry was on him. They toppled into the water and Landry piggy-backed on him, pinning the man's back with his knee against the rocks beneath the surface. Holding the swimmer's forehead with one hand and his chin with the other, Landry jerked the man's head back with as much force as he could muster. But his bad hand slipped, losing purchase, and his quarry pried at his hands with strong fingers. Landry kept the swimmer's head underwater, pushing him down into the silt and sharp rocks with his knee. This was incredibly hard to do—his legs felt as if heavy weights were tied to them. The swimmer's legs scissored—aided by flippers—and he twisted like an eel in Landry's grip—incredible strength driven by panic. One more time Landry took hold and jerked back, and this time he felt the neck go.

Even though he was sure the swimmer was dead, Landry held him a little longer, to make sure. They had a saying in the SEALs: "Never assume a frogman is dead until you find his body."

Finally, he released him and kicked away along the causeway to the gatehouse, where the two black SUVs were parked crossways in front.

Thinking: *One down.*

The helo was overhead now, circling. A news copter after all? The Bell JetRanger had a big white "8" on the side with the call letters WFLA NEWS. But the letters didn't look right—a rush job. The searchlight came on, blinding white and lighting up the ground around the gatehouse. Bursts of shot hit the water and came ever closer, smacking the pavement in a deadly pattern, smashing into the roof of the gatehouse.

He knew it was diversionary, but even so, they could hit him. He made it to the Suburban closest to the compound and crouched by the right front tire, hoping the engine block would stay between him and the helo until he could get into the vehicle. He'd left the keys in both vehicles for just this purpose. The helo hovered, like an angry dog poking its snout through a cat door. Landry launched himself in through the passenger side into the driver's seat. He floored the Suburban across the causeway, shot pellets shattering the back window. Jammed the brakes, shot forward again, slewing right and left like a slalom skier. At the boathouse he rolled out, rolled all the way into the brush. Crawled to the shelter of the boathouse and peered out the small back window, checking to see if anyone was around. That was when he saw the Carolina skiff pulled up into the reeds on the shoreline.

*　*　*

The cameras were out. Everything was out. It was the storm. Jolie *hoped* it was the storm. She listened, waited for the generator to kick in. Twenty seconds. Everything was dark. It was gloomy outside, the rain coming down hard, but in this shed it was very, very dark. Jolie rummaged around for the walkie-talkie.

A loud sputtering sound rent the heavily laden air. A cough, and the stench of gasoline. The lights flickered on. Automatically, she looked at the camera screens. Saw movement—two figures near the boathouse.

Just before the lights went out for a second time.

*   *   *

Jolie couldn't find the walkie-talkie. It had to be right near her. Her hand scoured the desktop. She needed to be able to communicate with Cyril. She could see the shapes of things in the gloom. Her fingers landed on the walkie-talkie, but she knocked it to the floor.

Reached down, feeling around her chair.

Hands running down the heavy links of the chain to the padlock.

Her fingers nudging the padlock as she fished around for the walkie-talkie.

Something sharp protruded from the lock. The key.

Relief poured over her, warm and welcoming. Followed by gratitude—Stockholm syndrome again. But the exhilaration of this moment was too great. Tears seeped from her eyes. He'd given her an out. He'd given her a chance to get away, or to go and protect her family.

Protect her family. Whatever their flaws, whatever they had done in the past, they were her responsibility now. They belonged to her, and she would see them through.

She held the chain, let it down to the floor quietly. She didn't want to attract anyone to this building. Jolie debated turning on one of the flashlights, but decided against it. She felt around for the gear bag with the arsenal Cyril had brought with him. She took a knife along with its scabbard and hitched it to her belt. She strapped her own Walther PPK to her ankle. She pulled on a dark windbreaker, took another .45 and stuck it in one pocket, and put the walkie-talkie in the other. She emptied the gear bag of everything but the remaining weapons and added three Maglites. Took one of the sound suppressors and screwed it onto a Heckler & Koch .45 semiautomatic. Time to go.

Her eyes had adjusted to the gloom. There was nobody in the doorway. Jolie wished she had power, wished she could watch the cameras, but they were useless to her now.

She remained crouched—a smaller target—and followed the wall to the doorway. Worried. Wondered if the men coming for them had FLIR scopes. Any minute, she could be dead before she heard the crash of the bullet—

Couldn't think like that. And in fact, she encountered no one. The shifting wind blew the rain against her back and then into her face, needles that were warm but somehow chilling, water trickling down her neck, but the windbreaker was good. She kept to the sides of the buildings, concealing herself wherever she could by bushes or trees, duck-walking where there was empty space.

She reached the octagon house and leaned against the side of the building away from the beach, away from the boat in the inlet. She'd have to work her way around to the basement entrance.

She heard something coming from the kitchen area directly in front of her—chains jingling, a ticking sound on the brick.

Small shapes, larger shapes, emerged from the gloom and into the blowing wind, coming through the mist toward her.

The dogs. They didn't bark. They wriggled, they panted, they surrounded her.

They followed her as she made her slow half circuit of the octagon house.

Worried they would attract attention, she moved faster.

She reached the steps. Followed by the dogs, she went down into the darkness.

60

Maybe she *should* have used a flashlight. Creeping her way through the gloom, dogs at her heels, Jolie aimed for a slit of light ground-level in the approximate direction of her grandfather's room. Their generator was still working. Her eyes adjusted to the darkness quickly, and she made out the heavy piece of furniture—a dresser—barricading them in.

She pushed away the dresser and opened the door.

Five pairs of eyes stared at her. Like a snapshot. Four of Cyril's captives sitting on the floor against the wall. Kay with Zoe, Riley next to her by a body's-width distance and still snuggled up close to her father. All of them stunned, except for Granddad in his hospital bed, sheet pulled up to his chin. His expression was vague—Jolie got the strong impression he'd gone back to wherever he'd come from.

For a moment there was silence. Jolie could smell the fear in the room and the undercurrent of desperation.

Then Riley said, "It figures that *you* would be okay!"

Jolie walked over to Riley and said, "Be quiet."

"You can't—"

"Riley, you might have a problem with me, but now is not the time. There are people out there who are trying to kill us. You need to listen to me like your life depends on it, and do exactly as I say. I am not kidding you about this. Do we understand each other?"

Riley stared at her, open-mouthed.

"Good." Jolie leaned down and sawed through the tape binding Riley's hands with her knife.

Jolie went around the room, cutting her family's bonds. Her family. She wished she could come up with another description of the people in that room. Other than Kay and Zoe, these people were nothing to her. But face it: they were linked to her by blood—she had to help them. When she came to Franklin, she said, "How did he get you to give that statement to the press?"

"He said he'd kill Riley."

"Do you know what his plans are?"

"He wants to lure someone here."

"Who?"

"Mike Cardamone."

"Did you know about the teams?"

"Teams?"

Jolie stepped into his space, and he stepped back. "Frank, this is not the time to play games. Do you know about the teams?"

"Yes! Yes…but I didn't run them. That was Mike's thing, not mine. I told him it was crazy."

"How many teams?"

"Two. It was a small part of the business."

"How many to a team?"

"I'm not sure."

"What kind of guys are they?"

"When it comes to something like this," he said, "they're the very best."

*　　*　　*

Jolie hustled them out of the room. She could hear a helicopter now, overhead, hovering. Not only that, but she heard automatic fire. That sobered up everyone in a hurry.

It took a while to get the old man to understand what she wanted. They had to pull along a portable oxygen tank. Jolie didn't know what a stray bullet might do, but she couldn't leave him behind.

He argued with her and quickly escalated to shouting. Jolie took hold of his shoulders and leveled her gaze at him. "Senator, please listen to me. You have to be quiet. I know you can do it. There are people coming to kill us, and you owe it to your family to take care of them. They are your responsibility. You all need to be quiet so they won't hear us, and you need to lead the way. Can you do that?"

He nodded. Then he zipped a finger across his mouth, pretended to turn an invisible key, and threw it over his shoulder.

"Thank you, Senator." She said to Franklin, "Where's the entrance to the tunnel?"

"It's through the pantry."

"This floor has a pantry?"

He motioned to a doorway ahead in the gloom.

"How do we get in and out?"

"There's no lock on the door. It's just hidden."

"What about on the other end?"

"They're hidden, too. No locks. We didn't install locks because someone could get trapped in the tunnel that way. Nobody's supposed to know about the tunnels."

"Luke Perdue did."

He glared at his daughter. "Yes, Luke did."

Jolie decided to park them in the tunnel between the pool shed and the boathouse. That way, should anyone come into the tunnel, they'd have at least one place to run, and possibly two.

She hoped the killers didn't know about the tunnels. But if they had a schematic of the island, they would.

The old man was losing focus, although he remained quiet. He sat with his back against the wall of the tunnel, zoning out. She didn't like his color. He seemed to be sucking at the air. The tunnel was stuffy and damp; it smelled of mold.

But she had done the best she could. She needed to know what was happening above-ground. The bursts of automatic gunfire meant that Cyril had already engaged the enemy. He might be dead already. She had no illusions about her own ability. She was a sharpshooter, but that was a long time ago. Her training was that of a cop, not of a soldier or an operative. She relied on the authority of the badge. That would be no use to her now.

She handed Kay the extra .45 she'd brought along.

"You're not going to leave us, are you?"

"You know how to shoot, right?"

Jolie knew that was true; Kay used to hunt with her dad.

"Where are you going? Why can't you stay here with us?"

"You should be all right here. I've done all I can." She realized she sounded just like Cyril. Felt it important to add, "If you have to shoot, shoot to kill."

*　　*　　*

The helo circled once, then flew away. Landry trained his rifle on the front hatch of the Carolina skiff, just in case someone was inside. The storm was getting worse. The water was pea-green, and swirling a mixture of tannin bark, foam, and trash washed in with the waves. Visibility was poor. The rain was a curtain, falling so hard on the dock it created a mist that rose into the gray sky like gauze.

His mind ticked over what he'd learned. First thing: a head count. There was the swimmer, the driver of the SUV, at least two men in the helo—the pilot, and whoever had shot at him. The helo would be for reconnaissance, surveillance, and communications relay. Command and control. If Cardamone had come with his men, he would be in the helo.

That was four people right there. Landry figured anywhere from two to four in the skiff. He'd take the higher number. If there were more than that, he probably wouldn't get through this, but where was Cardamone going to get those kind of operatives at short notice? So he'd guess there were eight total.

With the swimmer dead, that left seven.

The driver of the SUV had parked the vehicle somewhere nearby and come back on foot. Landry was sure of that.

The swimmer *had* managed to cut the cables to the lights and phone before Landry'd got to him, but at least one generator was still going—he could hear it. The helo was a diversion to pin Landry in one place while the rest of the team landed—probably one or two of them were disabling the generators now.

They would know he had access to a cell phone, that the people in the house had them, too.

But Cardamone also knew by now that Landry didn't plan on calling in the cavalry. He knew it was between the two of them.

With Franklin in the middle.

Because they would take into account the fact that there would be cell phones, they would go in fast, before the family knew they were in immediate danger.

Cardamone's team would fan out to all the structures on the island. The first place they'd go to was the main house. Two operatives, because they expected to encounter at least three people: Franklin, Riley, and the senator, and possibly the hired help.

The only question was, did they leave a man to guard the skiff?

The answer was no. If they had, Landry would be dead by now. The helo drove him here, into the boathouse—the obvious place to hide. Whoever was waiting for him would have picked him off like pheasant with its wings clipped.

It was the gap in their plan. They should have anticipated he would run for the boathouse, should have left someone there to kill him.

He made his way to the main house. He knew the enemy would have a simple diagram of sectors to search, and he also knew they'd stay within close enough distance to one another to offer support.

The rain fell harder. It seemed as if there was nobody on this earth other than himself. There was no movement except for the spatter of raindrops on foliage. The main house was dark—the generator out.

He went quietly into the dark house. The rain was loud, even from inside.

The operative almost blundered right into him. Landry saw his bulk, slightly darker in the half-light of the hallway, and stepped into the doorway of the room off the hall. The man sensed movement and crouched, pulling his knife and plunging it into Landry's side.

By that time Landry had his hands around the man's throat and broke his neck.

The man slumped, legs spread out in front of him. Landry's wrist hurt so badly he sank to his knees afterward, seeing little yellow dots against a sea of darkness.

The knife's blade had bounced off his Kevlar vest but grazed his armpit, and he could feel the blood leaking. Not serious, but it stung. He tore off his assailant's watch cap and shoved it hard against the flesh under his arm, holding it there for what seemed like an eternity.

The man's portable comm crackled. It was Cardamone. Landry thought about asking Cardamone's position, but he didn't think he could fake the voice. If the other op was near, he sure as hell didn't want to give away his location.

Two down, he thought. Five to go? Five, or maybe just three. He hoped it was three.

He was getting tired of the carnage.

He was getting just plain tired.

Landry hoped Jolie had taken the family down into the tunnels. Although Cardamone knew about the tunnels, and he surely knew about the three entrances, it was still their best chance. Like trying to kill a gopher in that old arcade game. Whac-A-Mole. Hit him here, he pops up there. Mole or a gopher? He realized his mind was wandering, he was getting a little off-kilter. It was the pain. He cradled his wrist against his other elbow, realized he needed to clear his head. Had to move this guy, now.

He dragged the man through the doorway into the small bedroom and into the closet. Closed the door quietly. Listened. Nothing but the rain drumming on the roof. Could hear his heart beating, the quickening inside him as he got closer to his goal.

What he wanted was Cardamone.

His eyes adjusting more to the light, he now concentrated on another sense: his hearing. Try as he might, Landry could not hear the helo.

He guessed that Cardamone had touched down somewhere, met up with the SUV. Or maybe a boat. He guessed this was the endgame.

He made his way slowly through the house—no one inside. Came out by the pool. The rain was coming in gusts now, blowing into his face. Sharp as needles. It seemed to wake him up, and he realized his mind had started to wander again. It was the wrist. The wrist was driving him crazy.

Landry had to discipline himself, remember his training. He made his way to the pool house, to the closet and down the steps into the tunnel.

61

Feeling her way through the tunnel, Jolie kept the H & K semiauto at her side. She would have to allow for the long sound suppressor screwed onto the barrel. Fortunately, the sights on the USP were raised to go with a silencer.

Abruptly, she was aware of cool air blowing in her way.

From a door opening and closing?

She waited, listening for something—anything. Footsteps, breathing, the sound of rubbing clothing. Nothing.

But with her eyes adjusted, she could see a mass of darkness inside the larger darkness. Familiar—at least she thought it was familiar. The shape. She held up her flashlight—left hand—and pointed the H & K with her right. "Who's there?"

"It's me, Cyril."

Her legs were rubbery. "Cyril."

"Don't whisper," he said. "Talk. But keep it low."

"Are they out there?"

"Yes. Pretty soon they'll look in the tunnel. You might be able to get them on the Hinckley."

"What about the helicopter? Wouldn't they shoot at us?"

"I can divert them."

Jolie said nothing. He would help her or he wouldn't. As glad as she was that he was here, she reminded herself that they had different goals. He wanted to kill Mike Cardamone. He also wanted to kill her uncle, Franklin. He didn't give a rat's ass about the rest of the people here. She needed to keep that in mind.

*   *   *

They straggled up to the boathouse.

Cyril left them.

"What's he doing?" demanded Riley.

"Making sure it's safe for us to go," Jolie said.

Riley leaned against her father, and Franklin gently ran his fingers through her hair. He looked beaten down. He mourned Grace, but it was even more than that. Jolie sensed he knew he was not getting out of this alive.

She wanted to tell him she would get them all out of here. But the words stuck in her throat. She wasn't so sure. She felt—it was a very strong feeling—that Franklin was doomed.

You don't know that.

Jolie looked at Frank, the way he kept running his hand over his daughter's hair. The way he stared into space, seeing nothing. As if the only thing holding him to earth was the repetitive movement of his hand on his daughter's hair.

Jolie had never really given much credence to blood ties. In fact, she'd despised her mother's side of the family. But now she realized that the Haddoxes, for all their wealth, all their power, all their connections, were just people who made mistakes. They were a mixture of good and bad and smart and stupid like everybody else. Like her, they were trapped by their own circumstances. Wealthy, yes, but unhappy. She was surprised at how unhappy they were.

Her studious avoidance of the Haddoxes, her attempts to render them insignificant, had in fact yielded the opposite effect. Instead of reducing their influence on her life, she'd made them loom large. The Haddoxes defined her view of wealth and power and set her on the path of outsider. She had made them larger than they really were.

Their absence had shaped her—

Until she met Kay.

She looked at Kay, at Zoe. They too were silent, but they hadn't disconnected. Behind Zoe's eyes was a lively intelligence. The two of them were still here, still hopeful. Jolie felt a surge of pride. Kay *would* be that way.

"I'm sorry," Franklin said to his daughter. "I'm so sorry for all of this."

"I miss her so much!" Riley said.

Jolie had thought he didn't really love his daughter, but now she saw otherwise. She thought Frank was stroking his daughter's hair because he wanted that to be the memory he took with him. If he didn't come out of this alive, he wanted his last moments to be real. He'd lost a wife today, but he still had Riley.

"Jolie," Kay said.

"Yes?"

"Do you think we're going to get out of here?"

Jolie lied. "Yes, I think we will."

*　　*　　*

Their chances got a whole lot worse in the next few minutes. Cyril reached her by walkie-talkie with the news. "They disabled the Hinckley's engine. There's no way to fix it here."

Jolie wondered if he was lying. She knew he wanted to keep control of them, particularly Franklin. But he'd likely tape them up and leave them—not play mind games.

"What now? You said they have a boat. Can't we take that?"

"It's possible."

He sounded distracted. This bothered her even more, because she realized how much she depended on him. She had no way of understanding his motives, but she'd come to respect his ability.

She walked deeper into the tunnel so the others wouldn't overhear. "What's going on? Just what are we dealing with?"

He told her there could be as few as three left or as many as eight. This shocked her.

"Two of them are dead."

Just two?

For perhaps the hundredth time, Jolie felt the same odd feeling that they were all disconnected from reality. "What now?"

"You have the sniper rifle?"

"I have it in the duffle."

"Get it and set up where I tell you."

"But what about—"

"Tell them to stay where they are. You said you were a sharpshooter, right?"

"I'm not a sniper."

"Then you're about to learn a new skill. No time like the present."

She listened as he described the spot. She would be concealed, but on high enough ground where she could set up the rifle and shoot anyone who came in.

"What am I looking for?"

He told her.

"You're sure?"

"It's what I'd do."

*   *   *

It took Jolie several minutes to get to the security center and retrieve the rifle and attach the sniper scope. "Rusty" wasn't a good enough word for her ability with a sniper weapon. She'd only shot a sniper rifle twice—all her expertise was with a handgun. She took the H & K with her, too—sans the sound suppressor—and made her way to a slight raised mound in the garden, hidden from view by royal palms and the low-hanging branches of a magnolia tree. She crawled in and started to set up the tripod.

As she was doing so, her ears registered the drone of a helicopter.

She sighted on the helipad, not thirty-five meters away. The rain had abated a little, but the island was shrouded in a gray-green opaqueness—Jolie could barely see the white cross on the lawn.

The helicopter was kicking up a racket now, circling the island. Loud and low, menacing. Jolie wasn't rattled. She brought herself down to the task at hand, looked through the scope, keeping the white-marked helipad in the crosshairs. Adjusting, a little higher. It would be nice to shoot the rotor, but she thought the easiest shot would be to get them as they emerged from the helo. Then they'd be sitting ducks.

For one second, the last vestiges of her law-and-order mindset rebelled. Then necessity shut it down.

The helicopter's rotors were deafening.

Jolie concentrated her vision through the sight and kept as still as she could. Willed her heart to beat slower. Got in the zone. The way she did in the sharpshooter competitions. A kind of Zen.

He'd told her to shoot between heartbeats if possible.

So quiet in herself, she heard another sound, even under all the racket—a car engine. Her ears were now hypersensitive, as was every other part of her. She kept steady on the scope. *Breathe.* The helicopter hovered but didn't touch down. She could see the chopper pilot through the window, headset ending in a comma at his mouth.

Then Jolie felt something zing past, split a leaf in two, and explosions of dirt all around her.

Someone was shooting at *her*.

Landry had half expected fire on Jolie's position. He'd given her the second-best sniper position, hoped that whoever was left on the island would concentrate his fire on the obvious choice. But the man was thorough.

Thorough, but vulnerable.

The fire came from the hedge at the side of the main house, closest to the cabanas. Landry made his way around until he was behind the shooter.

He hoped Jolie had not panicked. If she lay flat on the ground and remained concealed, odds were good she would not be hit.

He'd planned to take the guy out quietly. Instead, he shot the man from a distance to keep him from killing Jolie. He understood this was an emotional thing—he wanted the cop to stay alive. Not the smartest thing he ever did.

Now he'd drawn attention to his location and had open space to cross.

He made it across and grabbed up the AR-15. The magazine was empty. The helo began to rise. The pilot had created the distraction and now was done.

Landry fired his own rifle at the helo but missed. He headed toward the causeway, staying hidden wherever he could.

Jolie clung to the ground like a limpet. Head down, eyes closed, like the ostrich with its head in the sand. Fire only raked the ground near her once, before she realized the majority of the fire rippled off to the left, twenty yards away.

No matter how terrifying an experience, no matter how great the fear that quicksilvered through your system and shattered everything in its path, it could not last for long. Abject terror could not sustain itself at that level forever. At first, when the fire raked her position, Jolie had flattened out and put her head down and prayed. She felt as if Edward Scissorhands was chopping his way around her. Finally she realized the danger was past, and the bullets were hitting elsewhere.

They didn't know she was here.

They were guessing.

They'd fired on her position because it was a logical place to set up as a sniper. Now the shooting had stopped. The helicopter flew away.

But what did it mean? Had they given up?

It could be a trap. She decided to stay where she was, meld even more into the earth. The rain spattered the bushes and flowers and ferns and her windbreaker, her dark windbreaker that fit in with whatever shadows there were in this gray expanse of nothing.

If the helicopter came back, she would aim for the rotors and blow it out of the sky.

* * *

The SUV was parked on the road just beyond the gatehouse, already turned around for a quick escape.

Landry saw no movement. He guessed they were already on the island. He figured the driver of the SUV had rendezvoused with the helo farther up the coast, and Cardamone had come with the driver. For the second time, they'd used the helo as a distraction, tried to drive him into the open. It didn't work, but the helo had slowed him down.

Now he had to figure where they would go.

Plenty of options, but he thought Cardamone and the SUV driver would try the tunnels. That was what he himself would do.

The entrance closest to the causeway was the octagon house.

He retraced his steps to the cabana pool house.

Landry still didn't know how many there were. Three down. Best-case scenario, there was only Cardamone, the driver of the SUV, and the pilot. The pilot would be busy flying the helo.

In the little cupboard that led into the pool house, he radioed Jolie.

"They shot at me," she said.

"You're all right?"

"Fine."

"Time to get them out of the tunnel," he said.

"Now? I don't want to get shot at again."

"The man who shot at you won't be shooting anymore."

A pause. "You want me to go get them now?"

"Five minutes ago. There's a Carolina skiff at the dock the bad guys came in—you can take that."

"We don't have a key."

"I brought it around to the dock—the engine's running. Just go."

"You mean we could have gotten them out earlier? We could have gotten *away*?"

Her response annoyed him. He didn't expect her to understand the mission, but he wished she wouldn't waste time assigning guilt.

"Roger," he said, and clicked off.

Then he waited at the mouth of the tunnel.

If luck was with him, they would pass by.

And he would be behind them.

*　　*　　*

Turned out, it was one man and he came from above and behind.

Landry did not hear him.

Lifted off his feet in what felt like a massive explosion, Landry hit the ground on his right shoulder with an awful crunching sound.

He'd been hit—the sound of the gunshot came less than a second after impact.

He lay still and hoped the man would come to him.

Luck was with him. When the man reached down to check Landry's neck, he snared the hand, whipped around, and braced it against his chest, bending back two fingers till they broke. The man screamed. Holding his quarry's head steady with his bad arm, Landry shoved the palm of his good hand into the man's nose, dissolving the small bones inside and ramming the shards into his brain.

The shooter crumpled to the floor, an empty vessel.

At that moment, everything went out of him. Adrenaline deserted him, leaving him lightheaded. He felt as if he'd been stomped—it was so debilitating he could barely move. As if he'd been kicked in the balls, only his balls extended all the way up to his neck. His back was burned. He could picture it, glowing embers threaded into the Kevlar of his vest, branding the skin. If anyone else came down here now, he would be easy to kill.

He pulled the .45 out of its holster with his left hand and rested it on his knee.

Heard a noise behind him.

Swiveled, shot into the dark above.

Someone yelled, toppled. Landry stared into the darkness, but could see nothing. He thought this was because he was in shock. Darkness encroached on his vision. He felt dizzy. He heard slithering above, and the sound of someone rising ponderously to his feet. Cursing.

He was incapable of doing anything—just waited for the coup de grâce.

But whoever it was blundered away, out through the cupboard. Scared, maybe, of what he might find down here?

The darkness pulsed at the edges of Landry's vision, and pain radiated from his collarbone—the crunch he'd heard. His right arm was useless. His left hand had dropped the .45 and lay against his thigh, trembling. He stood up and leaned against the wall. It took him three tries to pick up his rifle and his duffle.

Then he dropped them and sank down against the wall of the tunnel.

Rest a while.

*　　*　　*

There was no one waiting for them at the skiff. The idling engine seemed loud even in the falling rain, obvious. Jolie herded everyone into the cover of the boathouse, told them to stay still.

Get the old man on first? He would be the most recalcitrant. She touched his arm. "We've got to go," she said gently.

He stared at her, bewildered. "I have to go to the potty."

Zoe said, "Grand, we have to go. It'll be fun. Like when you used to take us sailing."

He smiled at Zoe. "You keeping an eye on Riley? Don't you let her get knocked up."

Zoe put her hand under his elbow. "We've got to go, Grand."

He let himself to be led toward the boat.

Jolie heard a noise behind them.

Something dark in the rain, slithering like a lizard along the wall of the boathouse—a man, breaking abruptly from the overhang and running for the boat. Shoving Franklin, Franklin turning to grab him, pulling at the black pullover the man wore. The man was bloody, and Jolie couldn't see a gun.

But she saw the knife.

The man seized Zoe around the arms and catapulted her along the dock, pulling her against him with such force her head hit his chest, and the knife carved a shadow into her throat.

Zoe's eyes were wild, terrified. "Mom—"

"Shut up!"

Franklin yelled, "Mike! Don't do this, she's just a kid!"

The man pulled Zoe closer to his body, her hair tangling around his arm as he propped her chin up. Jolie saw the neat red line on her throat.

"Stay back!" he yelled, breathing hard, his hand moving with each exhale, the knife sawing a little against Zoe's neck.

Franklin approached him, slowly, hands out, as if trying to quiet a cornered animal. "Mike, let's talk about this. We've been friends for—"

"Shut *up!*" He shuffled backward, wrenching Zoe's arm behind her back, almost jerking her off her feet.

There was a sound, an almost inaudible crunch, and Zoe screamed.

Her arm was broken.

Jolie felt darkness coming down over her eyes—anger—and for a moment she lost track of what she was doing. Already in the stance, the H & K solidly in her hand, the other hand cupped around it, her finger near the trigger but not yet on it. "Drop the knife!" she yelled. "Do it now!"

A perverse part of her wanted him to defy her so she could shoot him between the eyes. She'd never in her life wanted to shoot anyone so much as she wanted to shoot the coward who had broken Zoe's arm.

And he was *laughing*. "This isn't a cop show," he said. "You stay right where you are. Just...stay. Right there."

He moved backward in an awkward dance, and Jolie saw blood seeping through his fingers. Zoe's face was pale under the veil of rain that seemed to get stronger, washing the blood into rivulets down her shirt.

Her eyes boring into Jolie's: *Help me.*

The girl was terrified and in incredible pain from the broken arm, but she managed to hold it together. Putting her trust in Jolie. Believing there would be a good outcome, that she would come out of this alive.

Jolie wasn't so sure.

Cardamone was at the edge of the dock now, his legs touching the gunwale of the skiff.

"Let her go," Frank said. "Just let her go and—"

"Frank, you are such an asshole. You think I'm going to give up my only ace in the hole?" Cardamone smiled, but it was more of a grimace. "Tell you what, buddy. How about a trade—you for her. Get in the boat now, and when we're away, I'll push her in the water."

Franklin went pale. "Mike, can't we just—"

"Get in the boat, Frank. Show some guts for once in your life. Do the right thing. Isn't that the legacy you want to leave your family? Grace is *dead*, Franklin, you fucking pansy. Don't you think it's time for you to make a decision about what kind of man you are?"

Frank stepped forward. Riley grabbed him. "Daddy, don't! He's just trying to get you to go with him."

Franklin seemed dazed. He looked at his daughter. "But what about Zoe?"

"She'll be all right. Won't you, Zoe?"

Jolie listened to this drama with half an ear. She adjusted her grip, felt the delicate trigger mechanism with her fingertip. Less than two pounds of pressure, all she needed. Cardamone staring at her. Nothing between them. He adjusted his grip on Zoe so that the tip of her head touched his nose.

Take all the anger out of it. All the emotion. Just make the shot.

She could make the shot. But suddenly, the dock swayed. Franklin walked forward, tramping on the wood.

Wait.

Out of the corner of her eye, she saw something moving in the hard-lapping waves by the boat's stern—washed-up debris, probably. The boat tossed, banging hard against the dock. It would be hard for Cardamone to step into the boat, but he was trying to do just that.

He lifted one leg and rested it on the gunwale. The boat tipping. The stern whacking repeatedly against the dock. He leaned forward awkwardly, almost losing his balance.

Jolie saw her moment slipping away. She couldn't shoot him now, not with the boat rocking, not with Zoe's head clamped under the man's chin.

"Mike," Frank said. "Be reasonable."

"Get in the boat, Frank."

Franklin stepped onto the dock. Riley screamed at him. "Don't! Daddy, don't do it! Please, don't do it! Daddy, *please!*"

Franklin was at the edge of the boat now. He reached a hand out to steady Zoe, who was in danger of falling between the boat and the dock, the knife now pinching deep into her skin. Another seep of blood.

Franklin lifted his leg to step into the boat. "Let me get her on the dock—"

Suddenly, automatic gunfire rattled from the direction of the boathouse. Everyone stopped—a tableau. Jolie swung around, gun trained on the flash of gunfire coming from the dark, her calculation split into tenths of a second—

And fired. Three times. Something fell hard in the darkness, and she heard the clatter of the rifle as it hit the deck and let out one more burst of gunfire before falling silent.

A moment of shocked silence, and then she heard Frank say, "Mike, can't you see it's over?"

She swung her H & K back in their direction, saw Frank standing in the boat.

In an instant, Cardamone plunged his knife into Franklin's side. Franklin staggered backward and sat down, fell over the gunwale and into the water. Surfaced, his face a mask of shock.

At the same moment, Cyril erupted from the water on the opposite side, pulling Cardamone's legs out from under him— just as Jolie shot again.

She'd hit Cardamone, but not in the head as she'd expected. Cardamone grabbed at his chest—Kevlar—and he kicked backwards at the same time, catching Cyril in the jaw. Kicked again, connecting hard, Cyril slipping back, sinking into the water, clawing for the boat with the bad arm still wrapped in duct tape. Zoe tried to clamber back to the safety of the dock, but the skiff surged backwards as Cardamone hit reverse. The dock line grew taut, and the boat heeled around in an unexpected shallow turn, the engine revving to a loud mosquito whine.

Cyril climbed up again, hoisting himself over the gunwale, and Cardamone hit him hard across the face with the paddle. Cyril fell backward into the water, and Jolie saw with horror he was too near the boat's propellers. She couldn't see, couldn't tell what was happening in the churning water. But she could hear his yell. Like the teeth of an electric saw, it tore through her and kept her bolted to the ground. Jolie had a clear shot now, but when she squeezed the trigger the magazine was empty.

Cardamone grabbed the dock line and started sawing through it with his knife, one hand on the wheel, pulling the boat in a circle that Jolie didn't think was entirely planned. She rushed the boat just as it pulled away, the water churning up silt and bark and foam, the engine screaming now. "Zoe!" she yelled. "Jump."

Zoe struggled in Cardamone's grip, her face a mask of pain. Blood leaked from her wound. Using her good hand, she pulled herself to a standing position just as the boat pulled the line free and catapulted forward, as if by slingshot. Zoe fell across the gunwale, her broken arm flopping like a ragdoll's. Jolie could see the protruding bone.

The boat shot out into the bay.

Jolie heard Franklin yelling, turned to look at him.

He was still holding his side, blood blotting through, his face pale. But he sat at the stern of the family's old skiff, hand on the tiller, ready to pull away from the dock. Jolie got into the boat. "Head them off at an angle," she shouted, and they took off.

Spray hit Jolie in the face as she tried to see through the rain and her wind-driven tears. They hit the Carolina skiff's wake, a thumping, punishing washboard, but Franklin's steering was steady despite his obvious pain.

Wounded himself, Cardamone was having trouble keeping the boat steady, running a zigzag course taking him back in the direction of the island—only fifty yards out.

Then he seemed to straighten out. It looked like he would get past them, but abruptly he veered back in their direction. Jolie saw why—Zoe was fighting him at the console, her good arm fighting for the wheel, and now the boat was right in their path.

Cardamone tried to turn again, but Franklin held steady until the last moment, when he turned slightly—clipping the Carolina skiff a glancing blow. Little more than a kiss, but Cardamone overcorrected, and the boat leaped in midair, coming down hard.

Everything happened in slow motion, as accidents do. Cardamone seemed to fly up like a jack-in-the-box, smashing against the console with a smack before cartwheeling into the water. Zoe was gone.

Franklin heeled the boat in a tight circle.

Jolie scanned the water, straining for any sign of Zoe.

"Anything?" Franklin's voice carried the thin edge of panic.

Twenty yards away, Zoe resurfaced, clinging to the flotation cushion. "There she is!"

They needed to get as close to her as possible to see if they could pull her into the boat. Jolie needed to be ready to go in.

As their skiff made another tight circle, Jolie pulled off her shoes and stripped down to her underwear. "You okay, Frank?"

"I'm okay," he said, although he spoke through gritted teeth. "But where'd she go?"

The cushion was there, but Zoe was gone.

Then she heard thrashing. It was Cardamone, holding on to a life preserver at ten o'clock. His face was a bloody mess.

As she watched, he dropped from view.

Pulled under?

She thought she'd seen—later she would come to believe it was just her imagination—something distinctly un-shark-like in the instant before Cardamone disappeared.

Jolie thought she saw an arm, a dull silver arm, wrapped around Cardamone's neck.

Cardamone's head bobbed up once more, his mouth wide open as he screamed. He was yanked under the whitecaps in a bloody froth. He did not resurface.

But Cyril was dead; she'd seen him go under the propellers.

Joe scanned the water again. "Frank, I think she's over there." She pointed in the direction they'd drifted from.

Then she spotted her—just a glimpse before the waves closed over her head, not twenty yards away.

Frank maneuvered the boat closer. Jolie stepped on the gunwale and launched herself off the boat.

As Jolie hit the water, panic seized her. She thought about the pond outside her house. In that moment, she was plunged into darkness—terrified. But a calm part of her mind instructed: *Kick to the surface.*

And yet she froze. For one terrifying moment, she could not move. She sank like a stone. Her mind told her to kick, to push herself up, but instead, she floundered.

And then Jolie heard the commotion nearby. She could barely see Zoe, but knew that the girl would die if she didn't come to her rescue. Jolie was a certified lifeguard. She had gone through training at the academy. There was no one else between Zoe and death—just her.

This galvanized her. Jolie kicked hard with her legs and used her arms to push to the surface, broke through, and breathed.

She had no swim goggles to see underwater, and the rain was coming down hard. But she had to get to Zoe.

Zoe was farther away—thirty yards?—gasping as she tried to stay above the waves. Jolie's training took over. She swam toward Zoe, amazed and heartened by the way her body cleaved the waves, her stroke as economical as a thresher.

Her fear of water gone.

When she reached Zoe, the girl grabbed hold of her neck and shoulders and pushed her downwards, her panic-driven strength amazing. She was a fear machine, desperate to stay above the water, to breathe, and would use any leverage she could to do it. Jolie managed to slip out of her grasp and propel herself downward, coming up to grab the girl from behind. This time she had her in the crook of her elbow, forearm pressed against Zoe's throat. She scissor-kicked, pulling Zoe in the direction of the boat.

The boat was now only yards away. Careful to keep Zoe face-up out of the water, Jolie fought her way through the swells.

But Zoe still seemed determined to sink them both. Wounded as she was, useless as one of her arms was, she had the strength of a determined wrestler.

Gulping salty water, Jolie spoke in a stern, strong voice. "Hold on to the flotation cushion. We're going to get you into the boat." That seemed to shock Zoe out of her battle mode. Her good arm grabbed harder to the cushion.

Frank bent forward and hauled Zoe into the boat. Jolie clung to the gunwale until Frank could bring her up, too.

She was too tired to do it herself.

All her energy was gone. Her arms started to shake.

Jolie watched Frank cover Zoe with his own jacket, and she said a prayer of thanks.

62

Landry drifted. In the downpour, he was in no danger of being seen. Rain splashed into his face and eyes from above and wavelets washed over him from below. He saw Franklin and Jolie circle around, pick up the girl, and return to the dock.

He let himself drift, because he was drifting in the right direction.

He took stock of his injuries. His right arm was still useable in the water, although he had limited movement. The duct tape helped. His back still felt wrong from the shot he'd taken in the tunnel. The vest had saved his life, but that whole section above his kidney throbbed, and he wondered if there had been a hairline crack in the bone and maybe some internal damage. Nothing he could do about that, so he took inventory of his other injuries. His nose was broken, and he bled profusely from a gash in his scalp. The propeller had nicked him close to his eye. Scalp wounds bled a lot. He managed to rip off his shirt, wrap it around his head, and put pressure on the wound, keeping his hand clamped hard against it. There were other, lesser injuries. He wouldn't worry about them now. He bobbed up and down in the water as he'd been trained to do at Coronado, his good arm keeping the shirt pressed hard against his head. Up, down, like a cork. Using his legs to kick up, then sinking back down beneath the surface, lower and lower, holding his breath, before kicking back up. He was drifting east, in the direction of the road leading to the peninsula.

A long way to go, but that didn't bother him. He had been trained for this. He kept up the rhythm. Down, up. Down, up. When he felt the wound had coagulated, he left the shirt tied around his head and treaded water with his arms.

Hours. The rain came down harder. It got darker. Sirens, lights. Cop cars racing down the strand, converging on the island. They were followed by a cavalcade of black SUVs—swift, dark, and silent. A police helicopter flew over, its light just barely missing him, and landed at the compound. He could barely see through the waves and the rain and the dark, but the lights blinked along with the pulsing pain.

He'd drifted too far to the north. The closest shore was due east. In the dark he looked at his watch, at the lighted numbers of the GPS. Changed his trajectory slightly, keeping the dark mass of land in his vision. Knew he could go all day, all night if he had to.

More sirens. More lights. More SUVs. Paramedic trucks, their lights and sirens off. But he was encapsulated in his own little cocoon of self-preservation. Just keep the direction…

*   *   *

When he made landfall, he crawled on his belly into the reeds. He did not move. He would not move until the early hours of the morning.

When three a.m. came and went, he followed the road north. The convenience store he'd spotted on his way to and from the compound was locked up for the night, dark—the only structure on the road. The store dated from the seventies, which was good news for him. An old place like that might have a pay phone on the wall outside.

And it did.

His brother answered on the first ring.

Landry said, "How's Ocala?"

"It's great, bro. Beautiful! Seen a couple of yearlings I like. Thanks for the trip."

"Good." Landry took a breath. Fatigue was beginning to set in. "Sorry, but you're gonna have to cut your vacation short," he said. "I need you to come and get me."

63

TWO MONTHS LATER

REAGAN NATIONAL AIRPORT, ARLINGTON, VIRGINIA,
CONCOURSE B

Jolie Burke walked past banks of television monitors on her way to gate ten. She didn't have to watch the screen to know what was on. The cable networks were following the story. The former attorney general of the United States had been indicted by a grand jury for his role in the cover-up of the death of Nathan Dial by the vice president of the United States.

Jolie had been a witness for the prosecution.

She'd been warned by the prosecutor that while there had been enough to seek an indictment by the grand jury, there was little direct evidence of the crime. Nathan Dial's body had never been recovered. While there was enough for a trial, he said, it was unlikely that anyone involved in the events on Indigo Island would spend a day in jail.

Milky sunlight came through the windows as Jolie approached the sitting area near her gate. The televisions continued to blare from every wall. She saw herself, dressed in a good suit, walking down the steps of the U.S. District Court in DC, a forest of microphones held up to her face. Her lawyer pushed their way through the crowd, shielding Jolie, saying, "My client has no comment at this time." That particular segment had been on cable news for the better part of an hour.

The worst moment for Jolie had come immediately after the indictment had been handed down and the grand jury was dismissed. She'd been ushered unceremoniously through a little-used corridor and had come face-to-face with Kay, Zoe, and Riley.

Kay, who had been crying, saw Jolie. She broke away from the group and walked up to Jolie.

"Why did you have to drag us through all this *now*? Why?"

Zoe came to stand by her mother. She looked mortified. "Mom, she—"

"Saved your life," Kay said, not taking her eyes from Jolie's face. "I know. And I thank you for that." She sounded anything but thankful. "But what's going to happen to Riley's *father*? Did you think about that?"

Jolie had no answer.

Kay turned away. Zoe stayed where she was for a moment, torn. Then she followed her mother down the corridor.

The trial would be many months away, but for Jolie, it was over in so many ways. She'd lost her cousin and best friend. She'd lost her livelihood—Skeet had finally found a way to lay her off. And she was a pariah in a county where Haddox money had always greased the wheels and kept businesses, large and small, going.

And what did they have to show for it? *Conspiracy to cover up a crime.* That was the only repercussion from a government-sanctioned killing spree that took the lives of Brienne Cross and so many others.

But there was little to no proof of these crimes.

The two white supremacists who had been charged in the deaths of Brienne Cross and the *Soul Mate* reality show contestants were released due to lack of evidence. Donny Lee Odell claimed he was at the Evergreen Tavern in Salida, Colorado, almost four hours away by car from Aspen, at the time of the murders. Two people had recently come forward to confirm his alibi. Jolie thought it was interesting that they had come forward *now.*

The tests of the blood found on the knife at Odell's home proved inconclusive.

Mike Cardamone's body was never found. The dead men on Indigo and the dead men in the house on Sea Oats Lane remained unidentified except for the FBI agent, Eric Salter, and a private investigator named Ted Bakus. The three other men in the house might have never existed at all. Their fingerprints were not on record. A raid on Cardamone's office provided nothing. Everything about the business was legitimate. There were no assassination teams. No names in the databases, no payment records.

Every byte of computer data they could find had been analyzed by an outside consultant.

There was nothing. The computers had been wiped clean, magnetized, and destroyed. Sanitized.

Whitbread Associates owned two jets. The manifests did show that they had been to Panama City and Tallahassee on the day of the firefight on Indigo. Their serial numbers had been recorded.

The FBI would look into it.

Meanwhile, the images of the dead men had been released to the media. But no one came forward.

Media requests to law enforcement on every level were met with disinterest.

Pretty soon a picture emerged. A rival Congolese megachurch used rioters to burn Reverend Wembi's church, which had been under investigation for money laundering. Experts posited that the megachurch also ordered a hit on Grace's family on Indigo.

No one came forward to refute this story. Not the FBI, not the state police, not any of the jurisdictions in between. Certainly not the Palm County Sheriff's Office, which forwarded all inquiries to the FDLE.

The narrative became a juggernaut. It was ridiculous on its face, a pack of lies and half-truths, but if there was an investigative reporter out there who saw the cover-up of the cover-up, Jolie didn't know about it. She knew there was no point in fighting it. At least she had managed to get justice of sorts for Nathan Dial. It was easier to pin a single crime on a dead man.

The announcement came on the loudspeaker. "Continental flight Five-forty-two, with service to Chicago and Albuquerque, will begin boarding in ten minutes."

Albuquerque was Jolie's final destination. She would go back to New Mexico, where she had spent the first ten years of her life. There was still family there on her father's side. She would go back home.

As she bent to grab the handle of her roll-on suitcase, something made her look up. Jolie only saw the man from the back, but she could swear it was the rogue operative she'd known as "Cyril." He moved efficiently through the crowd—mid to late forties, khaki trousers, knit shirt, expensive-looking carry-on bag. The same light brown hair, military cut. Big. She recognized the way he carried himself—a soldier. Not just any soldier, but one of the elite.

But Cyril was dead. She'd seen him go under the propellers.

Jolie checked her watch—there was time. She threaded her way through the crowd, not sure what she would do. Didn't know why she wanted to make sure. There was no point. Why not just forget about the whole thing?

Maybe it was because his body hadn't been found. There were plenty of solid reasons for that. A night hammered by a subtropical storm, plenty of sharks and fish to feed on his body. But it was one of the few questions that remained. Her life had been turned upside down, one phase ending and another beginning, and it would be good to know for sure.

"Cyril!" she called, just as a crowd of high school kids in matching shirts funneled onto the concourse from another direction. She kept pace with the group of passengers she was with, but she began to lose track of him.

And then, way up, there he was. Moving effortlessly through the crowd ahead.

"Cyril!" she called again.

He kept moving, but turned his head briefly.

Their eyes met.

He smiled.

And then he was gone.

THE END

ABOUT THE AUTHOR

Photograph by Ian Galley, 2011

J. Carson Black is the bestselling and critically-acclaimed author of eight books, including the Laura Cardinal crime fiction series. Born and raised in Tucson, Arizona, Black has found inspiration for her writing in everything from real life horrors to the headlines screaming today's news. She is currently working on her next thriller, to be published by Thomas & Mercer in 2012.